The Gladium Province is on the verge of civil unrest as humans and Morgons, the dragon-hybrid race, clash once more. But amid disorder can also arise passion…

When the bodies of three human women are discovered in Morgon territory—with the DNA of several Morgon men on the victims—it's just a matter of time before civil unrest hits the Province. But for ambitious reporter Moira Cade, it's more than just a story, and it may mean risking her own life.

Descending into the dark underworld of Morgon society, Moira is paired with Kol Moonring, Captain of the Morgon Guard, for her protection. Fiercely independent, Moira bristles at his dominance, and defies his will at every turn. Yet resistance proves futile when passion flares between them, awakening powerful emotions within both, body and soul. But as the killings continue, can their fiery newfound bond survive an even greater evil—one that threatens all of humanity, Morgonkind, and Moira's very soul?...

D1798955

Books by Juliette Cross

Nightwing Series
Soulfire
Nightbloom

Vale of Stars Series
Waking the Dragon

Published by Kensington Publishing Corporation

Waking the Dragon

A Vale of Stars Novel

Juliette Cross

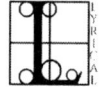

LYRICAL PRESS
Kensington Publishing Corp.
www.kensingtonbooks.com

For Rachel, my childhood friend and adulthood soul sister.

Keep reading & dreaming
RT16, Vegas
Best, Juliette Cross

Acknowledgements

Thank you to my beta girls—Julie, Jessen, Rebekah, Rachel, and Brooke—I love you ladies like the sky is wide. As always, I must thank my editor, Corinne DeMaagd, who is superwoman of the editing world, in my opinion. Your meticulous attention to detail and tireless efforts are more appreciated than you know. To my friend, Cora Cade, whose encouragement has lifted me up time and again. And finally, to the readers of fantasy romance—you are the reason writers like me are able to let our imaginations soar into the creative unknown, to craft heartfelt characters who yearn for true love, and to build worlds where dreams do come true. A heartfelt thank you from this humble writer.

Prologue

Tick.

Tick.

Tick.

The beautiful blonde froze.

Silence.

She peered down the darkened corridor of the cellar beneath the Vaengar Stadium. No one.

The Morgon with black hair and black eyes at the bar had told her the restroom was this way. The only sound was the wafting crackle of the torches. The only sight was long shadows cast by flickering flame. An eerie tendril of fear snaked up her spine. Even half-drunk, something primitive warned her of danger, like the innate foreboding a deer senses when the tiger stalks unseen from the trees.

She shook it off, flipped her long hair over one shoulder, and walked on, knowing the restroom must be just around the bend up ahead.

Tick.

Tick.

Tick.

She stopped again and spun around, unable to tell from which direction the sound came.

"Bennett? Is that you?" A hollow echo of her voice reverberated down the empty corridor. "Stop it! You're scaring me." The last came out a faint whisper. A presence—corporeal, malevolent, and drawing closer—plunged her into icy fear. Her pulse quickened. A hiss of wind pressed the thin fabric of her mini-dress to her thighs. The flame on the wall guttered to nothing, then relit anew.

Tick.

Tick.

Directly behind her. She whirled and stared up at a massive Morgon man who stood only feet away. A behemoth silhouetted by the flambeau. His pointed wings, half-open and huge, kept the rest of him in shadow, as if the light itself repelled him. She could see nothing but his eyes—amber orbs with serpentine slits, bright as the torch-flame. Her breath hitched in her throat. She fell back against cold stone, scraping her bare shoulders against the rough cavern wall.

He passed near a sconce, the light illuminating hard, angular planes, the ancestral lines of the dragon sculpting his face in stark relief—more beast than man. Her heart thrashed against her ribcage.

"I—I lost my way, I think. I should go." She gestured in the direction she had come, inching along the wall.

He moved with lethal grace, angling closer in slow, even steps.

Tick.

Her gaze dropped to his large hand. Claw-tipped fingers spread wide, the sharp nail of the index tapping the stone. She bolted left, only to find a wall of six Morgon men blocking her exit. They'd materialized out of the shadows in silent stealth. Unmoving, watching. Backing against the wall, she swiveled her head from those blocking her path to their master stalking closer.

"What—what do you want from me?" Her voice cracked, primal fear ripping through her gut.

By now, she'd reached the pinnacle of terror, petrified in place. Tangible evil seeped into her skin as the sinister creature loomed, enveloping her in his shadow. Something screamed for her to run, while a compelling power rolling from the beast kept her pinned in place. It was as if his very presence demanded obedience, subservience.

The beast braced one arm next to her head, her panic filling up the confines of their space. He inhaled a deep breath, drinking her fear in like the sweetest nectar.

"Will she serve, my lord?" A voice of authority from one of the Morgons in shadow—sultry but edged like a razor.

Her chest rose and fell, drawing the beast's gaze. He leaned closer, trailing one claw lightly over her swelling breasts. Viper-swift, he clamped her mouth with his other hand, stifling her screams, and continued his exploration of her naked skin with the blade-like nail. Her rapid pulse beat frantically at the base of her neck.

"Perhaps." One word, grating and broken. The voice of a monster.

He snaked his claw across the bottom of her throat, then down the line of her cleavage, pressing just enough to scrape the skin, a thin line of red rushing to the surface. Keeping her immobile with his crushing weight, he scraped a drop of blood from her breasts. He opened his mouth, revealing a row of sharpened teeth, the canines most prominent. Reeking of menace and power, he licked the tip of his claw.

"Perhaps." His voice fell to a raspy whisper. A rumbling growl rattled her bones. A flash of flame and shadow and all was black.

Chapter 1

I paused the image on the comm screen, swallowing the bile rising in my throat. Pale and naked, the mutilated woman was splayed spread-eagle on her back in the snow, her bloodless skin only a shade darker. Dirty-blond hair, matted and tangled, covered her face—all but one glassy, green eye. A slit made with precision and patience opened her entire cavity from throat to pubic bone, exposing internal organs. What seemed to be left of them, anyway.

"Did you get any close-ups?" I asked Macon.

"Yes. Your favorite smuggler is getting better at his illegal activities."

"You know I love you, don't you?"

"Stop sucking up. It doesn't suit you, Moira."

"But I do appreciate it," I said, setting his comm device in my lap. "Seriously."

"Well, when I get fired from my job, you can hire me here at *The Herald*."

"First off, you don't get paid as an intern at the precinct. And secondly, you can't write or edit worth a damn, so what could you do at a college paper?"

He rolled his eyes. "True. But payback for this will be you helping me pass my Ancient Lit class."

"Done. Now, show me what else you got."

Macon tapped the comm screen to play. "Here. Look."

Sure enough, his video panned to photos of the victim's hands and ankles, bruised from restraints. Just like the others. The last shot zoomed in on her lower torso and legs. Bright blood stained the inner slopes of pale thighs. I heaved in a deep breath and blew it out. "This blood doesn't look like it came from the mutilation."

"No. I asked my boss, Torrance, about that." Macon's voice dropped, grave and thick. "The tearing came from the sheer violence of the, uh…"

Macon swallowed hard. He seemed to be struggling to find words to describe such brutality to one of his best female friends. Finally, he cleared his throat, pushing his glasses higher on the bridge of his nose, and continued in a professional manner. "I heard our forensics guy talking to Torrance. Said the DNA evidence proves there was a multiple-rape. Like the others. But this time was much worse."

"Dear God."

I set down his comm device on the desk. Standing up, I stared out the window, unable to look at the images for one more second. My hands trembled. I crossed my arms and closed my eyes in an attempt to steady myself. But the images kept flitting through my mind on instant replay. A horror movie come to life. The torture and terror these young women suffered wouldn't leave me. Raped. Multiple times. Then torn open like sacrificial lambs. The fear they must've felt in those last moments. Anger welled inside, demanding justice for these young women. I twisted the medal that dangled on a silver chain at my throat, rubbing it for comfort between thumb and forefinger. Knowing that emotion was the one inhibitor of a journalist's investigation, a fault that could make me lose focus, I wiped away the thoughts and forced myself to the task at hand. Investigation.

"How—how many?" I asked. "Six of them, like the last two victims?"

"This time there were seven."

I whirled. "Seven?" Based on my theory that these heinous murders were committed by an exclusive cult of some kind, a new member didn't quite fit.

"Yeah. The DNA on the first two are from six different Morgon men, but the new victim has a seventh." The DNA for the human-dragon hybrid race was so distinct, there was no denying the murderers were Morgons. Macon pointed to the comm screen. "And look at this."

I sat back down while Macon scanned the photos, then paused on a shot of the dead girl's thigh. I frowned.

"Bite marks?"

"They slashed her carotid artery, then bit her. Well, one of them did."

"Let me guess. The new guy."

"Yep. The DNA around the bite mark matches that of the seventh culprit."

I peered closer at the photo on screen. "Why bite her? The Devlin Butchers have been methodical up to this point. Violent, yes, but also precise."

Some reporter had coined the phrase after they found the first body, saying she was split open like a slaughtered lamb. The horror these girls must've endured was one thing, but the repercussions for Gladium were exponential. While our city was one of the few which implemented desegregation laws for both species to live alongside one another, it was only in the past few years that amicable relations had begun to build beyond business. It wasn't uncommon to see interracial couples together in public these days. My older sister, Jessen, for example.

Since the Dixon Desegregation Act two decades ago, named for the former governor who founded the law and pushed it through Parliament, the dividing line between races began to blur, opening doors for cooperative trade and for businesses to flourish. Opening the door for even more. Humans and Morgonkind merged, throwing Gladium into a bright spotlight, whether we liked it or not.

When my sister, the eldest daughter of a powerful Gladium family, and Lucius Nightwing, the eldest son of the most powerful Morgon clan, united in marriage, our world tilted. Rumors of dissent and criticism from provinces abroad filtered into the city. Even so, professional and personal relations between the races had never been better.

But now, these Morgon murderers were specifically targeting human women. Why? There were plenty of human-only and Morgon-only provinces to reside if you didn't care for the mixing of races. And the murders carried some odd, ritualistic traits. Like the rapes by the same six Morgon men. And the precise slicing open of the victims' cavities. All the same. Until now.

I blew out a frustrated breath. "The bite doesn't fit our profile. A cult or gang ritual is precise and exact, like the first two killings. This new player is the one amping up the violence."

I stared up at the two young women smiling from their pictures on my bulletin board. One kicked the surf on the beach, mouth open wide in laughter. The other curled up on a park bench with a book, looking up as if someone just called her name. I kept them there to remind me what had been lost, what the world had lost now that they were no longer in it. And now I'd be adding one more picture to the board. A familiar anger burned through my gut. No more. It needed to stop. And if that meant me diving head-first into the Morgon world to find these fuckers, then so be it.

I sighed and turned my attention back to Macon. "The violence has escalated. We've got to look at this from a new angle. Figure out why the change with this victim."

"This one is a blonde, the others were brunettes," he added. "Another break from the pattern."

"I don't think our killers are seeking a particular type, except for—" I gazed back down at the comm screen, moving to more detailed close-ups of injuries.

"Except for?" Macon prompted.

"Except for the young and pretty."

A nascent thought, a memory from when I babysat my nephew two years ago, flashed to mind. Upon returning from the Vaengar Stadium where a popular Morgon sport was played, my sister's best friend, Sorcha, made a snide remark. *Yeah, doesn't matter if they're tall or short, human or Morgon. Vaengar players just like them beautiful, like that fucking blood cult.* Jessen had shushed her up, eyeing me in the corner of her kitchen. My overprotective sister had always been secretive about the Morgon world, though I never understood from what she was protecting me.

I sat back in my chair, staring at the morbid remains of the latest victim on the comm screen, one I still suspected was the result of some ritual cult. Perhaps the very one Sorcha mentioned with a slip of the tongue that time a few years ago. The signs were all there. I knew I was right. Whatever instinct policemen and detectives had, so did I. "I'm assuming her body was found in Devlin Wood. In Drakos."

"Yep. No different than the other two victims."

Drakos, a Morgon-only province to the north of Gladium. "And where was she last seen?"

"At the Vaengar Stadium here in Gladium."

"Just like the others." I combed my hands in frustration through my long hair before pulling a hair tie off my wrist and piling the dark mass into a messy bun out of my way.

"Well…" Macon straightened, his eyes following my impromptu hair-styling, "I think she—"

"These are much better photos than the others, Macon. Nice work." I scrawled some notes inside Maxine Mendale's folder, victim number three, then plugged my printer cord into Macon's comm device to get still photos for my file.

"Thanks."

"I'm sorry. I interrupted. You think she what?"

"Uh, I overheard Torrance say Maxine didn't leave with her whole party that night."

"I know that, Macon. She was abducted from the premises, so of course she didn't leave."

"I mean, they interviewed some guy named Bennett Cremwell, a friend of hers. He said they stayed behind for an after-party, some kind of hush-hush event. You have to know the right Morgons to be invited."

He had my full attention now. I stopped scanning the comm screen. "Okay. Let's go over this step by step."

I flipped open my journal with handwritten notes scribbled on every square inch and in no certain order. Not to the average eye, anyway.

"Why don't you just use your comm device for all that? It'd be much more efficient."

"I like paper and pen. Helps me think better." Macon scrunched up his brows, shaking his head at me. I flipped to a clean page and wrote Maxine Mendale's name at the top. "So victim number one, Sasha Blake, was also last seen at the Vaengar Stadium. However, her last contact with her friends was during the game itself. She disappeared when she went to the bar."

Macon nodded and nudged his glasses up again.

I glanced at my notes. "Sasha was also found in Devlin Wood in Drakos three days after her disappearance."

Leaning forward, he peered at my scrawl. "How can you even read that? There are arrows and dots and scratch-outs all over the place."

"I have a system." I blew out a short breath, moving on. "So the bruises and form of killing were the same. Victim number two, Clarice Mitchell, was last seen walking toward her car following the Vaengar Games. Her body showed up in Devlin Wood three days later."

"Right."

"But now, we have Maxine Mendale. Victim number three, found seven days after her abduction. I've checked the Vaengar schedule for who played our local team those nights—two from Drakos and one from another province farther north. Cloven."

"It doesn't matter." Macon sat on the edge of my desk, crossing his arms. "Morgons from all over come to the games. It may have nothing to do with Drakos or Cloven, as far as we know."

"Hmm. I don't know about that. I want to do some digging on this place, Devlin Wood." I tapped my pen on my chin, staring at the printer as it churned out photo after photo. I pulled one from the print tray, a close-up of Maxine's throat. I peered closer. "Macon. What are these marks?"

He leaned in, examining with me several centimeter-sized scratches along her throat in varying places. He pulled the other photos from the print tray. "Look. There are more here."

Little slashes along the inside of her wrist, even the inside of her elbows.

"On her inner thigh, too."

"Damn." I shuffled the photos. "They're not killing marks. Maybe it's part of the cult ritual. Or torture." Acid churned in my stomach.

"Yeah, but why?"

"You think I know the inner workings of a fanatical, psychotic, sadistic Morgon mind?"

I yanked open the other files with the photos Macon had pilfered from the first two victims. I only had long angles of these crime scenes. No close-ups. That's why I hadn't noticed them before.

"Look! Look at her arm." Even from the distant shot of the body, I could just make out small gashes on the inner arm from wrist to elbow. "Why the hell didn't I see this before?"

"Because from afar it just looks like scrapes, like the others on her body she could've gotten from captivity."

"Well?" I glanced back over my shoulder at Macon. "Did your boss Torrance say anything about these?"

"Are you serious? I'm an intern. The only information I get on high profile cases like this is from eavesdropping. I fetch coffee, make copies, and do what I'm told. You're lucky I got these at all." He thrust his hand through his hair in frustration, making it stick on end. A sure sign my faithful friend was at the end of his rope.

"You fetch coffee?"

"Stop it."

I shrugged, turning to my desktop comm. "No worries, my coffee-fetching, copy-making friend. There's someone else who can give us more information we need." I started typing. "Bennett...Cremwell." Hitting enter to scan the Net, three Bennett Cremwells popped on screen. "There are three in the Gladium Province. One is fifty-four and works at some robotics factory in the Warwick District."

"Not him."

I rolled my eyes. "Yeah. I didn't think she'd be hanging with a middle-aged, factory-worker at the Vaengar Games."

He smirked, flipping his brown hair out of his eyes and leaning his wiry frame over my shoulder toward the screen.

I clicked on the next entry. "Bennett Cremwell number two is thirty-five and lives with his wife and three kids on their country estate south of the city. Not him, unless number two was having an affair." I clicked the last name. "Recent graduate of Gladium University, currently an intern at Cade Enterprises in the technology department. Bingo."

"How convenient you have such easy access to Cade Enterprises."

I pushed away any hesitance. My need to interview Cremwell overrode my daddy issues.

"Isn't it?" I winked. "Hand me my boots over there. Underneath the desk." Preferring to work long hours in comfort, I often kicked off my shoes in my office. He picked up one boot from under the desk and tossed it, examining the other.

"Size ten? Damn, Moira."

"Shut it." I snatched it away from him. "I can't help it if I'm long-limbed."

True, not many human girls were six feet tall, but I liked that it gave me an intimidation factor with unwanted men. And annoying women. Fortunately, I was also born with an innate empathy for others—very necessary as a journalist for people to trust me with their stories. Part of getting people to talk was being a quiet, compassionate listener.

Boots on, I hopped up and grabbed my gray, wool coat off the corner rack. Macon followed me to the door. "Can I tag along?" He raised his brows, looking even more like the puppy dog he resembled.

I tilted my head and smiled. "I don't think that's wise. He might recognize you from the precinct."

His brow pushed together in a frown. "So how will you tell him you found his name?"

"I'll think of something."

I locked the door to my office. Macon shadowed me as we veered out of *The Herald* wing of the Literary Arts Department. Just as we reached the bottom of the steps, he pulled me to a stop. "Moira." His voice reflected the gravity in his eyes. "Please be careful. Don't get too caught up in this one. This isn't like the car burglaries or even the campus drug ring you covered."

I slipped my leather gloves on, wiggling my fingers into the tips. "Macon, if I plan to land one of the elite and rare positions on *The Gladium Post* next year, I've got to prove that I'm a serious journalist."

"Yeah. But at what price? Your own life?" His voice cracked with emotion. He really was afraid for me. Rightfully so.

I placed a hand on his shoulder for reassurance, giving him a friendly squeeze. "I know. I'm not stupid. I won't do anything without protection."

"I suppose you could always have your brother-in-law's security team trail you while you do your investigating." He chuckled. "Now that would be something to see."

I gave him a bright smile. "What a fabulous idea."

Nightwing Security, my brother-in-law's company, would come in quite handy if I managed to persuade him to help me out. That would mean persuading Jessen, too. Quite a feat.

"I'm serious."

"So am I. Don't you worry your pretty little cranium." I pecked a kiss on his cheek. "I have a dinner date at my sister's tonight. And she owes me about a billion favors in babysitting dues."

Macon tucked his hands in his pants pockets and watched me go, the winter wind blowing his hair in disarray. I jogged to my car at the curb and zoomed into the city toward Cade Enterprises. I needed to hurry and pay Bennett Cremwell a visit before he disappeared from prying, journalistic eyes.

As I sat at a light, a Morgon woman with slender silver wings stood outside of a shop next to a human girl. The human, a curvy blonde, gestured wildly with expressive eyes and a smile on her face. The delicate-boned Morgon tossed her head back and laughed, wings fluttering, her flaxen hair shimmering in the sunlight like golden silk. Friends. Just a decade ago, this would've never happened. Even with desegregation laws, the races merely had tolerated one another for business purposes. But not anymore.

Squeezing into a parking spot on the curb, I stepped out and cinched my coat tight, staring up at the towering skyscraper of Cade Enterprises situated in the center of the human business district. Who was I kidding? It *was* the center of the human business district. The lighthouse and beacon to which all other businesses aspired from afar, hoping to one day reach if they had a modicum of the success of corporate king, Pritchard Cade. My father.

I stepped through the revolving glass doors onto pristine, white tile and approached the receptionist's desk, wishing with all my might that I didn't run into him. I hadn't visited the premises in a few years, not since my financial separation from my father and an inherent need to avoid his towering kingdom altogether. My sister had cut herself off from him when she had married Lucius. Father was one of the few public figures who had rejected the intermarrying of the races. Of course, after my brother, Demetrius, married Shakara Icewing, my father had mellowed in his anti-Morgon ways. Demetrius had never told me all that had transpired during his courtship to Shakara that somehow softened my father's resolve. Though the animosity between both my siblings and our father had diminished over the past few years, resentment and old wounds still festered between them.

While my differences with him stemmed from refusing to accept his mandates to climb the corporate ladder he'd put in front of me, we still managed to have a civil relationship. The best way to avoid arguments was to steer clear of anything that might bring up his overbearing dominance and my willful disobedience. This is why I rarely stepped foot in his place of business. But nothing was going to keep me from my goal today.

I stepped up to the lobby receptionist's desk. "Hi, Cara."

"Hi." Her vacant smile told me she didn't recognize me.

"It's Moira Cade. I haven't been here in a while."

"Oh! Hi, Miss Cade." She straightened her spine and fiddled with her blouse. "So good to see you. Um, I apologize I didn't recognize you. Should I buzz your father and let him know you're here?"

She blinked rapidly. Good. She was nervous. I needed her to be so she wouldn't question why I needed to visit Mr. Cremwell.

"Actually, no. I need to speak with Bennett Cremwell in Technology. But I'm not sure what floor he's on. Could you look up his workstation for me?"

"Of course, I can." Scanning her comm screen, she tapped something onto her keyboard lickety-split. "Yes. He's on the thirty-fourth floor in Audio-Visual Systems. Room B sixteen. Would you like me to call him down for you?"

"No. Thank you. I don't want to drag him from his workspace. I'll just go right up."

I headed for the elevator before she could ask any more questions. A man in a sleek, navy-blue suit held the elevator door for me.

Early forties, well-groomed, and reeking of money, he turned a confident smile my way. "Floor?"

"Thirty-four, please." I kept my eyes straight, watching his reflection in the glossy doors when they squeezed shut. Taking in my shabby appearance, he probably thought I was a visiting friend of someone in the building. His eyes wandered the length of my jean-clad legs. I'd grown accustomed to people staring because of my height. What I could never tell by their inspection was whether a man admired a tall woman or thought them freakish. It didn't really matter. I stood even straighter, drawing his gaze to my eyes. His lips tilted into a wolfish smile. Thankfully, the elevator dinged, and I stepped out before the cradle-robbing businessman could strike up a "casual" conversation.

I strolled down B wing, ignoring glances from workers in their plexiglass cubicles, then stopped in front of room sixteen. The young man hunched over his desk, head in hands and staring at nothing, must be my guy. I knocked three times on the open door before entering and closing the door behind me. With messy brown hair, heavy bags under his eyes, and unkempt clothes, he sat behind the desk, sagging like an empty husk.

"Hi. Mr. Cremwell?"

Glazed, blood-shot eyes stared back, searching me for recognition and finding none. "Do I know you?"

"No." I extended my hand. "My name is Marina Creed. I have a few questions if you have a moment." I certainly wasn't going to use my real name. Hearing the boss's daughter's name might undo him altogether. He appeared to be hanging on by a thread. I couldn't blame him.

He didn't extend his own hand in greeting. Stress had obviously withered him down, making him fidgety and unfocused. I took a seat. "I wanted to talk to you about Maxine Mendale."

He flinched. "Maxine?"

I nodded. "I'm a reporter for *The Herald* at Gladium University. I've been following the disappearances and the murders of the three women. The first two were students at GU. Was Maxine a student, too?"

Dazed, he stared at me a moment. "Um, no. Maxine worked at a salon in the Warwick District on Lexington Avenue."

I flipped open my notebook and started jotting notes. Some of the stores in that area served both Morgon and human clientele. "Did she have Morgon clients at the salon?"

"I'm not sure. She never really said." He leaned forward, a sad smile creasing his pale face. "We didn't talk much about work."

"How did you two meet?"

"We have a mutual friend who introduced us at his club, Paramour."

I forced my eyes on my paper, refusing to show the jolt of shock that rocketed down my spine with this new discovery. Paramour just happened to be owned and managed by Mikal Lennox, my brother's best friend. And my ex-boyfriend of three years. I frowned and scrawled a note, feeling an acute headache coming on.

"Was the owner, Mikal Lennox, out with you on the night Maxine disappeared?"

"No. He doesn't like the Vaengar Games." A wave of relief washed over me. Though I'd hardly believe Mikal capable of any involvement in such a crime, it was nice to eliminate him right off the bat. "We actually started out at his club that night, but Maxine wanted to be adventurous. Said she wanted to check out the Morgons' idea of fun. Like a lot of girls these days."

He swallowed hard. I did, too. Poor Maxine never bargained for the adventure she would get that night. Nor did she deserve it. I reached across the desk and squeezed his hand. His weary expression softened at my touch.

"I know this is difficult. Just a few more questions, if that's okay with you."

"I already talked to the police about all this." He pulled away, combing his hands through his hair, his brow scrunching into a deep frown. "How did you know I was Maxine's friend anyway?"

He *would* have to make that astute realization now. I hated lying, but I couldn't tell him I had one of my best friends snooping around at the precinct for me.

"I have a few close friends in Nightwing Security." Actually, I was related by marriage to the owners, but general knowledge was better at the moment. "They were there that night. They found out your name."

He swallowed hard, his Adam's apple bobbing, his hands clenched together on top of the desk. "It was Morgons that did that to her," he whispered, voice laced with hatred.

"I know, Bennett, but I can guarantee you it wasn't the likes of my friends. The Nightwing clan wants justice for Maxine and the other girls, just as I do."

He must've seen the sincerity in my eyes. I hated to push people when they were stifled by grief, but time was of the essence. These killers wouldn't wait for us to mourn one girl before taking another. And I feared the repercussions of not capturing them soon. Gladium had become a haven for both races in recent years, a place where fear and ignorance had slowly faded into the background. And now, the Devlin Butchers were bringing all the prejudice and fear back to the forefront, rebuilding a wall we'd successfully torn down, brick by slow brick.

I implored Bennett with an expression I hoped conveyed both sympathy and earnestness. "Please."

He cleared his throat and gave me a short nod. "What else do you want to know?"

A swell of triumphant air filled my chest as I sped through the rest of my interview. I'd have good ammunition to get the favor I needed from my sister at dinner tonight.

Chapter 2

Jessen swung the door wide and wrapped me in a bear hug. "Muffin!"

"Are you ever going to come up with another nickname for me? I feel like I've grown out of Muffin."

"Never."

She ushered me through the foyer and into a split-level living room on the top floor of Nightwing Tower One. The top floor served as the residence, the second and third served as the guest suite and servant quarters. The remainder was used for whatever business and commerce the clan happened to own. Morgons counted from top to bottom as opposed to bottom up, so I currently stood on the first rather than the 103rd floor. The Nightwings owned several such skyscrapers in Gladium.

The warmth of my sister's home always welcomed me. Dark hardwood floors, a soft area rug woven in gold, red, and brown. A crimson velvet chaise and matching sofa, both scattered with plush cream and gold pillows. Flickering light from the six-by-ten foot fireplace and scattered candlesticks gilded the room in a warm glow.

Jessen took my coat and scarf as she closed the door, scanning my attire with a critical eye. Though several years older and a few inches shorter, she was my mirror-image in complexion—moon-pale skin and long, black hair. The one striking difference was my eyes—hazel-gold rather than deep brown. Still, we couldn't stand in a room together without everyone knowing we were sisters.

Those brown eyes were currently giving me the maternal once-over.

"What? What's wrong with what I'm wearing?"

"Nothing. You look great, but…"

"But?"

"Why don't you ever wear a dress or something? Aren't those faded jeans like a hundred years old?"

"These are my favorite jeans. Besides, you said this was a small get-together. Family and friends."

If she was up to her matchmaking schemes again, I was going to kill her. In a silver chiffon dress, black heels, and sparkling stud earrings, she looked a tad overdressed for a family dinner. However, she also appeared to be the elegant hostess and lovely wife of Lucius Nightwing. Just as stilettos and diamonds suited her, denim and boots suited me.

I narrowed my eyes as we moved farther into the room. "Is there someone specific I should be dressed up for?"

"No one special. Just Sorcha and—I just never see you dress up anymore. Such the grunge student these days. Do you need some money for shopping?"

I breathed out a heavy sigh, not ready to become embroiled in my struggling-college-student status again. "Who did you invite, Jess?"

Ignoring me, she called into the house. "Julian! Come see who's here!"

"Aunt Moira!"

Unable to stop the throaty laughter at the sight of my four-year-old nephew, I held my arms out to him. He was proof-positive that the Morgon DNA was dominant, beyond any shadow of a doubt, when the races intermingled. Standing a foot taller than the average human four-year-old, wearing only a pair of blue pajama pants, his mop of black hair flopped in his face as he ran to me. His thin black wings flapped furiously, lifting him like a glider when he leaped into my arms. Giggling, I held him low on the waist as he barely had control of his fluttering wings.

"Careful, big boy, or you'll lift me right off the ground."

He beamed, eyes a brilliant blue like his father's. His brows shot up. "You think so?"

"Well, maybe not just yet, but one day soon for sure."

Strong, little fingers clasped around my bare neck, my hair still pulled into a messy bun on top of my head. He pressed his forehead to mine, a devilish grin spread across his face, another trait he got from his father.

"You'll be the first one I take flying, Aunt Moira," he whispered.

"What are you two conspiring about?" Jessen called over her shoulder as she stepped toward the kitchen.

"Nothing," I said, giving him a wink.

"Promise?"

"Promise."

When Julian smiled, he lit me up inside, like sunshine in summer. I feared the things he would get away with as he grew older just from flashing that charming smile.

"Nothing!" I called out. He giggled, blue eyes glittering like glass.

"Come along, Julian." Brant, Lucius's longtime butler, valet, and all-around housekeeper had apparently added nanny to the job description. "To bed with you before your parents' guests arrive."

"I'll put him to bed, Brant."

The human male in his late forties visibly sighed with relief. "Thank you, Ms. Cade. I have a few things left to prepare in the dining room."

"Yay!" Julian's legs tightened around my middle, his wings flapping, blowing loose tendrils of my hair. "Will you tell me a story?"

As usual, I could deny him nothing. Sure, I wasn't ready to settle down and have my own family like Jessen, but I could certainly spoil this darling boy to my heart's delight.

"Sure." I carried him down the long corridor toward his bedroom, my boots echoing on the hardwood.

He whispered, "Brant's stories are boring."

I laughed. "I'm sure he tries his best. What story would you like to hear tonight?"

"Tell me another about King Radomis, the dragon king of the North."

Entering his bedroom, the chamber was bathed in serene, low light. I marveled at the cosmos above, a mirror of the night sky sweeping in slow circles on the domed ceiling. A crescent moon was beginning to rise from the left corner of his bedroom, as it surely was outside. Such a lovely invention by Nightwing Industries—a balm to send a child into sleep. So many humans categorized Morgons as creators of advanced munitions and security alarms, never seeing the simple beauty their minds could also create. Some prejudices and fear lingered long after laws tried to eradicate them.

"How about a story of the Golden Treasure in the Vale of Stars?"

"Nah. The treasure always changes."

I lifted his pajama shirt off the dresser and held it out for him. He slipped his arms through and then gave me his back so I could wrap the flaps around each shoulder blade where the wings protruded. "That's because no one knows what the treasure truly is." I buttoned along the two seams under each wing.

Wide-eyed, he asked excitedly, "Is the Vale of Stars a real place? Do they have a real treasure?"

I tapped him on the nose playfully, casting an air of mystery to my voice. "I don't know. But some say it is. No one really knows." Placing my little charge in his big, mahogany bed, I then tucked the white down comforter at his waist.

"That would be cool if it was." He flipped to his side, propping his head up on his hand. "I'd be the hero and go on the quest to find the treasure to save the world." His wings lay limp against the mattress. I stretched out beside him.

He referred to the version of the story that declared the treasure would one day save the world from evil, though no storyteller ever knew how. "So you want to hear that one?"

He shook his head. "King Radomis."

"King Radomis, huh?"

"I love your stories about him." He snuggled his head against his pillow, angelic eyes pleading.

"How about his queen, Morga?"

"Pfft." He waved his tiny hand. "She's just a girl."

I arched a brow at him.

"I mean, she's not like you or anything."

"Oh, really? How so?"

"Well, you're not a girl."

I laughed. "This is quite a revelation. Here, I thought I was."

A blush crawled up his pale cheeks. That was one trait he did inherit from his mother, milk-pale skin, like my own.

"I mean, you're a girl, Aunt Moira, but not a sissy girl."

"Ah." I bit my lip so I wouldn't laugh, forcing my face into a grave expression. "Well, it just so happens that neither was Queen Morga."

"But didn't you say she was a princess that had to be rescued by the king? That he saved her from those bad men?"

"You're a good listener. Princess Morga was fated to marry a man of her father's choosing, a cruel prince from a western kingdom. On the night before she married, she planned to escape during the traditional rite of bathing beneath the full moon."

One of Julian's wings lifted and fell higher against the pillow, his voice rising with excitement. "That's when King Radomis swooped down, shifted into a man, and rescued her."

I nodded. "Would you like to tell *me* a story? Or shall I do the telling?"

Sheepish, he mumbled, "But I know all that part."

"Well, let's skip further ahead to the part you don't know."

He nuzzled his head into his fluffy pillow. I combed dark locks away from his face. Brilliant eyes were intent on mine.

"When Princess Morga of the human kingdom in the West became Queen Morga of the dragon lair in the North, she was hated. Despised by all."

"Hated?" Julian stifled a yawn and curled a fist under his cheek.

"Because she was human."

Julian frowned. I knew he thought of his own human mother. And perhaps of me. "Yes, they did not share the more sophisticated views of today where humans and Morgons live peacefully alongside one another." I wouldn't burden my precious nephew with the fact that only *some* shared this view in our world. He had time enough to learn of hatred and ignorance.

"So what happened to her? They were mean to her?"

"Stop talking and listen, Julian."

He snuggled deeper as I caressed his bare cheek, sweeping gentle fingers along his shoulders and the thin arch of his wing, soft as suede. Having put him to bed so often, I knew what would send him into an easy sleep. I lowered my voice and drew out the syllables into a sonorous roll. What Julian called my *story voice*.

"It was worse than being mean to her. A rival female dragon, one who was pledged to marry Radomis before he fell in love with Morga, despised her so much that she plotted to poison the queen."

He opened his mouth on a gasp but said not a word.

"However," I continued, "Queen Morga was a smart woman. She knew envious eyes watched her all the time. There was a gathering of dragon royalty from every realm, dressed in full regalia in their human forms. When her rival, Balsheba of the Bloodback clan, toasted in her honor at a gathering of the courtiers, she suspected something at once. Balsheba raised a goblet in front of the whole assembly, saying, 'I drink to our new queen's health and long life, honoring her with this blood-ruby, my family heirloom.' After sipping the wine, she dropped the scarlet ruby into the chalice, passing the drink to her queen. Now, it was a longtime custom of the dragons that when a toast is made in honor of another, the receiver must accept by drinking of the same glass. Queen Morga had already realized the ruby was laced with poison. If she drank from the poisoned cup, she would die. If she did not, she would stir Balsheba's entire clan against her husband's house. Morga had no fears that her love, Radomis, would fight to the death for her. But she didn't want to be the one to divide the kingdoms, to be the cause of so much violence."

"What did she do?" murmured Julian before opening his mouth in a wide yawn.

"Well, it just so happened that King Radomis had been detained from Balsheba's toast by one of her minions. He walked into the throng the moment the queen took the chalice from Balsheba's hands, unaware of what had transpired. Morga turned to Radomis, raised the chalice and smiled at the assembly, saying 'Balsheba does me a great honor, and I accept her gift on behalf of my loving husband, Radomis. But it is a human custom that the king always drinks before his queen. My love, would you do the honors first?' Now Morga would never have let a single drop touch his precious lips, so she stood close by his side lest her plan not work. Balsheba's face blanched white, realizing that her deception would now kill the object of her desires. King Radomis took the goblet and tilted it in the air. 'To my queen.' And just as he lifted the drink to his lips, Balsheba's father leaped from the crowd and knocked the cup from the king's hands, sending it clanging across the stone floor. The blood-ruby bounced and rolled to Balsheba's feet, leaving a trail of poisoned red wine in its wake. 'What is this?' asked the king, his eyes blazing, realizing at once there had been some malevolent intent toward his queen. 'The drink was poisoned, my lord.' Balsheba's father knelt before the king. 'It was not intended for you. Forgive me. Forgive us.'"

Julian's droopy eyes slid closed. I waited for them to reopen to tell the rest of the tale. How Balsheba's father and three of her brothers were beheaded for the crime of treason, how Balsheba was exiled into the wastelands of the north and was never heard from again. But Julian slept sound. I tucked the covers close around his chin.

Jessen leaned in the doorway, arms crossed, a small smile creasing her lips. "Not your typical bedtime story," she whispered.

"Not your typical child."

"That's for sure."

We walked down the hall toward the dining room, arms linked.

"He loves you so, Moira."

"As I love him." I smiled to myself, catching my sister's watchful gaze.

"Haven't you thought of a family of your own yet?"

"Oh, come on, Jess. I'm twenty years old. I don't think my ovaries have shriveled up just yet."

"I know, I know. It's just that ever since Mikal, you've not once dated another guy. Are you still heartbroken over him? Or what?"

I let out a heavy puff of air. "I was the one who did the heartbreaking with Mikal, remember? He was a great guy. Seriously. He just wasn't… enough. I don't know how to say it. And I'm more interested in my career than I am in being a baby-making factory." I glanced down at the small swelling just starting to show. "No offense."

"None taken. I like being Lucius's baby-making factory." A naughty look.

"Gross. Too much information, thank you." Voices from the dining area drifted into the hallway. "So go ahead and tell me who you're setting me up with tonight."

Her cheeks flamed pink as she spit out a quick, albeit brief, description. "His name is Kraven Silverback. He works with Nightwing Security and is a friend of Lucius and Lorian's. He's a really good guy. He's intelligent and easy on the eyes. Just give him a shot. I know you'll like him."

I rolled my eyes. Jess didn't get it. Guys complicated my life, steering me farther off-course from my goal of becoming a serious journalist. They always wanted to put me in a corner where they could take care of me and keep me safe. Investigative journalists didn't sit in corners. They got in the muck of it right along with detectives sometimes, seeking the truth, no matter the cost. And now, she was setting me up with some overprotective Morgon who works for Nightwing Security. Not what I needed.

Hmm. Wait. Nightwing Security. Maybe this could be to my advantage. They supplied security for the Vaengar Games. And I needed to get into the games and mix with the Morgon crowd in order to find the man Cremwell described to me in our interview—*the black-haired, black-eyed guy with a facial tic*—who kept buying them drinks at an after-party in the basement of the Stadium.

"Just be nice, Moira. Please."

"I'm always nice."

She arched a brow at me, making a face I often made myself, meaning *I don't believe you.* "What are you plotting? I know that look in your eye."

I scoffed. "I do not plot. I plan."

"Hmph. Like when you planned your sixteenth birthday by sneaking out with Kris and going to a Morgon bonfire, getting grounded for six months."

My best friend, Krissa, who preferred Kris, and I had gotten into some trouble a time or two in our teen years. "Grounded? It was more like house-arrest. You're one to talk. I do believe you were the one sneaking out of your college dorm which landed you in a particular nightclub on the Morgon side of town. The night which got you all this." I gestured around us to the sprawling home.

Jessen heaved a sigh, one hand rounding her belly. "Do you always have to be so verbal when you're annoyingly right? You know, subtlety might do you some good."

"Not in my nature, Jess, and you know it."

"What happened to that little, wide-eyed girl I used to take to the park and buy ice cream for?"

I gave her a squeeze as we entered the dining room. "She grew up."

Lucius and Lorian Nightwing stood near the bar, drinks in hand, alongside another Morgon man. The brothers mirrored each other in stature and huge, arching black wings, both bearing an air that made most people want to take one step back in their presence. Lucius held himself with more grace than Lorian, Sorcha's mate and husband. Lorian's gaze often troubled me. With one bright blue eye and one amber-gold, it was hard to keep my features schooled into nonchalance. It wasn't just his eyes, but an unsettling predatory air that filled the room when he walked in. I asked Sorcha about it once. She simply whispered with a salacious grin, "It's his dragon. His beast keeps to the surface."

Though I didn't quite understand what that meant, I felt it clearly enough. While Lucius was certainly dangerous in his own right, he exuded confidence and a stoic charm. Lorian was a bit more...wild.

The silver-winged Morgon with his back to me turned as we entered. Brawny and broad-shouldered, typical Morgon build, his stony features relaxed into a smile when his eyes met mine.

Sorcha practically hopped across the room, her clingy green dress swishing with her hips. "Moira. There you are." Barely coming up to my shoulder, she swooped me into a hug. "Damn, girl. What is this? Shabby-chic week or something?" She stared at my plain black top and tattered jeans. "Girl, if I was you with those legs, I'd wear the shortest skirt I could find."

"Good thing you're not me."

She laughed at my sass, looping her arm through mine. "Come sit, so I don't get a crick in my neck from looking up."

"You have to look up at Lorian all the time."

"True." She added in a low voice with a smirk. "But my neck and head are typically resting on the mattress."

I punched her lightly in the arm.

"Ow! Are you still doing that body punching class or whatever?"

"Body boxing. And yes. It keeps me in good shape."

"And keeps plenty of highly attractive bruises on your skin."

I touched the bruise at my neck, remembering how my sparring partner and brother, Demetrius, had landed a swift kick yesterday. I shrugged. "It's worth it."

"There are better ways to blow off steam and keep in shape, Moira."

Sorcha was no longer looking at me, but gazing across the room at her Morgon man, a lascivious grin creasing her face. I shook my head, trying *not* to imagine what she was imagining.

Jessen waved us over. "Kraven, I'd like you to meet my sister, Moira Cade."

I withheld a heavy sigh. "Hi." I extended my hand. Thankfully, he shook it like a real person, not like I was a dainty flower that might break under the slight pressure of a man's handshake. No initial sparks, but I had to give the guy a chance.

"Hello," he said with a smile. "It's nice to meet you."

He walked with me toward the table, held out a chair, and took the seat on my right, folding his wings tightly against his back. If Morgons let their wings extend in the seated position, they could easily brush the person next to them—a gesture, either protective or suggestive, depending on the situation, saved for those in more intimate relations. Glad he wasn't being pushy on that score.

The table was set elegantly with bone-white china rimmed in gold. Glass votive candles lined the table runner of crimson brocade. Candlelight sparkled off the crystal-cut wine and water glasses. I unfolded my napkin in my lap, offering a small smile to Kraven as he did the same.

Jessen had hired two servers. The two human women, dressed in black and white livery, served us bowls of rich, brown broth with mushrooms and flanks of steak.

"Mmm. This smells great," said Sorcha, spooning a bite. "Did Ruth make this?"

Jessen's face contorted in mock-horror. "Do you think she'd allow any other cook in my kitchen? I'm sorry, *her* kitchen."

They prattled about cooks and domestic stuff, while my mind wandered. Cremwell had said the Morgon who seemed overly friendly, buying them drink after drink at the after-party, never did give them a name. He had gotten distracted by a fight in the Pit between two Morgons—some sort of main-event fighting match of the after-party—and when Cremwell looked back to the bar, the guy was gone. So was Maxine.

"I understand you're studying journalism at the University."

Kraven's brown eyes watched me as he stirred the soup around, not eating. He had a square jaw, and his nose crooked slightly to the left, a bad break that had never healed quite right. Still, it didn't mar his appearance much. Though rough, he had a calm, kind face.

"Yes. I graduate next year. And you work for Nightwing Security, correct?"

He nodded. "I do."

"I'm sure your job is interesting."

"Sometimes." He continued to stir the soup, never taking a bite. I glanced at Lucius and Lorian, both drinking glasses of red wine, ignoring the food.

"Is there a reason you don't like this particular dish?"

Morgon men had healthy appetites, so something was up. His expression showed surprise for a split-second before settling back into nonchalance. "You're quite observant, Moira."

"I'm a journalist. A writer. We tend to be watchers."

"Ah." He smiled, leaning closer to whisper, "Well, don't tell the cook, but meat cooked this thorough actually turns the stomach of most Morgons."

"Really?" The flank steak was tender and delicious, but it was indeed cooked completely through. "Why is that?"

He shrugged one shoulder, his wings relaxing a fraction. "I suppose it is the dragon in us. We like our meat bloody, I'm afraid."

"Interesting. I've never heard that before." I lifted the heavy glass goblet and took a sip of water.

"It's not something generally known or, should I say, confessed in mixed company." By mixed company, he meant humans and Morgons. "Not everyone likes to be reminded of our less civilized ancestry."

I glanced over his shoulder at the giant silvery wings shining by candlelight. "Well, it's kind of hard to miss."

He laughed. A very pleasant laugh. "True."

I shrugged. "My sister wouldn't care. Seems like something she would've picked up on by now."

"It can be easily overlooked. Humans and Morgons consume everything just about the same."

"Except red meat," I amended.

He nodded, smiling politely. The second course was pasta with a seafood cream sauce. All the dinner guests started to devour the appetizing dish.

"So, Kraven, do you ever work the Vaengar Games?"

He wiped his mouth with a napkin, sitting back. "I don't usually. Not anymore, anyway. Have you ever been?"

"No." I sipped my water, angling toward him, considering some of the information Bennett Cremwell had given me about what goes on at the after-parties in the Vaengar Stadium. "Do you go and watch fights in the Pit after the Vaengar Games?"

Silverware clinked against a plate as someone dropped a fork. The low conversations shushed altogether. I glanced down the table.

I shrugged. "What?"

"How would you know about the Pit?" asked Jessen, frowning.

The level of scowling by every pair of eyes at the table, except Sorcha, put me on edge.

Sorcha flipped dark-red hair over one shoulder. "Someone's been more involved in extracurricular activities than she led on."

"No. Actually, I haven't."

"What's this about?" Jessen's lips tightened into a grim line, the same look she had given me when I was a little girl doing something dangerous, like playing too close to the lake or the woods.

"I need some help with something. Some Morgon help, and I hoped Kraven was the one to give it."

Kraven angled toward me. "Would you be more specific?"

"Wait. No." Jessen tossed her napkin on the table, flipping out, just as I thought she would. "How the hell did you find out about the after-parties in the cellars of the Stadium?"

"You know," I accused.

Sorcha giggled.

Jessen rounded on her. "What are you laughing about?"

"You, Jessen. You still look at Moira and see your five-year-old baby sister. If you hadn't noticed, she's grown up. Taller than you, as a matter of fact."

"I don't care if she's six-feet tall or ten-feet tall, she *is* still my baby sister. And I don't want you going to those after-parties Ella told us about."

Lucius took Jessen's hand in his. "Perhaps we should hear what Moira needs help with. She's waiting patiently for you to calm down before she continues."

I loved Lucius. He understood me so well. Probably because our personalities were similar—quiet with a keen perception. And stubborn as a brick wall when we wanted to be. He held Jessen's hand, brushing his thumb across her knuckles, soothing her. The sight of the two so openly affectionate—a Morgon and a human—still shocked me a little, when only five years ago, no one had even heard of an intermarried couple like them before.

"Fine." Jessen inhaled and exhaled, putting on a poor show of being in control. "What help are you talking about?"

I folded and set my napkin on my plate, squaring my shoulders and facing the firing squad. "I need a Morgon, preferably a male, to be my guide in discovering the identity of the Devlin Butchers, who I believe are actually part of a Morgon cult."

Lorian jerked to his feet. A guttural growl swelled in a violent vibration, rippling down the table and shattering every wine and water glass, sucking the breath right out of my lungs.

Dinner was over.

Chapter 3

Sorcha held the stem of her broken wine glass mid-air, gazing up at Lorian, now towering over the table. Jessen stared blank-faced at me. An awkward, edgy silence filled the room.

Lucius stood, his wings flaring halfway open. "Let's all go to the living room where we can talk more comfortably. And calmly."

I didn't realize I was shaking until Kraven pulled my chair back. We followed in silence from the room, Lorian and Sorcha lagging behind. I caught a quick glance of her standing on tip-toe, cupping his face as she murmured in a gentle tone, "It's okay. I'm okay. That's all behind us."

What just happened? I expected some sort of outburst, but not *that*. I was definitely out of the loop on something.

Lucius paced by the crackling fire. Jessen sank into an overstuffed wingback chair, obviously bought specifically for her as Morgons didn't sit in high-backed furniture. I settled onto a sofa, pulling a pillow into my lap. Kraven sat beside me, leaning forward, elbows on knees, hands clasped together, wings slightly open. Finally, Sorcha and Lorian joined us. She stretched out on the chaise lounge. Lorian stood at her back, face frozen in stone-like rage.

Lucius paused, hands at his back. "Before we begin this conversation, I'll apologize for my brother's outburst." Lucius turned his blue-fire gaze in my direction, his dragon sparkling near the surface. "I'm aware that you may not understand why Lorian reacted in such a manner, and I'm afraid that's not a story for me to tell. It's Sorcha and Lorian's. Suffice to say, I think you just caught him off-guard."

Sorcha curled her legs underneath her. Lorian looked like a sentinel, guarding his queen. The journalist in me wanted to ask a million questions, but the survivor said to keep my mouth shut.

Lucius faced his brother. "Are we all capable of continuing this conversation more calmly?"

By all, he meant Lorian, who returned a sharp nod, saying nothing. His face didn't portray calm in any way, shape, or form.

"Now," said Lucius. "Why exactly do you need to discover the identity of the Devlin Butchers?" Lucius's arched brow and paternal manner told me he was no longer on my side. Or he might not be for long.

"I'm covering the story for *The Herald*. I've been—"

"A college paper, Moira?" Jessen snapped out of her stupor. "You can't be serious! You're talking about hanging in a place where girls are being abducted and murdered. Do you even know what they're doing to them?" Her voice rose to a screechy level.

"More than you do. I've seen pictures."

"Pictures. What pictures? How?"

"I can't reveal my sources."

"She can't reveal her sources." Jessen threw her hands in the air, ripping me with her sardonic tone.

"Besides, I'm not saying I'm running blindly into this. I'm asking for your help." I scanned the room, making eye contact with Lucius and Lorian. "I know this is dangerous. Believe me, I *know*." My voice cracked. I couldn't help it, imagining Maxine's mutilated body. "But I also have a lead on someone who might be involved in Maxine Mendale's abduction at the stadium at one of these after-parties. And I'm not sitting back and doing nothing. Jessen, I know you're worried about me, and I love you for that. But this is something I have to do. *Please* understand."

The room fell into silence again. I twisted the medal at my neck.

"What's your lead?" Lorian's first words, deep and gruff. And though his question was a compelling command, not a request, I wouldn't give them anything unless they gave something back.

I sat up a little straighter. "Did the stadium security cameras catch any footage of Maxine Mendale with a suspicious Morgon?" I needed to know if they'd already identified the one we were looking for. If so, then I had nothing to bargain with.

"Negative," admitted Lucius. "There was an electrical blowout earlier that night, knocking out the system. We're still investigating to discover if it was coincidence or more than that."

"Okay. Well, I have a good description of the Morgon man last seen with Maxine Mendale." I paused, sizing up my attentive audience. "Will you guarantee me a guide, someone to help me blend in? I don't even care if you have a dozen body guards there, as long as they're not hovering over me."

"What do you plan to do with the information you find, if anything?" asked Lucius.

"I'll take it to the Gladium Precinct. Of course, I'll demand exclusive rights on the story when I'm able to release it."

"Going to the precinct won't be necessary," said Lorian. "Nightwing Security is already investigating. We're working with the Morgon Guard in Drakos."

Nightwing Security was mostly a private-for-hire agency in Gladium, but their connection to the Guard ran deep. Lorian had a scrolling tattoo with the letters MG on the back of his neck. I had asked Sorcha about it, and she told me he was once in the Morgon Guard.

"The Morgon Guard?"

Lorian paced closer to Lucius. "They seek justice and retribution. Among other things."

I could only imagine what other things the Morgon Guard was responsible for as Lorian hadn't bothered to enlighten me.

I considered whether I was betraying my own race by allying with the Morgons, giving them information I denied the precinct. Though there were a few Morgons working for the GP and their elite forces, the police were primarily human. The inner-debate of where my loyalties lay took all of three seconds.

"Fine." I straightened, tossing the pillow out of my lap. "I'll tell you everything I know already and everything I discover from here on out, as long as you help me get into one of these after-parties."

Kraven stood and spoke up for the first time, hands at his back. "I can be her guide."

Lucius tucked his hands in the pockets of his black slacks, looking as if he were discussing the weather, not a multiple-murder investigation. "That'll work. You can take her to the game on Friday, as if you're just on a casual date."

A date?

"But we'll need more than one on-scene to ensure her protection. I won't let my sister-in-law go anywhere near that deathtrap unless she's fully guarded."

Lorian piped up. "Kol. He's leading the investigation for the Morgon Guard anyway. She may be able to give him some insight from the human perspective."

Lucius grinned. "Yes. And you know how much he appreciates the human perspective."

"Nevertheless. I'll contact him tonight."

Lucius faced Jessen. "Will that do, love? Kol Moonring will be her personal bodyguard. What more could you ask for?"

Kraven shifted from one foot to another next to me.

Jessen shifted in her seat, seeming to consider before giving a tight nod. "That will do."

"I'll say," added Sorcha, giving me a wink. "You won't have to worry about a thing, sweetie."

I'm not quite sure how the mention of this guy suddenly brought Lorian's temper in check and my sister to heel. As conversation mellowed into less volatile topics, all I could think was, who was this Kol Moonring?

* * * *

I was forbidden by both my sister and Sorcha from wearing my drab jeans on my "date" with Kraven. Sorcha's advice, "You'll never blend in looking like a homeless, college student." Thankfully, Kris was much more fashion-forward than I was and came to my aid. We had veered away from the uptown boutiques and had shopped in the Warwick District for something a bit edgier and more appropriate for a night out in the Morgon world.

Finally back at my apartment, I'd showered and dressed in record time. I zipped up my left boot and stood for her inspection. Grinning from ear to ear, she was sprawled across my bed, twirling a tendril of her light-brown hair.

"So?" I gestured to my outfit. "Will I blend in?"

"Honey, I don't know about blending in, but you'll put every other woman to shame. Human or Morgon."

"Please."

"Seriously. You look so hot. Why don't you dress up more often?"

"Now you sound like my sister. What's itching?" I peered over one shoulder, fumbling with one hand, trying to find whatever was scratching my shoulder blade.

"I got it." Kris popped off the bed, then turned me to face the mirror. "One of the laces is loose."

"Loose?" My reflection revealed a gold corset, embroidered with black-stitched roses on the front of the bodice. It may have been a lovely work of craftsmanship, but it was sucking the life out of me. Kris tightened and tucked the laces. I winced, both at the squeezing of my ribcage and the further heightening of my breasts. I'd never put myself quite on display.

"I don't know, Kris. I feel…overexposed."

"Isn't that the point?" She grabbed the short leather jacket off the bed and tossed it to me. "Here. This'll help."

I slipped into the jacket, glancing over my shoulder in the mirror at the copper-studded dragon in flight on the back. A leather-clad woman with a dragon stitched on her jacket would be a silent invitation to the more aggressive Morgons. I was hoping to draw the one Bennett Cremwell had told me about. Of course, I hadn't admitted a word of this to anyone else. A shiver of anticipation trembled through me. Was I pushing things too far? Still, I felt safe knowing several Morgon men from Nightwing Security would be incognito at the games. As well as Kol Moonring, whoever he was.

"Your outfit is hot. Hair looks great. Makeup is awesome. Because of me, of course."

I laughed, heading out of the bedroom. "Okay, Vaengar Games. Here I come."

"Isn't your date picking you up?"

"Morgons can't ride in cars, and I'm not letting him fly me there, so we're meeting at the stadium."

She followed me to the door of my studio apartment, picking up her bag off my thrift-shop coffee table on the way out. "Mmm, why not let him fly you there? Damn, if that wouldn't be cool."

"It's a business date. I told you that." I locked the door to my apartment, ignoring the flutter in my stomach at the thought of flying with a Morgon.

"Well, if it's business, you should've taken me along. I could've photographed the scene for you."

Hope laced her voice, but I didn't want to involve Kris on this dangerous mission. She was not only my best friend, but also an award-winning photographer and videographer for *The Herald*. I had no idea what I was walking into, and I wouldn't drag her into it.

"Not necessary." I hated seeing the disappointment in her eyes. "I'm just getting some preliminary info for a new story."

She shrugged, falling in stride with me on the sidewalk. "I still say you should've hitched a ride, business date or not."

"I'm not letting a man carry me around like some child. That's ridiculous."

"You're ridiculous sometimes, Moira, with all your feminist ideals. It's okay to let a man treat you like a woman. Being feminine isn't being weak."

"It's not that."

"Why not give this Morgon a chance then?" she asked.

"It's not that I'm a racist or anything, if that's what you think."

She burst into throaty laughter. "No. I never suspected you of being a racist."

Kris's unusual mixture of tawny skin and bright green eyes came from her parents' interracial marriage. Her father was from a dark people in the southern province of Nebea along the Sorrel Sea. Her mother was born and raised in Gladium.

People might raise an eyebrow at a human interracial union, but that's all. What ruffled society's feathers more was marrying outside your class. What rankled the aristocracy more than that, even with desegregation laws in place, even with high-profile marriages like my sister's to Lucius, was the mating to a Morgon. The old mindset was hard to break, despite the façade of being generally accepted in public society. Behind closed doors was another thing altogether.

We stopped at my car. My shitty old clunker with peeling paint was a daily reminder I was standing on my own feet, not allowing my father to rule my life. Kris might have had a point. Had I pushed my father away in order to appear strong? To be an independent woman who relied on no man to stand on her own two feet? In doing so, I seemed to have pushed all men away.

"Are Morgon men too tough for you to handle?" she teased.

I sighed, giving her a brief hug. "Let's talk gender politics in a male-dominated society some other time."

"You're avoiding my question."

"You're so smart. I'll call you tomorrow."

She waved over her shoulder. "Have fun on your *business* date!" She yelled into the night air, giggling all the way to her car.

Traffic was heavy, but I found a spot in the stadium parking lot and arrived at the entrance just in time. Kraven waited for me under the double-archway. His eyes swept over me in an assessing glimpse as I approached. He straightened, wings half open, expression unreadable. I hoped I hadn't overdone it trying so hard to fit in. "Is it too much?"

A smile cracked his square jaw. "No." He shook his head. "You look great."

By now I'd met him under the arch, but he hadn't made a move to go in. Inwardly, I cursed Kris for pushing me to wear this damn corset. "Are you sure?"

"I'm sure." He held out his arm, chuckling as if to his own private joke. "But so much for not attracting attention."

Deep breath in, then out. "Okay." I linked my arm through his. The charade of my first date with a Morgon had begun. "Let's go then."

Our plan was to arrive near the end of the game, so we could blend in easily with the crowd. I'd been to the Vaengar Games once before. I wrote my first feature story on this favorite Morgon sporting event. The Gladium crowd cheered our home team, the Sabers. Teams from Morgon provinces all over the place traveled to compete here in Vaengar Stadium.

We climbed the final ramp, and Kraven led me into the Box, opening wide to the vast arena. Energy and sound hit me like a tidal wave. The bell tolled to begin a match, and the crowd roared, sending vibrations through my chest. The Box was a sectioned off area with plush seating and a private bar, specifically for the elite Morgon clans and sometimes their fortunate human friends. I'd never been here before. Even with my tight connection to Lucius and Lorian, I'd never stepped foot into this realm of the Morgon world. A little uneasy, but I hid it well. One thing I learned in my upbringing among high society was to keep my mask on at all times. You never knew who was watching, waiting to find and exploit your weakness.

"Conn!" shouted Kraven, waving over a rust-winged Morgon with auburn hair. I knew him.

"Conn Rowanflame, this is—"

"Moira Cade," he finished, taking my hand in both of his. "We met at Julian's last birthday party, right?"

I nodded. "Good to see you again." As charming and handsome as ever. Many Morgon men bore a stern, sometimes forbidding, exterior. Not Conn. He smiled easily and wore a mischievous glint in his eye, promising he was up to no good.

"You're here with Kraven?" He raised an eyebrow.

"Yeah. She's here with me. So don't flirt too much."

"Me?" Conn looked appalled at the accusation, slipping an arm over my shoulder. "Never. Come sit in my private section." He waved Kraven off. "You go get us some drinks. What would you like, Moira?"

"A beer is fine."

"She wants a beer, and I'll have the same."

I laughed. Kraven just shook his head before moving through the crowd toward the bar. We'd mutually decided that our plan was to pretend we'd been dating for a month. It would make others more comfortable to open up to me. It would also be an outright challenge for Morgon men to test our connection.

In a quick briefing over the comm yesterday, Kraven explained that without a scent imprint in my skin, other Morgons would know I was still "available." Before I could even ask what a scent imprint was, he explained that when Morgons were serious about a female, Morgon or human, she carried his scent in her skin. Other Morgon men knew it immediately. Because I didn't bear his imprint, Morgon men would be vying for my attention. And hopefully, one of them would be the black-haired, black-eyed Morgon with a facial tic.

Fortunately, Conn's section was front and center with a great view of both the arena as well as the other tiers of fans. I had a feeling that Conn's appearance wasn't at all coincidental. The way his eyes darted across the crowd, searching for possible threats, reminded me of the way Lucius and Lorian assessed and observed. He must be on the Nightwing Security team.

Just as I sat, a silver-winged Saber flew past our section, the wind whooshing my hair back.

"Get 'em, Slade!"

"You know him?" I asked Conn.

"Yeah. A friend of mine."

Vaenger was basically a game of "capture the torque" where each team alternated playing offense and defense per match. The goal was to capture the golden torque dangling at the top of a spire welded into the cavern floor at the center of the arena. It was the job of the stealer on the offense to capture it before the bell tolled the ending of the match. And before being burned by a fire-breathing opponent on the defensive team.

Both teams played bare-chested, zooming through the air at ridiculous speeds. The opponents' stealer flew high above the players, circling in a slow, strategic way. He had wide, deep-purple wings, like the rest of his team. My blood pumped faster at the fanfare of dragonwings beating Morgons into the air, whipping their muscular bodies into a magnificent display of beauty and strength. A common spectacle for Morgons, I tried not to reveal how bewitching such a sight was for me.

"Who are we up against?"

I already knew, but didn't want Conn or anyone else to know that I'd spent the week in between dinner at my sister's and tonight researching every Vaenger team from here to Cloven.

"The Storm-gales, a rural team from outside Drakos called Violetvale, which also happens to be their clan name."

And also reflected the color of their wings. I nodded, sucking in a breath as a purple-winged player zipped past the box, blowing a stream of orange flame at Conn's friend who grappled with him in the air. The two went air-tumbling to the dirt floor of the arena.

"Here, Moira." Kraven was beside me, handing me a mug of beer.

I sipped lightly, wanting to keep sober. Morgon beer was stronger than human brews. Everyone knew their DNA differed from humans in many ways. One was their unbelievably high tolerance for alcohol.

"Conn. You going to the after-party?" asked Kraven.

Conn arched a brow, his gaze flicking in my direction. "Yeah. You're not bringing Moira, are you?"

"Why not?" I asked. "Kraven told me the fights in the Pit are pretty exciting."

I'd gotten a brief explanation that the after-party centered around a Morgon-on-Morgon fight match, surrounded by heavy drinking and carousing before and after the main event.

Conn leaned closer to Kraven. I pretended to be distracted by the players, the Storm-gale stealer sweeping down in a vertical dive to snatch the torque.

"It's not safe these days for humans, Kraven. Does Lucius know you've got his sister-in-law here?"

Kraven whispered something I couldn't hear.

"Right," was Conn's terse reply.

The crowd erupted as the Storm-gale stealer whisked the torque from the spire, crowning his team the winners.

"Come on," Kraven whispered close to my ear. "Let's beat the rush."

He threaded his fingers through mine, leading me out of the Box and down the corridor to a darkened stairwell. We descended, each curving flight lit by one flaming torch. My heart picked up pace. Kraven halted one step below me. His eyes shimmered in the dark, an animal's night vision.

"Focus on slowing your pulse."

"You can hear it?"

"I can feel it." He squeezed my hand, his thumb brushing my inner wrist. "But Morgons can sense fear. For the wrong kind of Morgon, it's an aphrodisiac."

"Isn't that the kind we're trying to find tonight?"

His eyes narrowed. "Slow your pulse."

A Morgon couple slipped past us, clinging to each other. Closing my eyes, I inhaled a deep breath, blowing it out steadily.

Opening my eyes, I nodded. "Lead the way."

Five flights down, the stairway opened to an underground tavern, one vast room with nooks and niches, bars and booths along one wall and a barred-cage surrounding a pit in the ground to one side. Lit by torchlight in sconces along the wall and a few wrought-iron chandeliers dangling on chains from the ceiling, the room remained mostly in shadow. Dance music pumped from somewhere. The entire scene was...seductive.

Still holding my drink, Kraven led me to one side, away from parties of drinkers already making noise.

"So this is it?" I took a bigger swig of beer, needing a tad of liquid courage.

"This is it. There'll be a fight later in the Pit."

"Do you see the Nightwing Security guys?"

"Yep. They're here."

"Conn doesn't know about this plan?"

"Lucius didn't want everyone knowing your involvement. They might give something away, guarding you too close. But with the recent abductions, he heightened security anyway. Everyone is on alert."

I scanned the crowds. No one looked our way. Of course, Lucius and Lorian's guys would be expert at disguise. I needed to move about the room, see if I could find my target. "I'm going to roam a bit."

His frown deepened. "I'll come with you."

"Kraven, no Morgon man is going to approach me with you hovering. Especially not the one we're looking for."

He must've seen the determination in my eyes, softening as I waited for him to bend. He scanned the room. "Fine. Just don't leave this basement for any reason."

"Don't worry." I wasn't stupid.

Taking another gulp for courage, I meandered through the crowd. Morgon men's eyes followed me as I passed, none of them matching the description by Bennett Cremwell.

Raucous laughter and cat-calls from a table in the corner drew my attention. I set my beer on a round-top, meandering toward the throng. Shielded by the winged-backs of Morgon men and a few women, I couldn't see what drew everyone's attention at the center. Inching closer, I heard a feminine squeal of laughter.

A strong hand wrapped my forearm in a firm grip, a voice rough as rock spoke one word. A command. "No."

A wall of heat at my back, I glanced over my shoulder at the tallest Morgon man I'd ever seen. I stepped away, pulling my arm free. He let me. He was hard in every way—demeanor, expression, posture, appearance. A cold slab of marble chiseled down into the statue-like physique of a dark, forbidding Morgon. He had a reddened scar slashing from above his left cheekbone to below his lip. His eyes were a midnight blue except for a pale ring circling the pupils. They seemed crafted by magic or some other

Juliette Cross

supernatural force as they glinted blue-silver in the dark. No one needed to tell me his name. It left my lips without my consent. "Kol Moonring."

Chapter 4

Dark hair fell in staggered waves to the nape of his neck and across his forehead. At six feet, I was accustomed to being eye level with most men, even Morgons. Not this one. He was the tallest I'd ever seen. He tilted his cleft chin down, taking me in. "You're tall…for a human female."

I straightened in my heeled-boots. "You're observant…for a Morgon male."

His eyes lighted on mine, no hint of a smile, but definitely a glint of surprise.

A trill of feminine laughter and masculine whistles erupted from the horde in the corner. I tried to walk around him, closer to the crowd. Without seeming to move, he stood in my path.

"What's the problem? Are human women forbidden?"

"Not at all. You're welcome to join them." He shifted his weight to one side, still blocking my way. "If you like strangers licking salt from your body and sticking their tongues down your throat, go right ahead."

Oh. Body shots.

"Just so you know, that group barely understands boundaries when they're sober. And they're nowhere near sober right now."

Within the circle of raucous partiers, a Morgon man's wings flared above the crowd, his actions hidden by the surrounding horde. His performance earned him a roar of cheers.

"Lorian asked me to keep you out of harm's way." He nodded in the direction of the rowdy bunch behind him. "That's harm's way."

I crossed my arms, deciding whether to see for myself or to follow his advice. As much as I hated to submit, my quarry would probably not be among the party-hard heathens in the corner. "I think I'll skip body shots tonight."

His gaze flicked to my chest. Crossed arms under a corset pushed my full breasts to new heights. I quickly uncrossed them, nearly earning me a full smile from Mr. Wall-o-Morgon. "Do you think any of that group was responsible for the victims?"

The hard planes of his face fixed into adamant, as if sculpted in ice. His jaw clenched. "No."

"Are you sure?"

One brow arched. "Quite."

A clamor of noise came from the entrance. The bare-chested players flooded into the cellar, their groupies trailing behind them. I watched Conn and the friend of his join Kraven to one side. One player from each team bee-lined for the cage to the whooping cheers of their fans.

"What's going on?"

Kol was a shield behind me. Though not touching, I could feel the heat of him pressing along the lines of my shoulders and down my back as I watched the scene unfolding across the room. His proximity put me on edge. Uncomfortably so.

"The main event." His voice had dropped low and deep, his breath brushing my hair.

Never one to let a man ruffle me, I eased a step forward. "I should go. Thanks for the warning about, uh, them." I gestured to the crowd behind us just as they surged toward the Pit en masse. Kol didn't move, effectively blocking me, as they stumbled past in a rough cluster.

"Moira! Hey, girl." Someone tugged my arm. "What are you doing here?"

Surprised, I spun to find an unexpected acquaintance. "Layla? What are *you* doing here?"

Layla was a student who worked at the reception desk in the Liberal Arts building, the same which housed *The Herald* offices. Usually meek and mild at work, I never expected to see someone like her in a place like this.

"Having fun." She winked. By her short skirt and low-cut top, she was out for more than fun. "I didn't think you ever came out of that office. Look at you, all hot and spicy." She grabbed my hand and dragged me with her. "Come on."

I didn't glance over my shoulder to see if Kol watched us go. I could feel his eyes well enough. Layla pulled me right up to the front of the cage. Kraven stood on the opposite side near the entrance gate, talking to Conn. The fighters were already down in the Pit.

"Hey, Drom," said Layla, pulling on the arm of one of the Morgons I instantly recognized as one of the horde hanging in the shot corner. "This is Moira. We go to GU together."

I offered to shake his hand, despising the arrogant tilt of his mouth and his sad attempt at smoldering eyes. Then it hit me. Layla might well have been the one squealing with laughter on the body shot table underneath this guy. He took my hand. Rather than shaking it, he pressed his lips to my knuckles, leaving a wet kiss. Gross.

"Hi." His eyes roved freely down my body. He pressed a little closer, releasing my hand, placing the other on my back, letting it drift low. "Where have you been hiding?"

I wanted to say, *from disgusting plugs like you*, but my goal tonight was to fit in. Blend. And see if I could find the guy who got Maxine Mendale drunk right before she disappeared. I gave him a semi-flirty smile, making me want to retch.

Kraven's bellowing voice drew everyone's attention to the Pit. He stood at the bottom, his arms raised with swords in both hands. As he used to officiate the fights a few years ago, it wouldn't appear odd if he entered the Pit for old times' sake.

"The pledge of the Obsidian Games apply," he bellowed. "Fight until one yields."

He tossed a sword to the Storm-gale player, the other to the Saber. At once, they went after each other in a clamor of steel on steel.

I wanted to ask what the Obsidian Games were. I hadn't heard of it before, but I refused to give Layla's "friend" a reason to get any closer. No need. One of his hands snaked around my hip as he pressed too close. Then Sorcha's warning clicked. Before she left the dinner party, she'd given me a hug and said, *Just know that violence amps up the libido of Morgon men. Those after-parties are ripe for sex and violence.*

Before his hand could drop any farther south, and his mouth could make contact with my skin, I slipped out of reach against the cage, giving him an apologetic smile. "My date is waiting for me."

Indeed, Kraven was scanning the crowd. Layla replaced my position, giving the slimy guy's hands a new victim. She didn't seem to mind.

Skimming along the inside of the cage, I pretended to be interested in the fighters in the Pit as I scanned the crowd for Bennett Cremwell's guy. Still no luck. I had to force my way through the bodies, pressing my own against others to make it to the other side. I squeezed in between Kraven and Conn, letting out a sigh of relief.

"Did you find him?" Kraven asked.

"No." I gripped the bars, feinting interest in the fight. "So tell me about the Obsidian Games."

"I figured your sister would've told you."

"Jessen withholds information sometimes." I blew out a frustrated breath. "I think she still thinks I'm ten years old."

Kraven smiled, giving me a nod, while watching the fight as I did. "The Obsidian Games is a rite of passage for Morgon men. The Games are held in Mount Obsidian near Drakos once a year."

I winced as one of the opponents barely dodged a fire-ball shot from the mouth of the other. The crowd *ooed* in unison.

Kraven blew out a low whistle. "That was close. As I was saying, all Morgon men compete at least once. That is, if you want to uphold your clan's honor. Young Morgon men, coming of age, battle against a champion of the Guard."

"The Morgon Guard?"

Kraven smiled. "Yeah. They're more than law enforcers."

I knew that already. The Morgon Guard had a reputation as the international Morgon police. No crime went unpunished, and there was nowhere a Morgon criminal could go without an MG officer hunting, finding, and dragging him before a Morgon Tribunal. Justice was swift and final. Punishment was immediate. No appeals. They had their ways of determining a criminal's guilt or innocence which remained a mystery to us. The mere mention of the Guard carried an air of trepidation for both races.

"I see." I finally acknowledged Kraven. I bit my lip as one opponent in the Pit pummeled the other guy in the face, gaining a roar of applause from the crowd. "So if a Morgon loses against a Guard champion, they lose their family honor? That hardly seems fair."

Kraven shook his head. "As long as the challenger doesn't yield, he still wins. A Morgon man, a *true* Morgon man, never gives up whether he's beaten or not. That's the lesson of the Obsidian Games. A lesson Morgons live by."

Another roar erupted from the crowd. The Saber was unconscious beneath his opponent. The Storm-gale held his arms up in victory, a trickle of blood sliding down his face, his teeth bared in a vicious grin, dark purple wings flared out in a powerful stance.

Kraven arched an eyebrow. "See," he said before opening the gate and entering the cage. His wings beated twice to bring him to the floor, so he could raise the arm of the victor.

I shook my head. I did see, but I didn't understand the relevance of letting someone beat you into unconsciousness for pride. The male ego—a dangerous force.

I sighed and glanced across the ring, my heart stuttering. Directly opposite me was a black-haired, black-eyed Morgon, gripping the bars. Something was different about him, the way he scrutinized the crowd, not enjoying the entertainment in the Pit as others did. I watched him with an unwavering eye. Then I saw it. His right eye blinked, his mouth twitching on the same side. My pulse pounded, a cold shiver crawling up my spine. He did it again, exactly how Bennett Cremwell had described.

He slid away from the Pit, vanishing into a sea of Morgons.

I pushed through the throng, weaving away from the cage. The music started again now that the fight was over.

He was at the bar, knocking back a drink. Perfect. I made my move, slipping into character, slowing my stride to exude sensuality rather than my usual swift step of determination. Moving like a woman transfixed by the mighty Morgon, I sidled up next to him, waving over the bartender—a slender Morgon female with hunter-green wings.

"What'll you have?"

"Hmm, I'm not sure." I turned to the man next to me, the man I'd been looking for all night who reeked of money in a silk gray button-down. "What should I have?" I laced my words like a sultry invitation. "I've been drinking beer tonight, but I need something a bit stronger."

His gaze slid over my face, neck, and hair, assessing every line. The hairs on the back of my neck stood on end.

"Brevette is always a good choice." His voice was a black, silky serpent—sexy and deadly in the same vein.

Brevette was a human-made whiskey. Strong and expensive. The perfect drink to lure in a human girl looking for a big-spender. I ordered a glass and reached in my back pocket for money. He flipped out a large bill. "Allow me."

"Thanks." I flashed a bright smile, leaning forward and flipping my hair over one shoulder. While watching the bartender, I felt his eyes following the design on my back.

"I've not seen you here before."

"This is my first time. Cool place." I smiled again, letting my eyes trail obviously over his wings in an appreciative manner. Sharp and strong, an odd shiny black, as if covered in shimmery scales, and cut more jagged than other Morgon wings.

He reached out a hand. "And who do I have the pleasure to be standing next to?"

I took his hand. "Who do *I* have the pleasure of standing next to?"

His mouth and eye did that tic motion, then his lips opened in a wide grin. He took my hand, not exactly shaking it, but not letting it go. Against all my instincts, I didn't pull away, fighting my natural inclination to narrow my eyes in defiance.

"My name is Borgus."

Hmph. Doubted that.

"Moira." I saw no reason not to give him my real name. Even if he discovered my last name and tracked me down, the only thing of interest he'd find was that I was a rich girl from an aristocratic family with a sister who intermarried with a Morgon. All my articles from *The Herald* were published under my pen name, Marina Creed. I wanted to make my own way, not on the coattails of my father's.

"Moira." He sang my name in a breathy whisper.

I had to physically keep myself from trembling.

"Beautiful name for a beautiful girl."

I smiled, slipping my hand from his to take a sip of my drink. He angled his body closer to mine. I forced myself to stay in place, his chest brushing my shoulder.

"I suppose men tell you that all the time."

"No. Not really." Truth. "Maybe they're intimidated by me," I teased, then lifted my glass of Brevette and let the liquor touch my lips rather than slide into my mouth.

He laughed. A deep-barreled sound. "Oh. That is certainly so."

Trying to keep my cool, I kept my expression flirty as his eyes wandered to my corset and what it held. He was appraising, measuring, knocking numbers off a checklist in his head. My heart rate picked up pace. Hopefully, he recognized it as excitement, not the fear shooting up my spine.

"You're not intimidated, are you?" I asked in a low whisper.

His black eyes glinted with something feral. Just as he was about to respond, an arm wrapped around my shoulder. "Hey, Moira! Where'd you sneak off to? I've been looking for you everywhere." Conn squeezed me in a tight grip. Thanking the heavens I hadn't given a false name, I whipped my head back to my suitor. Gone.

"Damn it." I shrugged out of Conn's embrace, peering over the bumping-and-grinding crowd.

"Moira, I'm not trying to come on to you, but that guy's a creep show. You don't want to hang with Morgons like that."

"Actually, I did." Ignoring his puzzled expression, I grabbed his arm and said, "Just tell Kraven 'he's here.' Okay?"

I stalked off, pushing through the crush of people dancing in the low light. The room was huge, but I caught the sharp shape of angular, shiny wings slipping toward an alcove. I followed as fast as I could, but that hulking creep I met with Layla earlier pulled me into a tight embrace and rubbed himself all over me. I pushed off with a violent shove. "I told you. I'm not interested!"

He leered. "Thought you needed more convincing."

No time for this shit, I gave him a swift hand-heel to the chin. His head snapped back and hands loosened their tight grip. Before he could retaliate in any way, I slipped away and took a few steps into the alcove, expecting another room, a bar, or something, but it wasn't an alcove at all. It was an exit. A stretch of dark corridor lay ahead with torches in sconces leading the way.

Don't be stupid, don't be stupid.

"Fine." I told the voice chanting in my head. I spun around, swallowing the yelp that came out of my throat.

Kol Moonring stood directly behind me, a scowl fixed in granite. Butterflies fluttered in my stomach. I blew out a quick breath, regaining composure after the shock of finding him standing there.

"Let me guess." I gestured over my shoulder. "Harm's way."

"You weren't seriously considering following him." Not a question from the Iceman.

"I didn't realize this was an exit. I thought it was just another room."

"It's not an exit. It's *the* exit. Two of the three victims were taken through this passage."

Glancing over my shoulder at the menacing darkness, I edged away, closer to Kol. He didn't move. Why wouldn't he move?

"If you're waiting for an apology or something, you'll be waiting a long time. It was a simple mistake."

"There's no such thing."

"As what? A simple mistake? Of course there is. I just made one."

"Simple can get you killed, Ms. Cade."

Ms. Cade? His condescending tone made me want to punch him.

"But it didn't. Now move your gargantuan self out of my way so I can get out of this creepy corridor."

A flash of blue-silver from fey eyes was a sign of the dragon riding him hard. I clenched my jaw, pretending he didn't intimidate me.

"You're Morgon bait in a tall, pretty package. You're going to get yourself killed. Or someone else."

I flinched, knowing that was certainly an insult, no matter that he called me *pretty*. He practically sneered while saying it.

"Excuse me?"

"You should go back to school. Write your stories, or whatever it is you do, and stay out of this world."

Fire lanced up my body, filling my cheeks. "Look, *Kol*." I refused to even give him the respect of authority. "You don't know me. You don't know *what* I write or *why* I write, so stay out of *my* world and out of my damn business."

I pushed past him, fuming. If I never saw him again, it would be way too fucking soon.

Chapter 5

When my comm buzzed me awake with an invitation for breakfast and a debriefing from Lorian, I accepted immediately, knowing it wasn't a request. I rolled myself out of bed, slipped on some sweatpants, a T-shirt, and a fleece pull-over, then headed to the Morgon district. Walking onto the terrace of Lorian and Sorcha's high-rise home, I squinted at the mid-morning sun skimming above the skyline. A shaft of pink-gold light shot across the top of Sorcha's copper hair, giving her an angelic halo. Of course, I knew my sister's best friend was far from an angel.

"There's our damsel causing distress, teasing those Morgon boys into a testosterone frenzy." She tipped a fluted glass in the air with a mischievous smile. "Mimosa?"

I took a seat at her breakfast table, framed by tall pillars of white marble, and gaped at the jaw-dropping view of the city. On this side of town, the skyscrapers took on a different shape. Rather than straight and linear, they slanted to a flat-top pinnacle. Some were a combination of stone and steel, rather than steel alone, jutting up into the sky like Morgon-made mountains. The tip-top was flat, of course, for lift-off and landing, and terraces jutted out around the uppermost floors, but the unusual design somehow made sense. The symmetry of Morgon buildings was more aligned to nature, creating a skyline of poetic beauty, rather than a statement of human might and power. I marveled at the rising sun, shielded by puffy clouds that softened the light pouring across the blue-tiled terrace.

"I didn't tease anyone into a frenzy. Where are you getting your faulty information?"

She giggled. "I can't reveal my sources."

With my words thrown back in my face, she pushed a plate of pastries toward me. I rolled my eyes and nibbled on a cream-filled one as she went on.

"The story is that you disappeared from Kraven without informing him of your whereabouts, flirted with the possible ringleader of the Devlin Butchers, then tried to follow him down the deserted corridor where two of the girls had been kidnapped."

My blood was boiling by the time she finished. "Are you kidding me?" I dropped the pastry on the plate. "I know who your *source* is. That damn Kol Moonring." This man was infuriating, butting in where his thoughts and opinions were most definitely unwelcome. "And I don't want him on my detail anymore. I——"

I stopped abruptly as their house servant, Vincent, appeared at the table, carrying a silver-covered serving dish. I reeled in my temper as he lifted the cover, revealing a tri-sectioned server of fluffy scrambled eggs, sliced ham, and a fruit medley. He leaned forward with a tight bow, then stepped soundlessly back into the house.

I spooned some eggs, strawberries, grapes, and sliced bananas onto my plate. Never one to pass up a free meal, especially one smelling as delicious as this, I forked a huge bite of the eggs.

Sorcha picked up right where we'd left off. "Moira dear, you were the one who asked for help, for protection," she remarked coolly, grinning like the wicked fiend she was, sipping her champagne-and-orange-juice breakfast, leaving the protein and pastries to me. "Begged, actually."

"Well, I want a replacement." I stuffed a whole strawberry in my mouth, chewed, then added, "Someone less asinine."

"He's the best. Lucius and Lorian insist on the best. Otherwise, they'll block you at every turn, and you'll never get your story. Besides, I wouldn't allow you to get involved if I didn't know you were sufficiently protected." Her tone fell to a somber note before she drained the rest of her mimosa.

"This has something to do with Lorian's outburst the other night."

She stared off across the city, the sun kissing the top of skyscrapers in the distance. "So perceptive. You always were, even as a little girl."

She pulled a silk wrap around her shoulders. The cool air, a whisper of winter, blew across the open terrace, brushing her reddish locks against her neck. Tucking my hands into my coat pockets, I waited as she poured another drink. Liquid courage for whatever she was about to tell me.

"Five years ago, when Lorian and I first started dating, I was abducted by a Morgon blood cult."

I sucked in a tight breath, holding it in my chest.

"Yes. I know." She took another sip. "It started with these anonymous gifts bearing a symbol on each card. The symbol was a sign of the

Larkosians, an ancient cult that sacrificed human women to honor their god, Larkos."

I wiped my mouth with a napkin and folded it on my plate. "As in the child of legendary King Radomis and Queen Morga."

"The exact one."

My major was journalism, but my minor was multicultural studies, including the elaborate history of Morgonkind. I'd done countless research, finding what information I could, though much of it was still barred from human eyes.

"Most of my information comes from old fairy tales and legends about the early Morgons. But I know the story of Larkos Nightwing killing his own father, along with annihilating the entire dragon race."

"Not just a story, Moira. It's fact."

My heart pounded a frantic beat, my palms sweaty in the cool morning air. I stayed still and waited, refusing to probe for answers. I instinctually knew when someone wanted to tell their story. The smartest thing was to be patient, wait, and listen.

Soon enough, she inhaled a deep breath and continued. "My knight in shining armor came to the rescue." She shifted, wrapping herself tighter. "Actually, he was more like a demon from hell to be honest. A marvelous demon." One side of her mouth quirked up as she remembered, her eyes seeing something in the distant past. "I wasn't kept long in captivity, just a few hours before they started the ritual."

I listened in complete thrall, taking mental notes of the differences in the recent killings.

"The ceremony involved the rape of a blood bride, then the spilling of her blood to honor Larkos. They thought it gave them some sort of mystical power or something. Thankfully, they didn't get to do either parts of the ritual."

"So you agree with me. You think the Devlin Butchers are actually part of this blood cult."

"No," came a deep voice from the archway leading into the house. Lorian walked toward us, controlled and steady—the opposite of what he was the other night. He leaned against one of the stone pillars. "We killed them all."

"But the similarities. Surely, one of them survived."

Lorian's eyes appeared even wilder in the morning sun. "None survived that night. I can promise you that."

I slumped back into my chair.

"However, the bastard who took Sorcha said something before I destroyed him into nonexistence."

I knew without a shadow of a doubt that he didn't mean a metaphorical destruction. Lorian had surely slaughtered the Morgon, then burned him into ash. My limited education on Morgon history listed countless executions of criminals, ending with burning them to cinders, erasing every part of them from this world as final punishment.

"What did he say?" I couldn't help but ask.

"He said 'the Larkosians are rising.' And they 'pave the way for him.' Sorcha would've been their first victim."

"But I wasn't." Sorcha reached out and gave her man's hand a squeeze. The memory had Lorian's eyes burning fire-bright. The strained muscles at his throat eased with her touch.

"If this is part of the same cult," he continued, "it's a new cell with the same agenda."

Sorcha and Lorian were lost in each other's eyes for a moment. Lorian's hand lifted, brushing a lock of hair away from Sorcha's cheek. I felt as if I were intruding on a private moment. Whatever happened with this past Larkosian cult, it locked these two together in a steel-tight knot—one that neither seemed willing to unravel.

Clearing my throat, I reminded them I was still there. "This *him* you referred to must be a new leader of the Larkosians, I would think."

Lorian finally shifted his fey eyes from his mate. "It can't possibly be the same faction. But with recent evidence of a new, more deadly player among the killers, I've been thinking it could be old fanatics, sympathizers with the group we wiped out five years ago."

"Then you've seen the police reports. The photographs."

"Of course. We gave them to the precinct."

I couldn't keep the surprise from my face.

He shifted behind Sorcha, placing both hands gently on her shoulders. "How do you think the Gladium Precinct got the information they have? The bodies were found in Drakos where humans aren't allowed or accepted. They couldn't march in and do their own investigation. The Morgon Guard is sharing their intel to appease the families of the victims from Gladium."

"But the Morgon Guard is leading the investigation, right?" I asked.

A slow nod. I kept my smile to myself, elated that I had such contacts. No other journalist would have access to the information I did. But it wasn't just about telling a story. It was about justice. An exhilarating thrill swept over me since I'd be a part of stopping this evil. That is, if Lucius and Lorian allowed me to move forward with my plan.

A sharp gust of wind and swift shadow fell across the table, drawing our attention to the Morgon landing on the terrace. Bristling at the sight of our newcomer, I breathed in a deep lungful of morning air, frustrated with my immediate reaction to his presence.

In the full light of day, his wings shone with a sheen of sapphire over deep black, rippling with thick-muscled framing. He was the first Morgon of the Moonring clan I'd ever seen. Most Morgons were named for their hue of wings, but Kol's clan was obviously named for their eyes. Unusual. In gray military-style pants and matching shirt, he stood stone-like next to Lorian, avoiding eye contact with me. If his skin were gray, he could've been a decorative statue on the terrace. But who wanted a scowling statue?

"Now that we're all here, let's debrief," said Lorian, taking a seat next to Sorcha.

Without a word, Kol sat next to him.

"Okay," I interrupted. "Can I finally ask why we're debriefing here and not with Lucius. No offense, Lorian, but I thought he was in charge of this little enterprise."

"None taken." Actually, he seemed amused. "Lucius doesn't want his pregnant wife stressing her mind or body about your whereabouts. So, while you're hunting your story, I'll be making sure you don't get yourself killed."

Kol made a grunting noise and shifted, still not acknowledging me. Whatever. Lorian gazed at me with those unsettling eyes. "Explain everything about your contact with your lead last night."

A chill crawled up my spine, remembering him. "Well, he's definitely got money."

Kol's eyes finally fixed on me with a lifted brow, an implied question.

"For one," I continued, "his shirt. It was Primean silk. I've seen enough of it to know the difference between less expensive brands."

Primean silk was a rare, shiny fabric made only in Primus, a human-only province to the west of Gladium. The irony was that Primeans still segregated themselves from the Morgons, yet they exported goods to other provinces to make their already wealthy city even wealthier. Greed, a powerful motivator.

"That's for sure," added Sorcha. "Seems like you and Jessen had a new dress in Primean silk for every ball you had to go to."

I ignored Sorcha's comment, not wanting to get into family history. "That leads to the other reason. There was an air about him. It's not something I can exactly point to, but only the aristocracy hold themselves that way and speak like him." I felt the weight of Kol's stare. I shifted my gaze to Lorian. "He also said his name was Borgus."

Lorian and Kol shared a look.

"Wait," said Sorcha. "I know that name."

"Borgus Fireblade," Lorian enunciated slowly.

Sorcha's eyes widened. "I remember! That was the cult leader of the original Larkosians."

"Yes, baby. But Borgus Fireblade and all of his clan died out five centuries ago when his fanatical religion was put to an end."

"Maybe this guy is a descendent of the original Borgus Fireblade, and he's carrying the torch, so to speak, and just adopted the name," I offered.

Kol fixed his eyes on me. "He wasn't a Fireblade. He's one of the Coalglass clan."

"Are you sure?" asked Lorian.

A sharp nod. "Definitely."

"Coalglass?" I asked Lorian. "I've never heard of them."

"Their name comes from the structure of their wings," said Lorian. "They're made for speed."

I remembered the way his wings were extremely sharp and angular, shiny, compared to other Morgons.

Kol looked at Lorian. "All of their clan resides in the Cloven Province, so he's far from home."

"Why don't you talk to Kieren, see if he'll help locate this guy and find out who he really is."

Kol said nothing. His face, neck, and shoulders went rigid. His hand on the table clenched slowly into a fist. Whoever Kieren was, Kol didn't like the idea of contacting him. Lorian held his gaze, waiting. Kol finally gave him a short, sharp nod.

Sorcha piped in. "Well, why didn't one of you just follow him and catch him? Bring him in for questioning or something."

"We're not dealing with regular criminals. Not even regular killers." Kol's voice fell to a deeper register. "Questioning one of them, even under torture, wouldn't do a thing. They'll die before giving us what we want."

I swallowed hard, not realizing torture was a viable interrogation technique for the Morgons. For all my historical education on their kind, I seemed to know very little.

Kol continued, "If he is one of the murderers, we need to get him to lead us to the others. The killings won't stop by capturing just one of them."

"Agreed." Lorian stretched his hand across the table, taking Sorcha's in his own. "What else did Borgus say to you?" he asked, glancing my way.

I shrugged. "Nothing worth mentioning."

Sorcha drew Lorian's hand into her lap, leaning forward. "He came on to you, didn't he?"

Kol shifted and pulled his wings tighter against his back.

"He was interested." I gripped my medal, twining it in my fingers, swallowing my fear. "That's why I want to see if he'll lead us to the others. I want to go back and try again."

Chapter 6

When all eyes swiveled to me, I had the distinct feeling I'd been here before. Except at the dinner party, I didn't have the Iceman's frigid stare boring a hole into my face.

Lorian clasped both hands together on the table, leaning forward. "You do realize that in order to lead us to the others, we'd have to let him abduct you."

"Yes."

"As in abduct you for the same purpose as the other women."

Sweat beaded along my hairline. "Yes. But of course, you'll track me to their hideout or wherever they take them before anything happens to me."

"No." Kol's only response. His eyes glittered brighter, drawing me in.

"Why not? You even said I was Morgon bait last night. So let me *be* the bait."

"No."

A scornful laugh escaped my lips. "Lorian is in charge here. Not you."

Kol's posture angled toward me for the first time. The harsh lines of his face, the grim set of his mouth, the taut strain of his shoulders underneath his long-sleeved T-shirt—all warned me he was as unyielding as a mountain. He tightened his white-knuckled fist till something cracked.

"*I* am in charge of this investigation." Steady words laced with ice.

A shiver rippled through me. "How so?"

Lorian smirked. "Moira, weren't you aware that Kol is Captain of the Morgon Guard?"

The blood drained from my face. Kol was most *definitely* in charge. I squirmed under the weight of tension rippling off the hulking man. A look of satisfaction cracked his frozen expression. I swear I wanted to punch him.

"And as Captain of the Morgon Guard, I won't allow it. You have no business inserting yourself into this." He turned his hard expression on Lorian, ignoring me once again. "There are other possibilities."

"Gaius has had some success then?" asked Lorian.

"I haven't received contact via comm since the second murder, but I did make one brief contact where he confirmed he was in."

"How did he make contact without a comm device?" I asked, unable to keep my questions to myself.

Kol's cold gaze slid over me, completely disregarding my question. "He won't be able to make further contact without jeopardizing his cover for some time."

I interrupted their semi-private conversation. "So, what I gather you're saying is that this Gaius is undercover for the Morgon Guard, trying to infiltrate the cult. That's perfect. Then I'll be in even less danger if I act as bait. Your mole can track my whereabouts straight into their lair and get information back to you. It's foolproof." I couldn't keep the excitement from my voice. Lorian actually chuckled. Not Kol. It looked as if he were about to explode.

"She's quick," Lorian mumbled to Sorcha.

Sorcha set her drink on the table. "Told you."

Lorian tapped his index finger on the table, wild eyes narrowed on the horizon. After a moment, he shifted back in his seat, angling toward Kol. "It's not such a bad idea. With your tracking abilities, the risk is little."

"See," I said reassuringly, "the risk is little."

"But there is risk," added Sorcha.

I glared at her, then settled my gaze back on Kol, realizing I had to convince him if this was ever going to happen. I refused to let Captain Iceman freeze me out. "What if your guy isn't able to gain their trust and get all the information you need?"

"Then you'll be in more danger."

"What I meant is that you'll need another way in. I'm it! I'm your way in. I know this Borgus guy is the key. I know I can get him to take me and lead us to the other cult members."

Kol's jaw clenched tight, his scar accentuating the hard planes of his face. Man, he sure did hate losing an argument. Silence stretched. The clouds thickened overhead. A wintry breeze gusted across the terrace, lifting the dark hair brushing his nape. Following the lines up his throat and over his cleft chin, I reached his eyes to find him staring at me. *Crap.* No, he caught *me* staring at *him.* I glanced down and brushed away a non-existent piece of lint from my jeans before returning my attention to Lorian.

Lorian cleared his throat. "She has a point."

Kol gripped the edge of the table, straightening and flexing his arm, the tendons tight ropes up his forearm to his bicep. He rolled his shoulder back as if trying to loosen a crick or muscle pull. The wing above his strained shoulder opened briefly before settling back into place. The subtle movements of his body distracted me. He was so large and broad, formidable, yet so lithe and graceful at the same time. The man was a walking, flying paradox.

I sighed, clasping my hands together on the table. "Look. I'm not saying we go barreling in there tomorrow or anything. I need to check out a few things first, and I need more information on the Larkosian cult as well as Devlin Wood, where they're dropping the bodies."

"These *things* you're referring to," said Kol, flint in his voice, "wouldn't happen to be other leads you failed to mention."

I paused a second. "I didn't withhold anything. I just forgot to tell you."

"Lie."

Damn it. He was right.

Lorian sighed. "She does need a proper education on Morgons and our history. More than her fairytales and university teachings."

"That's not my job."

"Fine. Then take her to someone who will. Petrus. Besides, he can give you more insight into the cult's obsession with dumping the bodies in Devlin Wood."

Kol dragged his gaze from me. "I can't take her to Drakos. You know that."

Lorian made a snorting noise. "He hardly lives inside the city limits of Drakos. He's more like a hermit. Like you."

"I can pass her any information from Petrus."

"Oh, no, no, no," I interrupted. "I don't think so. No offense. But you'd be the worst secondary source ever."

Cold blue pinned me again. "And why is that?"

"You're extremely…taciturn."

Sorcha snickered beside me.

I ignored her, focusing on Kol. "I need to speak to the primary source. This Petrus guy."

Without batting an eye, he spoke directly to Lorian again. "She can't drive there, and she has no wings."

Lorian arched a brow as if that answered the question.

Sorcha piped up cheerfully. "I have tons of flying harnesses."

I straightened. "I'm not flying with anybody, especially not *him*."

Did he just roll his eyes at me?

Lorian's otherworldly gaze settled on me. "How exactly do you think Borgus plans to take you, Moira? All of his victims have been abducted by flight. If you intend to follow through with this plan, then you'll definitely be flying. Better you get used to the sensation, so you won't be terrified and lose your wits if we're going to do this at all."

He was right. I swallowed hard. "Fine," I conceded quickly. "I'll go see this hermit, Petrus."

Lorian added, "And be aware that I'm not convinced this is the best course of action. As a matter of fact, your sister would flay us all just for considering the idea. Kol and I will have to discuss it at length before we decide to take such a risk."

"Fine," I bit out, trying my best not to sound petulant.

"Tell me the other leads you're withholding," Kol demanded.

"I've got an appointment to see the owner of the salon where Maxine Mendale worked"—I glanced at my watch—"in thirty minutes. And I'm visiting a bar owner tonight about the night she disappeared."

I could've easily visited Mikal at his house, but I didn't want to visit him in a place with so many intimate memories. No. I wouldn't give him hope of any kind of reconciliation by meeting in a place where we were once lovers. Still, I had to find out anything he could give me about Maxine and the night she vanished. I had to find him at his club.

I stood from the table. Kol stood with me.

"Where are you going?" I put a hand on my hip.

"*We* are going to the salon. Not that it'll be much help."

"If you don't think it'll help, why bother? I can just relate any information they give me."

"The same way I can relate any information from Petrus."

A stand-off. I narrowed my eyes and pressed my lips together, wanting to spit nails. He was infuriating to the nth degree.

"Fine. Meet me at Carella's on Lexington Avenue within thirty minutes." I stood from the table.

He scoffed. "I'll be there in five." His eyes gave me a once-over as if pitying my feeble human body. With a nod to Lorian and Sorcha, he took two long strides, and with one beat of his wings, shot straight up into the air, soaring higher and higher toward the gathering clouds.

"Show-off," I mumbled under my breath. I swallowed hard to lessen the fluttering in my stomach from watching the fastest launch I'd ever seen.

Lorian walked to the edge of the terrace, watching other Morgons in flight going to and from work. A white-winged Morgon of the Icewing clan stepped from his balcony across the way, alighting into the air with a grace and beauty I wasn't sure I'd ever get used to.

I glanced back to find Sorcha smirking at me with a mischievous gleam in her eyes. "What?"

"Ohhh, nothing." She sipped her second—or was it her third?—mimosa.

"Whatever you're thinking, just stop it."

"Yes, ma'am," she sassed. "Now, you just run along and go play, I mean, go investigate with your partner."

I rolled my eyes. "Thanks for breakfast." How did I ever get into this with that exasperating Morgon as a partner?

Mid-morning traffic was light, but it still took me twenty minutes to arrive and find a parking spot near Carella's. Kol stood in the shadow near its entrance, leaning with arms crossed against the brick facing, his wings tucked tight against his back. His eyes lingered on my car as I approached.

"You are Moira Cade, aren't you?" His tone dripped with sarcasm. "As in, the daughter of business tycoon, Pritchard Cade."

"What are you implying? Just spit it out."

"I'm curious what you did to make daddy disown you."

Ass. I crossed my arms. "What makes you think my father disowned me?"

"He apparently cut you off financially for you to be driving that thing."

My ten-year-old economy sedan sat in a forlorn state at the side of the curb. Yes, she was dinged to hell and back, but she was mine. And Kol was seriously pissing me off, intruding in my private life.

"My relationship with my father is none of your damn business." I stepped more into his space, glaring up at him.

He arched a dark brow, apparently unused to feminine aggression.

"Look," I said. "We may be stuck with each other for the duration of this investigation, but get one thing straight. I don't take shit from any man. Not even a Morgon one who happens to be a foot taller than me." I jabbed a finger in his chest, refusing to wince at how hard my finger bent back. Freaking slab of stone. "So keep your personal observations to yourself."

He actually smiled just a fraction, which only made my frown deepen. "Not a problem." He swept an arm toward the salon entrance. "After you."

I walked ahead, then spun back around. "You know. It might be better if you stay out here."

He sneered. "Not happening."

"I'm not trying to withhold information or anything. It's just that you're kind of big and intimidating. It might be better if you stay outside."

"Am I now." Not a question.

"Pfft. To *some* people, Iceman. Not to me."

Oops. Didn't mean to let that name slip. He moved into my space this time. I was suddenly rethinking whether I found him big and intimidating. I gulped dry air. "Relax. And just stay a little ways back. People respond well to me. Other than you, that is."

He tilted his head and cracked his neck. "Lead the way, Kittycat."

My mouth dropped. "*Excuse* me."

"You heard me." His voice was a low rumble, mere inches separating us.

"Don't call me that."

"Mmm. You sure enjoy judging others. Taciturn. Intimidating. *Ice*man. But you can't handle how others see you."

I clenched my jaw tight.

"Kittycat suits you. Sharp claws, watchful eyes, volatile when cornered." He flicked my braid over my shoulder. I batted his hand away. His grin made me want to scream. "See what I mean?"

Heat crawled up my cheeks. I was so pissed, but if I said a word, I'd only prove him right. I spun and marched to the salon door, shrugging off the sensation of seven feet of annoyance at my back, which was quite difficult.

Crooning alternative music beat a slow rhythm through the salon of sleek metallic chairs and glass-top surfaces. The waiting area sported smooth black sofas and a mirror on every wall. I felt like I'd just walked inside a crystal ball. A pretty blonde stood behind the clear glass counter wearing a skin-tight pink mini-dress and a syrupy-sweet smile.

"Good morning. How may I help you?" Even her voice dripped like honey.

She addressed me, but her come-hither stare remained on Kol behind me. Seriously? How could she possibly be flirting with him.

"I have an appointment with the manager, Ms. Carella."

"And you are?"

"Marina Creed, senior editor of *The Herald*."

"Of course. If you'll just be seated."

She waved to the empty waiting area and swept from behind the desk, making a dramatic display of smoothing her dress against her thighs. Please. Still, I glanced at Kol to see if he was aware of his new fan. He stood in his typical militant stance, his expression revealing nothing.

"Marina Creed?" he rumbled in a low whisper.

I cleared my throat. "My pseudonym. For the paper."

"Why do you need one?"

"Because I—" I blew out a frustrated breath, unwilling to confess my family drama to him. "Because I just want to use one. That's all."

"Mmm. Nice reason. Logical."

I cut a look at him, but he missed my death stare, facing the petite brunette with a blunt short cut in a black pant-suit who strode toward us.

"Ms. Creed?"

"Yes. Thank you for meeting with me," I said, shaking her hand.

Her gaze found my large shadow. "And this is?"

He stepped forward. "Ms. Carella, my name is Kol Moonring. I am leading the murder investigation for the Morgon Guard." His voice was much softer than usual as he offered his hand in the most polite manner I'd seen him adopt so far.

I stared at him, wondering where the Iceman had gone. Did I dare admit there were more layers to this man than the one he let me see? His hard glance dared me to say a word.

"Nice to meet you both. Please. We can sit in here." She waved to the waiting area. "We have a few minutes before my next client shows up."

I situated myself on a sofa next to Ms. Carella. Kol sat forward on a chair opposite us, opening his wings slightly so they wouldn't catch on the chair back.

"We won't be long." I pulled out my notebook from my bag and flipped to a clean page. "Can you tell us first whether Maxine had any Morgon clients."

The brunette shook her head. "No. We're a human-only boutique. No offense, Mr. Moonring."

"None taken."

Not surprising. This was obviously a high-end salon, catering to a wealthy clientele. Unfortunately, there were still many, especially among the aristocracy, who still preferred to live apart from the Morgons. Ms. Carella showed no signs of being a racist outright, but she was apparently aware her clients wouldn't take kindly to Morgons frequenting the place and might decide to patronize other salons. Business was business.

"Do you know if Maxine had any Morgon friends?" I continued.

"None at all. As a matter of fact, I was shocked when I heard she disappeared from the Vaenger Games. I'm not sure if she'd ever even gone to one before. But—" She stopped abruptly and stared at her clasped hands in her lap.

"But what, Ms. Carella?"

"Well, Maxine was sort of a wild one, you know? The fearless type. Always looking for the next adventure. One of the girls"—she waved toward the salon—"said Maxine had started talking about wanting to date a Morgon. To see what kind of adventure that would be."

Ms. Carella glanced at Kol, giving an apologetic smile, as if it might offend him to hear a woman speak of his race like a sporting event. I jotted the notes, shifting uncomfortably.

"I see. And had she gone through with this adventure of hers? Did she date a Morgon?"

"Not that I know of."

"Ms. Carella, your husband is on comm line two," came the saccharine voice from the receptionist area. "Do you want me to take a message?"

"Oh, um, pardon me, but this is important. Would you like to wait a few minutes?"

I said, "Yes" at the exact moment Kol said, "No."

I glanced at him, but he offered his hand and lifted Ms. Carella from her seat and swept a small bow over her hand. "We'll be in touch, Ms. Carella, if need be. In the meantime, please don't hesitate to call us if you think of anything you might feel is important." He slid a business card into her hand and gestured for me to go. "Come, Ms. *Creed.*"

Flustered, but not wanting to start a scene, I stalked out the door in front of him, ignoring the blonde ogling him as we passed. As soon as we were out the door and out of eyesight, I spun around. "What the hell was that? This was my interview, and I wasn't finished."

"She gave us as much as we needed. There's nothing more she could tell us." He walked past me. He'd apparently gleaned something that I hadn't picked up on.

"What did you discover? All she said was that Maxine wanted to date a Morgon. That's nothing special."

We were at my car. He stopped and turned so abruptly, I bounced off his chest and fell back against the passenger door. Ignoring and not apologizing for the bungle, he braced one arm on the roof right beside me, his forearm and bicep flexing.

"What else did she say?"

I reran the conversation in my head, scrutinizing every word. "Nothing. She was the adventurous type. I don't get how that helps."

"What else?" He waited, patient and still, fixed and focused, while my frustration mounted exponentially.

"That she was wild. So what?"

He remained silent as if pondering whether to continue toying with me or to let me in on his secret. I held his gaze, refusing to give him the satisfaction of knowing he'd gotten to me.

"Fearless, Ms. Cade," he finally replied, his voice low and deep. "Maxine was fearless."

My throat felt thick all of a sudden. "What does that have to do with anything?"

His mouth tilted into a devilish half-smile. Immediately, my heartbeat picked up pace, knowing I was in the presence of a dangerous individual, even with all my bravado of not being intimidated.

"Dominant Morgon men." He dropped his voice deeper, causing a rare fluttering in my belly. "We like a challenge."

"Are you telling me there's another *kind* of Morgon man?"

A grin cracked the hardness of his expression. "Some Morgons are more docile, preferring to keep their beast at bay. Others aren't." He inched closer. "We like our women spirited. Aggressive."

I swallowed hard. "So?"

His gaze swept over my face and neck, resting on my lips a split second before meeting mine. "So, Maxine was a challenge. This tells me that our Butchers weren't simply looking for a limp body, pardon the phrase. They wanted someone who might be a mate, someone who would fight back."

"I don't understand."

Kol's grin widened, showing teeth and everything. His facial scar drew tight, distracting me. Why was my heart palpitating so fast? I had to gain control and calm down before he sensed my heart racing and got the wrong impression.

"Maybe they're not looking for victims. Maxine lasted longer before they killed her. Perhaps they're looking for a particular kind of human woman. Perhaps the desired end result isn't murder and mutilation after all."

"Then what is?"

"I don't know." His hand came up, wrapped my braid, which had fallen over one shoulder, and slid his hand down the length. I shifted back, flipping it out of reach. He chuckled, a deep throaty sound. He was teasing me. Again. Trying to make me nervous. Aggravating the hell out of me. "But you're exactly the type to lure them in. Maybe you are the perfect Morgon bait."

I had no smart comebacks, reeling from the energy required to stay on top of my game in his presence.

He shoved off the car and out of my personal space, smiling at his own private joke. He walked away a few steps before lifting off into the air with intense speed, a wake of air brushing against me along with the woods-in-winter scent I now associated with him. I sucked in a deep breath, finally able to do so unencumbered.

Because I knew I was the perfect temptation for the Devlin Butchers, and even more because of the predatory spark in Kol's eyes, I was walking a course out of my control. One that would bring me to certain victory or to ultimate destruction. But as always, I was never afraid to take the unknown path. And certainly not if a righteous cause steered me forward. I'd do whatever I could to prevent one more horrific murder of innocent life. Even if that meant risking my own.

Now, regarding Kol, I was playing with fire. And I knew it. He wasn't one of those docile Morgons he mentioned to me. He was the raw, in-your-face, take-what-you-want, dominant Morgon man. That alone should make me run for the hills, because something in his eyes warned me he intended to be more than my partner in investigating this crime. And at this point, I had no idea how I'd respond to that.

Chapter 7

Paramour was a posh dance club in the human-only district. Mikal wasn't a bigot, but his father was. His only stipulation for investment in his son's business venture was that the club cater to the human population.

There were no laws preventing a human or Morgon from entering any store, club, or business they wanted. But just because it was legal, didn't mean you were welcome.

These were my thoughts as I strolled toward Paramour's entrance, glancing around for my Morgon partner. He materialized out of the shadows as I passed an alley. I started. "Don't do that," I hissed.

"Jumpy, Kittycat?"

Damn, the man had moves. No one his size should be able to come and go in such quiet stealth, then appear suddenly with his power-snapping aura. He was like a cool breeze one second and a lightning storm the next.

"Stop calling me that."

Covered in black from head to foot, he looked like night itself. His eyes shimmered a silver flame in the dark, a sign of his dragon lurking.

I cleared my throat. "I didn't tell the club owner, Mikal, that we were coming. But we're old friends, so I know he won't mind, but…"

He shifted forward out of the shadows.

I glanced at his vast wings. Even folded against his back, they made quite an impression. "Well, you may not receive a warm welcome in this place. Are you sure you don't want to wait here for me?"

His mouth twitched on one side. "Are you concerned about my feelings?" Though his features remained cold and passive, he was definitely laughing at me. "Touching, but no need. I'm a big boy."

A seriously big boy. The very reason I wanted him to stay outside. Gladium was accustomed to the Morgons who closed business deals and merged contracts by daylight behind corporate desks. But this was not that kind of Morgon. Kol was the reason some humans still veered to the other side of the street, the reason some double-checked their alarms at night, the reason some would never accept the desegregation laws put in place. An air of another world hovered around Kol, a mystique of aggression, strength, and an ancient beast lingering in his blood.

Realizing there was nothing I could do to camouflage or soften any of this, nor could I dissuade him from coming in with me, I shrugged. "Let's go then."

I walked across the street to the double-doored entrance. I wasn't so concerned about his feelings as I was my own. Humans could be cruel. I feared some ignorant ass would make me ashamed of my own race, as had happened numerous times before.

"Hey, Moira. Long time, no see." The burly bouncer grinned. His face fell as soon as he saw Kol behind me.

"Hi, Mitchell. Mikal's in tonight, right?"

He nodded, staring, but didn't say another word as we brushed past him.

At nine o'clock, it was already a crush. Lights and music pumped a hard beat. Bodies pressed in toward back-lit bars, others grinding on the dance floor. Fast techno-music vibrated through my chest, people speaking with their bodies more than their mouths. In one corner, a couple made out, while the crowd milled around them. No surprise. This was a pick-up and take-home place, not a quiet pub for bonding with friends.

Funny that the club didn't seem to fit Mikal. Right after we broke up, he opened Paramour with all of its glittering lights and fast, hard music, attracting fast, hard clientele. There was a need on this end of town, so his gamble paid off, and apparently, was still paying off. All the same, it still didn't match Mikal's personality. I knew he longed for something quieter, but then again, maybe he needed the distraction of loud music and bright lights. Did he take the glitzy-club route as some sort of rebellion because I'd broken up with him? He knew I wasn't a fan of this sort of place. Not my thing.

I hadn't been here since the opening premiere but knew where Mikal would be. Peering up to the second floor, I glimpsed Mikal in his VIP section. I tapped Kol's arm and gestured toward the second floor. He nodded. Kol's chest brushed my shoulders as we funneled through the crowd to the stairwell. His hand was at my lower back, guiding me forward. In a Morgon club, he could fly straight up to the next floor. But not here. Though dark, we still attracted a few stares. One girl yipped and spilled her drink down her low-cut dress.

On the second floor, I bee-lined for the white sofa that extended in a perfect square near the balcony. Mikal leaned toward a pretty brunette in a red dress, his sandy-blond hair falling forward, his warm smile charming the girl into a trance-like stupor. As if he sensed me, he glanced up, the easy smile slipping. I caught the twinge of pain in his eyes before he masked it. He stood to greet us and wrapped me in an embrace, brushing a light kiss on my cheek. "This is a surprise."

I smiled as best I could. "How are you?"

"Good." He tucked his hands in his pockets. "You?"

"Good." I nodded.

And so here we were again, stuck in nondescript, awkward dialogue. I'd tried to engage him a few times when he was out somewhere with my brother. It was always the same—polite isolation from anything real or important. I hated that we couldn't get past our past.

His gaze flicked over my shoulder.

"Mikal, this is Kol Moonring."

Mikal offered his hand to shake in a civil gesture, but I caught the strain on his face. Kol's broad, long-fingered hand, with scars along the knuckles, engulfed Mikal's well-manicured one. Mikal was clear summer and warm sunshine whereas Kol was stormy winter and biting wind.

"We're actually here on business. Kol and I are investigating the murder of Maxine Mendale."

Mikal's face tightened. "Why would you possibly be investigating that? For that damn paper, I imagine," he muttered the last few words. "You should leave it alone."

His tone of censure and disapproval instantly made my blood rise. "Kol. Would you excuse us for a second?"

He dipped his chin, his stony expression never changing. I walked to the corner, knowing Mikal would follow, taking deep breaths before I lost my temper. "I understand that you're concerned for me, but there's really no need."

"You always said that." Mikal took hold of my forearm. "You don't know what's happening to these girls, what happened to Maxine."

The deep concern in his eyes softened my anger. "I know everything that's happened. Kol is leading the investigation for the Morgon Guard."

He crossed his arms. "So I see you're well-protected."

"I know you don't understand my need to write for that 'damn paper,' as you call it, but you shouldn't concern yourself for me. Actually, you have no right to."

I regretted the last part as soon as it spilled out of my mouth, but I couldn't help it. Mikal was still clinging to the idea that we might one day mend our relationship and find our happily-ever-after. It would never happen. He would find some lucky girl to be the fortunate Mrs. Mikal Lennox, but it wouldn't be me. I cared about him. I even thought I'd loved him once, but when his thoughts had veered toward marriage and making me a happy little housewife, I knew we were never meant to be. The fact that he called my career choice a "fun hobby" on our first date should've given me ample warning that we were doomed from the start, but sometimes, I was a slow learner.

His jaw slackened, his mouth fell ajar for a heartbeat before he moved into my personal space, whispering close. "How can you say that? After everything between us." He tucked a stray hair behind my ear, his fingers lingering.

I inched back, hating the sickening knot in my stomach.

He pulled his hand away. "Still no chance, Moira? You won't change your mind?"

No question as to what he referred. I shook my head.

The stoic Morgon in military stance a few yards away waited with unexpected patience as he drew more and more attention. A nasty crew from my early bar-hopping days gestured toward Kol. They were pompous, self-absorbed rich boys who still found it funny to trip people and laugh at lonely, awkward girls. And I didn't like the way they were motioning toward Kol. Not that I feared for him. I feared Kol might kill one by accident, like flicking a fly too hard.

"This was a mistake. I'm sorry, Mikal. I didn't mean to hurt you by coming here. I just thought you'd help."

He caught my wrist as I turned away. "Wait." He released me. "Of course, I'll help. I'll always help you if I can."

We rejoined Kol, his eyes roaming between Mikal and me. Putting my business voice back on, I said in a quick breath, "Can you just tell us about Maxine the night she came here. Was she behaving odd in any way?"

Hands in pockets, a little stiffer than before, Mikal answered evenly. "No. She and Bennett had a few drinks, and she told him she wanted to go to the games. Nothing out of the ordinary. Not for Maxine anyway."

"Why not for Maxine?"

"She was a little reckless, always looking for a wilder party or bigger thrill."

"Sort of fearless?" I asked.

"Yeah. That was Maxine."

Kol and I shared a swift glance.

"Thanks, Mikal." I hugged him goodbye. "Let's go," I mumbled to Kol, moving ahead of him toward the stairs.

It was a crush when we walked in. Now it was unbearable. I wondered if Kol would struggle through the crammed club with his wings. I glanced over my shoulder. He'd fallen a few paces back, some giggling girls between us.

The crowd pushed me close to that group of guys I used to avoid like the plague. Assholes, every one of them.

"She's with the bat," one slurred in his drunkenness.

"Just like her sister. A Morgon whore." They chuckled together at my expense. Nothing I hadn't heard whispered behind my back a hundred times in the last five years since my sister married Lucius.

Ignoring them, I pushed on when a hand squeezed my ass. I spun to knock the guy off, only to find Kol with his hand around the ass-grabber's throat, bending him backward over the bar.

"Don't." I shuddered at Kol's voice, thick and gravelly, full of the dragon. The dude's friends backed off several feet, wide-eyed and speechless. Cowards, every one of them. They disgusted me. Kol's wings flared halfway, a hostile stance threatening violence. His jaw clenched, and I knew he was restraining himself.

With a lightning-swift move, he released the guy, who had actually pissed his pants. A wet stain was prominent on his crotch. If I wasn't stunned stupid, I'd have some snarky comeback for the guy, but Kol pushed me toward the exit before I could even gather my thoughts. Glued to my back, he kept a hand on my waist, propelling me forward. Fear skittered across the faces of those who caught sight of the Morgon looming behind me, moving with purpose. Once on the street, he gripped my wrist and tugged me into an alley. Dropping his hold as soon as we were in shadow, he fumbled in his jacket for something.

His eyes glittered so bright, I decided not to comment on his unnecessary machismo. Anger rippled off him in electric waves. He unrolled something. Buckles rattled.

"What makes a Morgon's dragon come to the surface like that?"

His movements were sharp and swift. He ignored me as he continued to fumble with straps of some kind. Shoulders taut, hands focused on unraveling whatever it was he held, he answered, his voice rattling, "Intense emotion. Anger. Sorrow. Desire." His glowing gaze finally met mine, the dark swallowing all else.

I gestured toward his hands. "What's that?"

"A flying harness. We're going to see Petrus tonight. Now."

"Now?"

"Yes."

One giant step toward me. Too close. I stepped back by instinct.

"You scared, Kittycat."

Definitely a challenge. Eyes narrowing, I refused to back up as he inched closer. Hell yes, I was scared. I'd never been flying with a Morgon. The idea of hurtling through the air with only a few straps between me and death petrified me. My hands on my hips, I tried to remain calm. "Are you a good flier?"

"The best." He lifted and unfolded his wings partway, a magnificent display.

"Modest, too, I see."

"Just stating a fact."

He snapped a length of the leather strap between his hands. I eyed them as if they were slithering vipers.

His gaze flicked to mine. "You don't like giving up control, do you?"

"No. I'm not fond of it."

"You're afraid."

I couldn't deny it. And I wasn't a liar, so I said nothing at all. His voice gentled. "Never let fear lead you. Not in anything." He moved closer, his intense energy lapping against me. "Just let go." My heart drummed an erratic beat. He gestured with one finger. "Turn around."

"What are you going to do?"

When Kol grinned, it looked unnatural but at the same time mesmerizing. "I'm going to help you step into the harness before I strap it to myself."

"I don't think I want you strapped behind me." My stomach flip-flopped at the thought of him standing so close.

His smile turned sheer wicked as if he could read my thoughts. "You could be strapped facing me, and that would be just fine by me."

"Stop it."

"Stop what."

"Using your"—I waved a hand at his chest—"manliness to try and intimidate me."

"Is it working?"

I wanted to say no, to lie to him, but my mouth wouldn't move. All I could do was consider how being strapped to this man might be worth facing my fear of flying. I spun around before he could read anything else on my face. "Fine. Let's do it."

"See?" Right over my shoulder, warm breath brushed my ear. "Not so hard, now is it? Just let go of your fear."

It wasn't just hard, it was downright impossible. My pulse raced as his arms bracketed my waist, rejoining in front of my torso, leather straps in hand. But this wasn't all from fear. Heightened anticipation of rocketing through the sky, strapped to Kol, made something else thrum wonderfully through my veins. An excitement that verged on insanity.

"Step in."

I stepped both legs into the leather harness and waited as he tightened the thick belt at my waist, then cinched the straps that criss-crossed my breasts. Sweat broke out on my neck and back as I listened to him buckle the part of the harness meant for the Morgon. Finally, he clipped the locking hooks on either side of his waist to the rings at mine, cinching the wrap-around leather strap one more time, pulling my body firmly against him. The back of my body was molded to the front of his. I hadn't been this close to a man in such an intimate way in quite a long time. Perhaps that's why my heartbeat skittered ahead.

"Where do I hold on? I have to hold on to something."

A rumbling chuckle vibrated from his chest to my back. He curled his hands around mine, engulfing them, and forcibly hooked my fingers around the straps at my chest.

"Is that better?"

"No." My breathing quickened. I was about to be flying through the air. This was insane.

"Just let go, Kittycat. I've got you."

That's what I was afraid of.

He curved both his arms around my abdomen, holding me tight. I felt his knees bend, mine bending with him. The snapping whip of his wings as they flared out stirred the air around us. A pulse of wind beat once right before lift-off. Looking up into the starry sky, I held my breath.

"Just let go," I murmured to myself the second before my feet left the ground.

Funny thing about fear. When you cling to it, the fear grows exponentially, a monster morphing into a suffocating mass. But when you face it head-on, conquering the beast before it swallows you whole, you find there was nothing there to fear at all. The chains break, and the whole world feels lighter than ever before.

Chapter 8

For several seconds, I couldn't even suck air into my lungs as we climbed higher and higher into the night sky.

"Breathe," Kol commanded close to my ear.

I inhaled, taking in the deep black above us behind a canvas of glittering stars. The buildings below grew smaller, their lights like pinpricks of candlelight. As Kol winged north of the city into the wilderness, the heaviness of the dark wrapped us in a cool embrace. At this height, he beat his wings little, letting us soar on a smooth, even path, skimming above the clouds. A half-moon shimmered a radiant glow on the thin blanket of vapor beneath us.

"What do you think?" he asked, his arms still braced around me.

My hands and face stung from the icy wind. Other than that, I was enthralled. Completely and utterly besotted with the sensation of drifting between earth and sky.

"It's cold," I managed to chatter between my teeth, "but it's beautiful."

"Next time, wear gloves and a thicker coat."

As if he'd given me any prior notice. And assuming there would be a next time. "Where does P-Petrus live?"

"East of Drakos. I'm taking you on a route to avoid other Morgons." He angled right, my hair flying across my face. He removed one arm from my waist and swept my hair aside, his fingers grazing the back of my neck. I tensed at his touch.

"Pull your hair back in the future. I keep getting a mouthful."

His other arm came back around my waist.

"Why must you hold me so tight?"

His arms left me. My weight dropped, straining against the harness straps. I sucked in a sudden breath, feeling as if I might fall, my fears slamming back into place.

His hands rested lightly on my hips. "I thought it might make you feel more secure. But if you prefer this—"

"No." I swallowed my pride. "It was better before."

"You're sure?"

I could hear the smile in his voice.

"Yes, damn it! Please, Kol."

His hands slid back around my waist, his arms bracing me back against the heat of him.

"Please." The way his voice rumbled against my ear made me shiver. More than I already was from the cold. "Now that sounds nice coming from you."

"Oh, shut up. How much farther?"

He banked hard to the left. I yelped.

"Not far now. Keep quiet. Voices carry up here in the air."

The humor had left him. He became rigid, muscles taut, as we moved below the cloud cover. What would happen if a human was found in the Drakos territory? Were we so hated that they'd try to harm me? I wanted to ask, but didn't dare open my mouth after his warning.

We flew over a dense woodland on the outskirts of a mountainous region. He whispered in my ear as if knowing my curiosity. "We're in the foothills of the Feygreir Mountains. That's Singing Wind Wood below us."

Singing Wind Wood! I'd learned so much about it in a class on Morgon fables and legends. Stories claimed magic lived in those woods. Supernatural animals roamed the forest, ethereal voices carried on the wind, mystical energy lived in the very trees. All fairytales and rumors, but I'd always wanted to find out if there was any truth to the legends.

A small clearing appeared out of the gloom. Kol skimmed above the treetops, the naked limbs stark and shining like bone under the moonlight, like spidery fingers webbing the forest in. As he beat his wings for a gentle landing, a cabin with a square window of warm light loomed before us.

It was an odd sensation, weighty, to be back on solid ground. I even felt a pang of regret as Kol busily unbuckled and removed the straps, his body heat vanishing as well.

"A cabin on the ground. Strange place for a Morgon to live."

Morgons liked to live closer to the sky. And now I knew why.

"Petrus lives here for the privacy. Not many Morgons venture into Singing Wind Wood. And even fewer search for dwellings on the earth floor.

"I hope you warned Petrus we were coming at such an hour," I said, stepping out of the harness. "It doesn't look like anyone's home."

My foot snagged on a strap, nearly tumbling me to the ground. Kol caught me by the waist and righted me so that I faced him. My hands gripped his biceps for support. A shimmer of blue-silver met my gaze.

"Petrus is the eccentric sort. He keeps no time. And we're friends. He won't mind." Kol still held my waist in a tight grip, not yet releasing me.

"And you believe he has some information to help us." My voice came out as a breathy whisper.

"He's the oldest historian living. If anyone has information we need, it's him."

He studied me a few seconds longer. I waited, unable to break the tension-infused moment by pulling away. Finally, loosening his hold, he let me go with a frown and then stepped toward the door before knocking with three sharp wraps. A fumbling and shuffling noise came from the other side of the wooden door, and it burst open.

A white-haired, white-winged Morgon stood there in brown homespun robes. He was of the Icewing clan, the only clan with such wings. My sister had confided in me that the Icewing clan had some kind of healing powers, but she hadn't elaborated. It was one of their clan who had healed a wound on her shoulder. The mark left behind was a radiant scar of an iridescent, scale-like pattern. I glanced at the reddened scar streaking across Kol's face, wondering why it didn't bear the healing mark of an Icewing.

Petrus had a kind face, wrinkles marking his brow and mouth, and twinkling gray eyes. He stood eye-level with me, which meant he was short by Morgon standards.

"Kol Moonring. What a peculiar surprise. Come in."

"I've brought a friend."

"I see that." His eyes swiveled, taking me in. "A lovely, lovely friend. Please. Come in."

The cabin was one large room, smelling of old parchment and heady spices. A fire crackled in a smallish hearth, soot stained at the base. A six-tiered candelabrum set on a desk piled with papers. Floor-to-ceiling shelves stuffed with books lined one wall. On the side of the fireplace stood a black, wood-burning stove, and in the far corner was a lumpy mattress piled with wool blankets, which I assumed was his bed. To say I felt as if I'd stepped back in time was an understatement. I knew that Morgons preferred natural elements like fire to electric lighting and stone to steel buildings. Something about their beasts was drawn to the natural.

Petrus had immersed himself in the most comfortable Morgon abode I could possibly imagine.

"Have a seat." He waved to a small couch, only enough room for two people. Petrus picked up a poker and stoked the fire. A log shifted and spit up sparks as I sat on the small sofa, nearly jumping right out of my skin when a cat-like creature leaped from the cushion to the arm rest. It was feline, no doubt, but I'd never seen a domestic cat like this before. Its legs were abnormally long, it's ears big and pointed, its tail a short stub. With silver and black stripes, its orange-gold eyes glowed like fire coals in the gloom.

"Oh, don't mind Seerie. She's a little witch, but she won't bite."

Seerie aimed her golden gaze on me as I sat on the low-back sofa—made to accommodate Morgon wings. Kol took the seat next to me, his thighs brushing against mine. Unfortunately, there was nowhere to push over. We crammed in together. It didn't seem to bother him, so I pretended it didn't bother me.

"I've never seen a domestic cat like her before."

"Oh, no. You never would. And don't let her hear you calling her domestic." He chuckled again. "No one owns her. If anything, she owns me."

"She's a necrominx, isn't she? I've read about them, but I've never seen one."

"Yes, yes. Only found here within Singing Wind Wood. I heard one clan tried to transport some of them to Cloven and domesticate them. Didn't work. They disappeared and returned here." Seerie began licking her paws, ignoring us with definite feline arrogance. "Now then, Kol. Please introduce our visitor."

"This is Moira Cade of the Gladium Province."

He took his seat in a tattered leather chair, angling away from the fire to face us.

"Well, now. The youngest daughter of Pritchard Cade."

I started in surprise. He chuckled. The sound was infectious. I had to smile with him.

"I know all about your family, dear heart."

Kol leaned forward, elbows on knees, hands clasped together. One of his wings brushed my back. I glanced at him, wondering if this intimate touch was just an accident. He didn't meet my gaze.

"We came to find out about—"

"Devlin Wood. Yes, I know. I've been waiting for you to come and visit, dear boy."

Dear boy? How old was this guy? And how did he know Kol would
come? Kol didn't seem surprised at all. Weird.

"So," I added, "you know about the women. The murders."

"I do live in remote isolation, but I keep apprised of the world. What
kind of historian would I be otherwise?"

He chuckled as Seerie finished her bathing and leaped across my lap
onto Kol's. She curled into a ball and purred in a low hum. Kol's large
hand stroked over her delicate head and neck in a steady rhythm. His gaze
caught mine. One side of his mouth lifted.

"What can I say?" He shrugged one shoulder, his wing grazing me
again along the spine. I shivered.

"The kitties like me." He brushed his hand from her crown, down her
neck, along her spine and tail. "Especially the wild ones."

Blushing heat filled my cheeks. Before I lost all reason and started
fantasizing about those hands stroking down my own spine, I flipped my
attention back to Petrus whose eyes had glazed in thought.

I cleared my throat. "Tell me about Devlin Wood, if you don't mind."

He popped up at the sound of a rising whistle. "Would you like some
tea? I nearly forgot about it when you two came in."

I nodded. He fixed two cups and handed me one. I glanced at Kol.

"Oh, Kol doesn't care for tea," Petrus explained. Kol's hand made slow,
lazy strokes over Seerie's coat, a broad hand that covered her entirely. Her
purring grew louder, her orange eyes drooping to tiny slits.

"Devlin Wood has a long history of witchcraft," said Petrus, settling
into his squeaky leather chair, dragging my thoughts away from Kol and
his steady hands.

My eyes widened in shock as I drank the minty blend, coughing on a
sip. "As in"—I cleared my throat—"as in flying-on-a-broom, cooking-in-
a-cauldron witches?"

He chuckled. "Yes, dear heart. Humans believe it the stuff of fairytales
and legends, but do not legends always have a grain of truth?"

I tilted my head. "Are you referring to dragon magic? The myth?"

"Morgon magic. And it's no myth. Morgons have gifts outside human
understanding."

"Because of their dragon heritage," I added.

He smiled, wrinkles crinkling around his eyes. "Now, not all Morgons
have abilities outside their dragon senses, like their heightened sense of
smell, eyesight, and so forth, but…some do." His pale-blue gaze roamed
from me to Kol who said not a word, petting Seerie into a pleasure-

induced coma. Now this was ridiculous. The first time I'd felt envy in a very long time, and it was of a cat.

I turned back to Petrus. "Like the Icewing clan...your clan," I added.

"You know of our clan?"

"My sister. She was injured and one of your clan healed her. I don't know exactly how, as she was very secretive about it. But the mark it left behind is extraordinary." Yes. Out of the ordinary. As in, caused by some supernatural gift. Why had I never considered this before? That the Icewing clan wasn't the only one harboring uncanny abilities.

"That's right. My clan has the power of healing."

"The Nightwings. What about them?" I had to know.

"The Nightwings are direct descendants of King Radomis and Larkos. Their gift is sheer dominance. No opponent ever wins against them. No one. Their dragon is too strong."

I mused about the clans that came about after King Radomis took a human as his bride and his queen. History told that other dragons saw fit to take human brides, thus populating the world with the varied clans of Morgons. When Larkos let loose his rage on his father and dragonkind, he allowed the Morgons to live, desiring them to become the superior race.

What gift did the Moonring clan have? There was a story behind those fey eyes, and I was going to discover it. Soon.

"Devlin Wood," he continued, "was a place of ritual and sacrifice. The witches I speak of are dragons who sought to use their innate gifts and amplify them with perversions of nature. Thereafter, there were a few Morgon witches. There actually still is one coven, the Syren Sisters. They live far to the north in the frozen Wastelands of Aria, outside the dominion of human and Morgon civilization. And the Syren Sisters profess to practice only good magic, using only animal sacrifice for their rituals. As far as I know, they speak the truth."

"But," I protested, "could there be others who've perhaps strayed from the natural path, who might still practice some sort of dark rituals?"

"Like what, my dear?"

"Like the sacrifice of blood brides." My mouth had gone dry. "The Larkosian ritual to honor their god, Larkos."

He smoothed his thumb and forefinger along his white beard. In deep thought, he grimaced. "The Larkosians used the site of Devlin Wood for ritual, as have many others before them. The original Larkosians used the deep caves of Mount Obsidian, but Devlin Wood has always held an air of mysticism. Dragon witches used spells, binding their powers with the sacrifice of flesh and blood, to gain more power. The witch Balsheba was one of the most prominent in dragon history."

"Funny, I just told my nephew the story of *Balsheba and the Poisoned Cup*."

The old Morgon's smile reminded me of one who'd seen too much of the world and wished he hadn't. "Of course, that fairytale you speak of is more fact than fiction. I bet you tell it where she dropped a ruby into the chalice, lacing the wine with poison."

Sitting straighter, I replied, "Yes. That's the story."

"Ah, but my dear girl. The truth is that the ruby wasn't poisoned."

I frowned. "Then how did she drink from the cup before she passed it to the queen?"

"The Bloodbacks were a clan with a dark gift. Poison pumped through their veins."

"Were?" I asked.

"Yes. I'm afraid their kind died out. Because of their lethal ability, they were feared. Few of them mated because other Morgons feared their fatal kiss, until eventually, there were none left. The last two daughters of the Bloodback clan disappeared almost a century ago. It is believed they were murdered, though bodies were never found."

"What do you mean by fatal kiss?"

"They had glands in their mouths that could release venom directly into a victim with a bite. Or a kiss."

My eyes widened. "Or with a sip into a cup."

He nodded. "In the story, before her attack on the queen, Balsheba had always been a vain creature, obsessed with prolonging her beauty and her life, one reason she sought a bond with the king. Naturally, dragon kings live longer than the average."

"Our history books claim he was nearly seven-hundred years old when Larkos killed him. Is that true?"

"Closer to eight-hundred actually."

I set my tea to the side. "Wow."

The average Morgon lifespan was three-hundred years old. This was why it was always so difficult to guess their age. Petrus must be nearing these upper years. I glanced at Kol, suddenly wondering if he was twenty-five or one hundred and twenty-five. One could never tell once a Morgon reached adulthood.

My hand went to the medal at my neck, fingering my most precious possession. Petrus shifted in his chair, watching me. "May I see your pendant"

I paused. No one had ever asked to see it before. "Um, sure."

I unclasped it and passed the coin-sized medallion on the silver chain to him. He examined it closely, a broad smile creasing his weathered face. "Saint Portia. The female avenger." Shrewd eyes fixed on me. "The martyr who sacrificed herself to save us from the evil of Larkos."

I straightened, proud of my patron saint.

"My dear boy," he said, looking at Kol who was certainly no boy, "do you know the history of Princess Portia?"

All this time, Kol had said nothing, hadn't even looked in my direction. "All Morgons do." His voice was rough and strained. "We're taught it from our earliest years."

"Well, let's hear it then," said Petrus.

Still stroking Seerie in his lap, he lifted his voice and told the tale that had haunted me all my life.

"When Princess Portia set out with her handmaidens and attendants to visit her sister, the queen of the dragonlands in the North, she had no idea she'd arrive to find blood and death. She'd sent messenger after messenger with letters. None of them returning. No word of what had happened. Knowing something was wrong, she armed a band of warriors and journeyed north to discover what had happened."

Kol paused and angled his body toward us, stretching his arm along the low sofa-back before continuing the story.

"Portia found her sister in her bed, death marking her cold body. When her husband, King Radomis, was killed by Larkos, their soulfire bond demanded that her heart stop beating as well. She'd lingered for a day after Radomis took his last breath, finally expiring with the setting sun. It was the way of dragons and their mates, and now Morgons and their mates, those bound by soulfire. One could not outlive the other. When Larkos entered his mother's chamber to say his final farewell, his heart seized at the site of beautiful Portia mourning at Morga's bedside. Though she was his aunt, he hungered for her so desperately that he wanted to bond in that unbreakable way of soulfire. Repulsed at the thought, Portia saw only one good if she could bear to tie herself to Larkos. She accepted the heartbonding of soulfire, the elixir to synchronize their hearts, allowing him to sate his burning lust on her body. When he had finished, the bond complete, she stabbed herself in the heart with his own dagger, ridding the world of the tyrant, Larkos."

Entranced by Kol's rolling timbre and heartfelt words, I jumped when Petrus finally spoke. "Well done, my boy." Petrus turned his gaze on me so fixedly, it was apparent he understood why I was devoted to Saint Portia.

"You know, don't you?" I asked in a whisper.

"Know what?" demanded Kol.

"What most Morgons don't know," said Petrus, his white brows pursed. "Princess Portia was married to the human prince of the west intended for her sister, Morga, before King Radomis took her as his bride. When Portia set out to visit her sister, she left behind a young son, knowing the journey might be dangerous for a human boy. Besides, her husband would not permit him to go. Princess Portia was extraordinary in the eyes of humans, not only because she sacrificed her own life for the good of others, but she did so knowing she left her son motherless. A true selfless act. Her son was the first of many in the powerful Kadenstar dynasty. Their descendants would shorten the name, when monarchies fell, to the surname Kaden. And about five centuries ago, one eccentric and rather racist descendant changed it altogether to Cade, desiring to distance his family legacy from the humans tied to dragon and Morgon lineage. My dear boy, you are sitting beside the ancestral granddaughter of Saint Portia."

Silence, except for the soft hiss of flames flickering. Petrus passed me the medal. I felt Kol's eyes heavy on me as I reclasped the chain around my neck.

"You even have the tell-tale ebony hair and fair skin," added Petrus, setting his tea cup down.

I swept my hair over one shoulder. "Yes. My brother and sister do as well."

"Lucius never told me this." Kol had finally found his voice, sounding almost strangled.

"He doesn't know. I only discovered it recently in an ancestry class when we had to trace our heritage."

"You've not told your own family?"

I shook my head. "I don't think my father would receive the news very kindly." Any attachment to the Morgons rubbed my father wrong. I had no desire to remind him that our own ancestors mated and bonded with dragons. "And Jessen and I haven't had much time alone the past few months."

Kol frowned, seeming to know I was telling half-truths.

"You know?" Petrus glanced between Kol and I. "That means that you two are distantly related. By marriage of course. Not by blood."

Kol stiffened.

I sat up straighter. "Um, excuse me? What do you mean exactly?" "You don't know the story of how the Moonring clan came to be?" I shook my head. He ignored Kol's jaw-clenching silence. "Ah, well. Diokles Nightwing was a very famous Morgon. He was the one who founded the Obsidian Games several centuries ago. You've heard of the Obsidian Games?" I nodded. "Good. Well, his wife bore him seven sons. When she was pregnant with the seventh, there was a festival just before the games beneath Mount Obsidian in Singing Wind Wood where all the clans had gathered. While fetching a pail of water, she went into labor at the pool, giving birth right there beneath the full, blue moon, glowing in the glassy pond. It is said she focused so hard on the image of the moon in order to distract herself from the labor pains, that the moon itself imprinted on her unborn child. The son she bore had dark blue wings and blue eyes with the exception of a pale ring circling the inside of his iris. A magical mark given to him by the forest itself. Perhaps that is why this place seems to respond so well to Moonring clan members. Even today."

I glanced at Kol with Seerie curled in a warm ball on his lap. Again, he avoided eye contact with me, as if he could ignore his heritage, the magical mark in question stamped directly onto his bright eyes.

Petrus mused. "How interesting that your sister and Lucius should find one another. That another Nightwing descendant should find a mate from the Kadenstar line."

He was right. It was as if fate had bound my sister to her Nightwing mate. Even my brother, who had once despised Morgons—a fault learned from our father—fell in love with Shakara despite his determination not to. In the end, Fate had her way. And I've never seen him happier. Did Fate have something similar in store for me?

"It's time we left." Kol interrupted my thoughts and stood up, setting Seerie on the sofa. She circled once and curled into a ball again.

"Thank you for your time, Petrus. It was a pleasure meeting you." I shook his hand.

"By all means. The pleasure was all mine. I'd always hoped to meet one of the famous Cades one of these days. You are welcome to come back if you should ever need."

"I'd like that," I said, meaning it, though I doubted I should ever have another occasion.

I glanced around at the rumpled stacks of papers, feathered quills, cluttered shelves of tomes, vials of potions, and pots of spices as I headed for the door. This place was haloed by everything good and whole and warm. I left feeling grateful for having met this eccentric, yet wise, old Morgon.

Once outside, Kol reassembled the harness with quick, sharp movements. A familiar vibration of energy surrounded him—a pulsing irritation emanating from within.

"What's wrong? Why are you so angry?"

"I'm not." He cinched the belt so tight around me, the air in my lungs whooshed out.

"Really? Because I think you are."

He spun me around fast, a large hand wrapping my neck, thumb pressing into the hollow between my jaw and neck. His other hand was at my hip, clenching. I braced my hands on his shoulders, caught completely off guard. A look akin to despair marked every line on his face, his chest rising and falling too quickly. He closed his eyes, his thumb brushing along the edge of my jaw.

"Kol," I whispered, knowing his dragon had him in some sort of desperate hold. "Are you okay?"

Slowly, he opened his eyes—pupils as thick, black slits, and irises glinting bright silver in the dark—full dragon eyes. I hitched in a breath.

"Fate is such a fucking, cruel bitch," he grated.

His thumb crossed to my chin. He held me close, my breasts pressed against the hard steel of his chest. His otherworldly gaze, full of danger and promise, traced my lips hungrily.

He was *not* about to kiss me.

"Kol." I gave a soft push against his chest. Immovable.

His thumb slipped down under my chin, sliding a sinuous line along the column of my throat to the hollow where my medal hung. He let his hand, gripping my neck, fall away from my body, seeming to come out of his weird trance.

"I need to fly," he said to the air, not to me.

After spinning me back around so fast I stumbled, he clipped the rest of the harness on, gripped me around the waist in his iron hold, and rocketed up into the night sky. We climbed higher than before, so hard, so fast, I thought I would be sick. One arm held me tight. I knew enough about Morgons to understand that sometimes they couldn't control their beast. Sometimes, the dragon controlled the man. For whatever reason, Kol's beast had dug his claws in, nearly strangling him. I didn't know why or what fate had to do with anything, but I did know I didn't want him to suffer. Jessen had once told me that gentle touch soothed her husband when the beast was riding him hard.

I wrapped my arm across Kol's forearm at my waist, trailing my hand up and down. He stopped our vertical ascent, evening out, and let the wind take us on a smooth ride. His grip loosened, but kept me close all the same.

When we descended into Gladium and landed near my car, he unbuckled and removed the harness in silence. I waited for him to say something, maybe apologize for losing it, but he didn't. Not a word. Not even a look. As soon as he was free of the harness and of me, he lifted back into the sky, melding with the shadowy night, leaving me in complete and utter confusion. And oddly bereft.

Chapter 9

Lorian's man escorted me to his study. Sorcha was at work at her family's marketing firm. Vincent took my gray coat and red scarf as he held the door open. Lorian stood by the fire and immediately cut off whatever he was saying to Kol, who faced the window overlooking the west side of the city. The sun had dropped beneath the horizon, painting the buildings an orange-pink hue. Kol's hands were clasped at his back, his wings pulled tight. He didn't turn when I entered the room.

"Moira, come on in."

Lorian met me halfway and led me to the sofa facing the fireplace. The room was decorated in warm mahogany tones except for a black marble desk near the window. Behind which Kol still stood, his back to the room.

"We've come to a decision." Lorian crossed his arms and leaned his shoulder against the wooden mantel. "We're moving forward with your plan."

I grinned, despite the impending danger.

"But *only* if you agree to all of our stipulations," he clarified.

I straightened. "Let me hear them."

"First, you cannot mention the operation to anyone. Especially your sister."

"Not a problem."

"This Friday is a big game with a Vaengar team from Cloven. We've deduced that most of the Butchers must be from this province."

"So you've heard from your undercover man, Gaius?"

"No. But before he removed his tracker, he was spending most of his time in and around Cloven. He most probably had to get rid of his comm device and tracker when he went deep undercover, standard procedure to cut all connection to the Morgon Guard. We're positive he's now immersed in our target group."

Lorian stepped over to his desk and lifted a syringe with a long, thick needle. I shivered.

"This is the next requirement. You'll have to agree to have a techno-tracker embedded under your skin."

"Won't a tracker be risky? If your undercover guy had to get rid of his, then they'll discover it on me, too."

"Relax." Hard to do as he walked toward me with that giant needle. "It's small enough that it won't be found or scented by the most adept Morgon."

"I've never heard of a tracker this small."

"That's because it's not on the human market," he said, squatting in front of me. "Quite frankly, it's not on the Morgon market. It was securely developed by technicians at Nightwing Enterprises for Nightwing security and the Morgon Guard."

"I see." I swallowed hard. I hated needles.

"If you'll remove your boot, I'll insert it between your toes. We've found this is the least conspicuous place. Morgon senses can be extremely acute, so the farther from a Morgon's nose, the better."

"Okay," I said shakily. "But why now? We're not doing the operation till Friday."

"I need to track your whereabouts for a few days beforehand to ensure it's working properly."

Frowning, I removed my boot and sock, aware of Kol behind me, though he said not a word. The plush carpet made of silky soft red fibers tickled my bare foot. Lorian took my heel in hand, glancing up. "It might be easier if you look away."

I turned toward the wall of windows and caught a silver-fire reflection. No expression at all from the Iceman, though his presence held me captive despite my will. I gripped the edge of the sofa. I felt a cool cotton swab between my first and second toe, then the sharp pinprick of the needle. Unable to withhold a little cry, I flinched and bit my bottom lip as a warm sting pierced the flesh.

"All done."

Kol remained in stoic silence behind the desk.

Seeing a small spot of blood, I wiped it away with my finger, feeling nothing under the skin. "How do you get it out if you need a needle to put it in?"

"I'm afraid that process is slightly more uncomfortable."

"Great."

I slipped my sock and boot back on, dreading the removal of the damn thing. What kind of monstrous tool would they use to pry my foot open?

Lorian stood to put the needle away and continued with the instructions on our upcoming mission. "We'll want you to bring a female friend this time, rather than a male escort. We believe it will increase the chance of this Borgus seeing you as an easy target."

"Hmm. That's probably a good idea. He vacated fast when Conn sat next to me at the bar."

"Exactly. Kraven will be your 'in' to the party, but he'll subtly disappear so it's just the two of you."

"I'll bring my friend, Kris, but you have to promise me you'll watch her like a hawk." Kris could be unpredictable, and I'd die if something happened to her because of me.

"There's no need to worry. I'll be there, as will Kol and a few other men from Nightwing Security and the Morgon Guard, to ensure safety. This leads to the final stipulation."

Lorian's eyes shifted to Kol who hadn't taken his eyes off me for several minutes and still hadn't spoken a word. Perhaps he was embarrassed about last night or something.

Lorian cleared his throat, striding before me in front of the fireplace. "I'm going to let Kol explain this one to you, but understand that it's non-negotiable." A ghost of a smile flitted over Lorian's face as he crossed the room and left me alone with big, bad Iceman.

The door closed with a definite *snick*. A heavy energy filled the study. I'd felt it often enough to know what it was. Kol's dragon was in the room with us. He met my gaze, all hard angles and taut muscles, primed for action. "We want to be certain we can track you before the Butchers do you physical harm." Something was off. His voice resonated too low for his calm composure.

"Yes. I understand," I said, a primal shiver trembling down my frame. The casual conversation belied the fiery energy sparking in the air. "You told me yourself that you're the best tracker there is. Plus, I have the techno-tracker embedded."

"True. But we're still not sure about their rituals. The victims' bodies tell us only that the women were raped multiple times—not whether it happens daily upon their imprisonment or as part of the ritual sacrifice. We believe it's part of the ritual, but we can't be sure."

I stood and stretched my palms toward the fire. I let the warmth seep into me, shaking off visions of rape and mutilation, refusing to let my own

Juliette Cross

fears seep into my psyche and affect the job I would have to do. After a moment, I turned my back to the fire.

"So, you have some sort of plan to prevent this, I suppose. In case you're delayed getting to me."

Danger seeped from him in a rippling aura, the sunset lighting his silhouette in orange-gold. "There is one way to deter them. At least long enough to give us the time we need to track you with stealth and surround the enemy in whatever lair they take you."

"That one way is?"

The focus of his gaze, the half-open arch of his wings, the flexed lines of his shoulders warned me that I should run. Fast. Feeling like a doe in the woods, knowing a predator drew closer, I froze for a moment, transfixed by the hunter.

"Morgon men hate the scent of another Morgon man on a woman he wants for himself. And the scent of a strong, dominant Morgon man will make them hesitate to do anything to you."

He circled the desk, making his way in a deliberate path toward me. A primitive instinct put me on high alert by the way his body moved with slow, steady purpose. Instinctively, I shifted away from the fireplace, putting the sofa between us. My heart spiked to a frantic beat. Fixing on his target—me—he flexed his chest and arms as he stalked closer.

"That strong, dominant Morgon man being you." I continued moving, mirroring his movements in the opposite direction around the sofa.

"I'm going to mark you"—his voice an icy edge—"and you're going to let me."

My boot caught on the tufted red carpet. I stumbled, then caught myself, giving him just enough time to ease around the sofa and corral me backward till I was once again by the fireplace.

He opened his arms, palms up, in a disarming manner, raising my alarm to red alert. "Unless of course you want to call the whole thing off."

"Of course not." I lifted my chin. No way was I backing out, though survival instincts told me to bolt right now. "I'm not going to have sex with you or anything."

"No need. I can get my scent under your skin without fucking you."

Crude words. They matched the man—hard, cold, devoid of emotion. His eyes roved the skin he planned to mark in short, quick order. So maybe a little making out. I could do that. No biggie. Just some kissing. Right?

"You're not going to bite me or anything, are you?"

"Oh." Closer. Closer. "Not too hard." His voice dropped several decibels.

"Kol—"

I had a split-second warning before I was pinned to the floor on my back. Kol's fingers wrapped my nape, spreading up into my hair around the base of my skull, his body heavy and hard on mine. His lips pressed, pried, commanded me to open my mouth. I did.

His tongue swept in—hot, invading, demanding my complete submission. He bit my lower lip, letting his teeth clamp just a little too hard. I made a soft cry before he melded firm lips over mine, giving me a punishing kiss. I braced my hands on his shoulders, pushing to catch my breath. Not that it did a damn bit of good. He was big. So big.

With a sharp crack, he fully extended his wings, creating an artificial night, closing me off to everything but him. He released my mouth and trailed nips up my jaw. The Iceman was long gone. All I felt was heat, simmering in my blood, melting through flesh to bone. His teeth grazed my earlobe. Desire coiled low and deep, tightening as his mouth worked on me.

"Let go," said the dragon. No sign of Kol.

Though my instinct was to resist the marking, my body had other plans, responding to every sweep of his tongue, every brush of his chest. His thigh pressed between my legs, spreading them, heat rushing to the place he rubbed. I moaned in the back of my throat, embarrassed by my unwilling submission, though not enough to make him stop. God, I wouldn't dare, it felt so good.

His hand gripped the collar of my shirt and wrenched it off my shoulder. The two top buttons popped. I didn't care. I'd never felt so consumed, so obliterated by sensation, my blood burning, rushing like lava through my body. Mikal had been a gentle lover. There was nothing gentle about Kol. And while my brain reminded me that this was to mark me for protection only, not for any kind of affection Kol might have, I was overwhelmed by his mouth heating my skin, by his powerful frame pressing me into the red-tufted rug. I bent my knees, caging him between my legs.

His mouth opened on the curve between neck and shoulder, biting down hard. I cried out, yet still my fingers wove into his black hair, pulling him closer, my body aching for more. His hand cupped my breast, squeezing till I arched up, yielding to his will. He licked the spot at my neck he'd bitten. My hips rocked up of their own accord, pressing against the thick length of him.

Control? I had none. I was riding on pure sensation. I'd lost my freaking mind.

His lips made their way back to my mouth. His tongue lined my bottom lip before sweeping in again. I kissed him back with the same intensity, sliding my tongue over his. He rocked in between my legs, the seam of my jeans a marvelous friction with what he pressed there.

"Kol," I breathed in desperation.

His fingers kneaded my breast. I rolled my pelvis up as he rubbed harder against me.

"Let go, Moira."

Frantic, I tried to hold on to some sanity, not wanting to give in to him, not wanting to let go, but it was impossible. He swallowed my scream when my nerves fractured. I never screamed with Mikal. Of course, I didn't always come with Mikal, either. And this wasn't even sex. This was…make-out marking.

Breathing hard and beyond embarrassed at my shocking reaction to his body on top of mine, I closed my eyes, willing myself somewhere else as a hot pulse still throbbed between my legs. I forced my fingers loose, still clutched in his hair and the front of his shirt, panting like some wanton. His lips hovered above my own, unmoving, lingering. I refused to meet his gaze. After a moment, his wings folded against his back with a whoosh as he lifted off my body. Heavy steps as he walked across the study and opened the door.

Sitting up, I gazed down at my top, gaping with the loss of two buttons. Within a minute, Kol walked back into the room carrying my coat and scarf. He sauntered over and pulled me to my feet.

Handing me my scarf, a smirk fixed on his face, he said, "You might want to use this to uh…" He motioned to my gaping blouse.

Fuming, I wrapped and tied the scarf, covering my exposed cleavage because *he* had torn my shirt. But what could I say after the way I reacted to his mouth and hands all over my body. Mortified didn't begin to describe how I felt as I yanked my coat from him and jerked it on, stomping for the door.

He caught me by the arm and whirled me around, leaning his head toward my neck.

"Stop it, Kol! Marking time is over."

While trying to pry him off with no success, he gripped my other arm, keeping me still. Damn it, I needed more body boxing lessons. Holding me captive by the arms, he nuzzled into my make-out-messy hair.

"Stop it," I gritted out.

"I'm just checking," he crooned. I wanted to die.

His nose grazed my neck in a fleeting soft touch. I shivered. He straightened, a wicked-as-sin grin plastered on his face. "Good. I'm well and deep under that skin of yours."

"Satisfied?"

He arched one dark brow as if to ask, *Are you?* I wanted to punch him in the face. For about the hundredth time.

"Not quite, Kittycat. But it'll do. For now."

I shrugged out of his hold. "Don't even think there'll be a repeat session, because there won't be."

I couldn't help the bitterness that had dripped from my voice. He hadn't violated me. He'd done worse. He'd made me lose complete control. He'd made me feel a shocking wave of pleasure unlike anything I'd ever experienced in my entire life, when I didn't want it nor had I asked for it. I didn't want to feel anything in that way. I didn't want a man in my life at all. Complicating things, steering me in a direction of his choosing.

What was I even talking about? It was nothing. Just a scent-marking. For protection. And if I *was* looking for a lover, which I wasn't, it sure as hell wouldn't be the infuriating slab of cold marble standing before me.

"See you Friday, Kittycat."

I stormed off, feeling slightly childish but unable to calm the anger brewing in my blood, the sound of masculine laughter behind me.

I needed to punch something. Hard.

Chapter 10

My roundhouse kick hit Demetrius square in the chest. He flew back, landing with a thud for the fourth time. Heaving breaths, I reached out a hand to haul him up.

"Damn, Moira." He puffed out between gulps of air. "You gonna tell me why you're kicking the shit out of me?"

"No reason." I panted. "Just got some excess energy."

He picked up a towel from the bench outside the boxing square and wiped the sweat dripping down his face, slicking his black hair.

"Does this excess energy have a name? You seeing Mikal again?" He sat on the bench, downing a water bottle.

I settled next to him, wiping my neck and face with another towel. "No. Of course not. I told you that was over."

I scowled deeper, annoyed with myself that I was so irritated about Kol, and I couldn't hide it no matter how hard I tried.

"Yeah. But he still talks about you. I thought there might be——"

"Don't go there, Demetrius. We're not suited for each other."

He stretched out his long legs, massaging his upper thigh where I'd probably given him a melon-sized bruise. He'd taught me a good maneuver to use when knocked to the ground and an opponent had the upper hand. I had proved I mastered the move when I kicked his ass.

He blew out a breath, slipping on a long-sleeved fleece. While hot and steamy up in our family's parlor-turned-gym, outside, the temperatures were steadily dropping.

Demetrius had started giving me self-defense lessons when I was fifteen and growing into a young woman. Those lessons merged into weekly sparring sessions until he moved out of our parents' home and found a place of his own with Shakara. And though I'd moved out a few years ago, we still chose to spar here. Old habits died hard. Or perhaps, there was some comfort in the familiar. No matter that this home held bitter memories and had created scars that might never truly heal for Demetrius, he always returned home and treated my father with respect, whether or not Father deserved it.

He aimed his brown eyes at me. "Not a guy. What then? School? Money?"

I shrugged, then retied my pony tail.

"Tell me," he urged before draining his water bottle.

His snooping was well-intentioned. When Jessen had fallen for Lucius years ago, he'd sided with my father, driving a wedge between him and our sister. Though he regretted it, and they'd mended things, there was still an air of tension between him and Lucius. He just couldn't help being the *big brother.*

"It's nothing." I slipped into my red hoodie.

"You know," he said, combing a hand through his dark, sweat-drenched locks. "All you have to do is say the word, and Father will give you whatever you want. He still has a trust fund waiting for you whenever you're ready to swallow your female pride."

"It's not money," I said with too much disdain. "And you wouldn't know the first thing about female pride."

"Thank God," he muttered.

I pushed him off the bench. He rolled and bounced to his feet, stifling a laugh. It was hard to be angry with Demetrius when he smiled, deep dimples in the corner. A sight I'd enjoyed more often since he married Shakara. Usually too sober for his own good, his smile could make the whole world feel right again.

"Seriously, Moira. You should give in to him a little. Let him help you."

"Oh, like you did?"

"Father and I both finally came to our senses." He smirked. "He's an ornery, old ass who will never change his ways. And I'm a brilliant genius who finally decided to use my gifts accordingly and better the company. Win-win situation."

"Yeah." I snorted. "And from what I heard a stand-off that nearly split the company in half." As well as the family.

He tilted his head, small frown in place. "When did you hear that?"

"I'm an investigative reporter. You thought I didn't know you and him had a falling out when you started dating Shakara?"

His frown smoothed. His stature softened. A goofy smile spread across his face.

I threw a towel at his head. "Jeez, Demetrius. Go home to your wife. And stop pestering me."

"With pleasure, dear sister." He hiked his workout bag over his shoulder but didn't move for the door. "Its money, isn't it? Let me loan you some."

"No."

"Stubborn woman. How the hell did you get that way?"

"It's in the genes. Trust me."

As supervisor in the technology department of Cade Enterprises for the past four years, Demetrius had yielded more profits than the entire decade prior because of his intelligence and business savvy.

"I want to *earn* my way. Like you. Even though I have no idea how you came out of that family crisis smelling like a goddamn rose as the dutiful son."

"Language, Moira. It's not becoming of you."

I slipped on thick workout pants over my tight boxing gear. "Since when is a girl of the aristocracy with a foul mouth *ever* becoming?"

"Touché. As to being the dutiful son, perhaps I am, but sometimes..." He wrapped the towel around his neck and clenched both ends. His eyes became glazed and distant, his countenance taking on that grave expression so typical of him. Funny. It reminded me of someone else with a frosty disposition.

"Sometimes?" I prompted.

"Sometimes duty does feel an awful lot like a cage. You've got to make sure your choices, even dutiful ones, are truly your own."

That's when I understood. Demetrius had once felt exactly as I did. And perhaps still did. He'd chosen to stay behind, to uphold the family legacy, to stay within the bars of Father's control, while my sister liberated herself by marrying a Morgon. It wasn't until Shakara came along and rocked his world that he finally broke free of Father's cage.

"Well, whatever it is. Don't let it bring you down. Life's too short to dwell on the negative."

"My brother, the optimist. Did hell freeze over and I missed it?"

He chucked his sweaty towel at me, hitting me in the face.

"Ewww!" I laughed.

"A smile. That's better than the scowl you wore in here. The workout seemed to help your crappy mood."

"It did." It had helped even more when I imagined Kol's face instead of my brother's every time I pounded him. "Thanks."

"No problem. Any time you need to beat someone up, just give me a call."

With a wave, he was out the door. I finished dressing and made my way down the wide, spiral staircase. Mother was out doing errands. Edda, our family's live-in servant since before I was born, greeted me at the bottom as she dusted the tall, wooden clock.

"Will you be joining the family for dinner on Friday? Your mother requested that you come."

I sighed inwardly. My mother still bore hopes of me snagging the most eligible bachelor in town and becoming the model aristocratic hostess for the most posh of high society. Like her. Though I loved my mother, another one with good intentions gone awry, I would never be the daughter she wanted. To avoid the look of disappointment in her eyes, I avoided her as often as I could, especially in the setting she so wanted me to be a part of.

"No, Edda. I'm afraid not. I have something to do for work."

"Of course." Edda smiled, surely knowing I may or may not have something to do with work. It didn't matter. I'd avoid the Cade party train as much as possible. "Well, work hard." She winked.

"I will," I promised as she bustled toward the kitchen.

I crossed the marble tile into the foyer, hearing papers shuffle from the front parlor. Frowning, I stepped in. Father was seated in the overstuffed chair next to the fire, reading the newspaper. This was the man I enjoyed spending time with, not the overbearing CEO I'd avoided at his office. At home, outside the realm of his professional kingdom, he was the man I wished he'd been during my childhood, before Jessen had left as the rebellious child he still spoke of with a pained expression. "Father?"

His usual steely gaze was somewhat wilted. "Moira. Come here, girl."

I obeyed. Though I'd relinquished his hold over the direction of my life, I still treated him with respect.

I sat on the ottoman at his feet. He folded the paper in his lap, twining his fingers together over a paunchy stomach. His face seemed more drawn, his eyes less severe, the mouth less grim. Time was softening the hard lines of a face I once feared. The man who never picked me up when I fell down, who never kissed a scraped knee or elbow, who never wished me a sound sleep at bedtime. No. The man who had taught me severity and tenacity was fading behind the graying hair and softening belly.

"Why are you not at work?"

"Oh, not much to do."

Since when did that ever keep him from work?

"I can catch up on local politics right here with *The Gladium Post*," he said, gesturing to the folded paper in his lap.

I picked up the paper, glancing at the headline, *When Will the Devlin Butchers Strike Next?*, written by Bard Woodblade, one of their lead reporters.

"So, girl. You still have your eye on *The Post*? Best be working hard if you do. Not many get the chance at one of their positions. Especially not women." His jab was meant to bolster my ambition, rather than discourage. I knew that now. Once, I would've taken offense, but I'd learned his ways.

"I'm working hard. No need to worry. As senior editor at *The Herald*, I get to choose from the best stories."

He pierced me with the grave look I'd grown up knowing so well. "Don't choose *from* the best. Choose *the* best. There is no other way to climb high and far. You're a Cade, whether you choose to acknowledge it or not. Remember that."

I glanced down at my fingers, pulling at a loose thread in my jacket. "I have no problem acknowledging who I am."

"Hmph. Really? Then who is Marina Creed? I'm assuming that's your pseudonym. Unless there are two senior editors at the university paper." My father had been reading my articles. My mouth fell agape for about five seconds before I took hold of my wits again. My father actually *read* my articles.

"I am perfectly proud of my given name," I said, clearing my voice of emotion. "I want to make my way on my own, not on the back of your accomplishments."

He rubbed his forefinger along his lower lip, an old habit of his when he fell into deep thought. He stared past me out the window. After a few minutes of listening to the steady crackle of the fire and the hollow ticking pendulum of the clock in the foyer, he gazed down at me with the old hard look I knew so well. "You know, girl. You're more like me than any of my children. You have a spine of steel," he said with an appraising stare. "Just know, that steely spine of yours can get you through a great many trials. But steel that is untested by fire is brittle and will break if it bends too far."

I considered his words as he went back to gazing over my shoulder out the window, rubbing his forefinger along his lip in pensive silence.

It made me cringe to be compared to the man who exiled my sister from the family because of his own prejudices against the Morgon race and who had once ruled over my brother like a tyrant. He was right. He was so right. I tempered the anger burning in my chest.

In childhood, Father was the one who forced me to get up when I fell down, who taught me to ignore the pain of scraped knees and elbows, who sent me to bed alone so I might learn independence rather than the life of a coddled child. In short, he made me the strong woman I was. After Jessen left and married Lucius, he demanded that I spend less time with my mother, a sweet but meek woman, and more time with Demetrius. My father made me who I was. Was it his regret of losing Jessen that made him change toward me? Or had he always seen my iron will as a reflection of his own?

"An early snow," he said, gesturing toward the window.

I stood and watched chunky flakes flurry down in a steady torrent. The sun blotched out by a pall of gray.

"Very early," I added.

"Best keep warm. It's going to be a deep, cold winter."

Chapter 11

The bell gonged, signifying the end of the game. To me, it sounded like the ominous toll of doom. Kris, part of tonight's cover, beamed her bright smile at Kraven, laughing at some joke, as carefree as ever. Forcing a smile, I wore my full façade of party girl. On the inside was an entirely different matter. I'd set myself up as meat for the slaughter. I was confident that Kol and Lorian and the rest of them would protect me. Still, the idea of where I might be by the end of the night should our plan come to fruition chilled my blood.

"Awesome! Let's go." Kris bounced out of her seat toward the door with Kraven close behind.

I'd been forbidden to tell Kris the details of tonight's plan, keeping those in the inner circle to a bare minimum. But she was my best friend, and everyone knew the unwritten rule. When you were sworn to secrecy about something, that included everyone *except* your best friend. So, of course, I told her everything. Besides, if I didn't tell her about my pseudo-seduction of the creepy Borgus guy, she'd think I'd lost my mind and scare him off as soon as he started leering at me. At first, she was hesitant, being more on the cautious side of care than me. But as soon as I told her there would be a bevy of Nightwing Security around the place, she was more than willing to be my accomplice for the evening.

We jostled into the corridor. Kraven stood at our backs, his wings partly open to keep others from running into us.

"Now, the espionage begins," she whispered in my ear.

I elbowed her. "Kris," I hissed in warning.

She winked, stepping aside so Kraven could sidle between us.

"You know, this isn't your typical club. It can get kind of rowdy down there," he said.

"Sounds fun to me." Kris smiled.

Kraven looked a little smitten. How could he not. Kris flipped her soft, honey-brown hair over her bare shoulder, tucking her jacket under her arm. Her halter-top of deep purple accentuated the blue-violet of her eyes. Kraven's gaze skimmed down her black-clad slender hips and legs when she wasn't looking. The poor guy was a goner.

Kris had dressed more modestly than me. After all, I was supposed to be bait. I needed to stand out. And I made damn sure of it. I wore skin-tight white patent leather pants with red criss-cross stitching on both outer seams from hip to ankle, and a blood-red corset under my black dragon jacket. I'd been the receiver of numerous lecherous stares by men and venomous glares by women the whole night, but the unwanted attention was worth it if I drew the one Morgon we were looking for.

I linked arms with Kris as we exited the Box and found the darkened stairs leading into the cellars. A parade of Morgons and a few humans were doing the same. I sidled up next to Kris with Kraven on the other side of her.

The house music pumped loud and hard as we descended into the basement. Nearly packed, the party must've gotten started early. The most shocking difference was the aura of blue light flickering from the sconces and black wrought iron chandeliers.

"What the heck?" exclaimed Kris. "How is that even possible?"

Kraven winked. "A Morgon trick." He glanced over Kris's head, giving me a knowing look. It was Morgon magic, not a trick. "They do this when the Riptides from Cloven play our team." The Riptides had vibrant sapphire-blue wings. For the first time, it dawned on me that most teams outside Gladium represented one clan, while our team bore members from several different ones.

"They're the Skyshadow clan, aren't they?" I asked Kraven.

"Yeah. They all live in Cloven." Kraven nodded toward the Pit arena. "I'm going to catch up to you ladies in a while. I need to check on the fighting match for tonight."

"Sure thing," I said, scanning the room.

I didn't recognize anyone. No sign of Kol or Lorian. Of course, the plan required them to stay hidden. Everyone knew Lorian and Kol's link to the Morgon Guard. We wanted the crowd to feel uninhibited. Kol informed me they'd be close, monitoring from a secure room with access to the hidden cameras.

"Come on, Kris. Let's go get a drink."

Weaving through the dancing crowd, I wasn't surprised to have to push my way through to the other side. A voluptuous brunette, human, had her arms wrapped around the neck of a Morgon man who had his tongue shoved down her throat. From behind her, another Morgon pressed close as his hands hiked up her skirt and trailed underneath. I hid my disgust as I pressed forward.

Damn, the sexual tension in this place was amped to a new level. Last time, I'd sensed the escalating sensuality following the fight, but tonight, there was an aura of sex heavy in the air. And the fight hadn't even started. This place would transform into a full-on orgy after the scintillating blood-bath. Now I understood why Jessen's face fell ashen when I'd mentioned the Pit. This place attracted the dregs of Morgon society. Not your typical nightclub party people, but the kind that let their beast roam to the surface, satisfying their animalistic urges without hindrance or regret.

"Moira," hissed Kris close to my ear as we finally made it to the bar. "Some dude just grabbed my boob."

I grinned. "Welcome to a Vaengar after-party."

"Yeah, but not all Morgons behave like that."

Kol flashed to mind. No, they certainly didn't.

"Kraven's nice," added Kris. "Why aren't you dating him again?"

I shrugged. "He's just not my type."

She snorted as she waved over the bartender, the same green-winged Morgon from last time, her hair dyed bright fuchsia. "What? A tall, fine hunk of male isn't your type? He's a gentleman, too. Best of both worlds."

The waitress brought us two Brevettes on ice. I clinked my glass against Kris's.

"You have a crush on him."

"What? Me? No! Pfft." She waved me off and gulped down half her glass.

"Whoa. Brevette is a sneaky drink. I wouldn't drink it so fast."

"Sure thing, Mom."

I shoved her with my shoulder. A roar of masculine laughter erupted from near the body-shot table. It seemed someone was entertaining the lascivious crew as usual. I caught a glimpse of a bare feminine leg between the Morgon bodies pressed close around the table. A girl squealed, then more laughter.

"What's going on over there?"

"You don't want to know." Some unfortunate girls giving up their dignity for a cheap thrill.

I sipped my drink, slyly checking out the room, not recognizing a soul. The grinding house music slowed to a more somber song.

"Kris." I turned at Kraven's voice to see a big smile beaming down at her. "Would you care to dance?"

She knocked her drink back and took his hand. "You don't mind, do you, Moira?"

"No. Of course not." I waved them off with a smile, happy Kris could enjoy herself while I grew more tense by the moment. "You two have fun."

Kraven gave me a sharp nod and guided her into the crowd. He was letting me be a lonely, morsel of Morgon bait all by myself. I'd nursed my one glass of Brevette for several songs and was on my second before the fish finally emerged from the murky waters and nibbled on the hook.

"We meet again, Moira."

I swallowed my breathless gasp and cooled my features before turning with a sensual smile. "Mr. Borgus. How delightful to see you again."

As before, he was dressed impeccably, from well-groomed hair to gold cufflinks. A starched, white Primean silk shirt, glowed under the blue light. A dark suit, finely tailored. A thin tie that shined silver in the dark. Even a triangle of handkerchief stuck out of the front lapel—an older fashion that certain members of the nobility still clung to.

"Please. Just Borgus. And the pleasure is all mine."

I extended my hand for him to shake. Instead, he took my hand and pulled me in, placing a kiss on my cheek, lingering close. I had to tamp down my urge to cringe.

When he pulled back, a glint of cold fire sparked in his eyes. He angled his head in an assessing manner, putting me on high alert. "You're dating a Morgon."

Oh, shit! How did I not realize he would smell Kol's scent on me before the planned abduction? I didn't even know what marking really meant in the crazy-ass mating rituals of Morgons. Did it mean I was taken? Or that I just liked one of their kind? Or that I'd just fooled around? Kol had tried to reconnect with me before tonight, but I had some "emergency" to deal with every time he had called.

I shook my head. "Not really. I was seeing someone, but I don't think he's the Morgon for me."

His mouth quirked up on one side, the one that didn't twitch. He seemed appeased by my answer. "Are you here alone?" One dark eye made the tic motion with his mouth.

"No, I'm here with a girlfriend, but she's, well, preoccupied at the moment." I waved in the general direction of the dance floor. "Would you mind keeping me company for a while?"

I shrugged out of my jacket, confident that my strapless corset would do the trick and reel him in. My dark hair slipped over one shoulder in a silken sheet. Though it had been several days, I still had to use concealer to cover the bruise from Kol's bite during our make out marking session.

Borgus shifted his body closer. "I would be delighted."

Seducing a possible murderer was new for me, making me feel as dirty as the girls doing unspeakable things in the dark corners of this room. But I blinked away my fear, thinking instead of the three girls pinned to the bulletin board in my office. I had a job to do, so I pasted on my sultry smile and lured him in.

I focused on maintaining calm, even breathing. Kol had warned me that Morgons could sense fear. Hopefully, if my heart accelerated with the look I had fixed on my face, he'd think I was only excited and aroused by his magnificence. This was tougher than I thought.

I waved over the bartender, forcing myself not to think of those girls, not to think what this man did to them. She slid me another Brevette on the rocks.

Borgus tossed down a large bill and waved her away. "So, Moira. Tell me about yourself."

I leaned my elbow on the bar, jutting out my hip. His face was split— half in shadow and half in hazy blue light, morphing his features to grotesque angles. Last time I'd seen him, I knew he was of the Morgon nobility, his features almost handsome. Now, the sharp contours and high cheekbones contorted into something frightening. Black eyes glinted in the low light with an unnatural luster. Matching their namesake, glossy black wings appeared like shards of glass sticking up over his shoulder. Coalglass.

I fingered an ice-cube, pretending to stir my fresh drink. "Well, I'm a student at GU, so that takes up most my time."

"What are you studying?"

"Multicultural Studies."

"Ah." One of his hands lifted a strand of my hair, twining it slowly. "And what made you choose such a field?"

"I've always been curious about other cultures and races. Especially Morgons. But now I'm interested in learning more firsthand." I gazed up from beneath my lashes, willing him to take the bait.

"Really?" His chest brushed mine. "I can certainly teach you whatever you'd like to know."

"I'm sure you can." Holding eye contact over the rim of my glass, I sipped the Brevette. "Don't you ever wonder about the other half of the population?"

He let my hair slide through his fingers and rested his hand on the curve of my hip.

"All the time." His mouth and eye ticked in unison. I pretended not to notice as his hand squeezed my hip, inching me closer. "Tell me what else you do with your time."

"I practice body boxing."

His eyes widened in surprise and obvious appreciation. "Human women do such a thing?"

"Oh, yes. Some do, anyway." I gave him my sexy smile. "A girl's got to keep in shape."

His eyes dropped to my breasts.

"Besides," I added, "I need a little aggression in my life."

He moved decidedly closer, his fingers sliding lower. I speculated whether suffering Kol's attentions to get his scent was worth the damn effort, but was so glad I did when Borgus's nostrils flared and a frown puckered his wide brow. Straightening, he dropped his hand from my waist and held out his hand. "Dance with me."

I took his hand and let him lead me to the stifling dance floor. He maneuvered near a corner and swept me into his arms in a waltzing fashion, one hand holding my hand in a loose grip, the other on my lower back, pressing me close. He smelled of a clean, masculine cologne. Disturbed that he should smell good, I pretended to be falling for his charms, letting his body mold to mine.

I tried not to think of Maxine as his fingers trailed down my spine. I tried not to think of those same fingers gutting her with a knife and tossing her carcass aside like trash. Were these the hands that did such a thing, the ones sliding sensuously over my body?

Sweat dampened the nape of my neck under my hair. My stress level was rising. He watched me with keen focus. I scanned the room as he guided my body in a slow circle. A Morgon couple backed against the wall. With his hands on her shoulders, the man eased her down onto her knees. In profile, her face lifted as she fumbled with his pants. He placed his hand on her crown, guiding her head closer before he shifted and whipped his wings out to shield them from view. Borgus followed my gaze. I looked away quickly, feeling small and alone in a sea of strangers.

"Does that bother you?"

"No. Of course not. I'm just not used to seeing that in a public place."
I struggled to keep my composure, hanging on by a thread.

Borgus chuckled, and I felt the hairs on my arms bristle.

"Not in Gladium, perhaps," he crooned. "Voyeurism is an aphrodisiac
in Drakos and even more so in Cloven."

Get it together, Moira.

I flipped my hair, putting both arms around his neck, feigning
nonchalance.

"I wouldn't know. It's illegal for humans to go to the northern Morgon
provinces."

"I wouldn't say it's against the law, but humans are not exactly
welcome." He gripped the base of my neck, his thumb stroking my collar
bone. "But it seems for the first time in history, the gates of the Obsidian
Games will be open to interested humans this year."

"Really?" No need to act surprised. This was news to me.

He leaned down, his mouth close to my ear. "Would you like to come?"

The sexual innuendo, implied in his lilting words, tied my stomach
into a knot. When his thumb brushed over the swell of one breast, acid
churned in my gut. Thankful his lips hadn't made contact with my skin,
I pulled back and peered into the shining black of his eyes. "Perhaps," I
answered in a coy, yet tawdry tone.

"You're flushed."

"It's just a little hot in here." I avoided his eyes.

"That it is. Let me buy you another drink."

He tugged me by the wrist back to the bar and tossed several large bills
on the counter, calling to the waitress, "A bottle of your best champagne."

Getting intoxicated would be completely stupid, but there was no way
to avoid playing along. Borgus untwined the top cap of the champagne
bottle, then popped the cork like an expert. Yes, he was accustomed to the
privileged life. He filled two fluted glasses and passed me one.

Voices clamored as the Vaenger players made their entrance,
streamlining for the Pit at the other end of the chamber. A gray-winged
Morgon girl flew to the chandelier above the Pit, inhaling a deep breath,
then blowing out a stream of flame to light the wicks, brightening the
view of the fighters entering the cage below. The crowd merged toward
the arena. Kraven's friend, the star player for the Gladium team, shirtless
and fuming, opened the barred gate and disappeared from view into the
bottom. A blond Riptide player with an arrogant smile laughed to one of
his teammates before following him.

"Would you care to watch the fight?" Borgus's voice had darkened, cutting like a blade. I forced myself to shake my head and pretended to sip the champagne, already feeling a strong buzz from the Brevette.

As the party at the shot-table broke apart and streamed our way, I wasn't all that shocked to see Layla mingling between a few Morgon men. Her top had fallen so low on her chest that I could tell she wasn't wearing a bra. Good Lord, she was a mess.

"Moira! You're back. Atta girl," she slurred, leaning drunkenly against me, knocking my glass. Champagne slopped over the rim onto my breasts. "Oops," she snickered.

Borgus stepped to the side when Layla sloshed her drink again in his direction.

"Is someone bringing you home?" I asked her.

There were no other humans with them, and I hoped she didn't plan on driving. A Morgon man loomed over her shoulder. "Hey, baby. I remember you."

I recognized the green-eyed sleaze-bag at once. "Take care of Layla, will ya?"

She'd already stumbled off with the rest of them. He didn't, easing into my space. Borgus just watched from the sidelines.

"Too bad she spilled that good champagne. No worries, baby. I'll wipe it off for you."

"Um, no you won't." I didn't need any acting for my next trick. As one of his hands came up, most probably to grab my breast, I gripped his forefinger and bent his whole hand and arm backward and upside down. He turned to avoid the severity of my hold, allowing me to twist his entire arm behind his back. He cried out as I pushed his hand closer to his spine and higher. Wings ruffled in my face when another Morgon grabbed him by the shoulder, dragging him toward the arena.

"Stop fuckin' around, Drom. I've got money on this fight."

His friend hadn't noticed what had happened in the blue gloom of the underground club. But I didn't miss the glare of malice Layla's beastlike friend, Drom, shot over his shoulder as he was hauled into the crowd.

"Well, now," said Borgus, clinking his glass to mine, half-empty from my struggle with Drom. "That was impressive. It's not every day I see a beautiful woman send an angry Morgon violently on his way."

I took a sip of champagne, letting him get a nice, long look at my vulnerable throat, deciding this was the moment. It was now or never. I needed to go for the jugular, or in this guy's case, the groin.

I set the champagne glass on the table and snapped his handkerchief from his front lapel to wipe the liquid from my breasts. I didn't need to look up to know he watched the slow move of my hand across my cleavage.

"I'd have to say"—I finished dabbing and folded the handkerchief in a perfect square, leaning my body against his—"that I'm not every woman." I tucked the cloth back into its place, smoothing his lapels with both hands, letting them rest near his shoulders, my breasts brushing the silk of his suit jacket. "And I'm picky about my men."

"Oh?"

"Strong. And confident, of course."

"Of course." He edged closer.

"A man with unwavering determination who knows how to please a woman. And one who understands what a woman wants, even if she doesn't know herself."

I blinked, realizing my description matched a certain Morgon with ice in his voice and fire in his kiss. A roar erupted from the crowd at the arena as I held his gaze, mere inches from his face.

"Do you know, Moira, that you carry the scent of another Morgon man?"

The fact that he was harping on this issue meant I needed to step up my game and convince him Kol didn't matter. I let my lashes fall, then lifted them in a provocative manner. "He doesn't mean anything." My stomach twisted. "I need a new Morgon man."

He slid a finger along my jawbone and across my lower lip. I didn't move, praying he wouldn't kiss me, wishing I had my medal for comfort. I had refused to wear it. A woman looking for a promiscuous liaison would never have something of that sort around her neck. My heart hammered despite my bravado. He leaned in close, his tone seductive and dominant. "Come. Take a walk with me."

I smiled, hoping no fear shone in my eyes. He wrapped a hand around mine, leading me away from the bar, winding around table-tops and the few couples engaged in amorous play rather than watching the fight. He led me toward the exit. *The exit* as Kol had warned me the first night I'd met him.

"Where does this go?"

He pulled me closer. "Outside."

"Oh."

My witty banter came to an abrupt halt. My throat felt thick. This was it. Soon enough, I'd be whisked away to God knew where. The noise of the cellar grew distant. The hollow clopping of my boots and his expensive shoes echoed off the walls, sconces of golden light tossing long shadows across the cavern. We rounded a bend. The silence heavier, I needed to say something just to ease my nerves. "Do you live close by?"

I shivered at the eerie smile I caught in the torch-light.

"We'll be alone soon enough."

A few more steps and he stopped, his grip easing around my wrist, holding me still.

"What is it?"

I stared up ahead, unable to discern anything in the gloom. An odd scraping or ticking sound reverberated from the shadowy recesses. A tendril of malevolence permeated the air, twining itself up my body and around my throat. I could no longer keep my pulse from pounding away. Something terrible lurked in the dark. Something terrible drew closer. My courage evaporated like mist. Suddenly, I didn't want to do this anymore. I didn't want to be the bait. Primal fear shook me senseless, screaming at me to run. Borgus tightened his hold on my wrist, staring fixedly into the gloom, willing whatever was there to come forth. My whole being drew back, sensing an evil otherness hovering in shadow, waiting to take me.

All at once, a stomping of several feet approached fast. I spun around to the sight of Drom barreling toward me, rage marking every strained line of his face. "There's the bitch."

"Shit," I mumbled.

Drom grabbed me at the same time three of his friends attacked Borgus. Then it was mayhem. Streaks of Morgon men flew into the melee, evaporating out of thin air. Growling. Yelling. The whoosh of flapping wings. I caught the profile of Lorian zip past me as Drom shoved me back against the wall. Scuffling and grappling filled the corridor.

Drom leaned over me, gripping one arm and wrapping his fingers around my throat with the other. "I'm going to teach you—"

He screamed. A horrible crack, then his head was hauled back. As Drom let me go, he gave me a violent shove toward the wall. I caught the flash of furious silver eyes right before my head whacked the cavern wall, and I slid down to the cold, stone floor. A haze swept my vision, dragging me under as I whispered, "Kol."

Chapter 12

Cold sweat slicked my brow. My head throbbed. I couldn't open my eyes. Voices sounded muffled and distant. I was still in the cave, but I was safe. Lorian's voice came clearly into focus.

"...needs a healer. I'll take her to—"

"*No.*" A powerful outburst, then quieter words. "I'll take care of her."

Lorian didn't protest. I doubted anyone would after that dominant command. I tried to open my eyes, to say something, to ask what happened, but all that came out was a soft moan as I was lifted into someone's strong arms. The crushing pain in my head increased. I slipped back into the black.

* * * *

When I awoke again, I could barely lift my lids. The sharp profile of Kol's face silhouetted against a moon-bright sky. My arms and torso were wrapped in something warm, though my cheeks stung from icy wind. I felt the familiar sensation of flying. Rather than in a harness, Kol carried me. My vision hazed as I went under again.

* * * *

Warm. I was warm in a soft bed, though I felt pin-pricks of pain on my upper left arm. I felt him nearby. A masculine woodsy smell wafted over me. Opening my eyes, there he was, large as life, bending over me in deep concentration. I peered at the spot where his hands were doing something. Pain throbbed.

"Are you stitching me up?" My sleepy voice sounded more scratchy than usual.

His eyes flicked up to mine, then back to his work. "Either that or let you bleed all over my bed."

His bed!

I tried to sit up. He splayed a firm hand across my upper chest, fingertips across my collar bones, and promptly pushed me back down before he went back to his stitching.

"You'll pop the stitches before I'm even through. Be still."

His voice was low and gruff, but no dragon lurked there. He sounded strangely calm compared to the voice I heard between unconsciousness and awake. The voice who had refused to let anyone take me but him.

A smooth gray stone arced upward to a dome-like ceiling. Somewhere, I heard water. Rain? Couldn't be. The first snow had fallen in a torrent. Rain was months away now. My head must be still fuzzy from whacking against that wall. I remembered Borgus, Drom, the cavern.

"Kol. What happened?"

"The operation failed." He continued to suture the gash in my upper arm.

"I was so close. We almost—"

He stopped stitching. His frown deepened over a narrow gaze. "We won't be making a third attempt. So don't even think about asking."

I said nothing, feeling mollified. He went back to work on my arm. I couldn't admit what a coward I'd become at the last second. How I wanted to back out, to call for help right before Drom and his oafish friends came barreling in, thus ending our grand plan. There was irony for you. The jerk I couldn't stand had saved me from going through what I knew now was a definite mistake. There was something else at the edge of my mind, trying to snake its way in. I pushed it back, watching Kol. His hands were so large—broad, long-fingered, yet gentle and deft at stitching.

"Did we get Borgus?"

Somehow, I knew the answer before he gave it to me.

"No. He slipped out while we took care of that asshole and his asshole friends. If Borgus's men were there, they were well-hidden and long gone by the time we'd dealt with the others." The asshole, no doubt, being Drom.

A white-waxed candle burned low on a side-table. From this angle, his scar stood out in stark relief, an angry line marking this Morgon man, making him more severe, more cold, more distant. Whether from being half-stupid from the knockout or just plain insane, I touched two fingers to the top of his scar. He froze.

"Did this hurt?" I whispered.

"Yes."

I trailed my fingers feather-light down the reddened scar past his lips to where it stopped beneath. "Does it still hurt?"

Swift and sudden, he gripped my wrist in an iron hold, pinning me with simmering rage. "Don't." He gave me one shake of the head. A warning. He angled his head lower and snapped the thread's end with his teeth. He was up and moving away before it dawned on me how stupid I was. What in the world had possessed me to do that? I must've hit my head pretty damn hard.

I curled onto my side, feeling constricted by my tight corset and painted-on pants. Uncomfortably so. I stared at the candle, watching the wax roll into pools in its cast-iron holder, wafting a soft honey-flower aroma into the air.

He returned with something in his hand. "Here. You might be more comfortable sleeping in this."

It was a long-sleeved black shirt made of a divine material—thick and petal-soft. It was also three or four sizes too big.

"Can you change on your own, or do you need my help?" The devil was back in his eyes. The tips of his wide mouth tilted up.

"No. I can manage." I pushed off the bed with my injured shoulder, winced, and buckled at the elbow. He caught me around the ribs and helped me into a sitting position, my legs hanging off his bed. Literally hanging, for I couldn't reach the floor.

"I'm fine!" I snapped.

He crossed his arms and stood there, blocking my way.

"Really. I was just a little dizzy. I've got it."

"You banged your head hard, but the worst injury is in your shoulder."

I touched the wound lightly, remembering how Drom shoved me. Yes. I had hit my head and scraped my bare shoulder on the jagged wall on my way down to the stone floor. The wound was clean, the stitches tight. I met the glaring Morgon's gaze. "What?"

"A simple *thank you* would suffice."

I opened my mouth to give him a sassy come-back, then snapped it shut. "Thank you," I muttered, examining the wound.

"It will heal quickly and leave a little mark. It's a surface cut, but will sting for a while."

I met his stern gaze.

"Change. Stay put," he snapped. "I'll have something for your head shortly."

He exited the room, the door nothing more than a stone archway carved into the wall. A very large one in order to fit his massive body and wings. Was his house in a cave? If so, then it wasn't deep underground. A fireplace stood on the far wall, the smoke filtering up somewhere to the open air through the stone chimney. From here, I could see large river rocks carefully embedded into the chimney up to the point where the roof sloped into a dome.

I unlaced the corset in the front, feeling instant relief when I removed it. There were indentions in my skin where it had supported me under my breasts and squeezed my ribcage. After peeling off my pants on top of the bed, I pulled on the shirt Kol had given me, luxuriating in the softness against my skin, raw from being bound so long.

Other than a low-backed chair next to the fire and the bed on which I sat, there was no furniture. As would be expected, the bed was massive—three times the size of my own in my little apartment. There were no posts or headboard, but there was a unique design carved directly into the slate-gray stone wall where a headboard would be. Swirls of vines crossed and interlaced into a pointed arch, meeting the edge of the roof where the dome began. I touched the carven image, running my fingers along the surface of a thorny rose. It reminded me of Kris's headboard at her parents' home.

"Kris!"

I jumped off the bed and took a few quick steps toward the doorway, unsure where I was going or what I planned to do. White spots filled my vision as the blood rushed to my head. I stumbled and fell on all fours.

Before I could even see straight, I was lifted by a cursing Kol.

"Damn it, woman. Can you not be so stubborn for once?"

His words were rough, his tone gentle—an intoxicating contradiction—much like the man himself. Instead of putting me back in his bed, he carried me into the next room and placed me in a chair before another fireplace, careful not to aggravate my wound. I waited while the world righted, then peered around. Kol poured something from a kettle on the stove along a wall farther off. This room was similar to the bedroom—a wide, open space encompassing the kitchen and living area with little furniture.

"Kris. Please tell me someone made sure she got home safely."

He crossed the room and placed a round, warm mug in my hands. "Of course. Kraven took her home."

I sighed with relief, thankful my friend made it out safely. "He told her you were feeling sick and left early."

"She wouldn't accept that. It's not like me to just disappear."

He leaned one arm on the mantel, made of dark wood, jutting out from a river-rock chimney like the one in his bedroom. "She protested at first, but Kraven can be very persuasive."

I remembered the way he looked at her. "I'm sure."

"Drink up."

I peered into the cup and smelled a soothing aroma. "What is it?"

"It's a Petrus concoction. Your headache will be gone as soon as you finish."

I sipped, expecting a bland medicinal broth. It was pleasantly herbed and tasty.

Kol stared into the yellow flames. I studied him over the rim of the mug, the throbbing in my head fading as he had promised.

This man. This man—hidden behind an icy wall, behind a façade to keep the world at bay—no longer aggravated or annoyed me. He intrigued me, lured me. Rather than let Lorian take me to a hospital, he insisted on taking care of me himself. Why? I wanted answers. I wanted to know more of the man behind the frozen exterior.

"So why did you bring me here? Why not Lorian's?"

Still staring into the fire, he didn't answer. I'm not sure he heard me at all. There was a rushing noise close by, other than the hissing flames.

"That can't be rain. Unless you live south of Gladium. But you work mostly in Drakos for the Morgon Guard, so that can't be."

He took the mug from my hand and set it aside, holding out his arm. "Come. I'll show you."

Curling my fingers around his forearm, I let him lead me just in case I decided to have another dizzy spell and fall on my face again in humiliation. I hadn't noticed the opening in the wall to the left of the hearth. The hall was dark, but pale light shone up ahead. As we drew closer to another archway, the rushing water grew louder, the cold more intense. Stepping out of the opening, I was instantly hit with a fine, misty spray and icy wind. I sucked in a quick breath. We stood on a ledge twelve feet deep and thirty feet wide where nothing but a cascade of water curtained the aperture. By the faint light on the other side, I could tell the moon was still up.

"A waterfall!" The rushing-water noise drowned out my voice. "You live behind a waterfall?"

"Good camouflage." He didn't have to yell. His deep tenor reached me easily.

Peering up at him, the rushing water reflected a soft pattern on his face. The harsh planes seemed gentler. His eyes roved down to my bare legs, which trembled from the draft, his shirt stopping at my knees. Glittering pools of silver met my gaze. My breath hitched. As if caught in a vise, I couldn't look away. He didn't pretend nonchalance as he drank me in—

my hair, cheeks, lips, eyes. Rather, he revealed open hunger—the look of a man who knew what he wanted, who was used to getting what he wanted, who would demand my submission if it so pleased him. And the sad part? I knew I'd submit. In less than a heartbeat. Not of my own volition. It was like my body was ensnared by a mystical web, resonating with his on an undeniable level. I couldn't figure it out. Did the marking give him some control over me?

He lifted a hand, then brushed his fingertips across my cheek, sliding down my jaw to my parted lips, grazing with unimaginable softness for such a man. Pulse pounding in my throat at the thought of being helpless beneath him like before, I let go of his arm. He dropped his hand and blinked slowly, breaking the spell.

"You need to sleep," was his command. Before I could take a step, he swept me in his arms and carried me back into his house.

"I can walk. I'm not an invalid."

He grunted, holding me tighter. I blew out a frustrated breath. But the truth was, this felt good. The woodsy, wintry smell of him filled my senses, drawing me in, wrapping me in sensual unrest. Why? Because he'd marked me with his scent? Was I now hooked on him like a drug addict needed a fix? I closed my eyes, willing the sudden arousal washing over me to be gone. No such luck.

He set me on his bed and pulled up the covers.

"Why did you bring me here?"

He blew out the candle on the side-table. "Get some rest."

He left me, snuggled in his warm bed with my question unanswered and my wayward thoughts wreaking havoc on my frustrated body. I stared at the shadows dancing on the domed ceiling for a long time and finally drifted to sleep, heedless of the darkness waiting for me there.

Chapter 13

I was chained to a stone slab on my back, arms and legs stretched outward, naked. Cold, damp air wrapped me in shivering fear. Borgus materialized from smoke and shadow near my feet, a lascivious grin stretching his mouth into a grotesque mask. With the tip of one finger, he started at my ankle, slid up my calf, crossed behind my knee, and grazed along my inner thigh.

"No!" I protested, unable to move an inch.

"No?" He continued up my thigh and over my pelvic bone, making circles on my abdomen. "That wasn't what you said in the club."

"I lied. I don't want you. I don't want this. I don't want to die!"

His finger left my skin. His sickening black-eyed gaze finished the trail up my torso to my breasts to meet my terrified eyes.

"You're not for me, lovely Moira. You're for someone special."

"Who?"

His mouth and eye twitched as he evaporated into wispy smoke.

An odd noise, like steel scraping stone, filled the dark chamber. Someone else was there. Veiled in a shroud of darkness, he loomed large at the foot of the stone slab. I could see no features, only the silhouette of a huge Morgon man and piercing fire-gold eyes. Smoky mist curled around him, hiding his identity. A familiar essence of evil crawled over my skin, seeping into my bones, filling me with sickening dread. The creature, for it was more monster than man, hefted himself onto the slab and over my body. A stench of rot and decay smothered me, choked me, as the thing's face hovered over mine. Still, I could see nothing but his eyes—full dragon with black, vertical slits dilated in burning amber.

He grabbed my breast with a rough hand and squeezed. I screamed.

"Mine." A broken, guttural voice. A demon's voice.

He lowered his putrid body between my legs, his veiled face coming closer, cold lips clamping over my own as I screamed and screamed and screamed.

"Moira." Someone shook me. "Wake up!"

I thrashed my arms, beating the air, beating someone else.

"*Moira.* It's me."

I grabbed the wrists of the hands cupping my face, finally fighting through the haze of the nightmare to see Kol above me. His eyes flashed bright, wrapping me in an unexpected sense of safety. I burst into tears and threw my arms around his neck, clinging like a child.

"Shhh." He lay in the bed next to me, the covers having fallen to the floor. Holding and rocking me against his warm, bare chest, one hand brushed over my hair and back. "It was a nightmare. You're okay."

I kept crying, unable to speak at first, letting the tide of fear wash away with each soothing stroke of Kol's hand.

"No," I sobbed. "It was more than that. I knew him. I'd felt him before." The tears streamed hot and fast down my cheeks, slipping sideways onto the pillow. I still clung to Kol, unwilling to let my protector go, the lingering effects of the dream still clawing my insides.

"I'd forgotten about him." I sniffed. "He was there. Tonight. In that exit where Borgus was taking me."

"What do you mean?" He continued to coax me with gentle hands and a soft voice.

"There was someone there. In the shadows. He was...evil. Dark as death. Waiting for us. For me." I sobbed again. Kol brushed away the tears, but they continued to fall.

"That's what I forgot to tell you. Couldn't admit. As soon as I sensed him, I couldn't go on. I wanted out of my dumbass plan. I wanted to run, far away. I was a coward! Those girls. That thing. Oh, God!" A fit of crying overwhelmed me.

"Shhh. Stop now."

His thumb brushed over the trail of my tears, a continuing caress as I tried to slow my panicked breathing. I pressed closer, not caring that I seemed weak, needing warmth and comfort to wipe away that horrific thing from my senses, needing to feel the strength and protection of his muscular body. Minutes passed while he soothed me with gentle hands, my nerves unwinding with each touch that slid over my hair and down my back. I inhaled and let out a jagged breath.

"You're safe." Something in his voice, an unexpected tenderness, called to me.

Prying myself from his shoulder, I examined the outline of his face by the dying embers in the hearth. I brushed my fingertips over the scar now hidden in shadow. His eyes glinted silver, sliding closed as I caressed him. Both of us sought comfort in the dark.

Heart pounding for a different reason, I let my fingers explore as I never would in the light of day—across his brow, along his granite jaw where a day's stubble scratched my fingertips, over his wide mouth and sensuous lips. Sensuous. I'd never noticed before. Or maybe I hadn't let myself notice. With all the coldness of Kol, his lips defied everything he appeared to be. His lips invited, summoned, lured.

Those lips parted. Two fingertips, shaky, skimmed a fraction inside, resting on a ridge of teeth. His tongue touched the tips. A half-moan escaped me as I pulled my fingers away. His hand combed into my hair, curling around the nape of my neck, his mouth brushing an intimate invitation against mine. I opened for him, and he came inside.

Gentler, but no less dominant than last time, he slid his tongue into my mouth, licking and tasting. Possessing me with his kiss. He shifted his weight over me. My body awakened to the bliss of having him so close again.

His mouth opened mine wider. He wanted more. So did I. In my right mind by daylight, when I wasn't drowsy from sleep, needy from a nightmare, warm beneath his comforting weight, and delirious with the sensation of his mouth marking me anew, I might have been able to push away. Might. But in such a state, I was helpless against his desire, against my own. All I could think was—

"Yes."

His lips trailed to my neck, nipping and licking a hot line down the tender column of my throat. My fear faded. An aching need coiled tight with every brush of his mouth on my skin. Although I couldn't see him in the dark, I could certainly feel him. My hands molded over the wide expanse of his chest, down the ridges of his abdomen. He found my mouth again, groaning as my hands wandered a soft path up and down. Lower to the thin trail of hair disappearing into his pants.

"Moira." A warning.

He gripped my wrists and pinned them above my head in a firm, yet gentle grip, speaking against my lips. "Stop that."

I bit his lower lip, swollen from hard kisses. "Why?"

"Because you're injured. And I'm trying to be a gentleman."

I let out a breathy laugh. "A gentleman? A devil, maybe."

He pressed a swift, hard kiss to my lips, then shifted back to my side. "Kittycat, you haven't seen anything yet."

Keeping both my wrists bound in one hand, his other skimmed over my bare thigh. He nipped down my neck, sucking the hollow at the base. I closed my eyes, letting my body have what she'd been craving ever since his mouth had left me during the scent-marking.

Long fingers found the apex between my legs, stroking over damp satin. If I was in my right mind, I might be embarrassed. But I wasn't calm-and-collected Moira. I was some other woman, driven by sensation alone. I moved my hips to match his stroking fingers. He growled. Or actually, the dragon growled.

"Keep your hands above your head." An order. I obeyed.

He freed my wrists and pulled my shirt up above my breasts, all the while still stroking between my legs, soaking the thin fabric.

"Beautiful," the deep-barreled voice whispered as his mouth opened over my breast, then sucked the tip hard.

My neck and back arched upward on a gasp. He slid my panties down over my hips. I bent my knees so he could slide them off my legs. He left them at the crook, one hand resting on a knee, keeping them bent and parted. His tongue circled my peak as his fingers teased down the inside of my thighs. Then his hands and mouth left my skin altogether. Wanting and desperate, I half-opened my eyes to find him staring into mine with a look of fevered longing, fixed and fierce.

"Don't close your eyes again."

I nodded, willing to obey any command.

Totally exposed. Totally vulnerable, my body thrummed for more. He bent his face close to mine, lips touching but not moving, holding my gaze in the dark.

A long finger stroked down my slick cleft, then slid back up in a slow, languorous caress.

"God, Kol," I whimpered.

No smile.

"Stay with me, Moira."

I did, lacing my fingers behind his nape as his finger probed my opening, then slid inside. I was so tight. It had been a long time since Mikal. Since anyone for that matter.

I made a choked sort of sound as my hips rocked up to meet his increasing thrusts. He pulled out.

"No," I begged, "Please."

He did smile then, sliding two fingers inside me, stretching me with divine pleasure. My mouth fell open on a cry. He smothered it with his own, his tongue thrusting deep. I rocked back and forth, my body knowing what it wanted, mounting higher.

I kissed him deeper, drawing him into me, wanting more of him. Burning. I was on fire. I whispered his name in the dark, a plea for something, for more. Clutching his shoulders, I moaned in ecstasy, like I'd never done in my entire life, coming hard and fast, my muscles clamping on his fingers. Squeezing my thighs, pleasure rocked through me.

What was he doing to me? This wasn't me. I didn't make-out with guys I barely knew or let guys feel me up that I had no intention of dating. I'd only ever been with one person and that was after a long time of courtship. Where the hell was Moira? I didn't recognize the woman panting and pleasantly sated beneath the behemoth of Morgon man. But God, I'd do it again in a heartbeat.

He pulled his fingers out and slid my panties back into place, then righted my shirt. He lifted the covers back on the bed, then threw two more logs on the fire. Sparks spit and crackled as the flames licked around the dry wood. Finally, he lay on top of the bed, stretched on his side. "Go to sleep."

I curled up on my side, facing away from him, ignoring what just happened as much as he seemed to be. I didn't understand Kol. During the scent-marking, he was all smug about his male prowess. Now, he was so grave, so serious.

"I can't."

"You won't have the same nightmare." He was close enough that his breath heated the back of my neck, but he didn't touch me.

"How do you know?"

"Remember when Petrus said clans have certain gifts?"

"Yeah."

"My clan has the ability to influence dreams. You won't have another nightmare."

I rolled over. "Seriously?"

His gaze was steady in the dark. "Dreamwalkers, some people call us."

"You can enter people's dreams?" I was already having trouble dealing with him in reality. The last thing I needed was him wandering into my dreams. "Wait. You won't do that to me, will you?"

The firelight brightened the room more than before. I caught his ghost of a smile.

"No. It doesn't work that way. We can influence the dreams of someone we're physically close to, though some of my clansmen can send messages, even visit the dreams of those we have a deeper connection with."

"Oh."

I curled my hands into the blanket under my chin.

"You won't have any nightmares, Moira. I promise you."

Feeling shy all of a sudden, I flipped over. I liked my name on his lips. His rough voice letting the soft syllables roll in a rumble made my heart trip a few beats.

I listened to the crackling fire and burrowed into the pillow, forcing my breathing to slow, willing myself to accept his promise as truth. So calm and serene in the warm room. There was a tug on my mind. Something pulled me away from reality, as if I were being carried into the other world of my subconscious. I drifted toward the world of sleep, floating in the tranquil place in between. Before I slipped over the edge, I thought I heard gruff, stern words.

"No one's going to hurt you. I won't let them."

And I thought I felt the gentle touch of a heavy hand combing through my long hair. But surely, I'd already fallen into a soft dream.

Chapter 14

I knew he wasn't in the bed from the moment my eyes opened. His presence had stamped itself clear and heavy on me. Wrapping a thick, down blanket around my shoulders, not yet ready to squeeze into my too-tight pants I wore last night, I then shuffled into the next chamber.

An alcove in the short corridor opened up to a spacious bathroom I hadn't noticed the night before. Against a smooth rock wall, three wide-mouthed spouts jettisoned hot water into one waterfall with the turn of a black lever. Not feeling comfortable enough to shower in his place, I twisted a similar faucet above a deep black-marble basin, splashing my face and rinsing my mouth with warm water. There was no mirror of any kind in the stark room. After finding a towel in a dark-wood cabinet, I dried my face and went in search of my host.

The living room was empty, though the fire burned bright.

"Kol?"

I couldn't hear the sound of rushing water. Stepping into the corridor leading to the waterfall entrance, I found a solid, metal door closed and alarmed. Though Kol lived in a home of natural elements, he still used modern technology for protection. Smart.

I wandered through the large living room, roving the bookshelf of texts—mostly historical, a few fiction works. I smiled, imagining big, bad Kol curling up with a novel. Something warm swirled inside my chest at the thought.

Strolling through the kitchen, grazing my fingers along the smooth, white-stone countertop, I surveyed the ceramic bowls filled with a variety of fresh produce—onions, squash, tomatoes, oranges. A butcher board and cooking knives stood on one end near the wash basin.

"He cooks?" I mused to myself, more impressed by the minute.

To wander the room filled with creature comforts like books, cooking utensils, soft blankets, a cozy fire, I'd never have pictured the owner of this pleasant abode to be stalwart, cold-as-ice Kol. I trailed a finger along the countertop.

"But he's not cold, is he?" I asked myself.

No. The façade he showed to the world didn't reflect the man beneath the frosty exterior. It took him mere seconds to get me all hot and bothered. I grimaced at my behavior last night, heat flushing my cheeks. Sure, he might have talents in the sensuality department, but I couldn't let myself get carried away by a sexy man when I was on the precipice of what could be a stellar career. Especially not a sexy, Morgon man, who might have plans to put me in a pretty cage and keep me there. I had to stay focused on the job at hand—finding the Devlin Butchers, writing a career-changing exposé, land the coveted job at *The Gladium Post*, and start climbing my career ladder.

By the way, where was that sexy man? Had he left me here all alone?

Wandering farther into the kitchen area, I opened a wooden door I thought might be a pantry. A chilling draft swept in. Stone stairs led up, like a castle tower.

My boots stood by the fire. I slipped them on and pulled the blanket tighter, then shuffled up the spiral stairwell. There was no landing, only a continual climb around and around till my leg muscles burned from the exertion.

Ignoring the blast of cold air at the top, I stepped out through an archway. An alarm system was set in the stone wall. Kol had left the door open and unlocked.

I stepped through the rooftop entrance. He stood against a parapet, looking out. The entire space was wide and open, walled like a battlement, jutting directly out of the mountain that was his home. A few flakes of snow danced in circles on the stone floor. A slate-gray morning dimmed the rising sun, muting the sky into a diaphanous smear of cloud-cover.

"Did you sleep well?" he asked, continuing to gaze out over the woods far below.

"Yes." I moved closer, cold wind nipping at my cheeks and nose. "Thank you."

Some wall had been breached, some bridge had been crossed or burned. The shield of ice Kol erected to keep the world at bay had melted to a thin sheet. Still stoic and rigid and strong, there was a definite change in him. Though no one else might notice, I certainly did. I could feel it in the air. A fragile web-thin barrier between us could be swept away, colliding our worlds if we so chose.

I joined him, gazing down at the frosted treetops far below.

"Where are we?"

"The northern tip of Singing Wind Wood."

Geography lessons flashed through my mind and what I remembered from my first flight with Kol to Petrus's home. Mount Obsidian was south of Drakos. Singing Wind Wood wrapped around the mountain to the southeastern edge of the Drakos Province where another mountain range hemmed in the eastern border of the woods.

"Your home is set in the Feygreir Mountains."

A tight nod. He did not move, as stone-like as his tower. His scar was softened by the gray morning light, blending with his features. He appeared more vulnerable, though no less powerful.

"How old are you?"

His attention shifted, eyes roving over my face. "Thirty-three."

Thirty-three? That was kind of old. Not by Morgon standards since they lived two or three centuries, but I'd never date a human that old. At least, I thought I wouldn't. Wait. I wasn't going to date him. What was I thinking?

His gaze, heavy and dark, made me retreat inwardly. "Too much man for you, Moira?"

I tightened my hold on the blanket.

"Look, Kol. No matter what happened last night, I'm just not, I'm not interested in dating right now."

"Dating." He laughed with a sarcastic lilt. "Humans." He shook his head.

A burning flush crawled up my neck. I hated it when he mocked me.

"I'm not interested in dating, either." He moved close. I backed up, my butt hitting the wall. He caged me in, arms on the stone balustrade on either side of me, the upward draft sheering across the mountain lifting my dark hair. "There's no such concept in the Morgon world."

"Morgons don't date? That's ridiculous. Of course, you do."

"We fuck. And we mate. There is nothing in between. No trying a guy on for size." His voice had dipped low, vibrating against my skin like a rough caress.

I tilted my head at a sassy angle. "Kind of beastly, don't you think?"

His mouth tipped up in a feral grin. "We are beasts, Moira. We scratch that urge when needed. We heartbind when the beast tells us so. No. You and I won't be *dating*." He said the word as if it were poison, leaning closer and inhaling a deep breath. "We're tied nonetheless. Whether or not it fits the pretty picture of your idealized future makes no difference. You—"

A strong gust of wind blew my hair across my face. With a violent turn, Kol snapped out his wings, guarding me against a sudden intruder I could no longer see. Shielded by Kol's massive body, I heard the crunch of boots on stone and the soft whoosh of large wings folding. The jovial rumble of laughter let me know this was no attacker.

"Seriously, Kol. Is this how you greet all your guests?"

Coiled tight, Kol's body loosened just a fraction, his wings sliding closed. He'd drawn a long dagger, now sheathing it back into its holster in his boot. I didn't even know he carried weapons. I stepped from behind him.

The sight of the Morgon man standing opposite him nearly knocked me on my ass.

Double. I was seeing double. Absolutely identical to Kol, but for the scar and the hair. The stranger bore the same sharp angles as his brother, but his smile, something I suspected he wore frequently, softened his features. His sapphire eyes danced with life, whereas Kol's burned with darker emotions. There was a difference in attire, too. The newcomer wore business casual pants and a starched, pale-blue shirt. His clean-cut hair was styled so that a heavy lock slid forward in a sexy sweep. So different from the wild, dark waves of Kol and his combat-ready clothes.

"Well, well, dear brother." His brow arched, and a smile widened in an expression that had surely seduced many a woman. "Who have we here?"

Kol heaved out a heavy, heavy sigh. "Kieren, this is Moira Cade."

"A great pleasure to meet you. I'd kiss your hand, but I'm afraid my brother would rip out my throat."

Kol's response was a low growl. I started to inch forward, but his rigid stance warned me to keep still.

"I had no idea Kol had a twin brother."

"Keeping me a secret, I suppose." Kieren winked. "Didn't want to take the chance of me stealing you away."

I would've stepped forward to shake his hand and clarify his wrong assumptions about me and his brother, but Kol cut off anything else that might've been said or done.

"Why have you come? You could've sent me a message via comm."

The merriment leeched from Kieren's sparkling eyes. "No welcome mat laid out for your brother?"

Kol said nothing, his body a line of tension held in an iron grip.

"No matter." He crossed his arms. A defensive pose. "I have information for you. Perhaps Ms. Cade ought to go inside while we talk."

I stepped farther in front of Kol. "If this is about the Devlin Butcher case, then I'm staying."

Kieren's expression widened in surprise.

"Go ahead," said Kol. "She's part of the investigation."

Taking a moment more to apparently process the idea that Kol was working with a human woman on the case, he cleared his throat. "The man you described going under the alias 'Borgus' is undoubtedly Barron Coalglass. His clan lives in Cloven and owns half the city. Barron is the youngest son of Titus Coalglass."

"Fuck."

"Exactly."

"Wait. Tell me why that's bad." My blanket slipped, a bare leg peaking out. Kieren's eyes followed the length of my leg, his mouth lifting in a half-smile I'd seen more than once before on his brother. I felt Kol's posture tighten. He shifted forward, just enough to put his body between me and his brother.

Kieren answered my question. "Titus Coalglass not only has money, shitloads of it, he also has political power. He's in the Cloven Senate."

I knew the Morgon provinces were governed by a Senate, each member holding equal power except for one consul, the leader of the Senate. His power rotated every ten years, ensuring no man or clan held power too long. A decade might appear a long term to humans, but it was a short span for Morgons. The Morgon Senate was not too dissimilar from the Gladium Parliament, except that our house had both human and Morgon representatives.

"So," I intervened, "even if we catch Barron, his father will get him off."

"Not necessarily." Kieren tucked his hands in his pants pockets. "But we'll have to bring him in alive and take him before the Tribunal. No *blade justice* for him or it could start a war among the clans."

One thing that hadn't been eliminated from human records was the history of *blade justice*, the unwritten law of execution-at-will upon a proven Morgon murderer. For centuries, the Morgon Guard had wielded supreme rule as the law enforcers in their society. Those offenders who had committed the most heinous crimes often fell beneath the sword before ever reaching a courtroom. I'd often read about how there was a tradition among aristocratic families that one son always served the Morgon Guard for a time—a trademark of duty, patriotism, and being born of the highest stock. This was because not everyone could "join" the Guard. One had to go through rigorous training and pass physical tests before being selected and branded a member. And by branding, I meant literally marked. I wanted to see Kol's sharp-lettered seal of brotherhood, the "MG" tattoo on the back of his neck, but he kept his hair too long.

I eyed him now, mulling over this idea that Barron was impervious to *blade justice.* "So, in any other case, Barron would be executed on the spot for his crimes. But because he's a politician's son, he gets special treatment? That's how it works in *your* society?"

Kol gave me an arrogant smirk, his eyes never leaving mine. "It's no different than in the human society."

Touché. But of course, I wouldn't admit it.

"You're also forgetting one vital detail," added Kieren.

I broke away from the staring contest I was losing. "What?"

"You haven't yet proven Barron's guilt. He is certainly the man you've seen hanging at this stadium club of yours, but we've yet to see blood on his hands."

The fact that I became dangerously close to getting that evidence last night, perhaps spilling my own blood on his hands, haunted me still. One, because we would've caught the Devlin Butchers and kept any other woman from a horrific fate. Two, because I'd wanted to bail the second I sensed some evil entity lurking in the shadows.

"We'll get our proof," promised Kol.

"So Gaius is definitely hiding in their ranks."

Kol gave a tight nod. "I'm sure of it."

Kieren stalked toward the parapet's edge. I noticed a slight limp in his gait as he favored his right leg. What struck me more was that his hair was short enough to reveal his nape. There was no MG tattoo marking him as one of the Guard like Lorian.

"Not sure if you're aware," said Kieren, "but Valla passed her Boards. She has only the Assassin's Trial left."

"I'm well aware." Kol's voice was deep and steady. "I speak to Valla daily."

Kieren turned a sharp look on his twin. "Of course you do." With a regal bow and a forced smile to me, he leaped over the edge, swooping down, then arcing back up into the clouds. I gasped, watching his steady ascent, always marveling at the grace of Morgon flight.

Trying to suppress any note of jealousy, I asked, "Who's Valla?"

Kol was behind me, his chest brushing my shoulders. "Our sister."

His warm breath swept across my neck. At once, I remembered his lips on my skin, shivering at the thought.

"What's an Assassin's Trial?"

"The final test before she earns a place in the Guard's Assassin Order. A division only for Morgon women."

Turning around with my back against the balustrade, I gazed up at him. "There are women in the Morgon Guard?"

A slow nod, eyes drifting to my lips. Subconsciously, or maybe consciously, I wet them. Sapphire flared.

"Morgons need national assassins?"

"Every nation needs assassins. Morgons simply choose not to hide what they are behind a name such as the Gladium Special Forces."

He got me there. "Why only Morgon women?"

"They're swift and silent. And like women of both races, they're good at deception."

Switching subjects. "Your brother has a limp. How was he injured?"

"I broke his leg." He clenched his jaw, forcing out the words. "Right after he cut open my face."

What? I'd always thought he'd been dealt that injury by an enemy, not his own blood. His twin.

Lightning-fast, he gripped my face in his large hands, power vibrating like an electric current. He could crush my skull, kill me in a heartbeat if he wanted, and the way he looked at me now, I feared he would.

"Don't you fucking pity me." Harsh, grating words. "Don't!"

His grip tightened, pressing at my cheekbones. A whispered cry escaped me. His lips were on mine—scorching, devouring, punishing me for whatever wrong I'd done. His tongue licked in, tasting me with fierce passion. He crushed my body against one of the stone pillars linking the stone balustrade to the mountain. Ice-cold at my back, a wall of Morgon heat at my front, my mind hazed, drifting from coherent thought to my needy body. One of his hands slid from my face to my throat, encircling it entirely as his assault with lips and tongue and teeth continued. A black shield of wings covered us, blocking out the cold, gray world, focusing my attention on him and him alone. Heat bloomed between my legs. I moaned. He growled, deep in his chest.

This was crazy. This was unbridled lust. Some innate desire to want the bad boy. That was it, nothing more. Right? And I wasn't the kind of girl to give in to such shallow passions, such superficial feelings. I wasn't an animal. I didn't need *to scratch that itch* whenever it arose. I was a strong, smart, reasoning woman.

I pushed him with great force, managing only to break our lips apart. "Stop, Kol." Panting like I'd sprinted a mile, the hoarse desire in my voice betrayed me. "This can't happen. I told you. I'm not interested in being with anyone right now."

He made a sound in his throat, something between a growl and a laugh. Removing his hand from my face, he kept the one around my neck, stroking his thumb down to my collarbone, causing a sensual tingle to zip down my body. "You can think whatever you want with that logical brain and defiant will of yours. It still won't change the truth."

I ignored his hand, the feel of his stroking thumb.

Tried to. Wasn't working. "What truth?"

He removed his hand, leaving me cold, leering down as if he wanted to bite and swallow me whole. "That you belong to me. You just don't know it yet."

Chapter 15

You belong to me?

His words circled in my head as I stared blankly at the comm screen, scrolling down a junior reporter's feature story on the struggles of the freshman student. I hadn't read a word. The story was meaningless next to other more pressing matters.

Even with the Devlin Butchers still at large, my wayward mind kept wandering to thoughts of strong hands and smoldering lips forcing me into submission. Lovely, sensual submission.

What was wrong with me! I didn't behave like this, like some swoony, smitten schoolgirl.

I couldn't wrap my mind around Kol's conflicting behavior, though. One minute he was coarse and rude, insinuating humans were beneath his notice. The next, he had his tongue down my throat, making my body sing with each passionate stroke. I squirmed uncomfortably in my office chair, remembering the heat in his eyes when he had laid that last searing kiss on me.

My office door swung open. Kris carried two thermal cups and a white pastry bag under one arm. "Coffee and chocolate delivery."

"God, Kris." I took a steaming cup and lifted the lid, blowing before taking a long sip of mocha heaven. "I love you, you know that."

"I know. And I love your door decoration out there."

I frowned. "Oh. Yeah. Lucius insisted I have a Nightwing escort wherever I go. It's pretty annoying."

This was, of course, right after Kol had demanded I stay with Lucius and Jessen because Barron Coalglass probably knew I set him up for an ambush and might retaliate against me. Morgons could hold a serious grudge. At first, I thought to protest being caged at my sister's place, but Lucius ensured I could come and go as I pleased as long as I had a security guard in tow. In the end, I knew they were right, much to my dismay. I bit my rebellious tongue, packed my things under heavy guard, and installed myself in the Nightwing's third floor suite, the one third from the top.

"Give him to me. I wouldn't mind him as an escort." Kris winked as she opened the pastry bag and pulled out two giant chocolate-chip, chocolate muffins, shoving one in front of me.

"I'm sure you wouldn't."

"He's not much of a bodyguard if he just let me waltz right in here without even inquiring my name."

"He knows who you are. He's been given a photo list of all my friends and co-workers. And no offense, Kris, but you don't look that threatening."

"None taken. So what's his name?"

"Wulfgang Icewing."

Kris grinned, set a muffin on a napkin, and marched to the door. Propping it open with her hip, she said to the Morgon out of my eyesight, "Excuse me. Wulfgang? Would you like a muffin?"

Thick silence. I could imagine his keen eyes roving her body. Whether Kris realized it or not, she had a body that magnetized men's eyes to every full curve. A barrel-deep voice replied, "No. Thank you."

Kris gave him a nod, let the door slide shut, and practically fainted in her chair.

"His name suits him." She lowered her voice, breathless. "He's got the look of the wolf about him. No doubt."

There weren't many of the male Icewing clan in the Gladium Province. I'd met a few Icewings before, but they were all women. Like the females, Wulfgang had silky, flaxen hair, worn long with braids at the temples. He watched everything with wicked-sharp, sea-green eyes.

Kris bit into her muffin and licked some chocolate from one finger. "He's pretty to look at."

"Don't let his pretty face fool you."

"I wouldn't dare." She grinned like a fiend. "Now. Tell me what the hell happened last night."

I rolled my shoulder by instinct, feeling the stitches pull tight, but there was no stiffness or soreness.

"That dumbass with Layla and his buddies came barreling into the tunnel, then Kol and the rest jumped into the melee. And our guy got away."

"Hmph. Did you get any good licks in there?" She took a huge bite of her muffin.

"I wish I had," I admitted sulkily.

"Well, don't hang your head about it. I mean, damn! I felt like a little fairy in that place, and I'm not exactly tiny."

True. Kris wasn't quite as tall as me, though still above average for a human female. And she was what men deemed *voluptuous*, curving a little more than was necessary, but in all the right places.

"I know what you mean," I agreed, remembering how it felt to be hemmed in on all sides by giant Morgon men. The only time I'd felt truly uncomfortable, however, was when I was in the arms of the enemy. "Our target, Borgus, is actually an aristo from the Cloven Province. His real name is Barron Coalglass."

"I don't want to talk about him," said Kris with a flippant toss of her honey-brown hair. "What I want to know is where you slept last night." She didn't even try to hide her grin behind her coffee cup as she took a sip.

"Kol's." I avoided her eyes, draining my coffee, but her naughty laugh fractured any chance I had of playing nonchalant.

"And tell me. What's it like sleeping with a Morgon?"

"Kris! I didn't sleep with him."

"Riiight."

"Okay. I slept *next* to him, but nothing happened."

A giggle. "Right."

"Seriously."

"Seriously. I can read you like a book. You're hot for this guy. I'll make a bet. If you did *nothing* with him last night, then I promise to swear off men permanently." She criss-crossed her heart with one finger and raised her hand in a mocking oath.

"Please. As if you could swear off men."

"As if you did nothing with that huge, hunk of Morgon man while you slept in his bed. Is he huge everywhere?"

"*Stop it.*"

"You stop it. I know you, Moira. I know the type of man that gets you all worked up."

"What do you mean? He's nothing like Mikal."

"Exactly." She rolled her eyes. "Mikal wasn't your type. You dated that poor guy for ages because he was safe. Because he didn't make you really feel anything, and there was no risk of losing your heart."

I blew out a frustrated breath and twisted my hair into a tight, messy bun, annoyed with this whole conversation. "What are you saying? That I'm heartless? That I don't have emotions?"

"Damn, you're stubborn. No. What I'm saying is that you're afraid. You're afraid to be with someone who might make you feel too much because then you'd open the door to the possibility of heartbreak." Lighthearted banter turned serious in a millisecond. Her brows pushed together, sorrow in her eyes as she squeezed my hand on the desk. "Because you don't want to end up like your father."

I flinched and popped out of my seat, then moved to the window and watched the light snowfall layering the walkway outside. Downy flakes drifted to the ground at a soft slant. So serene right on the other side of the pane.

"Sorry." Her voice was soft. Sympathetic. "But it's true."

My father had been deeply in love once. But not with my mother. He had loved and wanted to marry a Morgon woman, Sarasong. From a proud, aristocratic family, she had caved to the pressure of her parents' will and agreed to an arranged marriage to ally her clan with the most powerful Morgon family in the Gladium Province. She married Adicus Nightwing, and would later bear him two sons—Lucius and Lorian. Even so, she never shared the heartbonding of soulfire with Adicus. It was as if she could never give him her heart fully since it still belonged to someone else. My father. A man who would become so embittered over the years toward Morgons, especially toward the Nightwing clan. It was a sad, twist of irony when Fate led my sister to Lucius. Or perhaps not. Perhaps Fate was mending old wounds by tying the two together. Jessen and my father hadn't spoken to each other until after Demetrius married and mated to Shakara. But even so, bitterness and regret had kept them apart. Father had only seen Julian a handful of times since his birth. Another regret that hung heavy on my heart.

A young brunette strolled arm-in-arm with her boyfriend along the pavement. As they crossed under an overhanging branch, she unclasped her arm and tapped the branch, knocking the collected snow onto his head. Giggling, she ran. He chased her. She squealed with delight when he caught her in his arms.

I sighed, then glanced at Maxine Mendale's smiling photo, having pinned it alongside the others on my bulletin board. Maxine—beautiful, full of life and adventure. Her life ended way too soon. Here I was, always so sure of myself, so sure of my life's purpose, pushing toward an ambitious career with such determination. But Kris was right. There was one area of my life where I'd cut out all passion. Was I using my feminist ideals to build a shield around my heart, barring any man from entering that sacred place?

Juliette Cross

You belong to me.

I shivered. His lips on my skin. His hands on my body. My blood quickening with every touch. And still, I'd pushed him away. Hell, that was *why* I'd pushed him away. The thought of letting down my shield for him drove a spike of fear right through me. He had informed me emphatically that Morgons didn't date. So what was I? His wannabe fuck-buddy or his soulmate? If the first, I wasn't so sure I could resist anymore, knowing he would be a rough yet satisfying lover. If the second—

Someone jerked open my office door. Macon stood there, face flushed and eyes wide. "There's been another one," he panted.

"What?"

"Turn on comm screen TV on your desktop. Now." He hurried to my desk to do it himself.

"What channel?" squealed Kris.

"Any channel. It's on every damn one."

The first channel that popped up showed the still photo of a smiling, dark-haired student from Gladium University. I knew that smiling face so well. I'd seen it last night. Layla.

"No," I murmured.

"She was in my Psychology class," Kris said in a daze.

The reporter droned on. "The body of another co-ed from Gladium University found in Drakos. This may be the fourth victim of the Devlin Butchers...."

"They're not showing anything, Macon. Was she found in Devlin Wood? Damn it! This news station is useless."

"I'm not." Macon whipped out his comm device from his back pocket.

"You've already got photos?"

"Video footage. My boss, Torrance, received it at home from the Morgon Guard and sent it directly to me to upload to the inter-office database, wanting all officers on this now. There's something new here. A possible clue to the killers."

"What do you mean?" asked Kris, hovering over the other side of Macon.

He quickly pressed keys on his touch-screen pad.

"Well, one," I interjected, "they didn't keep her in captivity for any length of time. We saw Layla last night." My words stuck in my throat, dread settling in my stomach like a heavy stone. Poor Layla.

"This wasn't a ritual killing," agreed Macon.

I peered over his shoulder. "Then how do they know it's the Devlin Butchers at all?"

Macon pierced me with a solemn stare and pressed play on the video that he had pulled up on his comm screen.

A wide shot of Layla on the blood-spattered snow, stripped naked, limbs askew, one arm bent backward. Broken.

"Oh, my God," whispered Kris.

Horror and death glazed her sightless eyes. Her body was unmarked with the slashes we'd found on the other victims. Clearly, this was something done only to the victims kept in captivity. Layla was killed fast with fierce brutality.

Slit open from neck to naval. Similar to the others, but not exact. There was too much blood that had drained from her open cavity, pooling into the snow, lining her crumpled body in deep purple. Splatters of crimson streaked across her body and painted sharp lines of red in the snow, denoting savage thrusts of the knife during the killing. The camera panned to the base of a monument near her head.

"What's that?" asked Kris.

"Torrance said it's some memorial monument to Larkos Nightwing. Somewhere in Devlin Wood."

The camera flashed over the harsh depiction of a towering Morgon in stone before zooming in on Layla's upper body to a mutilation on her left breast, a carving in the skin over her heart.

"They believe this is some sort of clue, a message, which might lead to their identities. Layla was killed in a hurry, like the killer was rushed or angry, but this still has all the signs of being from our Butchers."

"Was she raped?" asked Kris.

"Unknown. Forensics hasn't had time yet to go over the body."

The camera zoomed in closer to the carving on the girl's fair skin. The fact that I was trying to decipher an image engraved in human flesh made my stomach roil, especially knowing I had talked to her last night.

Kris peered closer. "Looks like Morgon wings."

"That's what the officers are saying at the precinct. Along with the spear that crosses in front, it may be some kind of old Morgon warrior symbol or something. They're digging up records, but as far as I know, the Morgon Guard doesn't know anything more than we do."

"Hmm." I froze Macon's screen and zoomed in on the image. It lost some clarity, but I was able to determine something. "They're not Morgon wings. See this softened curve here? Morgon wings are sharp."

"Perhaps the killer slipped with the knife."

"Gross," muttered Kris.

"On both sides, Macon?" I arched a brow at him. "No. Looks more like angel wings. These soft lines here look almost like feathers."

"Maybe angel wings and a spear. Perhaps they consider themselves some kind of angelic warriors. A cult doing a service for heaven or something, I don't know."

None of that felt right. There was one thing I understood clearly, and it was the Butchers did *not* consider themselves angels. Gods, perhaps.

"This looks familiar," added Kris, tilting the comm toward her.

I gasped, jerking the device from her and turning it ninety degrees. My pulse pounded with a dawning realization.

"Holy shit." Macon gripped my arm to still the image in my shaking hands. All three of us looked straight over my desk to the emblem of *The Herald*'s logo—spread angel wings with a decorative pen crossing the center.

"Not a spear," I whispered. "A pen."

"Moira," hissed Kris. "He *knows*. Barron Coalglass knows you're a reporter. This was a message for you."

I stared in shock at the comm screen. The message was all too clear. Yes. He knew Moira Cade was also Marina Creed, exposé reporter and editor for the college newspaper, obviously working with the Morgon Guard to entrap the Devlin Butchers. There was no doubt Barron was the leader of this murderous band now. Ice flooded my veins, remembering how he had gripped me in his arms, how he had whispered in my ear.

"Moira, get back!"

Macon shoved me behind him as an enormous shadow darkened the entirety of my opaque-glass door.

My fear immediately transformed to relief. I knew the owner of that shape. "It's okay," I said, stepping around Macon as the door swung wide.

Kol swallowed the entire entrance, expression fixed in grave lines and sharp angles. He focused on no one but me, eyes blazing silver. Holding out his hand, his voice was full of the dragon—rough and fierce. "Come with me. Now."

Chapter 16

His hand encircled my forearm and whisked me out the door, barely giving me time to grab my coat and scarf.

In rapid fire, he ordered Wulfgang to follow Kris home and remain stationed there until further notice. Before I could utter a word, he had me out of the building and down the steps.

I shrugged out of his grip to button my coat before wrapping the scarf and tucking the tails under the lapels. "You could've at least said hello before yanking me out of the room. That's what normal people do, you know?"

"I have no time for polite etiquette."

"Is Kris really in danger?"

"Not likely, but we're taking no chances."

His hands slipped around my waist. Even through a thick layer of wool, I could feel the heat and weight of them. He pulled my body into an embrace.

"Kol. What are you doing?"

"Hang on tight, Kittycat." Steel arms banded me close as he bent his knees.

"Wait! No harness?"

"No time."

We rocketed into the mid-day sky. In the sheer panic of going from pavement to clouds in less than six seconds, I'd pressed my face into the curve of his neck and shoulder, cursing profusely under my breath. Blustery wind beat at my back, the sky an endless gray sheet. I burrowed closer. His pulse throbbed against my cheek. The panic eased into something else altogether. I turned my head so that my forehead rested in the crook, the edge of my lips grazing the sensitive skin at the base of his neck. He shivered, gripping me tighter against him.

What was happening to me? All he needed to do these days was put his body close to mine, and I lost all reason, cozying up like a cat in heat. A kitty cat. *Damn him.*

In no time at all, we landed on the top terrace that led into Lucius and my sister's home. Kol set me on my feet but didn't release me, keeping my body molded to his. Unable to resist his heady scent, I trailed my lips along a collarbone edging out of his T-shirt. He hissed in a breath, his hands squeezing my hips in a possessive hold. I stood on my tiptoes and pressed a single, soft open-mouthed kiss right beneath his ear. A silent invitation. Something was definitely wrong with me. Playing with fire had never been my thing. I was more the watch-where-you-step kind of girl. But apparently my cautious side had taken a leave of absence, preferring instead to swish past danger and wave a red flag.

The ring around his pupil, his namesake, glowed white-hot within shimmering sapphire. Gripping my hips tighter, he pressed a hard ridge against my abdomen. On purpose. My eyes widened. My breath quickened. He was big. Very big. Increasing my anxiety…and arousal.

He leaned down. Slow. So slow. A whisper-light brush of lips on mine. Soft, tender, while his body remained a steel wall. Gentle Kol made my heart do erratic things. Desire coiled low and deep, sparking heat within. I wanted to whimper, moan, plead for more, but I didn't make a sound. His teeth clamped my lower lip, just barely, letting it slide out. Piercing eyes held me captive, making a promise as one word left that dangerous mouth.

"Soon."

I started, snapping out of my desire-hazed stupor and stepped back. He released me and gestured toward the open archway leading into my sister's home. "After you."

As we passed under the awning and through the columns into the Nightwing home, I noticed two black-clad guards stationed in the shadows. Interesting that Kol would let someone see him in an intimate way with me. Surely, he knew the guards were there, watching. Wait a minute. *Of course,* he knew they were watching. That's why he held me entirely too close and too long. Another marking of his territory. I frowned up at him as we stepped down into the living room.

He arched a dark brow. "Do you have something you'd like to say to me?"

"There are lots of things I'd like to say to you."

"And do to me." That arrogant, crooked smile lifted half of his beautiful mouth, the cleft in his chin denting further, making him even more devastating.

Ass.

"You think you know so much." I scoffed and tightened the messy bun on my head, some hair having whipped out in the wind. "As if you have any idea what I really want."

He shifted behind me, leaning close to my ear. "I definitely know what you want." He nipped the shell of my ear. "And I'm going to explain it to you in full detail so there's no misunderstanding."

"Hah!"

"And show you."

"Pfft."

"Soon, Kittycat."

There was that promise again.

"Hmph." I shrugged away from him, so he wouldn't feel me shiver. When had I become a mindless nitwit, incapable of forming words? My only response to him had been a series of snarky sounds as he'd detailed how he would educate me on my *wants*.

Another shiver climbed up my spine, tingling the hairs on my skin. I shook it off, moving away from him. I needed distance in order for my brain to function properly.

Lucius stood at the fireplace, gazing into the flames. I heard the door to the outer terrace close behind us. I settled on a black velvet chaise. One of the Nightwing security guards tapped the alarm pad on the outer terrace wall, disappearing from view as the steel doors came down.

"Moira." Lucius held an amber-colored drink loosely in one hand, defying the tension in his shoulders. His typically tranquil gaze narrowed to a sharp edge. "I apologize for pulling you away from work, but we needed to ensure your safety. There's been another murder."

"I know." I took a deep breath. "The symbol on her skin. I believe it's the symbol for *The Herald*."

"You know about the symbol already? That hasn't been broadcast to the public."

Kol crossed his arms, leaning his shoulder against the corner of the mantelpiece. "Her friend, Macon, is an intern at the Gladium Precinct. He's been secretly getting video footage to her."

"What the hell, Moonring!" How'd he know that? I really wanted to slap that smug look off his face. "Stalker," I muttered.

"Good," interjected Lucius, still in deep thought. "I'm glad you're up to speed. The symbol is clearly a warning or a threat. We believe it is most probably directed at you, but there could be other reasons for displaying such a public message on the victim."

Jessen rushed into the room. "Did she—" Seeing me, she ran to the sofa and pulled me up, hugging the crap out of me. "Thank God you're all right."

I winced, shifting my shoulder away, biting my lip.

"Relax, Jess. She's safe," assured Lucius.

Still, my sister swept a critical eye over every inch of me in a millisecond, assessing any possible damage. I was glad she couldn't see my stitched shoulder.

"I'm fine." We both took a seat, and she snuggled into me like we used to when we were little on the living room sofa. "Lucius, you were saying there may be other reasons for making it public."

His eyes were on his wife, an endearing yet protective look.

"We believe there is another motive to these murders, other than an archaic ritual."

"Such as?" I asked.

Lucius swallowed his drink in one gulp and set the empty glass on the mantel. Kol's smirk had long-since faded to Iceman exterior. His lips tightened into a line as Lucius tucked his hands in his pockets and continued. "*The Herald* isn't simply a college paper. It's the most prominent publication on campus and is well-known even off-campus."

I glowed, knowing readership had dramatically increased since I'd become senior editor when only a sophomore. Lucius ruffled his large wings, then refolded them, an unconscious gesture. "Whenever there's a university event, *The Herald* is there, expressing the views of the student population, sharing the voice of the future leaders of the world. *The Herald* logo is synonymous with college ideals—liberty, equality, hope for the future."

"So"—I cleared my throat, sitting straighter—"you believe the Butchers are denouncing these ideals, trying to destroy that hope."

"I believe they plan to crush Gladium with fear, erasing the brighter future idealized by a free, desegregated nation, such as ours. I don't believe the murders are part of a cult ritual at all. I believe the murders are being used to make Gladium fall on a much grander scale." Lucius's voice vibrated with building fury. His eyes flared.

Jessen popped up, then walked to him and tucked herself in the curve of his body, arms winding around his waist. He cooled, stroking a hand down her hair and back, the other cupping her belly, his anger sliding off like a shell.

"I'm definitely missing something," I said.

Kol shoved off the mantel. Pacing to the plate-glass window, he faced the room, the garish light at his back casting him in shadow. "Immediately following the public release of the recent murder, the Gladium Parliament voted to close the doors of the Vaengar Stadium to all humans."

"What!" I jumped to my feet. "That's *illegal*. That's segregation. They can't do that."

Kol eyed me with a curious expression. "They can do whatever is necessary for the safety of the people of Gladium. Every victim was abducted from the stadium. Every *human* victim."

"But that's going backward." I put my hands on my hips, staring out the window into the city. "They can't do that," I bit out between clenched teeth, knowing I sounded redundant, but I was unable to articulate my swirling emotions of frustration and anger.

We'd come so far since the days of segregation and ignorance. Even my own father conceded that Gladium had turned the corner from a nation of two opposing populations to one of mutual peace. He hadn't said it in those words, but we all knew it was true. Morgons and humans were intermarrying and having children. Business professionals of both races had become mutually prosperous through alliances and merging companies. Politicians were no longer split Morgon against human, but falling into a division of ideals and morals rather than one based on race. It wasn't a perfect society, but Gladium was the first to prove that the two species could not only live amongst one another, but could cohabitate in peaceful union, could thrive and flourish.

I spun away from the city view. "This could reverse everything we've strived for."

Kol crossed his arms casually. "That's what they're counting on. A segregated people riding on fear are easier to conquer."

"What do you mean?" I asked.

"The so-called Devlin Butchers appear to be much more organized, more militarized than we first thought. They aren't mindless murderers. They're making calculated moves, which have the appearance of mindless butchery."

The white-haired cook, Ruth, clip-clopped to the living room entrance, wiping her hands on an apron. "Pardon me, Mrs. Nightwing, but how many will we have for dinner this evening?"

Jessen asked, "Will you be joining us, Kol?"

His eyes remained on me as he gave a curt nod. "Yes."

"Add two more, please Ruth. What was tonight's menu again?"

"Tarragon Steak," she said before returning to the kitchen.

I hoped Ruth didn't overcook the meat again, knowing how Morgons liked their meat rare. Kraven's admission ran through my head. *I suppose it is the beast in us all. We like our meat bloody.*

Like lightning, a vision crashed into my mind. A broken body, a slaughtered lamb, naked and gutted, gaping slashes on every pulse-point in her body.

"Oh my God," I whispered, jerking my comm from my coat pocket. "They're drinking them dry."

"What are you talking about?" asked Jessen, pausing in the kitchen entrance. She returned to my side as I flipped through the photo gallery on my comm. Lucius and Kol came closer and hovered over my shoulder. Jessen joined them as I finally found the shots of Maxine Mendale I'd saved. I zoomed into the marks on her neck and inner arms, holding my comm so they could see.

"I couldn't figure out what these slash marks were. They're on every part of her body where a strong vein would be accessible."

"Accessible," muttered Jessen. "Do you mean they're actually—"

I nodded. "For bleeding her. I don't have close-up shots of the other victims, but I could see these same cuts on them when I double-checked the photos Macon had given me."

Kol's expression sharpened into hard lines. "The victims were nearly bloodless. All but the one found this morning."

Lucius rubbed his chin thoughtfully. "But she wasn't taken for the same purpose as the others. She was taken to send a message. They very well could've been using the others to harvest blood."

"Maxine had a bite mark," I said. "I thought it was just some random act of savagery, but now it appears the murderer really was drinking her." I glanced from one man to the other, receiving no response. "Do Morgons really drink blood?" I persisted. A wave of nausea made me shudder.

"No," Lucius assured me. "Sane Morgons do not. However..." He glanced at Kol who stood stoic as ever.

"However what?" I demanded.

"There are some Morgons who have a break in their psyche. They go rabid, reverting back to their primitive dragon, submitting to bloodlust. This was what we thought had happened with Maxine Mendale. But it never quite fit."

"How so?" asked Jessen.

Kol pursed his brow. "The murders did seem to follow a ritualistic pattern."

"Like a cult ritual," I inserted.

Breaking from the circle, Kol stepped back, his wings fluttering in agitation. "If it were a cult, everybody would've been treated the same. But there have been differences, particularly the last."

"Right," added Lucius, pacing back toward the fire before turning to face us. "This last victim proved we're dealing with methodical thinkers, more like violent radicals with a cause rather than cult fanatics. Cults have no need to display their victims in so brutal, so public a fashion. Every murder has served a purpose."

"If not for some cult ritual, then why would they do this?"

The mechanic hum of the steel outer doors opening snapped all our attention to the terrace archway. Julian stood by the alarm pad, peering at the statue-like guards as they came into view with the rising doors.

"Julian!" Jessen marched after him. "What did I tell you? Do *not* open the door without permission."

"Aww, Mom. I just wanna see the Nightwing guards. They're awesome."

Jessen swung him up onto her hip and punched the key pad.

Kol stepped forward. "Hold, Jessen. Wait till I'm gone."

I frowned. Jess crossed the living room to the hall, whispering to her son. "You need a nap."

"No, I don't," he murmured, stifling a yawn.

Kol had already untucked his wings in half-open stance, readying for flight.

"Where are you going?" I walked with him to the terrace archway. "I thought you were staying for dinner."

"I need to visit Petrus at once. See if he has any theories on the blood drinking. I have an idea, but I need to speak with him first."

"I don't suppose he has a comm device so you can speak with him that way."

An arched brow. "Do you recall seeing a comm device among his feather quills and parchment paper?"

I sighed. "When will you be back?"

Kol stilled, rotating his body toward me, a beatific expression in place. "Why? Will you miss me?"

I pressed my lips together. He leaned closer and tucked a stray lock of hair behind my ear. A gentle gesture, a lover's touch. I couldn't breathe. "Don't go anywhere until I return and keep the doors locked."

He strolled onto the terrace and shot straight up into the air.

I punched the alarm pad, the steel door sliding closed. Ensconcing myself in the chair next to Lucius by the hearth, I sighed, frustrated and excited about the new discovery, as well as the man who'd just left after ordering me to stay indoors.

Once again, Lucius was lost in thought, staring into the flames. For a while, we sat in silence, both of us steeped in our own reveries.

Kol's gentle kiss when we'd arrived and tender caress when he left stirred something in me. I was uneasy, disturbed by his soft affection. And at the same time, all I wanted was for him to return right this minute and do it again.

"Lucius?"

"Hmm."

"How did you know my sister was your mate?"

A swift sidelong glance. "Soulfire." He steepled his forefingers at his chin. "Most Morgons don't speak of it, so I didn't recognize it at first." He grew quiet again.

"How so?" I encouraged.

He tilted a smile at me. "Ever the curious one, aren't you?"

I shrugged. "It's in my nature."

"I know." A smile ghosted across his face before he became serious with the memory. "It started as an ache right here." He pressed his hand to the center of his chest. "The hollow pain grew. When she was near, it flared, burning on the inside. The only thing to quench the fire was her touch. Even so, the burning never ceased."

"It sounds painful."

"It was, actually. That's how a Morgon male knows without a shadow of a doubt he's found his one mate. The pain is acute, but when she accepts him, they share the fire, their hearts bonding one to the other. The release of the elixir transforms the pain…into pleasure."

I swallowed, understanding completely. An aching need, pain, converting to pleasure. Something I couldn't stop thinking about these days.

Lucius's gaze fixed on me. "You wear his scent like it's your own, you know."

My heart jumped. "What?"

"Typically, this only happens with mated couples." All-seeing eyes watched me. "But you two aren't heartbound. Not yet."

"Heartbound? To Kol? I don't think so."

He smiled. "Too rough around the edges for you?"

"It's not that. He's just too, too…isolated. Within himself. I don't know if he wants a mate in that way."

He leaned forward, elbows on knees, hands clasped. "True. He has definitely built walls between himself and the world."

Walls. Yeah. I'd come to realize recently that I had my own. Mortared with endless hours of writing and copy editing, bricked with sleepless nights of research and investigating, topped with battlements made of innate stubborn will, and spiked with haughty, cynical feminist barbs that no man dared breach.

Until Kol.

"You know, Moira. When tragedy strikes, some of us are incapable of moving past it." Lucius never rambled. His stories and musings always had a purpose. I listened well. "Some of us react to tragedy, by say, building walls to protect one from future hardships. When my mother died, I had my father and Lorian to lean on. The grief didn't consume me as it very well could have otherwise."

"Kol lost his mother?"

"Both parents. They were heartbound." Morgon mates who shared soulfire also shared the beating of one another's heart. When one died, the other soon followed. "His father died of a stroke at work one day at the office. As you know, Morgon couples who share soulfire are bound in such a way that one can no longer live without the other. The surviving mate's death can take minutes, hours, even days."

"How—" The question caught in my throat. "How long did Kol's mother last?"

"Seven weeks."

I gasped.

"She lingered so long, the sorrow ate the flesh from her bones and emaciated her, stealing her famed beauty. Worse, the lingering reduced her to weeping almost incessantly till there was nothing left of the joyful woman she was—only a hollow shell was left behind."

Poor Kol. My heart constricted at the thought of him watching his mother waste away and die in misery.

"Needless to say, this devastated Kol and his brother. Kieren couldn't stand it. He bid his mother goodbye after one month, leaving Kol to wait with her at the bedside."

I found it difficult to swallow. "What about their sister, Valla?"

"You know of her?"

I nodded. "And I know Kol and Kieren had a falling out."

"Right. Valla was only seven when they lost their parents. As the eldest of the twins, by three minutes, Kol took custody of Valla."

"Was that what drove a wedge between them?"

"It was more than that. You'll have to ask him. What I can tell you is that the lingering death of their mother struck Kol the hardest. Our families grew up together. And Kol was always a fun-loving boy, always laughing. Before their deaths."

"Kol? You can't be serious."

Lucius smiled, a sad sort of smile, one of regret. "Tragedy changes us all, Moira. We get to choose how much. Some survive with a few bumps and bruises. Others wear their scars forever and build walls to block the world out."

Kol definitely had scars. There was the visible one given to him by his brother. But the one left on his heart by his mother bore much deeper. When had I come to care so much about his pain? When had he burrowed so far under my skin that I was afraid he'd leave his own scar behind on my heart?

Chapter 17

Dinner came and went without the return of Kol. I adjourned early to my own guest suite on the third floor down, knowing he'd join me soon enough.

I stood in the living room, staring out into the night, sipping a glass of red wine. After dinner and a long, hot soak in the bath, I'd been here in my knee-length silk nightgown, black and butter-soft. Waiting.

I'd washed my hair and let it air-dry in dark waves, falling down my back. I knew he loved my hair. I'd seen him stare whenever I wore it down. I'd taken time to shave and lotion my body with lavender scents. I'd made myself into a silken, sweet-smelling temptation—one he would no longer be able to resist. I didn't just want kissing or heavy petting anymore. I wanted all of him.

I'd watched the sun set beyond the Gladium skyline and Morgons return home from work to nearby rooftops. My eyes had adjusted to the dark, the city lights burning bright. Cars zipped here and there far below. Everyone seemed a world away while I waited in the dark for a certain Morgon to fulfill his promise. A promise that made my pulse quicken.

Soon.

I felt his presence rather than heard him when he finally entered. Slowly, I turned. A familiar silhouette moved in the shadows, silver eyes glinting. He circled the dining room table, angling closer to me. My gaze moved with him. Self-defense rule number one: never let the attacker have your back. And yes. He was going to attack. No doubt.

He moved past a wall sconce, the flame revealing his magnificent nude body. I swallowed hard. Kol didn't play games. He'd made me a promise, and he was wasting no time fulfilling it.

The air crackled, an electrical charge sizzling in the air. I'd sensed this before. The night Lorian lost it at dinner. A symptom of the dragon rising to the surface.

"You know my alarm code." I was shocked at the steady tenor of my voice. Not at all how I felt as the predator prowled ever closer.

"Of course." As expected, his voice rumbled like thunder, more beast than man.

I knew what I looked like to him—standing tall with the night sky at my back, barefoot, wine glass in hand, wearing nothing but a sheer piece of fabric clinging to every curve.

A click of the remote and the glass wall tinted black. No one could see in. I swallowed hard. Desire and a little trepidation flared at his intent.

Of course I wanted him. I wouldn't, couldn't, deny that anymore. Not even to myself. My blood rushed at the mere thought of his hands on my body. Still, I was never one to give in so easily. I never thought of myself as one of those women who played hard-to-get, but some inner demon wanted to provoke him. My defenses had mellowed with the wine, loosening my tongue. "I'm not so sure this is a good idea, Kol. This could muddle things in our investigation. I'm not so sure I want—"

His attack was fierce and fast. Knocking my wine glass clear away, I was pinned hard before it crashed to the floor. Cool glass at my back, his hand fisted in my hair, arching my neck just enough to meet his gaze. His other hand gripped my hip in a vise, his chest pressed to mine. A sconce above us flickered a pale flame, revealing his intensely serious expression.

"You severed ties with your father because he sought to lord over you. You left that Lennox boy because he wasn't man enough to handle you."

How did he know? I stared, mouth agape, unable to speak.

"I'll tell you what you want, Moira." His hand released my hip. Long fingers wrapped my nape, his thumb resting below my jaw, the other still clenched in my hair. "You want to be possessed, but not controlled. You want to be protected, but not smothered. You want to be dominated, but only in one way."

He stroked his thumb down my chin, forcing my mouth open. I couldn't form a thought, mesmerized by silver-fire and sensuous lips drawing closer. I slid my hands up his chest. I let one hand drift down to his waist, his hip, sliding over bare skin.

I gulped, my mouth bone-dry.

A fully nude Kol had me pressed against the glass. Though I was quite sure I already knew the answer, I could only think to ask him one thing.

"What—" Quick, unsteady breaths. "What do *you* want?"

His mouth curved into a wicked half-smile as he whispered against my lips. "I'm burning for you, Moira. An inferno flares inside every time you come near me." He traced his tongue over my bottom lip. "I won't go up in flames alone." He ground out the words. "You're going to burn with me. That's what I want."

Then he took my mouth, showing me what it meant to be set on fire.

Aggressive didn't describe the way he worked me with his mouth and tongue, his fist tightening in my hair. A soft moan lingered at the back of my throat. He moved to my jaw, my neck, descending, teeth grazing a trail. A strong hand skimmed over the layer of silk—rounding my hip, dipping at my waist, sliding up my ribcage, mounding my heaving breast. His thumb circled the peak as he continued to suck and nip my neck. Heat flared down low.

"This skin. Like porcelain. I want to mark every inch as mine."

"Why," I managed to breathe out. "Because I *belong to you*?"

"Yes."

"I won't be enslaved by anyone. Not even you."

A gravelly chuckle from the belly of the beast. He gripped the bodice of my gown and ripped it in half, letting the shredded silk pool at my feet. I gaped as he dropped to his knees, big hands spreading and holding my thighs apart against the glass. I uttered a cry when his mouth opened on me.

"Kol!" I grabbed his shoulders.

I tried to buck away, my core too sensitive for his hot mouth. But he was immovable, determined to taste me, licking to his beastly heart's content. There was no moving this man when he wanted something.

I gripped the arch of one wing to hang on, the bone thick and strong under soft, leather-like casing, making me think of another appendage on him, hard and covered in silken skin. I moaned. His teeth grazed. I tightened my grip on his wing, making him growl. He flicked his tongue, doing wonderful, wicked things. My head fell back against the glass wall, city life buzzing far below. Unable to control my body, I squeezed his shoulder, claws digging in, as I came harder than I ever had in my entire life, my hips undulating. I felt wanton and free, and I wanted more. So much more.

"Kol," I breathed on a sigh. "Inside me."

My knees buckled. Before I fell to the floor, he swept me into his arms and draped me on a chaise lounge on my back. No more words. Kneeling at the end, he pulled me by the ankles till my bum was at the edge.

Though his silver eyes and aggressive manner proved the beast had full control, he stilled, slowing himself. He skimmed his palms down the back of my thighs, bending my legs and gripping at the crook behind my knees. Spreading my legs wider, he nudged my entrance and sank in a fraction. He showed me how swollen he was for me, easing inside with a rumbling groan. I sucked in a sharp breath, his thickness stretching me to pleasure-pain. He inched all the way in, stopping only when he was sheathed to the hilt.

"Kol." I could think of nothing to say but his name. He filled me—physically, mentally, emotionally. All I could feel around me, as blood thrummed through my veins, my heart speeding away, was the powerful presence of, "Kol."

I reached up, skimming my hands along his ridged abdomen, across the planes of his broad chest, rounding his shoulders, and pulled him down to me.

Breathing labored and hot, mingling with my own, his voice vibrated against my skin. "From the second I laid eyes on you"—he slid out achingly slow, letting me feel every glorious inch—"this is where I longed to be"—he slammed hard and fast, just once, our thighs slapping—"deep inside you."

He held me there, my body sealed around him, tight as a glove, silver eyes boring into mine.

I rolled my pelvis up to meet him. "Give me more."

He gave it to me, pulling out slow and thrusting hard, steadily increasing until he pumped at a merciless rhythm. I clawed my hands into the sofa cushions, trying to hold on as he pounded into me again and again. Each time harder than the first.

I had no notes of comparison to Mikal. There was no comparing Kol to him. There was no comparing Kol to any man—Morgon or human. He ruled in a realm all his own. Right now, he ruled over me. And he knew it.

When he abruptly pulled out, I whimpered in protest, breathless and panting.

"Deeper," he growled, flipping me over with swift ease.

Deeper? He'd lost his mind. So had I.

Lifting me to all fours on the chaise, his broad hands slid along my waist to my hips. I heard his wings whip out to full extension, raising him to his feet behind me. One palm slid up my spine, pressing between my shoulder blades. He flattened my upper torso to the sofa cushion, then curled his fingertips over the curve between shoulder and neck. He gripped my hip hard as he pushed into me again, slow at first as my body accepted him. He ground against me with each pounding thrust. Marking me as only he could. I felt lightheaded from the intensity, unable to breathe as he entered me deeper and deeper.

Walls crumbled as he pushed my senses into oblivion. Barriers of stone and steel and my stubborn iron will collapsed into dust and gravel. As my body soared to his bidding, a revelation gripped me hard, repeating in my mind.

I belong to him.

He slowed, leaning forward to press his chest to my back, pulling me flush against him. One hand cupped my breast. The other slipped between my legs, two fingers sliding up and down my slick cleft, caressing me till I moaned his name.

"You got it all wrong, Moira," he whispered, his fingers matching the slow rhythm of his shaft inside me. "I am the slave." He thrust a little harder. "Every waking moment, I see you, smell you, want you." His fingers continued to caress and pinch softly, my senses reeling with pleasure. "I'm afraid once I feel you come with me so deep inside…your body clenching around me…I'll be lost forever…powerless to escape."

I reached back with both hands, one on his hip, the other wrapping his neck. Arching my spine, I rocked back against him, pushing him even deeper. He groaned like a desperate man lost at sea. He clung to me as if I were the only thing keeping him from drowning. A fine sheen of sweat made our bodies slide over and into each other, wave after wave of pleasure pushing us closer to the edge.

I turned my head, whispering into his ear. "Come with me, Kol. We'll be lost together."

I bit his earlobe and he came. Hard. His pulsing shaft ripping an orgasm from my body and a scream from my throat. He didn't let go, clenching me tighter as he spilled into me, a thunderous growl vibrating from his chest. For that brief moment, I understood what it meant to be consumed by another. My body, my will, my entire being was encased within the control of one man. And my heart soared at the euphoric sensation.

Minutes later, breathing heavily, still clutched in his arms, neither of us spoke a word. He pulled out of me, and I whimpered at the loss. Hauling my limp body into his arms, he carried me through the dark house to the bedroom, tucking us both into the guest bed. Curled around me from behind, we lay there in silence, both our thoughts too loud to let us sleep. I finally couldn't take it anymore. "What are you thinking?" I whispered.

No answer. I thought he might have fallen asleep after all, but then he spoke, shocking me with vulnerable, honest words. "I'm afraid of never waking again without wanting you. Needing you."

His arm tightened around my waist. I sighed, squeezing my eyes shut, knowing with bone-deep certainty I feared the same thing. "Is that really something to fear?"

"Yes."

Another honest answer. Another wall crumbled.

"I need you like I need to breathe, Moira. Like I need to fly."

Was it the dark that made him speak words he never would in the light? I didn't know. I didn't care. It was enough that he'd said them.

I turned in his arms and cupped his face, tracing my fingers lightly over his raised scar. I couldn't see him clearly, but I knew he could see my face with his dragon sight as if it were daytime. I let my eyes shine with a hope I knew he would understand.

"Like Morgons, I don't date, either." My fingers traced to the tip of his scar. "Nor am I the kind to sleep around to satisfy carnal cravings." I trailed lightly over his lips. "I need you, too, Kol."

I pressed my lips to his, prying them apart to slip my tongue inside. I kissed him the way a lover would kiss her mate. Boldly, shamelessly, like a woman who knows her right.

"I want you," he grumbled. "Again." Heavy hand on my waist.

His desire grew hard against my abdomen. I crooked my leg over his hip, opening for him. "Then take me."

And so he did.

Chapter 18

I rolled over to find him gone. With the terrace door sealed shut, I couldn't tell what time it was. My comm sat on his pillow, blinking a green light. An audio message.

Propping up on my elbows, I pulled the device to me. The time read 10:33 a.m. in the top corner.

"Damn. Talk about oversleeping."

I played the message.

"Good morning." Kol's deep rumble.

I couldn't help the silly smile from creeping across my face.

The recording continued. "I didn't want to wake you. Thought you might need your rest."

Boy, did I.

"I didn't get the chance to speak to you about my visit with Petrus last night. Lucius can fill you in till I return. I must meet with the Morgon Guard immediately. You're safe to move freely within the Nightwing Tower, but don't—"

He stopped himself. He heaved in a deep breath and sighed. His voice lost the note of tyranny, morphing to something gentler. "Please, Moira. Please don't leave this building. I will return as soon as I can."

"Not a problem, Captain."

Too tired to go to class or report to work, I thought a sick day was definitely in order. I stretched my body in the bed.

Before we had sex, I'd been able to pretend our attraction was just physical. Chemical. After last night, I could no longer believe this to be true. Nor did I want to.

But one thing puzzled me. I knew soulfire burned inside him. For me. He'd made his feelings quite clear. But he hadn't sad a word about it. Not that I was ready to leap into such an irreversible commitment, but I still wanted to know why he hadn't mentioned soulfire. Could I be wrong?

Juliette Cross

I scooted out of the covers and stood up. "Ow."

I was sore. Everywhere. My Morgon man had loved me long and hard. I smiled as I remembered and walked stiffly to the bathroom. Peeking at myself in the mirror, I laughed. Even my lips were sore. Swollen from many, many rough kisses, not one of which I regretted. I had a mammoth-sized hickey bite-mark on the slope of my shoulder. "Now, that's a doozy."

Strangely, the only thing not sore was the stitched injury from two nights ago. I lingered in a hot shower, then slipped into my favorite jeans and a comfy rose-colored sweater. After braiding my damp hair into a tidy rope down my back, I rummaged through my drawer and found the silver case I'd hardly ever opened except to take it to the firing range. Popping open the lock, I pulled out the sleek Volt handgun I'd packed.

About a century ago, the Volt gun was a weapon specifically designed by the Wellington Manufacturing Company in Primus to kill Morgons . While my father held animosity toward Morgons, the Wellington family openly despised every one of them. Because of their powerful political sway in Primus, they'd kept desegregation laws from ever passing in the human-only city out west. A Volt gun worked by using a Morgon's dragon DNA against them. Because of their dragon lineage, electricity voltage amplified the electric energy coursing through their blood and harnessed in their bones. A Volt gun essentially launched an electric missile, detonating on impact with a Morgon's natural DNA. Although the blast could kill a human by heart failure, most could survive a direct hit. A Morgon definitely could not.

My father had insisted I take the gun and practice shooting on the range when he learned I was venturing into Morgon territory to investigate stories. Though I never went anywhere I knew to be too dangerous, Father still worried about my sense of self-preservation. After seeing *The Herald* icon carved into Layla's skin, I had decided it was time to keep it close. Especially with Kol away. Strapping the harness around my waist against my skin, I then made sure the safety button was on and tucked it in place. My long sweater hid the harness. I didn't want to frighten Julian. For one, he would be terrified to learn why I felt the need to carry it. Two, he'd want an explanation of what the Volt gun did. I'd keep him from learning about the blind hatred of the world as long as I could. And three, he was a good kid, but also a mischievous one. If he saw it, he'd want to play with it, regardless of the danger.

My stomach rumbling, I meandered upstairs via the elevator to see what leftovers Ruth might have lying about.

Two brawny Nightwing Security guards stood outside the door in the foyer. The one with hunter-green wings and short-cropped hair gave me a tight nod.

"You're clear to enter, Ms. Cade." He tapped a code into the alarm panel on the wall. His eyes swept to the mark on my neck before gliding away just as fast. The other guard stepped visibly away from me, avoiding my gaze altogether. Weird.

"Uh, thank you."

As soon as the door closed behind me, I heard the alarm reset. Shuffling into the kitchen, I found Ruth rolling out some dough on a marble cutting board, flour dusted on her apron.

"Good morning."

She glanced up and out the window, the sun high overhead. "Well, now. It's nearly noon. Don't know that it's morning anymore."

"Right." I smiled. "Ruth, you wouldn't happen to have some of that delicious dinner left from last night, would you?"

She arched a brow at me, pounding her rolling pin right to left, then up and down, then the other way again. "I'm afraid not. But as soon as I get this crust on the chicken pies, I'll whip you up a bacon and cheese omelet."

My stomach growled just thinking about it.

"Seems you need sustenance sooner rather than later."

"Thank you. Yeah. Much appreciated." I ducked back into the living room to avoid her scrutinizing looks of I-know-what-you-did-last-night.

My sister walked into the room from the bedroom quarters. "There you are." She smiled, stopping in her tracks when her eyes saw my neck. "Whoa. Someone was a little…aggressive."

Self-consciously, I touched the mark, knowing my concealer did little, if nothing, to hide it.

"Sit down, sister," she ordered, pointing to the sofa. "We need to talk."

I didn't resist. Now that I'd settled in my mind I wanted more than a fling with Kol, I didn't care who knew we'd crossed that line.

"Spill it."

I folded my legs under me and snuggled a pillow into my lap. "There's nothing to tell."

Jessen threw her head back with a hearty laugh. "Um. Yeah. There definitely is. Kol has marked you in a way that screams to everything with a penis to back-the-fuck-off. And from what I can gather by your mood, you're pleased about it. There's butt loads to tell. So let's hear it."

That was something I could always count on with my sister—she was blunt and to the point. It was a comfort to know she'd always give it to me straight. No beating around the bush.

"Tell me something first. This whole Morgon marking, scent thing. Does it really make other Morgon men back off?"

She grinned at me, nodding. "Oh, yeah."

"That explains the two guards at the door. They acted like I had the plague or something."

"Of course they did. They don't want Kol stringing them up and flaying them for ogling or touching his woman."

"He wouldn't do that. How did you know it was Kol, anyway? And I'm not his *woman*."

"Puh-lease. The sexual tension between you two is ridiculous. Lucius and I had bets on how long it would take for you both to give in."

"What? You bet on my sex life?" I punched her in the arm.

"Ow! Don't punch pregnant ladies. We're delicate."

"Yeah. Right." I laughed but felt a tad remorseful as she was starting to get that soft roundedness of expectant mothers. "Sorry."

She waved me off. "I'm fine. So you're pretty serious if you've slept with him. I know you. You're not the sleep-around kind of girl."

I laughed. "That's what I told him."

"What did he say to that?"

"Well, he didn't do a lot of talking."

"I can see that. You look exhausted."

"And hungry."

As if on cue, Ruth bustled in with a silver tray and set it on the coffee table. "Here you are, dear. I've brought you some coffee and orange juice as well."

"Gah, Ruth, you're an angel."

I caught her smile before she clip-clopped back to the kitchen. I pulled the dish into my lap and started devouring the omelet. Pure heaven on a plate.

"Worked up an appetite, did ya, Muffin?"

"Shut it," I muffled with a mouthful of food.

She watched me as I finished it off and started on the coffee. By gradual degrees, I began to feel like a human being again.

"You said the guards were acting skittish around you?"

I gave a stiff nod, sipping my coffee. "Yeah, why?"

"So you haven't shared soulfire, yet."

Somehow, that made my heart twist. "How'd you know?"

She rested her hand on her belly. "When Morgons mark their mates, there's a period of time before the female accepts him that's sort of precarious. Most would-be suitors back off, especially if the marking was done by a dominant male."

"I'd say Kol is fairly dominant."

"I'd agree with you." Jessen giggled. "Any pursuit of you would be considered a direct challenge to Kol."

I realized then that Kol had marked me first under the ruse to protect me from the Devlin Butchers before our botched operation. He must've known even then that I was meant for him, choosing not to tell me.

"What's wrong?" Jessen placed her hand over mine.

"Nothing. It's just a lot to take in. I mean, just a few weeks ago, I was perfectly content to remain single, shoot for a successful career in journalism, and live my life blissfully free of complications. Now, I've got this extremely dominant Morgon man suddenly at the center. It's almost too much."

I sighed heavily, confused for the first time since last night. Everything was so clear when I was in his arms. When I wasn't, I only saw the problems that would arise in a relationship with someone like Kol.

"Is that what Kol is to you? A complication?"

"Yes…I mean, no." I shook my head, pulling on the tassels edging the pillow. "I'm just afraid of things being difficult for us. For me."

"How would they be difficult?"

"Well, for one, can you imagine him allowing me to enter harm's way to do my job as a journalist?" I scoffed. "Would Lucius let you?"

Her expression softened to one of sympathy. "No man, Morgon or human, would let the woman he loves enter into harm's way."

I set my coffee down, the cup rattling in the saucer. "That's what I'm talking about. Everything gets all muddled and confused when…when your heart gets all tied up with someone. Then you start doing things and making decisions based on their wishes and not your own."

Jessen laughed. "You mean when you love someone. I'm afraid that does tend to happen."

My heart skittered. Was I? Was I speaking of the famed four-letter word I'd avoided for so long? Was I in love? Mikal had confessed his love for me many times in our relationship, but never had I returned the gesture.

Needing to escape this conversation before my head exploded, I changed topics to something I was more comfortable discussing. "Speaking of Lucius, where is he? I wanted to talk to him this morning."

"He headed out to meet with Lorian and the entire Nightwing Security. Kol's visit to Petrus revealed something dangerous is definitely lurking in our midst."

"That's what I wanted to talk to Lucius about." I tossed the pillow in frustration.

"You mean, you and Kol didn't discuss it last night?" Her wicked grin was totally unbearable.

"I'll punch you again, Jess, if you keep that up."

"Fine." She glanced out the glass wall into another blustery gray day. "Petrus said blood-drinking was used by witches."

I followed her gaze. The thick cloud cover pressing down promised more snow. "He told me about some witches living up north when we visited. But they're supposedly nature-loving and the like."

"That may be so now, but according to Petrus, there were once dragon witches who used sacrificial blood, meaning blood taken from an unwilling human, to cast different spells. They used the life blood to enhance and sometimes twist the inherent gifts of their dragon."

"He mentioned something like that, but he never said they practiced blood-drinking. Of course, I didn't think to ask because that was before we deduced the victims were being harvested for blood."

Jessen's expression pinched with a pensive thought. "Kol said that there was even a witch in his own ancestry. She used the blood of innocents to twist their gift of dreamwalking. Empowered by blood, she could enter the mind of almost anyone and change their thoughts, their memories. She changed them to benefit her own power. She also used it to plague her enemies with chronic nightmares, driving them mad."

I stood up, mouth agape. Crossing to the window, I watched a white-winged Morgon land on a nearby rooftop, graceful and lovely. "Okay. But you're talking about ancient history. The dragons are all dead. What you're implying is that there are Morgon witches using these kidnapped girls for their blood in the here and now. It must be this coven of the Syren Sisterhood following the old rituals."

Jess nodded, her expression grave. "So you know about them."

"Petrus already explained that they exist, but live far away from both human and Morgonkind, living sort of like cloistered priestesses up in the Wastelands of Aria. They never leave, and allegedly only use their craft for good, using animal blood for their rituals."

"Until now," added Jessen.

"Until now. But that's a big *if* the Syren Sisterhood is involved. If they are truly a private sisterhood, living outside of society, what would be their benefit to aid a brutal band of raping, murdering Morgon men? It just doesn't make any sense."

We both stewed in silence. I contemplated the idea of blood being harvested for witchcraft. The idea of a coven living far to the northeast in the frozen wastelands connected to the Butchers defied any sort of logic.

"Did Kol mention his thoughts on this new revelation? What am I saying? Of course, he didn't. The man's mind is a steel trap. You won't get anything unless he wants you to."

"No." She smiled. "But I did hear him tell Lucius he's organized a party to go to the Sisterhood's stronghold to see what can be discovered."

"And the witches were always female?" I asked, pacing near the window.

"That I don't know. Kol was in a hurry to meet with the Guard in Drakos, one of his prime objectives being to send some men on this mission to the coven in Aria. Lucius briefed me quickly, then headed out the door to meet with his security team."

"Aunt Moira!"

I spun to find Julian barreling across the living room. He lifted himself with fluttering wings into my arms. My emotions in turmoil, it only took one tight hug from this kid to lift my heart back to where it belonged.

"Whoa!" I laughed. "Hey there, big guy."

"I like having you live here. I see you so much more."

Bright blue eyes sparkled. Jessen stood up, arching her back, making her mound more pronounced. "Come on, Julian. Let's get you some lunch."

"I'll take him, Jess. Why don't you get some rest."

She considered for about two seconds. "Well, if you don't mind, I would love that. A little nap would do me good."

"Go ahead. Julian and I will hold down the fort."

"Yeah, we've got it, Mom."

I set him down and took him by the hand. "Let's go see what Ruth has in the kitchen."

We found Ruth in full swing, popping chicken pies into the oven for dinner. I started for the refrigerator, but she shooed us to the dining room table where she already had a sandwich and chips with cold milk waiting for her youngest charge.

"Wow. I wouldn't mind having a Ruth at my place, you know."

"Mom wouldn't let you have Ruth," he said.

I sat with him as he stuffed his face. I probably looked much the same way to Jessen minutes before. "I don't think Ruth would want to leave with such a champion eater like you to wolf down everything she made."

He swallowed the last bite and gulped his milk, leaving a cute white moustache on his upper lip.

"Let's play a game, Aunt Moira."

"Okay. What would you like to play? I'm not very good at Morgon chess like your dad."

"Pfft. Let's play a fun game. Hide-n-seek! Mom's always too tired to play."

"I imagine she is." I laughed. "All right."

"Yay!"

The poor kid had definitely been cooped up too long already.

"But we have to be super quiet. Your mom is taking a nap."

"Okay, okay. You hide first." He raced back into the living room and jumped on the sofa. "This is base. If you get here before I find you, you win."

His wings flapped excitedly as he buried his head under a pillow and started counting. "One, two, three…

I slipped off my boots and socks and tip-toed toward the bedroom quarters. Stepping into Julian's room, I glanced up at his ceiling, reflecting the snow-gray sky outside, no sun to be found. His closet was a walk-in, pretty easy for me to find a corner and wait.

Not three minutes later of sitting in the dark, I heard the patter of his feet and a giggle outside the closet door. With his heightened sense of smell, I would lose every round of this game. Totally unfair.

He threw open the door. "Gotcha!"

I laughed and tickled him till he fell on the ground in a fit of giggles.

"Stop! I can't breathe."

I finally let him up. "That's the price for finding me too fast. It's not fair you can use your sense of smell. I can't do that."

"You want me to hold my breath?" he asked with a sincere expression. So sensitive, this little one.

"Of course not, silly," I laughed. "Your turn. I'll give you one minute."

I went back to the sofa and waited out the time. I started in his father's study, thinking he might venture outside the bedroom quarters to trick me. Not under the desk or behind the sofa in the study. My eyes lingered on the red-tufted carpet, remembering the last time I was in here, my cheeks flaming hot.

I peeked into the dining room, but there were few places to hide there. I tip-toed down the long corridor, housing the master suite, Julian's bedroom, and four guest rooms. The first bedroom was empty. So was the adjoining bathroom.

Walking down the hall, I felt a wafting breeze from the master suite. Surely, he wouldn't take the chance in waking his mother. Her door stood ajar.

"Julian," I whispered, slipping into their bedroom.

A small fire crackled in the hearth. Jessen lay sleeping on the bed on her back, one arm hanging off. Funny. She always used to sleep on her side. I supposed pregnancy changed lots of things.

A chill prickled up my spine. Something felt wrong. I tip-toed to Jessen, pressing my hand to her brow. Her forehead felt clammy.

"Jessen." I gently shook her. She made a soft moan.

The white, gossamer curtains hanging over the terrace archway billowed with a cold wind. The steel doors were open.

"Aunt Moira." Julian's faint voice echoed from the outer balcony.

"Damn it, Julian." He knew better than to open the doors, but a child didn't understand the repercussions. He must've thought since his mother was sleeping, he could get away with it.

The guard should've closed the door and sent him back in. I pulled the Volt gun from the harness under my sweater, edging toward the curtain rolling with the gusting wind. Pulse pounding in my throat, I parted the curtains.

The guard lay crumpled on the tile floor, wings obviously broken in several places, a pool of his own blood seeping across the entrance. From the crimson pool, tiny bloody footprints led farther out onto the terrace.

"Julian!" I screamed, running out onto the balcony, Volt gun aimed and ready.

I'd never known true fear until I saw what awaited me against the far wall of the terrace. Barron Coalglass held my nephew before him, clutching his tiny throat with one hand, bending one wing with the other. As a child, his wings were still pliant, but not unbreakable. I was more concerned about his throat.

"Put the gun down, Moira." Cold, commanding words. His arrogant sneer made my gut roil.

"Let him go, Barron."

He laughed, his black eyes never leaving me. "Good to know you've put your investigating skills to good use. Now that we both know who one another is, let me explain something. I have nothing to lose whereas it seems…you do."

He tightened his grip on Julian's throat. My nephew whimpered, round eyes wide and full of fear, his small body seeming more fragile and vulnerable in the shadow of a killer.

"Julian," I whispered. "It'll be okay."

"Well, now," said Barron. "It might and it might not be. That all depends on you."

"What do you want?" My hand trembled, my finger itching to pull the trigger.

"I thought that was quite obvious." He grinned. "You."

"The other guards will realize we're missing shortly. You're insane if you think you'll get away."

"I'm not as stupid as you think. Intel guarantees that the Nightwing men are gone from the premises and are quite preoccupied with their misguided attempts at capturing us. As for the other guards, well, they're all dead. Your sister and the servants are currently taking a chemical-induced nap. You see, there's no one to come to your rescue. You have no options."

I glared at Barron, trying to hold the gun steady, my eyesight blurring with angry tears.

"Moira." His tone lost its friendly note, dropping to threatening and deadly. "Put down the gun and come quietly, or I'll crack his neck and toss him over the side. Or maybe not. Maybe I'll break his wings, toss him over, and let the fall do the rest. Then Gor and Balisk behind you there will slit your sister's throat, after they have a little fun with her, and kill the servants. And still, we'll take you kicking and screaming."

I felt the two at my back, not daring to take my gaze from Barron. Malice gleamed from his eyes. He was right. I had no choice.

"If I come without a fight," I choked out, "you'll not harm my nephew or my sister or anyone else."

"I promise." He smiled.

"How can I trust you? You're a bloody murderer."

"True. I suppose you'll have to take that chance."

I'd never known hatred like I did at that moment, helpless to do anything but what he wanted. It shook me, along with the fear and anger vibrating through my frame.

I dropped the gun. My hands were pinioned behind my back at once by the two Morgons behind me. One of them roped my wrists together, leaning toward my neck and sniffing like the animal he was. "She's been marked."

"I see that," said Barron. "Violently so. By a very dominant male. Seems we're taking someone's prize."

I held my head high. "Yeah, and he'll kick your ass if you hurt me."

Disregarding my comment, he marched closer, guiding Julian by the wing. "It's no matter, our master is more dominant than all of them put together. He'll wipe that scent right off."

I started to struggle. "Let Julian go, Barron."

"Ah, yes. Our deal. Gor, break all of the comm devices in the home and lock him inside. The others will be out for hours. That's all we need."

A hand holding a chemical rag covered my mouth and nose. A cold sweat swept over me as the drug pulled me under, and arms wrapped me in a steel grip. The last thing I heard was Julian screaming my name.

Chapter 19

I awoke to the damp smell of earth and a pain in my left foot. I jerked upright, chains jangling. My right ankle was cuffed and chained to a stone wall. I lay on a filthy mattress on a dirt floor. Dark droplets stained the cushion. Blood.

"Oh, God."

I jumped up, knowing other victims had been here before me. I wobbled at a wave of nausea and dizziness. Whatever chemical they used to knock me out left a horrible headache in its wake.

At least I was still wearing my clothes. Remembering the photographs of the victims—naked and mutilated— a violent trembling shook my body. Whether from the aftershocks of the chemical or from bone-deep dread, I wasn't sure.

I glanced down at my throbbing foot. A bandage wrapped between my toes. I squatted and peeled it off. Five stitches closed a thin wound.

"Shit."

They'd found the techno-tracker. It was supposed to be advanced, secret technology of Nightwing Security. How'd they know I'd have an embedded tracker?

Barron had slipped by telling me his intel informed him of Lucius and Lorian's whereabouts. Only an insider in the Guard or Nightwing Security would have that information. Of course, Barron probably didn't count on me getting out of here alive, so it didn't matter what he let slip.

A square table stood against the far wall near the arched entrance of the room. The arch was large to fit a Morgon-sized man through the door. A cross-hatched iron gate sealed the entrance. A small sconce in the wall cast a dim light. The walls were built of stone and earth, like tunnels underground. The overwhelming sensation of dense weight above convinced me of that.

I had no idea how long I'd been out or how long it had taken to travel here. If I did, I could've at least guessed how far away they'd taken me.

The table had a drawer on the side. I shuffled toward it, but it was out of reach. I jerked on the chain, scraping the thin skin of my ankle in the process. "Damn it!"

Now I knew why one ankle of each victim was so chaffed. Except Layla's. Looking around, I'm not sure if she had it worse or better than the others. At least her terror and suffering was over quickly.

I yanked on the chain links tethered to the wall. Didn't budge. I banged the lock of the steel cuff against the stone, only managing to make my bare ankle bleed.

Curling my knees to my chest, I feared how poor Julian fared after I left. Alone in the house with his mother and the servants unconscious, having watched his aunt be abducted. I felt a pang for Jessen, knowing the fear she'd feel when she awoke to find me taken. I thought of Kol, wondering where he was right now. But of course, I knew the answer to that. He'd be looking for me. My heart constricted. I had to find a way out of this.

"Think, Moira. Think."

I twisted the medal of Portia in my fingers, praying for an answer, some help, anything. Tucking the chain back into my sweater, I stared at the table.

If I stretched out on the ground, I might be able to reach the table leg and drag it to me. I was surely the tallest woman they'd held in here. Lying flat on my stomach, I scrambled toward the table, my middle finger just barely reaching the closest leg. I sat up and pulled the chain taut, stretching out again. Two fingertips touched the table leg. I curled them, moving the leg an inch to the right. Closer. "Come on."

Wiggling my fingers, I scooted an inch the other direction, now able to curl three fingertips around the corner. "Yes."

An inch closer and I could wrap all four. I pulled it toward me, tightening my whole fist and dragging the table over. Sitting up, I jerked open the drawer.

"Nothing. Come on, damn it."

I pulled the whole drawer out. A metallic edge gleamed. Wedged in between the side was…a fork? Better than nothing. After finally managing to pull it from the crevice, I hurried and slid it into my back pocket. Footsteps approached.

I jerked to my feet and cracked a table leg off with my foot, giving me a sharp-ended stake. Scrambling until my back hit the corner, I waited.

A key jangled in the lock. The door swung open. Two Morgons stepped into the chamber, both with bright yellow wings, tan skin, and long, blond hair. I'd never seen Morgons of this clan before, but I knew from my studies they were of the Sunsting clan from northern regions. Barron stepped in behind them. All three were dressed in black tunics, hitting just above the knee, and leather, sleeveless tops. All they needed were swords and chest plates to match the Morgon warriors from history books.

"Where's the battle, boys?"

Barron smirked, his facial tic winking one side of his face. "Apparently, right here." He laughed. The other two chuckled, finding my attempt at self-defense humorous. They wouldn't be laughing long.

"Really, Moira. How can you possibly think to escape with a splintered piece of wood and chained to the wall."

"If you think I'm going down without a fight, you're out of your fucking mind. If I maim just one of you cult-following, murderous assholes, I'll die a happy woman."

"Cult?" Barron's black eyes narrowed as he slithered farther into the room, flanked by his Sunsting henchmen.

"The Larkosians," I hissed. "Isn't that what you call yourselves? With your blood-drinking rituals and sadistic mutilation of innocent girls." I choked back a sob, my emotions welling to the surface in a torrent.

He glanced at the others, grinning. "If you think we are that pathetic, fanatical sect Fallon Greyclaw tried to resurrect, I'm afraid your deductions have been wrong. But not entirely."

What the hell did that mean?

Lucius and Kol were right. The murders were an act of war, a way to break the peace between Morgons and humans. So what about the blood-drinking?

"Get her, Gor," commanded Barron.

He lunged, grabbing my wrist without the make-shift weapon. I stabbed in and out with a quick thrust, hitting just below the shoulder. He cried out, backhanding me against the wall, the wooden spike flying from my grasp. The other one came for me. I slipped the fork from my back pocket and swung high, scoring his cheek.

"Bitch!"

Gor wrapped me from behind, grabbing my arm with the fork and banging my wrist against the wall until I dropped it. The one I'd gotten across the face gripped my throat and leered down at me, his eyes pale yellow like his wings, the gash on his cheek bleeding.

"You'll pay for that, bitch," he grated out.

"It's an improvement." I smiled, masking the fear racing through my veins. "Trust me."

He hauled his hand back.

"Stop!"

He did.

"We'll not have her looking any more battered before the master receives her. Bring her."

Gor leaned down, pulling a key from somewhere and unlocking the cuff. I gave him a swift kick to the jaw before he could duck away.

He definitely wanted to kill me. Malice gleamed in his eyes.

"No, Gor," said Barron coolly.

Gor rubbed his jaw and squeezed my arm much tighter than necessary. They dragged me through an earthen tunnel, dark and narrower than I expected. Sconces lit the corridor every three or four yards.

I knew where they were taking me. To the evil one. That thing I sensed hiding in the shadows the night I offered myself up as bait. The thing that claimed me in my nightmare. Nausea boiled in my gut, overwhelming terror threatening to make me vomit.

We passed another cell like mine. Empty. We passed a second where I caught a glimpse of an unconscious human woman in jeans and a T-shirt strapped to a table, her arms straight out, open veins draining into bowls beneath her elbows.

"Wha—?" I dug my heels into the dirt, only managing to slow myself, not stop. "What are they doing to her? Barron!"

"No worries, lovely Moira. That will not be your fate."

More women. They were abducting them from other provinces. Gladium wasn't the only target. *My God.* My mind reeled at how many other young women had been taken for this sadistic, twisted band of murderers.

"Where are we?" I asked after our third fork in the tunnels.

"You can call it home, dear girl. But we call it Palace Prime."

After several turns, Barron leading the way, they pulled me out into a large open cavern. Stalagmites rose up from the floor, stabbing upward, mirroring the stalactites hanging down, like stone swords armed against each other. A cleared ring in the center bore a painted symbol I didn't recognize—a giant Morgon, wings outspread, crown on his head, holding a scepter in one hand, a sword in the other. Torches encircled the symbol, casting everything else in deep shadow.

The Sunsting guards dragged me to the center and stopped, forcing me to my knees. Barron stepped a few feet forward, blocking my view.

The familiar sensation of malevolence filled the air, the one I'd felt that night in the tunnel of the Vaengar Stadium's basement. There were others hovering in the shadows of the cavern around us, keeping still and quiet. But it was the presence of someone, something more menacing than all of them put together, that had me trembling. The one who remained out of sight.

"We have brought her, my lord." Barron bowed, sweeping backward and to the side. Barron, subservient?

Whoever he spoke to was shrouded in shadow, sitting on a massive throne of stone. Fire-gold eyes pierced me through the gloom. The same eyes from my dream, my nightmare. He stood and stepped forward.

From sheer dread, I averted my gaze to the floor, my chest heaving quick breaths, my pulse pounding in my head. A cold sweat broke out on my skin.

"Look at me, human." His voice, a deep-barreled frightening sound, made me want to obey. Instinct prompted me not to. I shook my head.

Gor gripped a fistful of my hair and yanked my neck back, forcing my face upward.

A monster stood before me.

I sucked in a breath. And couldn't exhale.

Huge. A beast, bigger than Kol or any Morgon I'd ever seen, towered over me. Bare-chested, wearing a leather kilt and a gold torque around his massive neck, his black hair hung long, his massive, black wings jutted over his shoulders. Black wings. Like the Nightwing clan. Impossible. His appearance didn't frighten me nearly as much as his face. His brow was too large, his jaw too wide, his chin and nose jutted too far, like the muzzle of a...of a dragon. He was more monster than man.

At the moment, his piercing gaze had left me to pin Gor, who still had his fist in my hair. With a swift movement, the monster grabbed Gor's arm and snapped the bone. Gor yelled, letting go of me. The creature took his head in his hands and cracked his neck, dropping the body to the floor.

Not a sound. The only surprised gasp came from me. I glanced at Gor's glazed expression, alive only one second before.

The monster stared at Barron. "She is not a bleeder and will not be handled as such."

"Yes, my lord. Of course."

The beast squatted down to me, his serpentine pupils dilated, observing with predatory intensity. Malevolence rippled off him like a foul odor. I was looking at death himself, except death would've been more kind, promising some blissful afterlife. In his eyes was endless emptiness.

His massive hands bore long, extended claws. He used one to tilt my face upward, his claw digging into the tender flesh under my chin. I refused to whimper or cry, forcing myself to hold his gaze, no matter the fear trembling through me. He turned my face to one side, then the other. He pulled the tie holding my braid in place, unraveling my hair with his clawed hand, lifting the dark waves to his nose. His eyes finally caught the mark on my neck, hidden before by my braid hanging to one side. His eyes flared a fiery red. He became preternaturally still.

"Who touched her?" he asked low and deep.

"None of us, my lord," assured Barron, stuttering. "She's taken a Morgon lover. Very recently."

A moment's pause. He smiled, revealing a row of sharp fangs, canines protruding. My heart raced faster. He was an abomination, some mistake of nature. A horror story come to life.

"Then she can take another."

He released my chin and stood to his full height, his voice bellowing in the cavern chamber. "She is to be my breeder. No one will take his pleasure on this one."

A unison of "Yes, my lord" rang out.

In a lower voice, he waved to someone in the shadows. "Commander Gaius. Take her to be bathed and put her in my chamber. I want her upon my return."

"Yes, my lord."

He whirled toward the shadows behind him, his knotted spine jutting out and stretching the skin on his back. He flared mighty, black wings. Footsteps fell in line with him and filed out an exit in the wall behind his throne. He was leaving on some other mission. Thank heaven!

Gaius!

Tall, dark-skinned, shaved head, and fierce expression, I would never in my life have taken him for a traitor to this cause if I didn't know it already. His skin and eyes matched the cocoa-brown of his wings. He was a Woodblade, the only one I'd seen so far in this place. He gripped me by the upper arm, lifted me off of my knees, and led me out a different corridor. I glanced over my shoulder to see Barron following his master along with a troop of others.

Where was I? This wasn't a cult, that was certain. This was a new society, made of Morgon soldiers who did everything they were told on penalty of death. Ruled by a mighty Morgon god, a beast of unparalleled proportions, who reeked of violence, power, and blood.

As Gaius led me away, four Morgon guards flanked our front and our back. Trembling from the encounter I'd just escaped, I glanced up at the one Morgon who might help to get me out of here. He didn't even look at me. His expression was hard and focused, like all of the others in this place, and I feared Kol was wrong. Gaius might have switched allegiance to this army of murderers. Or perhaps some dark magic had ensnared him to their cause. I trembled. My best hope may not care one way or another whether I lived or died.

Chapter 20

We wound farther into the cavern. The yellowish rock walls sparkled with a sheen. We came out into a circular chamber. Water dripped from stalactites on the ceiling. Thick humidity and steaming pools of all sizes made the place feel like a public bathhouse. Vapor filled the smaller chamber, dampening my skin. I suppose this *was* their public bathhouse.

A russet-winged Morgon, a Rowanflame clan member like Conn, lounged in a pool, his arms resting on the edge, his wings laying flat on the stone, while two scantily-clad women massaged his shoulders. My heart stammered at the thought of one of Conn's clansmen, distant relation or not, being a part of this foul group of Morgon men. Conn would beat him senseless for shaming the family name if he knew.

Gauis snapped to a halt. "Out!"

The Rowanflame, unaware of us, launched to his feet, revealing his full naked body. Like the other men here, he was in fantastic shape. But it was horrifying rather than enticing. Strong soldiers with sadistic minds and an even more sadistic leader—the combination terrified me. I dreaded I might never escape. I looked away.

"I see we have a new recruit, Gaius. I don't mind sharing. Bleeder or maiden?"

"Neither."

"I'll break her in for you either way."

"No. You won't. She belongs to the master alone, and he doesn't want anyone's hands or eyes on her. Get. Out."

Gaius's voice was a brutal blade. Enough that the Rowanflame took all of one second to move into action. He grabbed his clothes hanging on steel rods pegged into the cave wall and shook the water from his wings before he vanished through another tunnel. Wherever we were, it was vast with a never-ending string of tunnels. Without help, I'd never make it out of here alive.

"Stand at your stations. No one enters," barked Gaius to the other guards.

They marched to the entrances of the room without hesitation. Gaius had rank.

"Tend to her," he snapped to the two young women, standing like statues next to the steaming pool the Rowanflame had just vacated.

Both of them were delicate and dark-skinned with pale green eyes. They were from Primus, a human-only province to the West. Their coloring was unmistakably that of the native people there. The two young women, close to my age, wore identical white, gossamer tunics, roped with gold belts around their waists. Their hair was braided into many plaits, coiled and pinned to fall in a stream down their backs. I couldn't help but notice the bitemarks on their necks and shoulders. Not skin-breaking bites. Morgon-marking bites. They also bore gold-linked chains around their necks with a dangling loop in the front. Most probably to chain them up at night. Were they concubines of some sort? How many lovers were they forced to have? My stomach twisted into a tight knot.

They stepped forward to gently take my arm, guiding me toward the other side of the pool.

"Dress her in a maiden's gown," commanded Gaius. "But *no* throat-chain."

I glanced over my shoulder, pleading with my eyes. "Gaius," I whispered, knowing he could hear me with his dragon sense of hearing. "Do you know who I am?"

He gave me a sharp shake of the head, his eyes softening a fraction, before his voice bellowed across the cave. "Do as you're told, woman, and you will live."

His words were an order, one the others listening at the doors would hear and understand to be another harsh command. But I read in his eyes that it was a promise. *I would live.* I nodded, signifying that I understood, even though I still trembled from this suffocating atmosphere of brutal domination.

Gaius turned, giving us his back, but not moving away from the pool. I noticed he didn't have the MG tattoo on the nape of his neck. He must be in a special unit for undercover work. Of course he wouldn't have anything on his body to break his cover.

The two girls started to undress me, lifting my sweater.

"I can do it myself. Please." I pulled away and removed my own clothes.

They frowned at the empty harness around my waist, hidden under my sweater. Too bad I didn't still have that Volt gun. I'd blast every bastard in this place. I shed everything except my medal. I eased into the steaming pool. So bizarre to have these silent women rub soap on my skin and shampoo my hair. As if I were in another time and era altogether.

"How long have you been here?" I asked.

They didn't respond and continued washing me with gentle hands.

"Can you not speak to me?"

The one soaping my arm shook her head before averting her eyes again. They were both so pretty and meek, though one of them had a look of defiance marking her cold expression. It broke my heart thinking of them in this insane captivity, serving as sex-slaves to these monstrous men. I bit my lip to avoid screaming, trying to keep my temper under control. I needed to be level-headed and focused.

They took their time shampooing my hair several times and bathing me with soap, smelling of rose and mint. They wrapped me in a robe and guided me behind a rock formation that served as a private dressing area. Shocked to find the area raised above the cavern floor, tiled in red and decorated with a white, fluffy carpet, I stood there until one of them nudged me up to the platform.

One of them urged me to sit on a pedestal with a smile. I did. She was the softer of the two. They must be sisters or relations of some kind. The shape of their eyes and mouths were so similar.

They combed and braided my hair, weaving gold ribbons into my plaits, letting them fall loosely around my shoulders.

The gentler one leaned close to me and whispered, "It will hurt less if you don't fight."

"That's a lie, Lena," snapped the other. "It will hurt all the same." Flinty steel glittered in her eyes before she cast them down as before. "Now quiet, Lena, before the commander renders punishment."

I glanced back to where Gaius still stood facing outward near the pool.

"Does *he* punish you?" I asked.

The angry one held me in her green gaze, hard and cruel. "They all do."

As they applied powder and rouge to my face, a sickening nausea curdled in my stomach. What if Gaius had already switched sides? They said he punished them. Did he do it as part of being undercover? Was that part of the Morgon Guard rules? To keep the cover at all costs, even committing the same heinous crimes of those he was trying to catch?

The one called Lena used a lip-brush to gloss my lips with oil from a blue vial.

"What is that?" I asked, the aroma strangely familiar but covered over with honey.

All conversation was over. They didn't answer me.

Removing the robe, they toweled me dry and rubbed floral-scented oil all over my body. This was the most disturbing part because they didn't miss an inch. The realization of what they were preparing me for iced my blood.

His *breeder*? Like an animal to be kept here to sleep with him and bear his children. Bile rose in my throat. I swallowed, more determined than ever to get the hell out of here. I inhaled deeply as they wrapped some of the fine gossamer material over one of my shoulders, letting it drape down to mid-thigh, much shorter on them since I was so tall. After tying a gold-braided rope around my waist and putting satin slippers on my feet, I was escorted back to Gaius.

He turned, assessing me with an emotionless sweep of dark eyes. "Come," he bellowed across the chamber to the other guards, not to me.

He led, expecting me to follow. What other choice did I have? We exited through a different corridor than the one we entered.

"Wait! My clothes."

"You won't need them," he snapped.

"But—"

He continued walking on. One of the other guards nudged me none too gently to keep me moving. I followed, shivering in the cold corridor, now that we'd left the heated bath chamber.

I glanced back once more. The two slaves, Lena and the fiery one, stood mute and at attention, hands cupped and heads bowed in obedience. Slaves. The unbearable humiliation and suffering those girls must feel. And how many others were there? These bastards had to be stopped.

I twisted Saint Portia between my fingers, sending a silent prayer up for those two young women, hoping with all my heart they survived. Hell, I needed to be focusing on my own survival. The pitiful possibility of escape weighed heavy on my spirit as we wound through the tunnels.

Then something came to my attention. We were ascending. The cavern floor sloped upward. We were heading for the surface. My heart skittered faster.

Gauis halted abruptly outside a chamber with steel double-doors. They'd carved them into the cave itself, fitting the giant doors on fist-sized hinges.

"Stand guard," he ordered the others. They obeyed without a blink, snapping to attention.

Gaius opened the door and guided me into a darkened room. He puffed out a thin flame from his mouth to light the candles on a tiered gold candelabra on a black-wooden settee. He sucked in another deep breath and blew a flame to light the gold-caged sconces on the walls, filling the room with warm light. Plush cream carpeting spread throughout the vaulted room. Crystal chandeliers dangled from the ceilings. Along one wall stretched a massive bed covered in satin black-cased pillows and a furry, crimson coverlet. The headboard was the depiction of a Morgon battle carved in gold. I had a feeling it was solid, not plated. I licked my lips, feeling faint. This place did not look like it belonged at the bottom of a cave. It looked like a madame's room in a high-end brothel.

"Gaius," I hissed under my breath.

He returned from lighting the room, his expression grave but no longer bearing the stern look of a mindless commander.

"Please tell me you have a plan of escape." I licked my lips again, that nasty lip-gloss smeared all over them.

"Yes."

"Great. We need to move fast before that thing comes back."

"We can't go. Not yet."

"Not yet?" I was screaming in a whisper, knowing Morgons had ultra-sensory hearing, not wanting to alert the guards outside.

"Number one. You've been drugged and may pass out in a matter of minutes."

"What?"

He clamped a fist over my mouth and glanced toward the door, then glared at me, his voice low and dangerous. "That balm on your lips is a kind of sedative. It doesn't last long, just long enough to keep you calm and docile till he returns."

I yanked his hand from my mouth, my words tight and fierce. "Why didn't you warn me what they were putting on my lips?" I rubbed the back of my hand hard across my mouth.

"Because I need everything to seem as normal as possible until the very last second. This brings me to the second reason we can't leave now. He'll be back within the hour. That's not nearly the head-start we need. He has too many men and resources, spies hidden away, even in the Morgon Guard. If we're to escape and actually survive, we need several hours of a lead."

"How will we get that?"

"Listen," he snapped. "I have about twenty seconds before one of the guards peers in here to make sure I'm not fondling the master's merchandise."

He held out a syringe filled with clear liquid and a stopper on the end. "Take it."

I did.

"Once he's in this chamber, he will order no disturbances till morning because he'll want all night with you."

I swallowed but had no spit left.

"Get close enough to stick him with this. It's a high concentration of poison and sedative. The sedative will knock him out. The poison will do the rest. Don't miss the mark, or he'll kill you instead. I'll be waiting outside this door."

"Commander?" One of the guards opened the door and stepped in. I hid the syringe behind my back, staring submissively at the floor.

"All is in order," he barked, swiveling and marching through the door. "See that no one enters until the master returns."

"Yes, Commander."

They left, sealing the doors with a loud clang. I winced, gazing around the room, feeling trapped in a very opulent cage. Only one way out, and I couldn't escape by force. I glanced down at the weapon Gaius had given me. I'd have one chance, and I couldn't fail.

My head drooped. The drug made my legs shaky. I climbed onto the bed, scooting to the headboard. Unstopping the syringe with trembling fingers, I then placed it carefully underneath the pillow. I curled into a ball and lay there, fear gripping me hard. All the failed scenarios tripped through my mind: the syringe slipping from my fingers, the creature holding me down by my wrists, my captor pulling me from the bed and overpowering me. Maxine Mendale's bloody and mutilated body flashed to mind.

"No," I whispered, squeezing my eyes shut.

As soon as I closed my eyes, a pull, deep and strong, compelled me to relax. I did, slowing my breathing. Before long, my pulse eased, and serenity swept over me. As if two hands cradled me in their palms, keeping me safe, I followed the sensation, wanting to be held, slipping further into a dream.

Jessen and I were at the park. Sunshine poured from a summer-warm sky. Jess looked around sixteen, sitting with her back against an oak tree and a book open on her knees. Six years her junior, I skipped in the sunlight, picking white pansies from the field.

"Don't go too far, Moira," she warned, turning back to her book.

"I won't," I promised, picking and smelling, then prancing farther afield with light steps and a light heart to make a crown with yellow buttercups.

A cool woodland edged the park. I glanced back at Jessen, engrossed in her book, then stepped closer to the woods. Something waited for me there. My whole being yearned to be in the shade of those trees.

Seeking the one who awaited me, I walked faster. When I crossed from sunlight to shadow, dropping my flowers at the edge, I became the young woman I was now. And found the one waiting for me.

"Kol!"

He opened his arms. I leaped into them, feeling them close around me in a possessive embrace. He nuzzled into my hair, holding me as if I were the dearest thing in the world to him.

"Kol," I whispered. "I'm so afraid."

"I know, Moira."

I pulled back to see him, eyes pure blue-silver, whites and all. He cradled my face. This felt...real.

"This isn't an ordinary dream, is it? You're dreamwalking."

"Yes. Please, Moira, tell me you're all right. They have not hurt you, have they?"

Though I still felt safe in his arms, even in this dream, I could read every line of pain etched in his face. His fear was as great as mine.

"I'm all right," I assured him, kissing him.

In this dream, our lips met with tenderness, something we'd not experienced together in reality. Before I could get lost in his passion, he pulled away, still cradling my face in his hands.

"Tell me where you are. They've removed the tracker. I'll go mad if I don't find you soon."

"I know they did. I'm not sure where I'm at. It's a large, winding cave that goes deep under the earth. I believe they dug their own tunnels deeper. The walls seem to be made of a shining sort of rock, maybe limestone. It's cold in the tunnels, but there is one part of the cave where there are natural steaming pools. That's all I know. But Gaius is here. We have a plan to escape."

"Good. I've been unable to reconnect with Gaius since he left Cloven. There are several possibilities of where you could be, but those kinds of tunnels are far into the wilderness. I'll be searching with the Morgon

*Guard constantly. When Gaius gets you out of there, tell him to take you
to Safehouse X."*

"Where's that?"

"He'll know."

*I clung to his shirt, wanting to burrow right inside of him, tears
streaming down my face. His hand stroked down my back. His powerful
frame held me tight, his lips brushed my temple.*

*"Don't be afraid, Moira. Be strong. You'll be out soon, and I'll find
you."*

*I shook my head, choking on a sob. "Kol. There's a monster here.
That's who rules them."*

His face darkened. "A monster?"

*"He's Morgon, but he's not. He's hideous, with claws, fangs, and he's
massive. He must be eight feet tall. And he wants—"*

*No. I wouldn't tell Kol what he planned to do to me. I wouldn't burden
him with that fear.*

Kol's entire being became rigid and cold. "What does he want, Moira?"

*I shook my head and kissed him hard. Though he moved not a muscle,
his arms squeezed around me. I poured my heart into that one, lingering
kiss.*

"Tell me," he growled, dream-eyes shining bright.

*I broke free, running for the sunlight. Before I crossed over, I glanced
over my shoulder. "Find me, Kol."*

He reached for me. "Moira!"

"Find me."

I leaped out of the shadows.

My eyes shot open. My body trembled with violent shaking.
Instinctually, my fingers searched my throat for my comfort, my medal.

Gone.

Bolting upright, I saw it...dangling in the clawed hand of the king of
this underworld.

Chapter 21

I inched back against the headboard, my hands braced on the pillow, knowing what lay beneath. He continued to gaze at the medal, eyes observing every detail. When he spoke, the deep, broken tenor struck me again as unnatural.

"You humans still honor your saints and your God."

Still? How did he not know this? Our religious practices weren't a state secret.

"Speak," he commanded, shifting his gaze to me. "I know you want to."

Willing myself to breathe evenly, I tilted my chin up, holding my head high. "We honor what is good. Not what is evil."

He smiled. If you could call it that. Sharp teeth, two canines longer than the rest, jutted out. My heart tripped faster.

"There is no good or evil. There is only power, and who has the most."

I begged to differ. Evil incarnate stood not two feet from me at the edge of the bed. He rubbed a clawed thumb over the face of the medal, finally dangling it from the uppermost tier of the candelabra on the nightstand. Ropes of muscle rippled and bunched with every movement he made.

"So you honor your saint. I assume she has her own order."

Many of our saints did. Portia certainly did. The Sisters of Light were a peaceful order who lived reclusive lives southwest of Primus. They devoted their lives to helping the poor and less fortunate, especially orphans. But I sure as hell wasn't telling him.

He moved closer, a slow, primitive movement from someone who knew his prey could not get away. "You are afraid, which proves you are intelligent. You are also angry, which ensures you have strength. For a human female, you are well-muscled and have a strong body. You also show signs of being fruitful."

His eyes raked over my breasts, the transparent fabric giving him a good view. He inched closer, his giant wings opening in a gesture of dominance. His wingspan demanded awe. I sucked in a breath.

"You may fair better than the last."

I gulped air, refusing to think about what happened to the last woman he used as a breeder. Or tried to.

"Who are you?" I managed to ask without stuttering.

He reached down a clawed hand. I forced myself not to move, not to grab the syringe now and launch myself at him. I couldn't take the chance of missing. If I did, he'd snap my neck in two seconds, just like he did to Gor. I needed him closer. Bracing one hand on the bed, he leaned toward me, then trailed his knuckles over my cheek, along my jaw, and gripped my chin in strong fingers.

"I am your lord and master, your king and sire. I am your sun and moon, your every breath, your every waking moment. I am your summer and winter, your entire world, your everything."

An invisible pulse beat and rippled in the air. I gasped.

While my brain scrambled to comprehend what just happened, I felt split in half. Panic vibrated through my bones, a primal instinct screamed for me to get away—fast. Another part of me wanted to bow down before him, to do anything he wanted, to worship him. An aura of power, pure and strong, hovered around him. His dragon gift of dominance threatened to tear me in two.

I felt like a butterfly pressed to a collector's board. Fluttering my wings would only tear them, rendering me helpless, unable to fly. So instead of trying to flee, I lay there petrified.

"What did you just do to me?" I asked, voice shaking, recognizing the presence of Morgon magic.

"What is within my power and is my right." He lifted his chin in a dominant gesture. "Now. Lay down and spread your legs."

Shit! I was doing it, his dominance a pulse against my skin. Morgon magic bent my will to do his bidding, not my own.

Looming above me on his knees, he unfastened the belt holding his tunic, readying himself, my nightmare coming to life.

"You won't breed from this mating," he said in a gruff voice, dragon eyes brightening. He removed his tunic and tossed it aside. I stared at the ceiling, definitely not wanting to see that part of him.

"How do you know?" I asked, trying to entice him into conversation, stall him. I reached both hands above my head, angling my body into a submissive pose, letting one hand slide just under the edge of the pillow.

"We know when our women will breed. We can smell her when she is ready."

I'd known about a Morgon's heightened senses, but I didn't know they could scent a woman's hormonal changes. The fact that he lowered himself to me, knowing I couldn't breed, sparked a new fear inside me.

"Then why bother with me now?" My body obeyed his dominance against my own will. And still, I couldn't keep my mouth shut. "Let's just wait if there's no purpose."

He laughed, crawling over me, above me on all fours, willing me to look at him. I did, captured in fire-and-gold. Dread gripping me as it had in my nightmare.

"There is purpose." One of his hands rested beside my head on top of the pillow. The other lifted my woven braids of hair. "I want you. That is reason enough." He sniffed my hair. "And we must break your body in so that it knows mine and will open to my seed."

I couldn't breathe. He grinned, the hairs on the back of my neck rising. *Saint Portia, help me!*

"But the most important reason is I want to scrape the scent of your man from your body." A new panic overwhelmed me. I didn't want to lose Kol's scent under my skin. I didn't want to lose any part of him.

"No," I muttered under my breath.

Flaming eyes caught mine. His shoulders stiffened. He'd heard me.

"No?" Fury laced this one, gruff word.

He gripped one of my thighs, his claws pricking into my skin. I cried out, tears pooling in my eyes, as my hand groped under the pillow.

"You are mine and will obey." His mouth came over mine, a long tongue snaking inside, nearly choking me. I squirmed and whimpered, yanking my face to the side. Sharp teeth nicked my lip. He weighed me down with his chest. "Your former lover marked you hard," he growled close to my ear, licking my neck with that long tongue, right where Kol left his bite. I cringed. "But I will mark you harder."

My fingers fumbled, making contact with nothing. His chest rumbled with a sinister laugh, the hollow sound full of darkness.

"Looking for something?"

I met his leering gaze, horror dawning.

"I had no intentions of being stabbed with your little needle while taking my pleasure." I couldn't form a word of response, my mouth agape. "If you can get to it, be my guest." He made that horrible sound in his chest again, meant to be laughter. I caught sight of the syringe on the table against the far wall.

He squeezed my thigh, his pelvis dropping, preparing to thrust inside my body. On instinct, I used the first move Demetrius had taught me, a short-distance hand-heel punch directly up into his nose.

Crunch.

"Ah!" He whipped up onto his knees, his wings wide. I twisted out from underneath him, landing a swift upward kick with my foot to his jaw so I could scramble away. I shot off the other side of the bed and onto my feet.

His feral smile found me, anger blazing on the tight lines of his monstrous face. My gaze flicked to the syringe. So did his, then back to me. I launched myself toward the needle. With one beat of his massive wings, he crashed into me, an arm around my waist. I fell against the table, knocking it over, both of us tumbling to the floor.

The syringe fell and rolled a foot away. On my stomach, I reached for it right at the edge of my fingertips. He gripped the backs of my thighs, claws pricking the skin. I cried out, ignoring the pain as I curled the needle into my hand.

"Yes," he ground out in a demonic voice. "You'll make the perfect breeder for me." He hauled me back, preparing to take me from behind. "Maybe even more than that," he ground out, voice full of hard lust.

I subconsciously thanked myself for pushing my body into maintaining flexibility and agility. With one hand, I shoved my weight off the ground, twisted on my knees, and plunged the needle right into his throat. The shock made him freeze. I pumped the liquid in and scrambled away. All of which took about three seconds. My body trembling, I prayed.

Dumbfounded, he pulled the empty syringe from his neck. He wiped his finger over the spot and sniffed his fingers.

"Black Hellebore." He chuckled, rising to his feet. I couldn't help but glance at his groin and be thankful he hadn't finished the job. He wouldn't have broke my body in—he'd have broken me in half. "You do have strength." His words slurred. "I am afraid you will be disappoi—"

Before he'd even collapsed to the floor, I leaped across the room, snatched my medal, and swung open the iron door.

"What are you doing?" A Sunsting guard pivoted, marched for me and, reaching out, crumpled into a heap. Gaius stood behind him, bloody dagger in hand. He shoved the body into the chamber, closing the iron doors. Blowing a fine line of flame all along the frame, he melded the doors shut.

Tossing me a burlap sack, he hissed, "Put these on. Fast!"

I stripped and pulled on my jeans, dirty sweater, a pair of wool socks, and a long, black trench that was too big while he watched for others. I didn't ask who the socks and coat belonged to. I didn't care.

Gaius put one finger to his mouth, ensuring I kept quiet. I knew all about Morgons' extra-sensory abilities. No way was I taking a chance in getting caught now. I nodded and followed up the corridor, which sloped higher and higher at a steady angle. Ignoring the pain in my thighs where his claws and teeth had punctured, I rode on adrenaline alone and the need to get as far away as possible. Whatever signal Gaius gave me as we moved fast and silent, I obeyed. Within a hundred yards, we came to an opening where snow gusted in.

Gaius flattened me against the wall, mouthing, *Wait*, as he pulled out his dagger. With soundless stealth, he rounded the corner. I heard a short scuffle, then a gurgling, then nothing at all. He returned, grabbed my hand, and pulled me out onto the edge of a land of sheer rock.

The moon shone tonight, gleaming over the flatlands as far as I could see in every direction. Two Morgons lay dead near the entrance.

"Here. Step inside this." He held a canvas object in his hands.

"A body bag?"

"I can't be seen carrying a human," he spat out quickly, holding the straps open. "That's not done in Cloven, which is where I'm taking you. A Morgon carrying baggage won't cause suspicion."

"Baggage? Nice," I said, stepping in. I shivered, wondering how Gaius had easy access to a body bag. Was this how they carried their victims and dumped the bodies?

"Better that than being spied by one of the many scouts."

Gazing into the night sky, I asked, "Are there many?"

"Many. The patrols don't stop, so we have no time to waste."

"I'm ready."

"Good."

For the briefest of moments, I wondered if I could trust him. What the angry Primus girl had said caused me to wonder. But logic proved he was on my side. Otherwise, he wouldn't have risked his own life to get me out. And I had just watched him kill a few of the enemy to do so.

I gave him a sharp nod. "Zip me up."

"There are slits here"—he pointed—"so you can reach through and hold onto these straps."

Somehow, he understood that hanging inside a bag without a place to grip could drive a human crazy. As he zipped past my neck, I stopped him. "Gaius. Thank you. I thought I…back there I mean—" I broke off, an aftershock of emotion pouring down my cheeks from the fear of what could have been and the relief that I'd survived.

"No need. This is my duty. If I can save one, then I've done well." He zipped the bag to the top. I heard him belt the bag to him in three places.

"I've cut a patch out on your right and replaced it with mesh so you can breathe more easily."

"Thank you," I whispered.

He lifted off with a strong beat of wings. I never thought I'd be so grateful to be helpless in a body bag, hovering thousands of feet in the air.

"Gaius. Can you hear me?"

"Yes." Strangely, the bag didn't mute his voice much. "We need to remain quiet until we reach a safer zone."

"But, Gaius. Kol told me that when you got me out, we should go to Safehouse X."

His wings beat harder as we lifted above the clouds. Through the mesh, I could see a blanket of white, moon-bright and rolling, like a cotton-soft sea. Cold air rushed through the opening, making me feel less claustrophobic, more at ease.

"He visited you in a dream?"

"Yes."

"Then that's where we'll go."

"Is Safehouse X in Cloven?"

"There is one in every Morgon Province. He will have back-up waiting for us at each one."

Tears spilled anew. Kol would have men scouring every territory searching for me. Soon, I would be safe in his arms. My spirit soared at the thought, reminding me that the man of ice had chiseled his way into my heart.

My gut clenched tight. I'd never known fear like I had in that cell, when I thought I would die there and be separated from Kol forever. I'd never known fear like I had when that monster held me like I was his possession, when he nearly took me in the way only one man had the right to. I was desperate to be with Kol again, to tell him exactly what I thought of walls and isolation and separation from the world and the ones you loved. Life was too short to waste, harboring bitterness against family and cherishing loneliness like it was his own precious pet. Life was too short to waste on ambition alone, pretending it was enough for me. I wanted more. I wanted Kol. I wanted…love.

Chapter 22

We flew for nearly two hours. Gaius used evasive maneuvers, never staying on the same altitude or flying in a direct path. He plummeted to the ground and hid us in a copse of trees, silencing me as he peered overhead. He wrapped me in his arms, enveloping us both in his wings, camouflaging us in the trees, even to a Morgon's keen eyesight from above. One great advantage of having wings the color of nature.

"Scouting party, heading northeast to the palace," he said in a hushed whisper.

After ten minutes of utter silence and stillness, he whipped open his wings and lifted off again toward Cloven. The monotonous rhythm of his beating wings lulled me to sleep. When I awoke, I peered through the mesh at an amazing sight—Cloven.

I couldn't make out whether the buildings were made of stone or steel in the dark, but the shapes were pyramid-like with flat rooftops. For landing, of course. Some of them had full-pointed peaks. Others were a jagged construction, mimicking a natural mountain, but the squares of yellow light proved they housed Morgons inside. I peered down, finding only darkness and shadows below. No cars zipped along streets. No cars. No streets. No humans. The city was an artificial mountain region, built for beings who never needed to set foot on earth, lifting themselves closer to the sky where they belonged.

"Wow," I whispered.

Gaius skirted the city, banking away from its center. A river wound a sinuous path far below. Fewer buildings in the same pyramid structure, but with more space in between, lined the far side of the riverbank— private residences. We veered parallel to the river, arcing toward a white-stone building, gleaming under the moonlight. This building was different than the others. From above, it was shaped like a giant crescent, the tips reaching toward the river. On the flat roof was a clan crest in tiles, similar to what Morgons did on their top terrace in Gladium homes.

The crest was nothing but a full moon on a midnight-blue background, a paler shade of tiles ringing the moon. Though I'd never seen it, I knew this could be the crest of only one clan—the Moonring clan.

We landed with a rough jolt. I lost sight through the mesh opening as the bag shifted.

"Stay quiet till we're inside."

Gaius unbelted the bag from his vest harness and lifted me in his arms. I couldn't see where we were going but heard a door slide open.

"Quick," commanded a familiar voice.

We were inside. A door shut. An alarm pad beeped. We were airborne. I gasped, not expecting flight indoors, then just as quickly we were on solid ground. I was set upright, and the bag unzipped. Inhaling a deep breath, I took in my surroundings.

My heart skipped a beat when I thought Kol stood before me. Kieren's brow pursed into a frown so similar to his brother's. He wore the same high-fashion attire I'd seen him wear on the day we'd met. "Are you all right, Moira?" Sincerity in every word.

I nodded, needing a minute to process where I was and who was here.

"Kieren, do you know about my sister? My nephew? Are they—"

He held up a calming hand. "They're fine. All of them. The cook had quite a knock on the head, but she'll recover. However, the Night Security guards were all killed."

I winced, my heart dropping for those men who were only trying to protect us.

"Come on in." He ushered me farther into the room.

Another Morgon, on guard, stood looking out a curved wall of glass. The room was a breathtaking open space with a domed ceiling thirty feet above our heads. A platform jutted out near the ceiling, the door leading to the rooftop we'd just entered. It was more than a little disconcerting to stare at the exit so far above my head, unable to escape if I needed to. A white marble fireplace stretched the entire length of the wall, a stark pillar against the warmer-hued stone. Low flames emitted the only light in the room.

"I've double-checked the security alarms downstairs. All good," said a Morgon woman in dark combat gear, appearing right out of the floor.

There was a giant hole dropping straight into the room below. No stairs. Of course. Why would they need them?

The Morgon woman crossed in front of the fire, the light casting a warm glow on her blue-black wings, shining a halo on her white-blonde hair, falling like silk over her shoulders and down her back. She drew closer to me.

"Whoa. You reek of him!" I froze, afraid the monster had marked me, despite my unwillingness. "Kol sure got under your skin." She grinned.

I sighed relief. She stepped forward and offered her hand, meeting me eye to eye. "I'm Valla Moonring."

I shook her hand. "I'm Moira Cade."

"I know." She smiled, revealing how truly beautiful she was. "You've met Kieren already, and that's Bowen." She gestured to the one silhouetted against the window, her flaxen hair shimmering in the orange firelight. The twins had inherited darker looks, though they all shared the same midnight-blue eyes with a pale halo around the center.

"No time for chit-chat," snapped Gaius. "We can't stay here, but I need to give you what information I can before we go."

"My home is safer than any other place," said Kieren, his charming demeanor no longer present. He was more like his brother than he had let on when I met him. "Besides, Kol told us to stay at Safehouse X and make contact the moment she arrives. He's in Drakos, but could be here in two hours. I'll contact him."

"No!" Gaius lunged and grabbed his comm device before Kieren could punch in a number. Everyone's attention riveted to him. "No, Kieren. It's not safe."

Gaius moved to the fireplace. I took a seat on a cobalt-blue, velvet sofa.

"Why not?" asked Valla, her playful tone evaporating. She sat next to me, whipping her wings behind the sofa-back in a swift move. Unlike a Morgon man's large wings, hers fit her frame—long, sleek, and elegant.

"He has spies everywhere. Even moles in the Morgon Guard and elsewhere. They've been able to intercept communication sent via comm devices. Don't ask me how. I was never included in the intel briefings. I was used"—he turned away from us, staring out into the moonlit night—"for more brutal purposes. I couldn't warn you because we were forced to take injections every day to prevent Moonring clan members from infiltrating our dreams and stealing secrets. They know well enough how many of you are in the Morgon Guard."

"Injections of what?" asked Kieren, voice dropping to a lower register. He sounded so much like his brother.

Gaius shrugged. "I didn't ask. It would've been suspicious. This operation runs like a militant machine. You do what you're told. I couldn't receive or give any more messages to Kol once I was assimilated into their ranks and taking the injections."

"Wait, Gaius." Kieren thrust his palm out. "Who is the leader? That's what we've been unable to discover."

Gaius faced us again, the fire at his back, his dark features hidden in shadow. "I don't know. We... They called him lord and master. When I came on scene, Barron Coalglass was in charge, abducting girls for their blood and for...other purposes."

"Their blood?" asked Valla. "They were really drinking human blood?"

"I believe the king was drinking their blood," said Gaius before blowing out a tired breath. "Our orders were to harvest the blood, and that was all we knew. But I know of one instance where he bit and drank from a victim directly."

I shivered. "Maxine Mendale."

Grim-faced, Gaius nodded.

The other Morgon who'd been standing guard near the window joined us. He wore his long hair in a cue. His eyes shined pale green by the firelight, his wings a deeper shade of the same color. One of the Huntergild clan.

"So where did he come from? This lord and master," asked Kieren.

"I can't tell you. I can only say that one day, not long after I joined their ranks, Coalglass called an assembly at Palace Prime."

"What's Palace Prime?" asked Kieren.

"There are several palaces, as they call them, which are more like hidden lairs. I've only been to the one, where Moira was taken, but I know there are others. Anyway, Coalglass called an assembly and announced that our king had finally come. The king who would bring order back to our world and put humans in their rightful place. In chains."

An audible gasp escaped Valla. My fingers went to my throat where I'd replaced my medal around my neck. My stomach clenched into a ball. I'd almost lost it forever. It cost little to buy another, but I'd worn this particular medal for so long. It had comforted me for so many years, giving me the will to become a woman of strength—free-spirited, determined, independent. Then the beast had taken my medal, as if he had the right to strip me of my dearest possession, as if he could strip me of the woman I'd become.

But I'd gotten it back.

Kieren, Valla, and Bowen gazed at me. "What is it?" asked Valla.

I shook my head, shaking off the fear and torment of that place where the monster ruled with a brutal will. "Nothing."

Kieren turned to Gaius again. "But *who* is he? Where does he come from?"

"I wish I knew." Gaius stepped forward. "I did hear Coalglass once mention something about a Syren sister, a defector, who has allied with them for their cause, their revolution. I heard her name mentioned long before the king made his arrival."

"So it's true." I clasped my hands together to keep from wringing them in nervous agitation. "The Devlin Butchers aren't butchers at all. They weren't murdering those women and putting them on display for some cult or for some kind of sick enjoyment. Their plan this whole time has been to start a race war."

"Their plan is to dominate all of humankind," added Gaius. "And Morgonkind as well. It won't just be a monarchy led by this king. It will be a totalitarian state with a sadistic dictator on the throne."

The beast's words filtered through my mind. *There is only power, and who has the most.*

Silence. I stood up. Realization dawned on all of us at once. It wasn't just the freedom of humanity that was at stake. It was the freedom of everyone. Every race.

Valla rose to her feet next to me, shaking her head. "I just can't believe it."

"What is he like?" Bowen asked, meeting my gaze.

"He's a monster. He's bigger than any of you." I eyed Kieren's large proportions, identical to his brother's. "Even you," I added. "He's malformed. Claws instead of hands. Sharpened fangs, like that of a—"

My fingertips unconsciously brushed along the seam of my jeans near the punctures in my thighs.

"Like that of a dragon," Valla finished for me in a small whisper, watching my hands.

I folded my arms to keep them still and nodded. "But we don't need to worry about him anymore. I injected him with poison to escape. He should be dead by now."

"That doesn't mean his army will give up their quest," added Gaius. "Coalglass is his second-in-command, and he's maniacal."

"They had other girls there." I stepped toward Gaius.

Bowen tensed as tight as a bowstring, his expression darkening. "How many have they taken, Gaius?"

"There have been dozens of girls from every province, every human village imaginable. Not just the four from Gladium. They've kept it quiet, but soon, human police precincts will make the connection. And now the Guard will know." He paused, his brow pushed into a deep frown. "I believe...their blood made him stronger, made him more dominant."

I scoffed. "More dominant."

The others glanced at me.

"He wielded it like a weapon."

"So," interrupted Bowen, "they *have* been the ones responsible for the missing girls in Primus."

Gaius nodded. Bowen pivoted back to the window, fists clenched at his sides.

"I'm afraid the blood was for other reasons as well," continued Gaius. "Coalglass and the king kept the army divided in a way that each faction was responsible for particular missions, no one knowing what others knew. It was the king's way of keeping control. Only Barron has full knowledge of the greater plan. But I can tell you, he bled a lot more girls than he was drinking. There's more to discuss, but we must move from here. Immediately. There's no guarantee the locations of any safehouse known to the Morgon Guard is still confidential."

Kieren stalked toward the hole in the corner. "Give me thirty seconds to change." He dropped through the floor. I heard a soft whoosh as he landed below.

Gaius pulled a leather pouch from his pocket. He opened the pouch and handed a small object to Valla. A comm micro-drive.

"I've stored my logs on these micro-drives." He handed a second one to Bowen. And a third to me. "I hope to give a full report to my captain, but I need to know if we're separated or I'm captured—or worse—that what I've endured was not in vain." His voice dipped low, filled with an anguish I hadn't detected before now.

Valla placed her hand on his arm. "You will deliver your intelligence to my brother yourself. But know that I will keep this safe. Just in case."

His captain. Kol. How I longed for him, wanting so desperately to send a message via comm. But I trusted Gaius. I wouldn't risk anyone's life for my own peace of mind or to still my restless heart. I'd have to wait.

Kieren reappeared, newly attired in dark clothing, a huge scabbard strapped to his thigh. Again, my heart leaped at the sight of him, looking so much like his brother. He gave me a wink. "Well, Moira darling. If things don't work out with Kol..." He swept his arms down his body as if gesturing what I could have.

I shook my head with a light laugh, the first time since I'd tickled Julian in his bedroom. My laughter faded fast, wondering how my sweet nephew fared after witnessing such a nightmare in his own home.

"Let's go," snapped Gaius, picking up the body bag.

Bowen was at my side. "May I assist you to the roof?"

"Please." I let him put his arms around my waist, and with one beat of wings and a swift jolt in the air, we were thirty feet higher on the platform leading to the rooftop.

Bowen let me go as soon as I regained my footing, all of us following behind Kieren as he disabled the alarm and ushered us out the door.

"If I may ask,"—came the deep, quiet voice of Bowen—"did you see any young women from Primus in captivity where you were?"

"I did. I met two from Primus."

Pain creased the man's brow, making me feel even more miserable that I hadn't helped them. As if I could have.

"Did you get their names?" His green eyes glittered under the moonlight, so familiar.

"One was named Lena. The other I didn't find out."

His eyes closed, then it hit me. His features, though more masculine, mirrored the girls I'd met in that horrible place. Specifically the older, angrier girl. Was he somehow related to them?

I continued softly. "They couldn't speak to me very much, and I only saw them a short time." I wouldn't tell him they were being used as sex-slaves for those beasts, for he knew and cared for these human women. I wouldn't add to his pain, but I *would* give him hope. "I don't know much, but I can tell you they looked strong, determined to survive."

"Thank you." He gave me a sharp nod, his eyes full of heavy emotion as he spun away to the edge of the roof.

"Hurry, Moira." Gaius held open the body bag.

"Wait!" shouted Bowen, expression taut and strained.

I'd stepped one foot inside the bag and froze right before the wind was knocked out of me. Someone slammed me to the ground. Kieren stood above me, swinging a dagger at a yellow-winged Morgon in a familiar black tunic. Balisk.

The whip of wings and boots hitting pavement sounded just before the sliding of steel on steel and the pounding of fist into flesh. Bowen swung a long, thin saber in deft arcs. His opponent, a Sunsting, dipped and puffed a lungful of air, blowing a burst of fire at Bowen who somersaulted above and out of danger. He landed behind him, swinging his silent blade and severing the Morgon's head from his body. The head bounced on the pavement. My stomach churned. Before the body hit the floor, Bowen engaged another enemy soldier in combat.

Gaius launched himself at the towering Balisk, while Kieren fended off another coming for me. Barron wasn't in this crowd of Sunsting soldiers. Gaius stabbed one in the shoulder just as Balisk came up from behind and locked a thick arm around his neck.

"You should die slowly, Gaius, but I want your death too much."

Gaius flapped his wings, partly trapped by Balisk's body. A flash of silver. A line of red. Gaius gurgled and crumpled to his knees.

"No!" I screamed.

Balisk pulled his arm back and swung full-force through the air, slashing one of Gaius's wings in half. A post-mortem humiliation. Hatred burned inside my chest. My days of body boxing didn't prepare me for full-combat mode amidst falling bodies. How ill-prepared I was for this entire investigation, for this ruthless world.

Balisk stalked toward me with a feral grin and yellow eyes penetrating through the dark, looking more demon than Morgon or man. A primal shiver tingled up my spine. I scampered back, trying to get to my feet.

Kieren dispatched a soldier and shoved me back behind him. "Stay down."

Balisk circled, obviously angling for his target. Me.

"Didn't take you for a human lover, Moonring," he growled, ducking Kieren's swift slice through the air with a thick short-sword. Kieren dodged another swing of Balisk's dagger, saying nothing. Balisk pivoted closer to me.

"I'd like to gut her for what she's done," he grated, "but my orders are to bring her back alive." He swung high with his sword. Kieren dodged and spun away.

"Too bad," said Balisk. "She'd make a pretty corpse."

All the rage I'd held bottled inside behind the fear boiled to the surface. For myself, for Maxine Mendale, for Layla, for the Primus slave-girls, for every young woman taken against her will. For the rapes, the beatings, the terror, the murder, the mutilation, and for Gaius, I swallowed that fear and used the anger to do something besides cower and wait my turn.

Lying on my side, I swung my leg the way Demetrius taught me to when I needed to do serious damage. I felt a crack when I landed a hard kick sideways against his knee, sweeping Balisk to the ground. Before he landed, I lunged, using all my weight to keep his head pinned with my bended knee, grinding it into the tile roof. One of his hands jerked up, grasping for my throat. Kieren lowered to his knees and shoved his short-sword directly into Balisk's heart.

"You're so lucky"—Kieren's voice ground out like crumbling stone—"that I'm the one killing you and not my brother. He'd keep you alive to cut your heart out slowly for what you threatened to do to his mate." Balisk's hand squeezed my forearm. Kieren twisted the blade in his body and gave it a violent jerk. Balisk sputtered blood out of his mouth, wide eyes glazed, his arm going limp and dropping away from my arm.

"Get up, Moira."

I did. Kieren took hold of one of his wings, dragged him to the edge of the roof, and launched his body over the edge.

I crawled to Gaius's side. His eyes stared up into the night. A slow blink and the faintest of breaths told me he still lived. I angled his face toward me. "Gaius. Can you hear me? It's going to be okay."

I knew it would never be okay, but thoughtless words of comfort still spilled from my mouth. He blinked again, focusing on my teary gaze. "No," he choked out. "I don't want to survive this." What was he saying? "I had to become one of them, you see." He gasped for breath, pleading me to understand. I listened as I always did when someone wanted to tell their story. "They threatened to kidnap my sisters, my mother, to do to them what they did to the others." Blood gurgled and streamed from his mouth. "I became one of them. My sins are so great." He gasped for breath, a line of blood trailing from his mouth. "But you. When you came...had to get you out. My captain's mate, I couldn't leave in their hands."

His breathing was shallow and raspy. He closed his eyes as he exhaled one last breath. I held in a sob welling in my chest. "Sleep, Gaius. Rest now."

"Kieren!" Bowen bellowed from across the rooftop. "*Go*. Get her out of here."

Jolted from the somber scene at Gaius's side, I glanced up to see Kieren storming in my direction, having just fought and killed another Morgon. Bowen and Valla were in combat with the last two soldiers. Valla defended herself with swift moves, leaping through the air and slicing her opponent across the face with the twin rapiers in both hands. She literally kicked him in the ass after she ducked and slipped under his lumbering form, knocking him off balance.

She glanced over her shoulder. "Go! To Blind Bird Falls!" she yelled, ducking her attacker as he tried to snatch her by the hair. She twisted away, slicing him across the face.

Kieren sheathed his sword and pulled me off my knees. "Arms around my neck, Moira darling."

I wrapped my arms around him, locking one hand on the wrist of the other arm. He lifted my legs, holding me in a tight embrace, took three long strides, and leaped off the building. My stomach dropped out from underneath me. He banked hard right away from Cloven, winging high up into billowy clouds.

"Where are we going?" I asked, teeth chattering. From fear or cold, I wasn't sure. Probably both.

"A special place. Hang on tight. My brother would never forgive me if I let anything happen to his mate."

Chapter 23

Did he say *mate*? Just like Gaius had. But I wasn't.

Teeth chattering, we flew into a spray of misty sleet.

"Cover your face," he commanded, sounding so much like Kol. "I'm going to speed up. This'll sting."

I turned my face into his neck, the flap of my collar forming a tent across my cheek. We rocketed forward, flying at a speed that would have me dizzy and nauseous if I were looking.

"Morgons have skin of leather, t-t-too?" I stuttered.

He chuckled, the sound dying on the biting wind. "Our bodies relegate temperature much differently than humans."

"I n-noticed."

He wore nothing but a long-sleeved black shirt as a second skin and wasn't fazed at all by the freezing cold. I, on the other hand, was suffering rather badly, even wrapped in an insulated trench coat.

"How f-far is Blind Bird Falls?" was all I could mutter between my teeth.

"Not far. It's not a place, actually. Blind Bird Falls is a childhood game Kol and I used to play with Valla at our summer home. That was Valla's clever way of telling me where to go."

He dipped out of the clouds.

"Sorry about the cold. I'll have you warm soon enough."

The lower and farther west he flew, the less my teeth chattered, till finally I was just plain cold and miserable, rather than freezing to death and waiting for a limb to fall off. Kieren skimmed deep into a valley, one story above the earth.

A lake spread wide like a multi-fingered hand, jutting into perfect, tree-lined coves. Ideal for a summer home, a getaway from the world, tucked into a lush valley. Of course, even under the cloak of night and full cloud-cover, I could see that nothing was green and the trees were bare. But in summer, it would be lovely.

"It's so beautiful," I murmured.

"That's Pearl Bottom Lake."

The moon broke over the wind-rippled water like slivers of white glass, sparkling iridescent like pearls. Cool mist rolled along the edge. Kieren cut a sharp left into a dense growth of evergold trees. There weren't many in or around Gladium, but I loved them because they kept their leaves the longest, falling finally in the dead of winter. The moonlight shone on the golden leaves, gilding the lakefront area in a vibrant halo. One of the trees was huge, four-men thick, with branches stretching out like a great beast to protect its lair.

Kieren swept under the ancient tree, lighting not thirty yards into the grove where a river-rock cabin stood. It blended so well with the woods that I gasped in surprise when he set me down.

Kieren stepped up to the alarm panel and punched in a lengthy series of numbers, letters, and symbols. A stone door slid sideways into the wall. He swept an arm for me to enter, glancing over my shoulder.

"Not completely rustic, is it?"

He tapped the alarm pad, sealing the door shut behind me. "After my father died, Kol had an alarm system installed in the place, complete with twelve-inch thick granite." He laughed in a bitter sort of way. "At the time, I thought he was acting a bit overzealous and paranoid. But now I'm damn glad he did." He said the last with an edge of regret.

I peered around the room, hugging my body, shivering. Thick wooden beams cross-hatched cathedral ceilings, opening the room into a wide space. Morgons liked their rooms big and open. Two huge, round skylights were symmetrically placed in the ceiling, both sealed off at the moment. There was a second floor loft, but no stairs. White cloth draped the furniture. Kieren whipped off a blanket from a plush, earthy-brown sofa. The cabin had a familiar feel to it, like that of Kol's place in the Feygreir Mountains.

"Sit. I'll get a fire going."

He opened a door next to the river-rock fireplace and pulled dry kindling and logs from a pantry. I sat down while he blew a puff of orange flame, licking a fire to life. Must be nice to have warmth at their fingertips. Or at the tip of their tongue, actually.

Though still cold, I had stopped trembling.

"I'll get you some towels and a blanket."

He disappeared into what must have been a bathroom, returning a minute later. He tossed me a clean towel, using another to dry his hair. He reached one hand behind his back to unzip the back flaps of his shirt under his wings. As he was about to pull the shirt over his head, he paused, realizing he was about to strip half-naked in front of me. And damn it, I was staring. Not because I found Kieren attractive, but because I found Kol mind-blowingly sexy. And he looked too much like his brother. Perfectly defined bronzed abs peeked out from where he'd lifted his shirt, his upper torso broadening at the shoulders. But he wasn't Kol, and no sparks flared as they would for him.

I glanced away, remembering how Kol used his body on me, how he'd made me climax over and over till I was a bag of bones, how he'd held me against him all night long afterward, tucked safe in his arms.

"I think I'll change upstairs." He winked. "The way you're carrying my brother's scent, it's like he's in the damn room." With two beats of his wings, he landed on the loft and shouted down, "And I won't be accused of coming on to you or anything. He'd kick my ass, and I wouldn't blame him."

I was glad he left the room, so I could be alone a moment with my thoughts of seeing Kol soon. What would I say to him? Forced together out of necessity, we'd been reluctant professional partners, never behaving very professional at all. Then we'd become more than willing partners of another kind. Sex had broken down barriers, wiping away our walls of isolation. Yet, neither of us was comfortable with vulnerability. And neither of us had voiced emotions beyond profound pleasure and desire. I told him I needed him. And I did. Not just my body, but something else deeper inside yearned for his presence, his scent, his...everything.

Kieren returned in dry clothes, his shape so much like his brother's, my heart ached. He must've seen it in my eyes, throwing me an apologetic glance.

"I had to borrow some of Kol's clothes."

"You don't have your own things here? I thought this was the family summer home."

He grunted, stoking the fire with a cast iron poker. "Once, yes. Not so much anymore."

His expression hardened as he stared into the flames. That wasn't a subject I wanted to broach with him. He glanced back at the door. "The others will be along soon."

"You're not afraid for your sister?"

"Valla?" He snorted. "No. I might be more afraid for the Morgons on the other side of her Drakonian steel."

I laughed, remembering how she moved like liquid, dodging every thrust of her opponent's sword, slicing through the air as if her weapons were a part of her. Her enemy had never landed a blow before Kieren had hauled me out of there, concerned for his brother's *mate*.

"Kieren, you said you wouldn't let anything happen to Kol's mate. But…I'm not his mate. I mean, not in the way Morgons…that is…" I felt like a stammering child, unable to express what I meant. I wanted to say, yes, Kol and I were lovers, but we hadn't shared soulfire. And Kol hadn't offered or even mentioned the idea. We'd only recently crossed that particular intimate line.

Kieren shifted his focus from the flames to me, a broad grin fixed in granite planes. He opened his wings partway, then refolded them, as if stretching.

"Moira. I realize you're human, and you're unaware of Morgon ways. And senses. But let me explain something to you."

If I wasn't dying to hear what he had to say, I would've smacked him for his condescending tone.

"There are levels of dominance when a Morgon man wants a woman. When he wants a lover, he'll mark her as such, a subtle trait to let other Morgons know she's off-limits, unless the woman deems otherwise and rejects his scent. When they're through with each other, she'll shrug off his scent like an old coat."

I frowned. "Rejects?"

He propped the poker against the river-rock hearth, then clasped his hands behind his back, ignoring my question. "Then there's the marking a Morgon man gives when he claims a woman as his own. His one and only. This is very different, the scent acting like a palpable barrier, a physical threat to other would-be suitors."

"So, what you're saying is Kol has claimed me."

He shook his head.

"More than that,"—his smile widening—"you've accepted him as your own, as if you were already mates."

"What?" I shook my head. "That doesn't make any sense. He didn't even ask anything. I sure as hell haven't consented to anything."

A bark of laughter escaped him. He crossed his arms, his smile no less arrogant. Now I really wanted to slap him.

"Yes, Moira darling. Apparently, you have. There's no way he could burrow that deep otherwise. The marking is…violent in its possession.

Only the seal of soulfire will ease the fierce nature of the aura he's cast over you." He gave me a mischievous wink. "You must've consented in some way other way than using words."

Had I? Perhaps I had. Why didn't that anger me?

I pondered the reactions of Morgon men around me since Kol and I'd spent the night in each other's arms. All of them had been hesitant, edgy around me. Even the Nightwing guards back at Lucius and Jessen's place. All of them except the king. But he wasn't a normal Morgon. He was something…other.

Even Gaius, who had only touched me out of necessity, seemed wary. Gaius. I still couldn't believe he was gone. I couldn't believe his confession at the end. Forced to become a murderer to save his own family. And in the end, he saved me from untold horrors. He ended his life well, despite what he'd become in the viper-pit of Palace Prime.

My emotions see-sawed, my thoughts flipping from one thing to the next. Rather than being furious by Kieren's revelations about scent-marking, I had a wonderful, unexpected reaction. My heart soared at the thought of bonding with Kol. I wanted even more. I wanted to be heartbound. I wanted soulfire.

Kieren stoked the embers, adding another log. The door alarm beeped. I jumped off the sofa as Kieren stepped in front of me. The door slid open. Valla and Bowen rushed in and sealed the door behind them.

A red slash cut across Bowen's shoulder. Valla was perfect, untouched.

"They're all dead," she reported almost cheerfully. "Bowen, there's a bathroom through there. A medicine kit in the cupboard."

He crossed the room in swift silence and shut the door behind him in a bathroom off the main living area.

"No injuries, Valla?" asked Kieren.

"No. Of course not."

"You'll make a good assassin, sister."

"I *am* a good assassin, brother."

She stepped in front of the fire near me. "Now, we need to make contact with Kol and let him know what's happened and where we are," she said, eyeing Kieren.

"Right. I'll take care of it. I'll use a bedroom upstairs." Kieren whipped out his wings and flew up to the loft as he did before.

I already knew what he planned to do. "He's going to dreamwalk, isn't he?"

"It's the safest way since we don't know how much of our comm net has been compromised. We need to keep this place as secret as we can.

Obviously, our safe houses are no longer confidential. The enemy knew we'd be there."

I stood next to her, letting the damp towel fall from my shoulders.

"Surely Kol won't be sleeping. How will Kieren make the connection?"

She eyed me, still damp and cold. "Come on, let's get you into something dry."

She slipped through the kitchen and led me through a door on the other side. She twisted a knob at the entrance that lit four gas lanterns ensconced on the walls around the room. Many Morgons used electric lighting, but it seemed everything was done old-school at this hide-away.

The huge canopied bed was draped in shades of lavender and gray. Valla opened and stepped into a walk-in closet. I studied several photos on the wall above the vanity. One of her as a young girl squeezed between two smiling brothers. My heart leaped at seeing Kol, unscarred, before the rift between the brothers. There was another picture of a lovely Morgon couple—a dark-haired man with a square jaw, broad brow, and intense blue-fire eyes wrapping his arms around a beautiful platinum blonde with soft, almond-shaped eyes, her white wings open and out of the way so her lover could hold her close. She looked more like a butterfly than half-dragon woman, the love she felt for the man at her back shining in her eyes. I hadn't known Kol's mother was of the Icewing clan. I thought of Petrus, wondering if there was any family connection. I strolled, finding another of a scarred Kol and an older Valla. She held two long daggers in both hands as if showing off a gift. I laughed inwardly. While my father was buying us Primean silk gowns for balls, Kol was buying Drakonian steel weapons for his little sister, Valla. Funny that I felt such a connection with a stranger I'd just met, yet we were raised so differently.

The last photo on the vanity was a family portrait of all five of them, here in front of the lake at this home. Their mother now had black wings, her mouth open in laughter. Kol smirked, an arm around his brother's shoulder, while Valla and Kieren laughed. Their father mirrored Kol's expression. Their mother had different color wings than in the other portrait. I marveled at Morgon women, giving up their identity to accept the transformation of heartbonding, letting go of their clan colors to match her mate's. It was more than a woman giving up her last name. They sacrificed a part of who they were to tie themselves completely to their love, a physical representation of the bond for all to see. Did Kol not want to give me soulfire because a human woman couldn't show her full devotion to the world? Without wings, how could we ever match the union he admired so much between his parents?

"You asked about dreamwalking," Valla called from the closet. I returned to her, shaking off darker thoughts. "Kieren and Kol don't need to sleep to dreamwalk. Must be the twin thing. Kol once told me they can feel the pull of each other when they need to connect in the dreamworld. They go into a trance-like state, not needing to actually sleep."

Valla perused through her clothes, pulling a pair of pants from the hanger. "Here. This should fit you. And try this top. We're about the same size."

I gazed at her slim, lithe body, unbuttoning and sliding off my jeans. "Except I'm a bit rounder and wider."

"If you mean bigger boobs and full hips, well then, yeah. But trust me, you wear it very well."

We giggled. Not needing to unbutton the back flaps of the cream-colored top, I slid it over my head. I had to squeeze into her brown leather pants, sucking in to zip the zipper.

"Moira. Do you need some antibiotic?"

I glanced up. She gestured toward my legs, having seen the tiny marks before I'd pulled on the pants.

"No. It's fine. He didn't—he wasn't able to go deep." I needed to know something only she could tell me. "Valla, can you smell him on me?"

I had to be sure there was no trace of that monster, knowing Kol's reaction would be violent in the extreme. Not against me, but it would jolt Kol into a suicidal crusade to kill every one of them, even if I had killed their king.

Valla stepped closer and leaned toward me. She smiled. "No. Only my thick-headed brother's scent is on you."

I sighed relief, exhaling a puff of air.

"Do you want to talk about it?" she asked in a quiet voice.

"No," I replied, stealing a look at myself in the vanity mirror.

Her clothes certainly fit. Like a glove. They looked obscene on me.

Shaking her head, she grinned, looking very much like Kieren.

"What?" I asked, self-conscious. "What's wrong?"

She laughed. "Not a thing. But this better not tempt any of those boys to touch the merchandise. Kol wouldn't like it." She opened the dresser and found a pair of black, knee-high stockings. "I think I have some boots downstairs." She tossed the stockings to me. "I don't usually keep footwear here, but I'm pretty sure I have a pair I left last time."

I sat on the edge of the bed, then rolled a pant leg up and slipped on a black stocking.

"Valla. Tell me about this place. It speaks of family and love, but Kol and Kieren—" I didn't know if I should mention their obvious rift.

"My brothers." She snorted. "Yeah, they're total dumbasses."

"What happened?" I couldn't keep my curiosity from getting the better of me any longer. Prying or not, I needed to know what had put that scar on Kol's face, the limp in Kieren's gait, the darkness between two brothers who had once loved each other dearly.

She sat on the bed next to me as I slipped on the other stocking.

"Do you know about my parents' deaths?"

I nodded.

She blew out a breath that lifted her fair bangs off her forehead. "My father served as a member of the Cloven Senate. His death was diagnosed as a heart attack, but Kol thought otherwise. Father had spoken to him of leaving Cloven altogether, as he'd been opposed so often on the Senate, not always sharing their views."

"Views on what, if I might ask?"

Her blue eyes shimmered emerald in the warm light of the lantern on the wall. "Race, politics, Morgon dominance in the corporate arena. There were some clans pushing for Morgon dominance, a boycott of Gladium where Morgons were merging with human companies."

"I imagine the Coalglass clan was one of them." My stomach twisted at the thought of Barron.

"True. But they weren't the only ones." She tucked one leg under her, sitting on her foot. "So my father was one of few who opposed the majority. There was a significant vote looming that would boycott all imports and exports from Gladium. My father was on the side of Morgon and human merchants in Gladium who did business with open-minded Morgon merchants in Cloven. Because the taxes were too high for small Morgon merchants to ever make a significant living inside Cloven alone, many had reached out to Gladium to export their goods. They'd always have to bow and scrape to the nobility, who kept them under heel."

"Then your father died. Before the vote."

She smirked. "Smart girl."

"And Kol believed it to be something other than a heart attack."

She nodded. "Though only the eldest by a few minutes, Kol should've taken Father's place on the Senate, but he renounced his position. However, Kieren wanted his place in government. As the son next in line, it was his right. Kol forbid Kieren from taking it." She flipped her hair over one shoulder. "You can imagine that didn't go over very well. So the two idiots got into a scuffle, which escalated into maiming one another."

"I can't believe it," I said, glancing at the family portrait and the two happy brothers.

"Believe it. Men are fools. Morgon men are worse." She hopped off the bed, hands on hips, looking at the portrait on her vanity. "Unfortunately, I happen to love those damn fools. I just wish they'd forgive and forget. Move on." She led me toward the door. "I will say that since Kol has been investigating the disappearance of the Gladium girls, he's talked to Kieren more in a month than he normally does in a year."

We walked through the kitchen to meet with Bowen and Kieren, both seated in the living area. The gas lanterns were lit around the room, covers removed from the furniture. The cabin was truly charming. I wanted to see it by sunlight, the windows uncovered, the open sky through the skylights. They quieted when we walked in, masculine eyes travelling over me.

Looking quite different than I did in my baggy jeans and borrowed trench, my hair still in braids twined with gold falling halfway down my back, I wasn't so naïve to not know how I looked to the opposite sex. I crossed my arms and sunk into a chair, trying to steer attention away from me.

"Hey. Boys. Stop thinking whatever it is you're thinking," snapped Valla.

Heat crawled up my cheeks. Bowen stood swiftly. "I'll watch for them outside."

"Them?" I asked, wanting, needing to change the subject.

Kieren stood, crossing his arms. "Kol was already en route to Cloven, having gotten a tip from someone in Cloven that Gaius was spotted flying toward the east bank with a large bundle strapped to him."

"So you talked to him?" I asked.

A stiff nod. "I relayed all of the information Gaius had given us. And of course, I told him that you are safe."

"Sit," said Valla. "Relax. I'll get us some tea."

Sit. Relax. No way in hell could I relax, my stomach flipping somersaults. Still, I sat, wringing my hands, and waited.

Valla returned a few minutes later with hot tea in a saucer, a pattern I recognized from Gladium.

"This is a Bridewell pattern, isn't it?"

"Yes." She smiled. "The set was an anniversary gift from my father to my mother."

"How beautiful." I admired the teacup, not so much for the twining-vines pattern, but because it reflected the love of Kol's parents.

"Remember those merchants I mentioned earlier?"

I nodded.

"The Bridewells were one of the human families my father fought to allow to trade in Cloven."

I took another sip. The alarm at the door sounded. My teacup clattered in the saucer. I set it on a side table, hands shaking.

Standing, we all faced the door, waiting to see if it was Bowen or—

A snap of wings folding, seven feet of fierce Morgon man barreled through the entrance, pure dragon eyes blazing silver. The Morgon honed in on me in a millisecond, my heart leaping into my throat.

"Kol."

Chapter 24

He stood in the entrance, still as death, an electric charge rolling off his body, filling the room with his broad frame and larger-than-life presence. I'd stopped breathing the second I saw him. With predatory gait, he came for me. Scowl deep, jaw clenched, scar taut against the hard angle of his face, I trembled, watching him storm closer. Not from fear. From agonizing anticipation of his touch. The need a visceral torture.

With five long strides, blue-black wings half-extended, he gripped me in a vise, molding my body against his, fisting my hair, sucking the breath right out of my lungs as he crushed his mouth over mine. I slid my hands over his shoulders, around his neck, nothing but tight, flexed muscle beneath. Ignoring our audience, I tried to pull him closer.

His body a rigid wall of flesh-encased steel, I couldn't help the small sound of pleasure that escaped my lips. He jerked back, pulling us apart a fraction. Without even glancing at his siblings, eyes still for me, only for me, he scooped me in his arms and leaped upward, winging us to the loft. Three more strides and we were in a bedroom, his foot slamming the door closed.

Pitch black hemmed us in. He had me stretched out on the bed in less than a second, covering me with his body, devouring my lips once more. Nipping. Biting. Sucking on my tongue. Groaning like a dying man. I opened wider—my mouth, my legs—wanting more of him. His breathing was jagged, his movements shaky, hands trembling as they roamed over me, my breasts, my ribs, squeezing my hip. He shook as if he were borderline hypothermic, his body in shock.

"Skin," he growled.

He ripped my pants down my legs and off my body, no panties underneath. He stripped off my shirt before I knew what had happened, pinning me before I could even take a breath.

"I want skin, too," I murmured against his lips.

Fumbling in the dark, I found the zippers of his back flaps underneath his wings and pulled. He yanked off the shirt and tossed it away. Pressing me into the mattress, I sensed his wings spreading wide above us, a cave of heat walling us in. Seeing nothing but slits of silver, I smoothed my hands up and down his shoulders, arms, roving over his chest, twining in his hair. That electric charge snapped in the air, warning me of his volatile state.

"Moira, I can't stop. I need, I need—"

He hovered over me, holding his weight on his forearms, knowing his dominance had him knotted and ready to spring. He needed to be inside me, to be as close as he possibly could after fearing for my death for so long. He needed the deepest, most primal level of connection. Because I did, too.

"Shhh." I nipped at his jaw, light feminine bites and kisses as I slid my hands lower, unzipping his pants. He didn't move, holding himself above me, letting me take control. Sliding my hands lower, I stroked his thick length, surprised that I'd already had it inside my body. There would be pain again, but pleasure, too. Great pleasure.

I sighed, spreading my legs, scooting my pelvis up so I could guide him, our fevered panting the only sound. He pierced my slick heat, thrusting hard and deep the way he needed to. The way I needed him to. I cried out, the sharp sensation of pain lost the second his throbbing shaft sheathed to the hilt. He took my mouth, groaning as he licked and tasted, his tongue stroking deep. All of him stroking deep. A wave of emotion flooded through my body to have him once again fill me.

Letting me have some of his weight, he pounded into me, over and over. I wrapped my ankles at the small of his back, anchoring myself to him, letting him drive as hard as he wanted, the sensation spinning me higher.

"Kol," I whispered in his ear. "I needed…"

Before I could form another thought or say another word, I cried out, coming hard and fast. Too fast.

He sheathed himself deep and stilled, cupping my breast in a possessive hold, letting me ride out the orgasm, wave after wave, as I whimpered beneath him. I felt a tear slip from one eye and across my cheek, the release of emotion too much for me. Kol kissed up the damp trail left behind, drying the path with his lips, moving again inside me, slow and sweet.

The hand on my breast slid beneath my bottom, gripping one cheek as he rolled his spine, thrusting in a steady rhythm, again and again. His lips brushed against mine, less desperate, more gentle. Less frantic, more sensual. His tongue teased my lips. I opened for him on a gasp. He sucked my lower lip, tasting in a tender way.

"Moira." His voice, gravel-on-stone in the thick darkness of the room, heavy with lust and need and something much, much more. "I can't live without you." A deep stroke of his shaft, slamming hard, but slow. "I want you. Always."

His words, his body, and his hard, demanding desire drove me near madness. Loving me with an intensity that burned fire-bright, he pushed me to the edge before calling me back again.

"Is this"—I rocked my hips up to meet him. He hissed in a breath— "your declaration of love?"

"Yes," was his instant, broken reply.

My heart skipped a beat. His often brutal, and now vulnerable honesty, cut me like winter wind. I wound one hand in his hair, pulling his mouth down to my own. A moaning growl rumbled through his chest to mine. I kissed him deeply, stroking my tongue along his, matching his need, his aggression, as best I could.

He pulled away, panting as he continued to pump inside me. "You're making me insane." He sucked my neck, marking me, driving his scent deeper into my skin.

I fisted my fingers into his hair, pressing him harder against me, begging for more. He buried his face against my neck. What was it about him that made me feel powerful and powerless at the same time? I was the strongest woman in the world when he said my name with such adoration, loved my body with desperation, and pushed me higher toward climax as if my pleasure was all that mattered in the world. And yet, I was the most vulnerable I'd ever been—caged beneath his massive body, enveloped by his powerful wings, and captured within his sensual embrace. Soaring higher and sinking faster was the most glorious sensation I'd ever felt. I wanted, hoped, he felt it, too.

Nipping his earlobe with my teeth, I whispered, "Show me how you feel."

His other hand cupped beneath me, both large hands gripping my bottom, fingers digging into flesh, his weight spreading me wider. He tilted my bottom up, stroking till he hit the sweetest place. "What you do to me, Moira," he panted against my skin.

I moaned. "Oh, God."

I clawed down his back. White-hot passion racked my body, wringing me out, stroke by stroke.

"Tell me who you want, Moira. Tell me who you belong to."

Pounding me with fierce unrestraint, I was engulfed by something rare, something raw, something so deep and real. And I knew I would never feel this way with anyone but him. There would never *be* anyone but him. Ever again.

"You." I gasped, my inner walls pulsing around him.

He stiffened, buried inside me, releasing his seed into my body. For a split second, I feared pregnancy, even after that monster king had said I wasn't "breeding." Never before had I considered having children, but after the brief time I'd been intimate with Kol, I wanted to give him children. I wanted to give him everything.

I loved him.

So I pulled his head down and whispered that very thing in the pitch dark, our sweaty bodies aligned and intertwined as one. I was unable to say the words too loud, only in a whisper, afraid they might change this moment in some terrible, irrevocable way. But all I felt was the loving sweep of his mouth over mine—no tongue, no penetration—only lips on lips, brushing a tender caress. Acceptance of my gift, my open heart. As I accepted his.

After a moment of silence and sweet touching, he slid out of me. I heard him moving, though I could see nothing. He blew a bright line of yellow flame, lighting a three-tiered candlestick on the bedside table.

Disinterested in the room, I took in the sight of my magnificent man by candlelight. He lay on his side, wings folded to his back, eyes roving over me. Unaccustomed to being examined in the nude, I wasn't shy for some reason. Not with him.

One of his hands traveled a light trail over my hip and across my ribs, circled my abdomen, then back up between my breasts, stopping suddenly. He gazed at the mark high on my cheek, his expression darkening to a storm.

"Kol. I'm okay." His expression remained unchanged. I cupped his face between my hands, forcing him to look at me, the dragon vivid in hard planes. "I'm safe."

Finally, he blinked, stony expression softening. "Tell me what happened."

His fingers resumed their petting trail up and down my waist, brushing in soothing sweeps, reminding me that I was now safe in his arms.

He seemed to be forcing himself to slow his breathing, to calm the rage after seeing the mark on my cheek. So I told him in quick, clipped succession how I was taken, chained, and held captive, leaving out how close the monster king came to making me his breeder.

Kol's fingers rounded my hip and stopped, his gaze finding mine. "Who gave you the mark on the cheek?"

Gor. "He's dead."

"Good." He pulled loose one of my braids, untwining the plait and lifting the gold ribbon to his nose. "And who were you made into a concubine for?"

My pulse sped ahead. "Why would you say that?"

He proceeded to undo the braids hanging by my temple with gentle fingers, pulling the gold ribbons and tossing them away.

"Long ago, dragon kings kept human concubines, but never sired a child with one. Radomis was the first to take a human woman as a wife." The ring around his iris glowed white within a sea of deep blue. "There are millennium-old paintings in some of our museums depicting the ancient ones, their slave girls dressed in white tunics, gold ribbons braided into their hair."

"Why gold?" I managed to ask evenly.

"Gold is the element of royalty, a dragon king. It labels them as his property." His voice dipped low and soft as a whisper. "So, tell me, Moira. This bastard of a king had planned to keep you as his concubine, hadn't he?"

Pause. I nodded. Now I knew why Kieren's mood was so dark after his dreamwalking chat with his brother. He'd told Kol all about this monster Morgon who led this dark charade. I decided the best thing was to be honest with him about my experience.

"Concubine sounds rather kind. He was looking for a breeder, not a lover." I winced at the memory of those monstrous hands on me, his eyes raking me as if I were a precious piece of livestock. "But, Kol, I injected him with poison. Gaius gave me a way to escape, gave us both a way to escape."

Kol's eyes slid closed, a tremble shuddering through him. "I'll be forever grateful to Gaius, for what he risked in saving you."

There was no need to point out he risked his life. And lost it. There was more to tell about Gaius but not now.

Kol's sharp features seemed kinder in the candlelight. His hands threaded through my hair, draping the long strands on the mattress. We lay sideways in the bed, never making it to the pillows. His fierce passion had consumed us both.

I stared at the line down his cheek. "Kol."

"Hmm."

"Why didn't you have an Icewing heal this?" I traced a finger there. "Not that I mind it at all. Actually, I kind of like it, but—"

He stopped my mouth with a soft kiss.

"No need to explain." He sighed, seeming to remember. "I didn't want it to be healed. I wanted the reminder of what I'd done. I regretted what I'd done to Kieren, injuring him that way, my own blood." Regret laced every word. "But I couldn't take it back. I thought, well, I thought I deserved the scar."

I leaned up and kissed the center.

"Perhaps it's time you two let those wounds heal."

A tender smile from my not-so-icy Morgon man. "Perhaps."

My eyes dropped to the pulse in his neck, still thrumming hard. I remembered the heat of his kiss, languishing in the near-memory. A small sigh escaped me.

His mouth ticked up into a half-smile. "What, Moira? I can see the wheels turning in your head."

I shrugged one bare shoulder. "I was just wondering something."

"That something being what exactly?"

If I wanted to know, I had to take the plunge. "Soulfire."

His fingers curled to wrap my waist. "What about soulfire?" No inflection.

"I wonder…I mean…" I tried to find the words, the courage to ask him what I needed to know. He slid his hand over the curve of my hip and back up to my waist, waiting patiently.

"Why haven't you mentioned it yet? If you feel the way you do about me, isn't that something you'd want to share with me?"

Sex with Kol was mind-melting, but I knew he hadn't given me soulfire. My sister had once told me it wasn't something she could express in words, but something you'd recognize the instant it happened.

His gaze left the contours of my body, meeting my own. "I won't bond with you in that way, Moira."

My heart fell, my blood running cold. Clearing my throat, I managed to ask, "Because…it doesn't burn that way for me?"

His hand continued its exploration of my body. He gave a sort of snorting laugh. "Oh. It burns that way." His gaze raked over me, his words telling me the fire wasn't remotely extinguished. "The truth is that my mother suffered terribly when my father died. They were heartbound, and the pain she endured was unbearable." His fingers curved around my waist again, tightening. "I'd never do that to you. I don't wish you to suffer. Ever."

His words were ice, his eyes were molten—soft, filled with affection. My blood warmed at once. "But, Kol. Don't you want that bond? Isn't that what Morgonkind longs for?"

He shook his head. "Not at that price."

I frowned. "You'll suffer instead." I lifted a hand, tracing his scar in the half-light. "Lucius told me the Morgon male is in pain around his mate till he can release it."

"Lucius should keep his mouth shut." He brushed a lock of hair off my shoulder. "Don't worry about me. Just tell me you'll have me."

"I'll have you." I smiled. "As many times as you want. You're not all that bad in bed."

His hand drifted south again and pinched my bottom. "Kittycat likes to tease, does she?"

I laughed, squirming to get away. He threw a heavy leg across my thighs, leaning his chest partly against mine, easily containing me. Though in all honesty, I didn't really want to get away.

"Moira, Moira, Moira. What am I going to do with you?"

I laughed, my chest rising and falling with the exertion, drawing his eyes. My brain hazed when he got that look, full of stricken desire—for me.

"Be still, Kittycat. I want to pet you."

"Pfft." I rolled my eyes, casting off an air of bravado, while my insides turned to jelly. "I'm not an animal, Kol."

His hand trailed down my abdomen, sliding along the slick apex between my legs. I gripped his bicep, sucking in a sharp breath, feeling the muscle tense and ripple. No way was he budging.

"No. But you certainly like being petted." I closed my eyes on a sigh, sinking into the sensation of his fingers working my sensitive cleft in a gentle rhythm. "Don't you, Moira?" He spoke in a hoarse whisper. His voice moved closer. His thumb massaged my nub, making me even wetter as another finger probed my entrance in a slow circle, teasing. "Don't you?"

I wouldn't lie to him, not even when he was performing delicious torture on my body that deserved a false response. I would erect no more walls between us now that I'd crossed that threshold, giving myself to him body and soul.

"Yes," I murmured, rocking up against his steady strokes. His mouth opened over mine, tongue taking possession of its domain.

Then he punished me for my teasing. And I knew I'd tease him again as soon and as often as I could.

Chapter 25

I awoke to muffled voices coming from downstairs. The candles on the three-tiered candelabra had burned down to one-inch stumps. I'd snoozed a long time.

A light shone into the room from a connected bathroom. I decided a shower wouldn't go amiss, knowing the extrasensory Morgons could sniff out any scent on me. I blushed at the thought.

The bedroom was stark—no furniture but a bed and side table. Definitely Kol's room. In the bathroom, sealed river-rock tiled the floor and standing triple-man shower. Four spouts poured from the ceiling when I turned the faucet. I had never considered the idea Morgons needed to wash their wings as well as their bodies. And even for Morgons, Kol was exceptionally large. Exceptionally.

After a quick shower in steaming spray, I redressed in Valla's clothes and wound my damp hair into a long, tight braid. I pondered Kol's refusal to take the step into heartbinding. Of course, I never thought I'd be so eager to commit. I was many things, but a liar wasn't one of them. Not even to myself. Kol was everything to me. I wanted to be the same to him. An impossibility if he withheld the one thing that all Morgons held as the pinnacle of a mated pair's intimacy.

I shook off my anxiety and walked out onto the loft balcony. A host of faces stared up at me as I stood on the edge. There were a few newcomers—Lorian, Kraven, and Conn.

Kieren's face tilted into a smug smile. "That's quite a predicament, Moira darling."

Hand on hip, I dared him to say another word.

Kol gave him a scathing look as he stood from the sofa. With one beat of his wings, he landed in front of me, blocking out our audience. "Sorry."

I shrugged, wondering how difficult it might be to try to fit into his world. My sister didn't seem to have a problem, but Kol didn't live in

Gladium. He visited. His world was Drakos and Cloven and places like this—ones that didn't factor in the needs of a human.

Kol lifted me close. "Are you okay?"

I nodded with a half-smile as he brought us back to the ground floor.

"You might need to install stairs there, brother." Kieren grinned, but Kol made no remark, making me wonder what exactly our relationship status was. He wanted me, he had said. But he didn't want the final binding that would tie us to each other forever. Was this truly about his mother? Or that he didn't plan on this being long-term?

Lorian stepped closer. "Are you all right?"

"Yes." I managed a weak smile.

"I had orders from two hysterical women to ensure you were safe and unharmed."

"I'm sure that you did. Rest assured." I squeezed his arm. "So what's the plan?"

We all faced Kol in a semi-circle, some sitting, some standing. Valla moved to stand by me, handing me a pair of long, lace-up brown boots. I leaned against the arm of the sofa to slip on the first one.

She leaned in close. "Glad you got rid of that floral scent. It was overkill."

Tilting my head as I tied the laces, I whispered, "No weird smells, now?"

"Well"—she winked—"my brother. And he's a little weird."

I smiled, slipping on the other boot just as that same brother cleared his throat.

"We're all aware there's a spy either in the Morgon Guard or in Nightwing Security," said Kol.

"Or in both," added Lorian.

Kol gave a tight nod. "Which is why I've chosen you to escort us back to Gladium. Lorian's top men." He gave a nod to Kraven and Conn. "And mine." He glanced at Bowen, then to his brother. Kieren wore no smirk now—his expression grave and...proud. Lastly, he dipped his chin at Valla.

"I'm not one of your best *men*, brother."

"No, but you might as well be. You're deadlier than just about every soldier in the Morgon Guard."

Valla grinned at that.

"Our plan is to speed directly for Paxon Nightwing's place in Willow Woods outside of Gladium." Paxon was Lucius and Lorian's cousin. Their fathers were brothers. Paxon's mate and wife, Ella, was expecting her baby any day now, so I knew it was serious for us to descend on them. "Their home is known only to direct family members, and would be an unexpected place for us to hide away from the city. But we need somewhere isolated where we can further evaluate the information Gaius was able to smuggle out to us."

Heavy silence weighted the room, remembering Gaius.

"What we do know," Kol added, "is that scouting parties will be flying between Cloven, Drakos, and Gladium to intercept us."

Kol whipped out a map from his inside jacket pocket. After spreading it on a low table, he pointed to the valley region southeast of Cloven.

"We're here." He trailed his finger along the valley near the mountain region of Feygreir where his home was. "If we skirt the western side of Drakos, past Singing Wind Wood, we can keep outside the area where scouting parties expect us to be."

Kieren nodded. "That should be the safest route."

"Agreed," said Lorian. "If we're lucky, they may believe we already gave them the slip and have called off the scouting parties."

Kol's piercing gaze scanned each one of them. "Let's go then."

Valla tossed a pair of leather gloves to me. "You'll need these."

"Thanks."

Kieren and Bowen slipped into another room off the living area. As Kol took my hand, leading me to the door, I noted it was a small armory. Swords, daggers, jagged weapons of steel lined within a wall-to-wall glass case. Kieren handed Bowen a quiver of steel-tipped arrows and a bow.

Kraven must have been well-armed as he marched directly outside.

Conn stood to one side, thumbs hooked in his front pockets, staring at Valla with a mischievous grin on his face. "You don't need to arm yourself, Blondie?"

She passed right behind him, nose in the air, twisting with brutal speed, whipping out her rapiers from concealed sheaths, and criss-crossing them at his neck. If he were an enemy, she could behead him in two seconds.

Conn grinned wider. "Someone's a bit sensitive."

"I'm not sensitive, *Red*." His smile slipped. "I'm just always armed. Best remember that."

"Oh, I don't think you'd ever let me forget it."

"Got that right."

She whipped her rapiers away, the steel-on-steel zinging a vibration in the air before she sheathed them in scabbards sewn into her pants. I'd thought they were just odd-shaped pockets.

Kol tugged me along as I'd craned my neck to watch the display.

"What was that all about?"

Kol shook his head. "Those two have hated each other from afar for a very long time. Whenever they're forced into one another's company, they always exchange a few barbs."

Considering the heated exchange, I imagined what might happen if that anger transformed into another kind of passion. Maybe they fought to avoid other emotions brewing under the surface. I didn't have any more time to consider it as we stepped through the cabin door.

Once in the night air, a cool mist wrapped me in a chilly embrace. Billowing vapor hovered on the lake and around the cabin, curling slowly in the breeze, layering the night in white.

Behind me, I heard buckles clink together. Kol unfolded the harness we'd used before.

"Why do you call this place Blind Bird Falls?"

I cinched the harness strap around my waist and buckled it tight. Kol had strapped his part of the harness to himself already.

"You see that tree over there?" He pointed to the massive evergold, the one with arm-like branches stretching far and wide.

"I do."

"Kieren and I used to play a game with Valla there. We'd hide a bread roll somewhere in the branches and blindfold her. Using her Morgon senses, she had to find the prize."

"What if she fell?" Yanking the harness tight across his chest, he arched an eyebrow. Then it hit me. "Wings. How could I forget?"

"She was never in any danger."

"Still"—I finished the last strap—"it seems kind of dangerous as a child's game."

"The Morgon world is different than the human's."

I'd begun to see that, wondering if I had any place in his world. Perhaps Kol was right in choosing not to heartbond with me. Maybe his instincts were better than mine.

He spun me around and pulled me flush against his chest, buckling us together. Leaning down, he whispered, "I like the way you feel against me like this."

I lifted my chin in the air, refusing to meet his heated gaze over my shoulder. "I'm sure you do. I think you just like having me bound to you and at your mercy."

"Oh. No doubt of it."

"Hmph. You'd best just keep your eye on the sky and your head out of the gutter."

His arms wrapped around my front. "Later." A quick kiss on my neck as he braced me in his arms.

I stared up at the smudge of moon hidden behind billowy clouds. "Fly, Moonring."

"As my mistress commands."

With one bend of the legs, we rocketed into the night sky, flying low over the lake, moving south. I gripped the straps crossing my chest, the best place to "hang on." Though I had no real control at all. I hoped Kol understood how much trust this took for a human, placing my life in his hands. Literally.

Flanked on our right were Kieren, Valla, and Bowen, their wings dark against a mist-gray night. To the left in V-formation were Lorian, Kraven, and Conn. Because of the haze, we steered closer to the ground, rather than find cover in the clouds.

We moved swiftly over and out of the valley, crossing a rocky, barren wasteland. We finally drew close to Gladium, flying over the frosted forest of Singing Wind Woods.

I'd muffled my face behind the collar of my trench, but still the cold seeped into my cheeks and gloved fingers. Kol's arms tightened around me. "You're shivering."

I snorted a laugh. "Humans aren't built for flying in the freezing cold." I couldn't hide the tone of bitterness from leaking into my voice.

"What's wrong, Moira?"

"Nothing. I just—"

Slam!

My body jerked sideways. Someone gripped my arm. I caught a flash of yellow wings. One of Kol's arms left me, then the other as he grappled mid-air with two, maybe three Morgons. We spun toward earth. I punched at the Sunsting soldier gripping my arm, my fist glancing off, landing nowhere. A flare of silver. A dagger. I screamed, kicking and struggling. The whole time we were surrounded and gripped by the enemy, wings flapping, all of us falling in a mass of grappling limbs.

The cries of mid-air battle echoed above us. A fireball burst from someone, beaming across the inky sky. The distinct singing of Valla's Drakonian steel clanged against another. One of Bowen's arrows whistled through the air, hitting a large target.

The solder who gripped my arm swung his dagger toward me. No, he wasn't aiming for me. It was the straps linking me to Kol.

Juliette Cross

"No!" I screamed.

I was yanked away from him. A bellowing growl filled the night. I glimpsed Kol held by two Morgons as we still spun mid-air—one trying to stab a knife in his chest, the other attempting to stab him in the back. He had both men by the throats, squeezing the life out of them, his face contorted in rage. The one with a death-grip on my arm sliced through air, severing the other strap.

"Kol!"

Feeling our bonds broken, silver eyes whipped to mine. His great wings beat furiously to free himself from the grips of the other men. I dangled in the hold of my captor. He laughed, his hand wrapping my wrist.

"You want her, Moonring? Go get her."

The vise on my wrist released me, tossing me into the night. I screamed. So did Kol. "Moira!"

Falling, falling, falling.

Breathless. I flailed my arms, helpless to save myself.

Treetops filled my vision. Frozen, craggy branches stabbed upward, as if rocketing toward me, though it was my body plummeting down. I closed my eyes, unable to watch my death come closer. I stilled my limbs and opened my arms, finding peace in no longer fighting for control, because there was none to be had. I pictured the one who meant the most to me in all the world—hard planes, icy stare, warm hands, warmer heart.

"I love you," I whispered into the wailing wind.

Arms wrapped around me from behind. We sped toward the earth, avoiding the trees.

"Tell him so the next time you're alone."

"Kieren!" Tears streamed as he shifted me in his arms so I could hold onto him.

"Hang on, Moira darling. I've got you."

In the dense growth of trees, he didn't set me down, but flew close to the ground into the heavier woodlands where massive evergolds grew close together. "I need to hide you."

I could hear someone yell not far behind us. "Moonring!"

Barron Coalglass. My heart hammered against my ribcage. Kieren banked hard left toward a fat, hollowed-out tree. He dropped me inside, but it was too late. Barron was upon us. Kieren whipped around, wings up. I burrowed farther into the hollow of the tree, loose bark crumbling on my shoulders.

"I know she's there," crooned Barron. "As soon as I kill you, I'll find her."

"You make it sound so easy, Coalglass."

"It will be. You've spent too many days in the Senate, Moonring. Your hands have grown soft, your hide thin."

"Is that so?" Kieren circled, leading Barron away from the tree. "I'll give it to you. Even leaderless, your operation seems to be functioning well." He drew him farther away into a clearing.

Barron laughed. "Leaderless?" His chilling tone pierced me with cold hatred, his voice a viper's sting. "She tried. But failed."

My heart plummeted. I couldn't read Kieren's expression from this distance, but the silent pause told me he digested the truth of the statement. Barron wasn't bluffing.

"Your king lives?"

"Oh, yes." Having circled around, Barron was now opposite Kieren in the clearing, facing me. Arrogance and triumph dripped from his voice. "Poison has no effect on my lord and master. Unfortunately, the sedative she dosed him with did. Even so, he no longer wants her for just a breeder."

Relief washed over me until he spoke again.

"He wants her for much more. *After* he punishes her."

My heart sank, stomach clenching tight. Barron's black eyes found me in the gloom. "And I intend to help him do just that. As soon as I dispatch you"—he glanced upward—"he'll be along shortly, so let's get this over with."

Barron lunged, lightning-swift with the aid of his wings, slicing a concealed dagger across Kieren's chest. Kieren cried out. The two grappled and fought, steel swinging, wings flapping. I cringed, watching the two fall to the ground. A crunch of wings. Barron bellowed, blowing a line of orange flame, singeing Kieren. Another cry.

I glanced up through the barren trees, fearing I'd see the monster, looking for help, finding no one. A panting struggle. Blood gurgling in someone's throat. The two Morgons collapsed, one on top of the other.

Both still as death.

Terrified, I tip-toed into the open, crunching fallen leaves beneath my feet. Kieren splayed unmoving atop Barron, whose staring, black eyes showed no spark of life. Careful of Kieren's wings, I pulled him by the shoulder, rolling him off of Barron. Kieren's short-sword was buried to the hilt under Barron's ribs, blood pouring a dark pool into the ground.

The front of Kieren's shirt was burned away, his entire chest a mass of seared flesh. But his chest rose and fell. Alive.

"Oh, Kieren."

I didn't dare touch him further, knowing the pain of the burn probably knocked him unconscious. I curled into a trembling ball next to his body and waited.

No one came. Time stretched. My shivering grew more violent, wracking my body from teeth to toes. So cold.

I heard nothing but a night bird in the tree above me, a scurrying animal in the fallen leaves, the wind singing a solemn tune through silvery branches. My fingers stopped stinging. My breath grew shallow.

Singing Wind Woods.

Petrus said there was magic in this place. That it clung to the Moonring Morgons because their clan was first born in these woods. Would it protect me because I was beloved by Kol? Would it keep me from dying?

"Please protect us," I whispered to the woods, voice broken.

My thoughts hazed. My mind drifted. I wasn't cold anymore. I couldn't feel my fingers or my feet. I couldn't feel much at all.

Something slunk close to the ground along the trunks of trees, drawing closer. A flash of orange-gold light, then it vanished. Or so I thought. It reappeared among the roots of the closest oak. Thin, spindly limbs, like these branches. Feline. Familiar.

"Hello?" My voice was hoarse, hardly making sound at all.

It meant me no harm, slinking nearer. Round, golden eyes peered close to my face.

I smiled. "Seerie."

Petrus's pet, the necrominx. She lowered her black nose and touched it to mine, shocking my body with a spark of vibration. Warmth spread into my blood, flowing into my chest, my limbs, fingers, and toes. I began to shake, my teeth chattering.

She burrowed into the curve of my abdomen, radiating mystical heat straight into my body. I could feel the blood pumping faster into my cheeks and nose. Soft fur brushed under my chin.

There was no doubt now. Magic did live in these woods, and I was favored. Blessed. I wouldn't die. I would have the chance to see my love again. Such a precious gift made me weep with joy. Seerie shifted, licking the tear from my cheek, tongue rough but tender. I laughed, chest aching from the slow thaw of my body.

"Th-th-thank you."

The necrominx snuggled under my chin, a rough purr rumbling against my neck.

I wouldn't waste this gift. I must swallow all fear, all pride, and tell Kol what he truly meant to me. That even without the bond of soulfire, he was everything to me.

The wind blew a sweet melody, whistling and singing through the trees, as if angels lived here, carrying their ethereal song to those it loved best. Silver branches waved in the wind, brushing and rustling, making their own music of the night. I felt cradled in warmth and safety, the necrominx close to my heart, wind-song caressing my soul. I whispered again to the spirits here, lips trembling. "Thank you."

Seerie lifted her head and pricked her ears. She stepped lightly to the edge of the tree line, staring back, imploring me with orange eyes to follow. She was right. We had to find Kol and the others. With warmth in my limbs, I moved to follow, touching a hand to Kieren's cheek. "We'll bring help. Hold on."

He appeared lifeless, though a pulse still beat in his throat. I forced myself to leave him, knowing Seerie would lead me to Petrus's cabin.

Seerie slipped through the woods more urgently, stopping every few yards to glance over her shoulder. Her fey eyes darted in all directions. She hopped over a protruding root from a thick-trunked tree. These evergolds were old, branches hanging thick and heavy, their knotty and gnarled roots protruding high out of the earthen floor.

Seerie paused, her gaze shooting straight into the sky. Hissing, she implored with her eyes for me to follow.

I stared up, seeing nothing, but obeyed anyway. A prickling of fear crept up my spine. She crawled into a deep groove between jutting roots. I did the same, crouching down, back against the trunk, curling my legs into a ball. Seerie pressed her body against my legs. The familiar spark of necrominx magic enveloped me, darkening the shadows around the tree to deepest pitch just as the sound of great wings beat overhead.

Sucking in a breath, I froze, watching the monster king land a short distance away, folding massive black wings to his back. I felt a growl quiver in Seerie's belly. The beast-like Morgon pivoted his head in all directions, lifting his nose into the air, inhaling deep. Then he swiveled his head toward us and stepped forward.

Trembling in the dark, I prayed that whatever magic this little feline had, it was enough to hide us from the creature stalking closer. His voice rumbled when he spoke, like boulders rolling down a mountain, sending a shiver through my frame. "I can smell you." The crooked grin creasing his sharp-angled face made me cringe. He opened his arms, clawed hands extended. "Come to me."

He laced those three words with a pulse of dominance, which rippled outward from his body. It beat against my chest, snatching my will and forcing me to move forward. I was no match for Morgon magic.

"No," I whimpered, tears pricking, unable to withstand the compulsion to obey.

Seerie hissed when I moved out of her supernatural shadow, bounding away into the woods, leaving me alone…with him. I stood, my back ramrod straight, my body yielding to his will as it had done before.

With a feral gleam in his eyes, he puffed up his bare chest and moved toward me—controlled, powerful—with slow, purposeful steps. His prey caught, there was no hurry.

Wrapping his fist around my braid, he gave a tight yank, tilting my chin upward. I yelped. He curved his other hand around my waist, claws digging into my back through my clothes.

I trembled under the scrutiny of his serpentine eyes with slit pupils gazing their fill. He bent his head and inhaled my scent. "You've fucked him again."

I couldn't respond. His eyes narrowed, mouth drawn in a tight line. "I'm not accustomed to my servants defying me." His voice grated against my skin, claws piercing my skin.

"I'm n-not your servant."

His grip tightened in my hair.

"Ah!" I gasped.

"No. You are not a servant." His mouth cut into an obscene smile, revealing a row of canine teeth. He relished my pain. "You will be my queen. There is only one way to scrape your lover's scent from your skin."

Heart hammering, I pushed against his shoulders to no avail. His grip held hard, his motive sure. He wanted…

"Soulfire," I whispered, nearly choking on the word.

"Yes."

I kicked and fought with my arms and legs, the rest of me pinioned against him.

"Be still!" His voice thundered with Morgon dominance. I bowed my back, the torture of defying his will paralyzing me. "Succumb to me, and the pain will go away."

"No." I shook my head, frantic.

"You must." His beastly features contorted to reveal the savage monster he truly was. "If you do not, everyone you know will die."

Captured in his fiery gaze, I saw the crumpled bodies of Lucius and Jessen in a pool of blood. I saw my parents ripped into pieces on their living room floor. I saw Lucius tossed off the roof of a high-rise with broken wings. I saw Kris, Macon, Sorcha, Lorian, Valla, Kieren, Kraven, Conn—all of them—glassy-eyed and lifeless. Finally, across my mind flashed an image of the one I loved most, stretched on a floor, beaten beyond recognition with the cool, void expression of death frozen in place. I didn't know whether he put those images in my head somehow or whether I conjured them myself. The impact was the same.

I swallowed the lump swelling in my throat. I had no choice.

"Yield to me," he commanded. His eyes flickered to the medal dangling at the hollow of my neck. "Be what she never was. Be my queen."

Saint Portia.

Oh, God. This beast, this abomination was...Larkos? It wasn't possible, and yet I knew it as surely as the stars hung in the sky, as the wind whispered through the trees. Larkos Nightwing, the first Morgon who wiped out all of dragonkind, held me pinioned in his arms, demanding that I be his queen, be what Portia never could.

I *could* be what she never was. The death of him.

Something had happened between them. Their heartbond wasn't strong enough. She killed herself in vain, unable to seal his fate as well.

But I could.

I could bond him to me, accept his horrific embrace, his barbaric body, his heartless heart. I could wind him around me in a way where my death would unequivocally equal his. I could kill this beast clutching me in his arms as if I were already his possession.

Kol would never forgive me. But he would live. As would my family and friends.

"Yield," he growled, tightening his grip on my braid, my scalp pulling in pain.

"Yes." Pulse pounding a death knell, tears streaming in hot protest, I gave him my consent. "I will be your queen."

Triumph spread across his face as he lowered his lips to mine, a growl vibrating from his chest. The moment he sealed our mouths, something slammed into us both. We tumbled sideways. I rolled out of his grip to the cold ground.

Kol loomed over the beast, rage vibrating an electric current in the air, sword slashing forward. The king flung his weight upward, knocking Kol to the side, but not before his sword lanced across his shoulder.

He yelled, swiping a sharpened claw through the air, just missing Kol's face. Ready for him, Kol swung, silver glinting, catching the tip of the beast's hand.

The creature screamed, clutching his bleeding hand. Three shadows swept into the clearing—Valla, Conn, and Lorian.

The beast's face contorted into a dark mask before he skyrocketed up into the night, breaking branches of trees as he spun upward. Lorian and Conn trailed in his wake, cracking more branches. Twigs and leaves falling like rain.

Kol flew to my side and scooped me off the forest floor.

"Kieren." I pointed the way I'd come. "He's hurt."

"Bowen and Kraven found him already," said Valla, gaze fixed on Kol. "You get her out of here." She vanished into the heavy darkness above.

Clinging tight, I pressed my cheek into the curve of his neck and shoulder, sighing at the instant warmth of my heart, safe in his arms again. But the tightness of his jaw, the steely glance of his gaze, and the iron-clad embrace nearly stopped my breath. He knew what I had nearly done. What I would have done, willingly, had he not come.

We flew under the treetops, not over. I closed my eyes and waited, hoping we didn't have far to go. Somehow I knew where we'd end up. Sure enough, when he landed and I opened my eyes, we stood within sight of Petrus's cabin. A square of yellow light glowed in the near distance.

He set me on my feet with a violent jolt, gripping my shoulders, eyes blazing like a madman. I felt his agony, a visceral lash in the air against my skin.

"You would have *bound* yourself to him?"

"Kol—I—I—"

"*No.*" He clutched me in his arms, an embrace of desperation and longing and sheer panic. One hand cradled my nape, fingers firm. The other spread against the small of my back. "Never." His words ground low, like a stone wall sliding open. "Never will you sacrifice yourself for me, for *anyone!*"

"I could've stopped him if you'd let me. I could've killed him." My ire rose with his, my fingers curling into fists against his chest. "He threatened to kill everyone—"

"I don't give a fuck if an entire *city* burns to the ground. I would have *died* without you. Don't you understand?" His hands came up, cradling my face, fingers spreading into my hair along my scalp, his hold too tight. "This is no longer your body, your heart, or your soul. It is *mine.*"

A sob escaped. "But it's not, is it?" Voice shaking, I have no idea how I could challenge such a man with the undeniable edge of insanity filling his eyes. Even so, I pushed him to the brink. "Not without soulfire, I'm not. I never will be."

The old fear skittered across his face.

"Someone once told me to never let fear lead me." I swiped the back of one hand across my cheek. "But you do. How long will you let fear lead you?"

I knew the second he snapped, the moment he took what fate had offered. I caught a glimpse of possession, obsession, and devotion from the piercing blue. Then he made me his, once and for all.

I don't know how, but a second later, I was on the ground underneath him, his glorious body pinning me to the earth. His mouth opened over mine, a brutal taking. His tongue stroked in deep. He pressed harder against my body, sealing our love with a kiss only Kol could give.

A blazing wave of liquid fire melted from his mouth into mine, streaming into my blood, rocking me through muscle and bone. I flinched at the electric shock. He pressed me harder into the cold ground, as if I needed to feel the force he wielded, the power of his love, sealing us with the flames of soulfire. My pulse pounded an erratic rhythm as molten pleasure flooded through my veins. I moaned, sucking on his tongue to feel another wave pound through my body, a rush of flowing flame.

Jessen was right. There were no words.

A growl rumbled against my chest...then I felt it. A syncing, interlocking snick, my heart beating in perfect rhythm to his. Breathless and panting, I pulled apart.

Yes. He felt it. His expression reflected my own—a profound knowing of one another locked into place. Fixed, like the brightest star in the darkest night. We didn't just belong to one another. We existed on the same plane, every breath a comingling of our love, growing, expanding, as long as we lived.

For many minutes, we did nothing but touch each other and absorb the sensation into our skin, as if love itself were a tangible blanket wrapping us in an unbreakable bond. When he pulled away from me, I was exhausted, and yet ached for more at the same time.

"Now," he said, voice like black velvet, "you are mine." He pressed his mouth more gently against my lips.

The sensual sting of soulfire slid down my throat, pouring straight to the heat between my legs. "I am yours."

He trailed his hot mouth down the tender column of my throat.

"Forever?" I asked.

"Yes." As always, Kol gave me the immediate truth, a promise that nothing could sever us in this world.

He let his teeth scrape before he licked and kissed a trail lower. Though my brain fogged and could hardly function when his mouth and hands worked on me, I needed to know something. "Kol?" My voice was little more than a whisper.

I'd avoided this question till now. I couldn't let a sorrowful answer change my decision of being bound to him. I wanted nothing more in my entire life, and I wouldn't let my own fears stand in the way.

"Yes." He lifted his head, meeting my gaze, eyes a cerulean sea. His thumb stroked a tender caress along my jaw as if I were a precious treasure he feared he would break or lose if he pressed too hard.

"Will you live my lifespan? Or, will I live yours?"

Morgons lived much longer than humans. I feared my earlier death would doom him. Yet, I had been too selfish to ask, wanting all of him no matter what the consequences might be.

Kol smiled. A wicked, lascivious smile. "Moira, my love. We are the dominant species. In all ways. Your heart will stay strong, linked to mine. And now that I have you, I plan to live longer than Petrus himself."

I laughed. He pressed his lips to mine again, soulfire singing down my throat. I whimpered, tasting the Morgon elixir of love, life, and eternal belonging. I nipped his lips.

"Can we do this again when we're alone? When we're back home." I could only imagine the pleasure of soulfire when we were bound in the most intimate of ways.

"It's my first priority."

"Of course it is."

He brushed a lingering, sensual kiss along my lips, teasing with slow precision. A soft moan escaped me. "I wish we were back home. And alone."

"So do I." He shifted over me, showing me how much he truly wished we were.

I laughed, joy buoying me up after the near-death experience in the woods. Kol grew serious all of a sudden. "Which home would that be?"

"Yours. I want to live with you."

"You'd leave Gladium for me?"

"In a heartbeat." I smiled.

"I wouldn't do that to you, Moira. We'll find a place in Gladium together, where you can do your work and I can do mine."

"What about your place in the Feygreir mountains?"

"We'll go there when we want to hide from the world."

I nipped again at his lips, so tempting. "Sounds like heaven."

"You are my heaven." His arms squeezed me tighter against him.

"And you are mine."

After Mikal, I'd decided that love wasn't all that important. That marriage could be found in some distant future of my own choosing. And the husband of my choosing would be conciliatory and passive, allowing me to chase my dreams without his interference.

What I hadn't imagined was that an exceedingly dominant man would come into my life and rattle me to the point that I didn't give a damn about my dreams, because life with him had become most important. What I hadn't imagined was that this same man—knowing my heart as well as his own, knowing my life would be incomplete without fulfilling those dreams—would insist on being my equal, my partner. Never my master. I hadn't imagined this man would be my silent, steadfast protector so that I could have every wish my heart desired. I hadn't imagined...Kol Moonring. The one who orbited my life and encircled my heart with a love beyond imagining. He was Fate fallen from the sky.

Chapter 26

The anchorwoman stood in front of the Vaenger Stadium, listing the names of the four murdered girls. Their still photos, the ones I had scanned and sent to her from my bulletin board, popped up briefly on the comm-screen.

Then she launched into the latest news. "The leader of the Devlin Butchers, Barron Coalglass of the Cloven Province, was killed in an attempt to bring him to justice by the international Morgon Guard and Gladium's own Nightwing Security team. We have Chief Jackson of the Gladium Precinct here with a statement."

The forty-something human, graying at the temples, with steel-gray eyes, stared into the camera. "Barron Coalglass was the undeniable ringleader of the so-called Devlin Butchers. Many of his gang were also killed in an attempt to apprehend them. Those who got away are in hiding, but we'll find them. There is no evidence that the escapees will continue their leader's criminal path. Therefore, the Vaenger Stadium here in Gladium is open to all of the public once again. Our forces will be vigilant in protecting the people of this city until all perpetrators are brought to justice. Thank you."

Chief Jackson gave a stiff nod and slipped off-screen.

Kol stepped into the living room of our high-rise apartment on the edge of Gladium. Less than a week since it all had happened, I moved out of my old place and into this one with him.

Kol buttoned up the front of his starched gray shirt, listening to the reporter wrap up her story. I walked behind him and started buttoning the back flaps beneath his wings. "It's a lie."

He opened his wings to give me better access. "A necessary one. If we want a world of peace, some lies must be told."

"Hmph. You're sounding more like a politician. You sure you don't want to take a place in the Senate?" I finished up the last of his buttons.

He folded his wings, turned, and took me in his arms. "No, Kittycat."
The nickname that once made me bristle now made me smile. "No?"

"I'll leave that to my brother." He brushed a light kiss across my lips.
"Though I'm afraid Kieren will have to stay in hiding for now."

"Is he really in danger?"

He scoffed. "Titus Coalglass is a powerful son of a bitch, and he won't
turn a blind eye to the *blade justice* committed on his son. Kieren will be
absent from the Cloven Senate for a time. We'll keep him well-hidden."

That was only part of the current agenda of the Morgon Guard and
Nightwing Security. Another was the scientific analysis of Larkos's
pinky finger. Kol had severed it clear from his hand. A lab technician
in Nightwing Security forensics was currently dissecting the digit to
discover if this monstrous Morgon could indeed be the first Morgon from
ancient tales. How DNA tests could determine this was still a mystery to
me. At the moment, Kol and I were alone in believing the Butcher King
was in fact the first Morgon to ever live. Even Lucius and Lorian were
skeptical. No Morgon in recorded history had lived a full millennium,
much less four. Historical records dated Larkos Nightwing's birth back to
forty-two hundred years ago.

There was also the question of the mole in our ranks, but no one had an
inkling who that could be, either. Kol had set certain pieces into motion,
but for now, we felt safe. All signs of the Devlin Butchers had vanished,
though we knew it was only a matter of time before the world tilted in the
other direction.

"So..." I trailed a finger along the sexy V where his shirt dipped
beneath his throat. "You and your brother have made amends."

His hands slid down my back, finding my hips, the silky fabric of my
black dress clinging to my curves.

He sighed. "Not exactly. But I think he's beginning to understand I
could've been right about our father's death."

"You know, Kol. He saved my life."

"For which I'm eternally grateful."

"Valla says you're both fools." I kissed the patch of skin at my eye-
level. "Actually, she says all men are fools."

"Valla is a smart, young Morgon woman."

His hands glided lower, fingers inching up the fabric of my black dress.
His lips found my neck.

"Kol—"

"Mm?" His mouth melted my insides to goo.

"We don't have time." My protest sounded like nothing of the sort as his hands slid up the back of my bare thighs.

He let them linger. He swept his lips along my neck and brushed a kiss on my pulse. Finally, with a heavy sigh, his hands disappeared, smoothing my dress back in place.

"You're right." A quick peck on the lips, he gripped my hand and led me to the terrace. "Where's your cloak?"

"Here." I pulled it from the back of the sofa. I slipped into the loose sleeves of the crimson-colored, velvet cloak, flipping up the hood. The luxurious wrap draped to my ankles. "I don't know how I'm going to wear a harness in this thing."

"We won't need one. The ceremony isn't too far."

"I wish I didn't have to be toted around like a baby-doll."

"I'm so glad that you do." He swept me up in his arms. "I like the feel of you at my mercy."

I rolled my eyes. "Valla was definitely right. Men are fools."

He nipped my bottom lip. "Yes. But I am your fool. Yours alone." My heart fluttered.

He stepped farther onto our terrace and lifted us both up into the pink twilight.

"We won't be late, will we? The sun is already setting."

"No. The ceremony begins when the sun has dipped beyond the horizon."

From this side of Gladium, it was a short flight before we were flying over the foothills of the Feygreir. Other Morgons flew in from all directions, landing on a flat outcropping just below Pike's Peak. I was relieved to see more than one carrying a human—Lucius and Jessen, Lorian and Sorcha. We landed in silence, surrounding the unlit pyre. A gray-haired Morgon priest, white-winged in snowy robes, stood like a sentinel guarding his treasure, fingers steepled before him. I'd never seen a Morgon priest up close, having never been to a funeral rite or heartbinding ceremony. Kol informed me that no one speaks at a burial rite. No one but the priest. So I knew not to ask any questions. They'd have to wait till tonight in the warmth of our bed.

Gaius lay atop a thin slab of stone, a mount of kindling circling him. Body and wings wrapped in a brown shroud, the color of his clan, one hand was left exposed, gripping his sword. Warriors were buried with sword in hand.

Kol shifted me in front of him. I kept my hood up, a glacial wind raking over the precipice. Jessen gave me a warm smile, Lucius protectively at her back. Lorian and Sorcha stood on our right. His stance the same.

I scanned the Morgon faces, recognizing many from the Morgon Guard and a few from Nightwing Security. Bowen. Kraven. Valla. Conn stood a few feet behind her, eyes glancing at her platinum hair whipping in the wind. The flaxen-haired Morgon who guarded me outside of *The Herald*, Wulfgang, stood across the pyre, staring stone-faced at the body we'd come to farewell. He'd finally been released from guarding Kris, who I'm not sure was happy by his absence.

The crowd opened. A line of brown-winged Morgons marched in stoic silence, surrounding the pyre in a semi-circle. The head of the line was a hard-faced Morgon, Gaius's father, next to a slender, brown-haired female. Three sisters followed, tears falling in quiet mourning. The others must've been more distant relations, all still within the same clan.

The priest stared at the horizon, watching as the orange sun slipped beyond Mount Grimm, Feygreir's highest peak, casting the sky in deep purple.

He opened his arms, white robes and wings spread wide. "All spirits move from one plane to another. It is not our right to judge when one has come and gone. The Great Creator breathes them into existence, giving us mortality to experience the earthly world before sending us onto another, higher plane. We thank Him for our time with Gaius Atrius Woodblade. We honor His call to gather our son's soul from this world. We send Gaius with grace and blessings and love."

Gaius was many things to the loved ones encircling his body now. Without him, we would not have known there were three other lairs out there where they were building armies, nor would we have gathered the intelligence that their purpose was much greater than enslaving and murdering humans. Rather, they planned to start a civil war. Our society was being held over a precipice. Without the good of both races working together, it would certainly fall.

To me, Gaius would always be the one who freed me from a hell I could not have escaped alone. I sent up my own prayers with the priest for his soul to finally be at rest.

The priest lowered his hands, palms up, taking three steps back from the pyre. I marveled at how much he reminded me of the human priests I knew—benevolent and wise. We were all not so different as some might believe.

Gaius's father filled his lungs with air and blew a great powerful flame straight into the kindling under his son's head. Gaius's mother and sisters followed, one sister wiping her tears before she could muster the strength. Finally, the other clan members followed suit until the pyre blazed bright against the darkening sky.

A shadow alighted on a crag just above us, a delicate Morgon woman. I gasped at her beauty. Her wings were a fan of color, beginning with the roots, a deep indigo graduating to sapphire, then sea-blue, cobalt, brightening to fire-gold, tipping the outer ridge in white. I'd never seen multi-colored Morgon wings before. I'd never seen anyone of this clan before. Her ebony hair shimmered with blue highlights against moon-pale skin. But the oddest thing of all was that even from here, I could see her eyes were the brightest gold—an unnatural color, setting her apart even from Morgonkind.

I glanced over my shoulder at Kol. He gave me a tilted smile, squeezing my waist to let me know he knew I had questions and would answer them later.

A sound unlike any other filled the evening sky. The Morgon woman's song swept over the billowing fire, surrounding us with a sorrowful lament. It pierced the heart, bringing tears to my eyes, then slid away with a warming melody, ending her requiem in a harmony of peace and a wave of silence.

When she was done, and all was quiet but for the burning pyre, the family marched out and leaped off the edge toward Drakos. One by one, Morgons lifted away. Kol gathered me close. I slipped my arms around his neck, burying my face against his chest, and we flew into the night, the first pinpricks of starlight peeking from the distance.

Without asking, Kol answered my question. "She was of the Starfell clan. They are gifted with song."

"Her voice." The wind whipped against my face. "I felt it in my bones."

"Some say they're no better than witches, their song is so powerful. Those are the jealous ones. Yet, at every Morgon funeral rite and heartbinding ceremony, there is always a Starfell clan member to celebrate in song."

I said nothing. He flew lower, taking us from the frigid air, city lights sparkling in the distance. Kol shifted closer to my ear. "I'd like to have one at our *wedding* ceremony."

He had my attention. I stared at him, the wind tousling his hair. "So, you don't mind having a human ceremony?"

"I know it would make you happy. Why can't we have a combined one with two priests like your sister did?"

My heart ached at the thought of Lucius and Jessen's wedding ceremony. "My father forbid me to attend. I didn't get to see it."

He swept his lips against my temple. "Sorry, love. But I'll bet he attends ours."

"I don't know about that."

"I do."

I frowned at him, just as we landed on our terrace. He set me on my feet. "Your father is getting old. And from what you've told me, he loves you. Just as much as he loves your sister. There's something about aging men that weakens the stubborn streak of their youth. Age is humbling to a man. He'll want no more regrets. He'll come."

I smiled, hoping and believing this could be true. "You'd do this for me? Stand before an audience of humans and Morgons and hand over your heart in public."

His eyes glittered silver by city lights. "Oh, Moira. I gave you my heart so long ago. I don't give a damn what others see or think."

I pulled him down, opening my lips over his. Our tongues slid over each other's, a sensual lure. I instantly wanted to crawl into bed and drag him with me.

"Mmm. Don't you have a rather important story to finish writing?" he teased.

"Later."

He laughed, a full, hearty, wonderful sound. His hands slid into the opening of my cloak, trailing down to the hem of my dress. "Now where were we?"

"Seems you've already found where we were."

His hands slid higher over my bottom. "I have a great memory."

"You have a great many things." I arched a brow. "However, I wonder if you have any surprises left."

Predator-still, he let the dragon peer down from slit-pupil eyes. A deep-chested growl rumbled against my chest. "A challenge, Kittycat?" Before I could utter another word, he had me indoors, spread on my back on the kitchen table. "I will do my best and let you be the judge."

I laughed at his sudden reaction, which faded quickly as he whipped open my cloak, leaving it clasped around my neck as he undressed the rest of me, hands gliding, knowing every curve and line of my body.

Caught in the hot blue as his lips sealed to mine, I marveled once more at the heartbond, drawing us ever more in sync. My Morgon man was full of fire and love, and as I would learn over the years, full of many, pleasurable surprises.

Meet the Author

Juliette calls lush, moss-laden Louisiana home where the landscape curls into her imagination, creating mystical settings for her stories. She has a B.A. in creative writing from Louisiana State University, a M.Ed. in gifted education, and was privileged to study under the award-winning author Ernest J. Gaines in grad school. Her love of mythology, legends, and art serve as constant inspiration for her works. From the moment she read JANE EYRE as a teenager, she fell in love with Gothic romance--brooding characters, mysterious settings, persevering heroines, and dark, sexy heroes. Even then, she not only longed to read more novels set in Gothic worlds, she wanted to create her own.

Turn the page for a special excerpt of Juliette Cross's

Soulfire

In a world divided by prejudice and hatred, only love can bridge the chasm.

Tensions are rising in the Gladium Province. The boundary between humans and Morgons has begun to blur. While the human aristocracy strives to maintain distance between their daughters and the dragon-hybrid race, fate has other plans.

As the daughter of the corporate king, Jessen Cade is duty-bound to honor her arranged marriage to a man she detests. Feeling trapped by family duty and a loveless future, she longs for more, straying to the Morgon side of the city.

Lucius Nightwing is the eldest son of the powerful Morgon clan, and the greatest enemy of Jessen's father. When a bar-room brawl thrusts Jessen into his arms, his dragon roars to the surface, craving to sate his carnal hunger in the brown-eyed beauty. The beast in Lucius recognizes her as his own, even if the man refuses to admit the truth.

On sale now!

Chapter 1

I swung one leather-clad leg over the balcony railing and froze. Straddling the stone balustrade, I gazed upward, willing my heart to still. A crescent moon cut a half-smile in the starry night as if mocking my rebellion. Or perhaps encouraging it.

Don't look down.

A smudge of cloud blurred over the moon, nudging me into the darkness. Deep breath in, I swung the other leg over and shimmied toward the ivy trellis. My long legs helped me maintain balance on the stone balcony, making it easier to climb down. Of course, I had to have the villa suite on the top floor—an obscene luxury for a college student. *Only the best,* my father would say. I knew the truth. He tucked me away in an ivory tower, complete with armed guards, imprisoning me to watch my every move. It had nothing to do with protection. Not mine, anyway.

My maroon silk blouse snagged on a tendril of ivy. I slipped it loose and dropped the final few feet to the grass below. I peeked around a manicured shrub toward the front of the complex. One of the guards leaned against the entrance, nearly dozing. Smiling to myself, I crept across the shadowed lawn to the side street.

I jumped into the sleek, black coupe waiting at the curb and turned to Sorcha. "Let's go."

She grinned and tore off into the night, away from Cade Heights.

"I don't get it." Ella leaned forward from the back seat. "Why can't you just walk out the front door like everyone else, Jessen? There's no curfew or anything."

I flipped down the compact mirror above the passenger seat, checking my hair. I plucked a leaf from the black waves falling past my chest. "Ella, have you actually met my father?" I wiped away a streak of dark liner from below one eye. "Sorcha, where's your eye shadow?"

"Check the glove compartment."

I touched-up the tawny shade of color on the outside corners and smeared a glossy cream on the bottom lids, setting off my light brown eyes. Pleased my hair and makeup looked fresh, and not like someone who just crawled down an ivy trellis, I flipped the mirror shut.

"Yes, I've met your father. You know I have." Ella didn't get the concept of rhetorical questions. Her glazed look, as always, made her pretty features more child-like. "So?"

"So!" Sorcha careened around the next corner, veering deeper into the city. "That man could suffocate a person with a glance."

I sighed. "Forget about him. Don't you ladies want to know our destination tonight?"

"Oooo, I do love it when you're sneaky, Jess. So what's the big secret? Why am I decked out in my highest-heeled boots and shortest skirt?"

I pulled the glossy flier from my back pocket and handed it over.

"Oh, yeah. That's what I'm talkin' about, baby." Sorcha turned down a side street, heading for the farthest edge of the Gladium Province.

"What is this?" Ella snatched the paper from Sorcha's hand. "We can't go there. It's a Morgon club, Jessen! We're not allowed."

"Oh, Ella. Relax." I snatched the flier back and pointed at the headline. "Do you see who's playing tonight? We have to go. For moral support."

"Yeah, for moral support," agreed Sorcha with a mischievous grin, tossing her dark red locks over one shoulder. "And to play with a little fire."

I laughed. Ella didn't.

"You two are crazy. Out-of-your-minds crazy. I don't care if Jed's band is playing. He knows we're not allowed on that end of town, much less in one of their clubs."

"Calm down." I twisted in my seat. Ella looked like a wide-eyed doe frozen in the headlights. "First of all, that's not true. It's not illegal to go to a Morgon club."

Ella needed a refresher course on desegregation laws, and how it was illegal for either race to bar anyone from a public place. Of course, my father might let a Morgon come into his place of business, but he'd never let one step foot in his house. Not unless there was money riding on it. Unlawful or not. Ella's parents also fell into his line of thinking.

"Look. Other humans go all the time. Jed told me. I mean, why the hell would they hire a human band to play if it were against the law? Times are changing." I wanted to believe it was true, whether or not my father was stuck in the dark ages of bigotry and discrimination.

Ella heaved a small sigh, voice almost a whisper. "But, my mom, she told me never to go to their side of the city." I glanced over my shoulder. She twisted a blond curl around her index finger, a sure sign of distress for my timid friend. "It's dangerous, Jessen. Your dad would kill you."

"Hence, the very reason I snuck out of my apartment rather than let his henchmen tail me all night long, as usual."

Sorcha zoomed into the Morgon district, the buildings transformed to suit the dragon-hybrid race—sharper, wider, taller, like mountains made of glass and steel.

"I don't approve," protested Ella.

Sorcha squeezed her car into a parking spot on a street where glittering clubs lined the block, then popped open her purse and applied a fresh coat of cherry-red lipstick in the rearview mirror.

I gave Ella my reassuring expression while Sorcha primped. "I know. Don't worry. Jed wouldn't invite us if he wasn't sure it was safe. Now, come on. Let's have some fun."

"Wait!" Sorcha passed me the lipstick. "You look good in this."

I applied and handed it back. "Better?"

"Luscious." She winked. "Look out Morgon men."

We walked the block in silence, taking in the towering sight of Acropolis at the end. At least ten stories of Gothic stone with wing-like buttresses and spires stabbing into the darkness above. Grotesque gargoyles glared down. The stone creatures drew my eye with their long limbs, sharp claws, wings spread wide, and gaping mouths, tongues lolling. Was this some kind of subliminal warning to beware of winged beasts?

Sorcha glanced up at one particular fiendish gargoyle, seeming as if it would leap off its pedestal at any moment. "Mmm. I'm feeling like a damsel in distress. How about you, Jess?"

"Um, isn't this owned by the Nightwing clan?" asked Ella, sandwiched between us.

"Yep," I replied.

Sorcha added more sway to her walk. "Awesome."

Though the exterior reeked of an ancient time, an electric blue sign burned above a black door—*Tonight: Red Dream*. My heart skittered at the sight of the man checking IDs. I'd never seen a Morgon this close. We'd had a guest speaker in my Multicultural Literature class, but the Morgon woman, a poet, stood on the stage a good distance from the audience.

This guy was huge, a wall of bulging muscles. His brawny physique wasn't what kept the three of us riveted to the spot. Massive wings—

leathery, jagged, and magnificent—held us spellbound. The man cleared his throat to get our attention, gesturing inside with a crooked smile. "Welcome, ladies."

"Such a gentleman," said Sorcha, batting her bedroom eyes. As we stumbled into the club, she grabbed my shoulder and leaned in. "I think I'm in love."

"Slow down, Sorcha. There are plenty more inside."

Sure enough, there were. Sorcha bee-lined for the bar. I followed, scanning the décor. I'd never been inside a Morgon building. Maintaining the Gothic style in black leather seating, low-lit sconces, and wide, gold-trimmed mirrors on every wall, the space didn't feel stifling or closed-in as expected. Rather the opposite. The bar lined one side of the ground floor, the stage the other. The center of the room was the dance floor that opened all the way up to the tenth floor. The skylight in the ceiling framed a deep, inky night. On both sides of the club, wide stairwells spiraled upward. Wrought iron railings barricaded each floor, maintaining the sense of open space. I was standing at the bottom of a giant birdcage. I smiled to myself. Of course I was.

"Jess! Come here!"

I'd stopped midway to the bar, stunned by the vast and opulent interior. A throng of Morgon men surrounded Sorcha and Ella. *Oh, hell, Sorcha.* Ella looked like she was about to bolt, a frightened rabbit hemmed in by wolves. I sauntered up, well aware my body drew attention. Though not as voluptuous as Sorcha, I stood much taller. With black wavy hair brushing my hips, I straightened, thankful for my gift of height. In a biology book on Morgons, which I'd smuggled from the library in my teen years, I'd learned the average height of an adult Morgon male was six-foot-seven. The average. Just like the one with platinum blond hair currently raking me with hungry eyes.

"This is my friend, Jessen," Sorcha introduced. She turned to the two chestnut-haired Morgons on her other side. "This is Conn and Corbin Rowanflame. They're twins." Sorcha winked. They nodded in unison with identical expressions of my-mouth-would-make-your-knees-buckle. I didn't doubt it. I nodded in greeting, examining the deep russet hue of their wings. Sorcha turned to the platinum blond whose ravenous gaze didn't waver for a second. "This is—"

"Slade Silverback," he interrupted, taking my hand and sweeping a kiss across the knuckles. His wings shimmered silver-gray under the lights.

"Is it true each clan is named for their wings?" I asked.

He kept my hand in his, pulling me closer. "Yes. It's true. The coloring is distinct to each clan. The dragon inside us is patriarchal." He puffed up his chest. "Children always have the wings of the father."

I tilted my head. "What happens when a Morgon woman marries…um, I mean heartbonds, to a Morgon of another clan?"

He leaned closer, too close. "Her wings change color to match her mate's."

"Because of soulfire, right?"

He didn't answer my question. "Why don't you let me take you flying? I could make you soar." Silver wings twitched at his invitation.

Did these cheese-ball lines actually work for him?

He kept inching into my space. Though he assumed I was flirting, I wasn't. I'd always been curious about Morgons, their more personal information forbidden to us. This was my first flesh-and-blood conversation with one, and he was stripping me naked with glittering green eyes. "I'm sure you think you could, but no thanks."

"Whoohoo! Come here, Jess." Saved by Sorcha.

I scooted up to the bar between her and Conn, avoiding the too-close attentions of Slade. The bartender, a young human woman about our age, lined the bar with shots, each glass in front of a pint of beer.

"What's this?" I asked.

Corbin winked and gestured for us to step away. "Watch, ladies."

We shuffled back a foot. Corbin sucked in a lungful of air, held it a second, then blew a stream of flame from his mouth along the row of shot glasses. Ella squeaked. Sorcha laughed, throwing her head back. I marveled with a smile as a line of red-orange flame licked and lit the top of each glass. Fire danced around the rims as if Corbin controlled it. He grinned, making me wonder if he did. "Drop the glass in the beer and down the hatch. Quick!"

One by one, we dropped the shots, dousing the flames, and guzzled the liquor-spiked beer. Sorcha beat us all, slamming down her mug. "That was badass. Do it again, Corbin."

The guy blushed. I didn't blame him. Attention from Sorcha could make any man☐any species☐crumble. I wiped the back of my hand across my mouth, glimpsing two Morgon men at a side door. Dressed all in black, they reminded me of the burly guy checking IDs. Giant, rock-like statues with military awareness in their watchful gazes.

"Hey, Corbin." I pointed to the stone-like guards, reminding me of the gargoyles squatting on the roof of this place. "What's up with the extra security in this place? Looks like we've got a celebrity coming or something."

"Huh?" He glanced toward the guards. "Oh. Nah. Typical Nightwing security."

My fascination with Morgons led me down a specific research path during my adolescence. Much to the consternation of my high school history teacher, I'd read everything I could get my hands on regarding the hybrid race. The Nightwing clan were direct descendants of Prince Larkos and the dragon king, Radomis, himself. Because of their royal ancestry, they continued to be the most powerful clan among their kind.

"What do you mean typical?"

"They protect their family investments. And they take extra precautions when there's a human band on site, knowing there'll be more mingling of the species."

I'd read an article recently about the Nightwing financial holdings in Acropolis and other new nightclubs, attracting more and more patronage from humans. I'd heard my father cursing the fact on a number of occasions.

Nothing irked him more than corporate competition. For his lead rival to be a Morgon clan made his blood boil on a regular basis. I knew, because I witnessed his rants and tirades more than once to my brother, Demetrius, over breakfast. Mornings were such a delight at the Cade household.

"What you really mean," I said to Corbin, "is they suspect violence is more likely to break out, and are preparing for said violence."

Corbin's mouth tilted into a boyish smile, which was odd and adorable coming from someone his height. "You're a smart young woman. And who said human women were dim-witted?"

"Excuse me? Are you saying Morgon men think we're stupid?" Heat flooded my face.

He grinned. "No. I just wanted to see you get angry. We like feisty women. The way your eyes get all wild and your cheeks turn pink. It's hot."

I punched him in the arm, only making him laugh. "How's that for feisty?"

The pounding of drums and the screech of a guitar pulled our attention to the stage. There stood Jed in all of his golden-boy glory, smiling at the crowd. In torn-up jeans and a raggedy T-shirt, he still had a line of women—Morgon and human—clinging to the stage at his feet.

"Welcome, everyone," he said, voice rumbling. "It's a pleasure to be here. We are Red Dream, and we want to hear you scream!"

He winked and laced the words with so much sexual innuendo, I thought the groupies would faint. The women in the front row erupted in squeals when the first song vibrated to life.

"Come on!" Sorcha grabbed my hand, dragging me into the crowd. Ella held back with Conn. Fear no longer lingered in her eyes. Perhaps it had something to do with the brawny guard, making sure no one bumped or jostled her. Since she was in good hands, I followed Sorcha into the sweaty mix.

Slade sidled up and handed me a blue-bottled longneck—Scale Ale, a microbrew import from Drakos, one of the pricier ones. I took it with a tight smile, not wanting to be rude, not wanting to encourage him either. He watched me take a sip. The dark, rich lager slid down my throat with a kick. "Good stuff," I said, giving him a genuine smile.

He winked with a lop-sided grin of his own. I sipped the beer and bobbed my head to Jed's insane lyrics about star-crossed lovers, broken hearts, and death being his love's true paramour. I swear, the girls panted and swooned at his rock-star antics.

When the first song ended, Sorcha nudged me with her elbow, a frown creasing her lovely face. "Don't look now, Jess, but Demetrius and his entourage are here."

"Shit! Where?"

She gestured toward the wall to my right. I glanced over. Demetrius saw me. "Damn it. And Aron is with him." They stalked straight for us.

"Shit is right." Sorcha downed the last of her beer. "Party's over."

Demetrius yelled over the pounding music. "What the hell are you doing here, Jessen!" He grabbed my arm and twisted me to face him.

"The same thing you are, Demetrius." I smiled too sweetly. "Here to watch the show."

I glimpsed his best friend Mikal over one shoulder. A grim line replaced the light-hearted smile Mikal usually wore.

Demetrius ground out his words in anger. "You do *not* have permission to be in a Morgon club. *Ever.*"

My brother had the same chocolate-brown eyes and black hair as mine. If he didn't look like he wanted to bite something all the time, he'd be gorgeous. Lately, we were always fighting. Possibly because he was becoming more and more like our father every day. He gripped my arm tighter.

Protective brother was one thing, but dominant jailer was another. Anger flared in my gut. "How come you have the right to be here, but I don't?"

"Because you're a woman. You don't know what you're doing, what Morgon men want from you."

Um, the same thing human men wanted? Hypocrite.

Sorcha stepped up. "You are *such* an asshole."

He ignored her, yanking my arm. "You're leaving. Now!"

"No, I'm not." I jerked free of his hold.

Slade sidled in beside me. "The lady doesn't want to leave with you, dude. Let her go." Corbin and Conn were there two seconds later, hovering behind him.

"She's my sister, you fucker!"

An electric charge snapped in the air, resonating around the Morgon guys. Having read about their extraordinary dragon senses in a book, and feeling them electrify my skin into gooseflesh, were two totally different experiences. Slade's wings opened partway, a distinct stance increasing his size to scary proportions. The cold, fixed gaze of Conn and Corbin made the hair on the back of my neck stand on end.

I raised my hands in a calming gesture, hoping to crush the rising tension before they came to blows. Restrained violence rippled around the Morgon men in a tangible wave. Then Aron's dumb ass stepped forward and opened his mouth.

"Back off, boys." He looked ridiculous and out of place in pristine jeans and a cream-colored sweater. What an idiot. Calling Slade and his friends "boys" was exactly the wrong thing to say. Leave it to Aron.

"And who the hell are you?" Slade asked, a head taller than Aron.

"I'm her fiancé." He gestured toward me.

I rolled my eyes. "No. You're not, Aron. How many times do we have to go over this?"

He moved closer, his chin jutting out at an arrogant angle, making me want to punch him in his aristocratic face. "Yes, Jessen. We are engaged to be married, and I won't have my fiancé in a place of ill repute."

"A place of ill repute? Does this look like a brothel to you? It's a club, Aron. That's all. I'm watching one of my closest friends play in his band, or trying to watch. Until you showed up."

"This is no place for my future wife." His words grated out through clenched teeth.

"Perfect. Because I'm not your future wife."

He grabbed me by the arm and all hell broke loose. Slade's wings flared wide. Demetrius launched himself fist-first through the air. Corbin tossed Sorcha out of the way, slamming a fist into Mikal's head, which snapped back with the force. I ducked and shoved through the sweaty bodies and swinging punches. Glancing back, I saw Conn slam an elbow, then his head, into some guy I'd never seen before, scooping Ella off the floor and carrying her out of the mayhem. Before I could slip out of the way, someone shoved and pinned me to the wall by my shoulders. A body pressed against mine. Aron. Anger burned darkly in his cold eyes.

"You are mine, Jessen." He glared down, his tone possessive and furious. "And I won't have you here for these creatures to leer at."

"Let—me—go."

"No. You're coming with me."

I struggled to free myself. He gripped harder, then started dragging me to the door. I feared what confrontation awaited me in the parking lot. Or worse, back at his place. He'd tried to corner me alone at my parents' house more than once, but I was always wary of him. I never liked the look in his eyes, especially when my parents mentioned a possible wedding in the near future. He might have my parents' blessing for this archaic-as-shit arranged marriage, but he didn't have mine. And never would.

"Let me go!"

Aron opened his mouth to say something. He froze, eyes glazed, then hit the floor.

Decked in black with midnight wings and eyes of blue-fire, a Morgon man towered before me like an angel of death. A fitted shirt outlined his broad chest and powerful frame, filling my vision. My breath caught in my throat. While chaos whirled, he wrapped vise-like arms around my waist, crushing me against a wall of steel in a rough embrace. I opened my mouth to scream. No sound came out. He bent his knees a fraction before two beats of vast, black wings lifted us with a jolt. I clung to his muscular shoulders for fear of falling, the masculine scent of him wrapping my senses into a tight knot.

I hadn't noticed from below there were breaks in the railing for Morgon flight. He dropped me into a chair in an empty VIP section. Rising to a mountainous height, electric-blue held me captive. Piercing, his gaze reached deep inside, as if he could see the secret part of me, a part I tucked away from the world, kept hidden behind a mask of indifference and strong will. Someone screamed below. Hard angles contorted into a fierce mask. Snapping his gaze away, he spun, took two long strides and fell from the edge, plummeting out of view.

CPSIA information can be obtained
at www.ICGtesting.com
Printed in the USA
FFOW04n1701100216
21336FF

9 781616 507244